Kandy Shepherd swapped a career as a magazine editor for a life writing romance. She lives on a small farm in the Blue Mountains near Sydney, Australia, with her husband, daughter, and lots of pets. She believes in love at first sight and real-life romance—they worked for her! Kandy loves to hear from her readers. Visit her at kandyshepherd.com.

After ten years as a television camerawoman, **Ella Hayes** started her own photography business so that she could work around the demands of her young family. As an award-winning wedding photographer she's documented hundreds of love stories in beautiful locations, both at home and abroad. She lives in central Scotland with her husband and two grown-up sons. She loves reading, travelling with her camera, running and great coffee.

Also by Kandy Shepherd

One Night with Her Millionaire Boss
Their Royal Baby Gift
From Bridal Designer to Bride
Second Chance with His Cinderella

Also by Ella Hayes

Italian Summer with the Single Dad
Unlocking the Tycoon's Heart
Tycoon's Unexpected Caribbean Fling
The Single Dad's Christmas Proposal

Discover more at millsandboon.co.uk.

PREGNANCY SHOCK FOR THE GREEK BILLIONAIRE

KANDY SHEPHERD

THEIR SURPRISE SAFARI REUNION

ELLA HAYES

MILLS & BOON

First published in Great Britain 2022
by Mills & Boon, an imprint of HarperCollins*Publishers* Ltd,
1 London Bridge Street, London, SE1 9GF

www.harpercollins.co.uk

HarperCollins*Publishers*
1st Floor, Watermarque Building,
Ringsend Road, Dublin 4, Ireland

Pregnancy Shock for the Greek Billionaire © 2022 Kandy Shepherd

Their Surprise Safari Reunion © 2022 Ella Hayes

ISBN: 978-0-263-30224-0

08/22

MIX
Paper from
responsible sources
FSC® C007454

This book is produced from independently certified FSC™ paper
to ensure responsible forest management.
For more information visit www.harpercollins.co.uk/green.

Printed and Bound in Spain using 100% Renewable Electricity
at CPI Black Print, Barcelona

PREGNANCY SHOCK FOR THE GREEK BILLIONAIRE

KANDY SHEPHERD

MILLS & BOON

To three lovely friends I've met through the world of romance writing: Cathleen Ross for her constant support, Efthalia Pegios for her help with Greek language across several books, and to wonderful reader Helen Sibbritt— Helen, this gorgeous Greek hero is for you!

CHAPTER ONE

CLAUDIA EATON STARED at the name on the client booking form for so long the type began to blur. *Stefanos Adrastos*. It couldn't be him. Impossible. It must be a common enough Greek name. A coincidence. That sudden jolt of her heart at the sight of his name meant nothing. She forced a deep calming breath.

The booking for her company, People Who Pack, had come just days ago from a relocation agency that regularly contracted her to pack up their clients' residences. A last-minute cancellation had allowed her to slot it in for this morning. She'd hastily noted the address, but hadn't had time to take notice of the name buried further down in the details provided by the agency. It was one of many of the smaller jobs that were the bread and butter of her business.

If she had noticed the name there was no way she would be standing on the steps of the imposing converted Georgian house, waiting to be buzzed up to an apartment. She would have sent someone else from PWP to check on his identity. She could now, having got this far, turn around and flee—pretend she'd got the time wrong. But PWP had a reputation to uphold. The relocation service sent a lot of business her way, and she couldn't afford to let them down. Not just because the name of the client struck a chord from her past.

This Stefanos Adrastos—surely not *her* Stefanos Adrastos, who was a long time and an ocean of heart-break ago—was moving his personal effects from an apartment in Bloomsbury to an address in Athens. Her Stefanos had never wanted to live anywhere but Greece—certainly not central London. He was the heir to his family's shipping business, probably holding the reins of it by now.

She tried to convince herself that this client named Stefanos Adrastos was an elderly scholar—this area was within a hop, skip and a jump of the British Museum, the British Library, numerous university colleges and the homes of many lauded literary figures. Or perhaps a young student whose wealthy parents could afford accommodation a cut above the usual student digs.

The sooner she discovered for sure that this man was not her first love—last seen ten years ago when she was nineteen—the better. Then she could get on with the job she'd been contracted to do.

Nevertheless, her voice was an unrecognisable croak as she spoke through the intercom to introduce herself as 'Claudia from PWP'. The imposing front door swung open to a marble-tiled foyer. She took the small elevator to apartment number three, which took up the entire top floor. Before her knuckles could rap on the door, it swung open. A tall, broad-shouldered, dark-haired man stood there.

She recognised him instantly.

Him. Stefanos. It was him.

Claudia stared at him, unable to believe it really was *her* Stefanos and that he was here in London. *After all this time*. The man who had been her first love, whom she'd thought she could never live without—until she'd had to.

His smile of welcome froze as he stared right back at her. 'You,' he said gruffly.

'Y-yes, me,' she stuttered, unable to say anything more substantial.

'Claudia. Just Claudia. No surname. That's who I was told was coming to pack for me.'

His English was perfect, as it had been back then, with just a trace of a charming accent. As he had done then, he called her *Cloudia*, in the European way, rather than Claudia—she had used to like it.

'I didn't know it was you. Or I… I…' She was going to say *Or I wouldn't have come*—but could she have resisted the opportunity to see him again? Even after the bitterness of their parting. Would *he* have cancelled if he'd known it was *her*?

She couldn't tear her gaze away from him. Ten years had wrought differences. The last time she'd seen Stefanos he'd been a boy of twenty. Now he was very much a man—black curls cut short, the dark stubble on his chin halfway to a beard, his skin a pale olive rather than a deep tan. He seemed taller, more substantial. *Even more handsome.*

Shock piled upon shock: the shock of his presence, of the undisguised hostility in his eyes, of her own visceral response to him. *She'd never forgotten him.* A flush burned hot on her face and neck—a curse that came with red hair and fair skin. She'd never fainted in her life, but she suddenly felt woozy and clutched onto the doorframe for support. In doing so, she lost her grip on the clipboard containing the paperwork for this packing job. It hit the ground and papers scattered across the threshold and into his apartment.

'S-sorry,' she stuttered, still barely able to claim her own voice.

She bent down to collect the papers from the floor at the same time he did, and their shoulders collided. The action brought them close…intimately close…her cheek nearly touching his face, his scent achingly familiar. He was *too* close for the strangers they now were to each other.

Abruptly, she stepped back to break the contact. 'Sorry,' said again, although ten years ago he hadn't wanted to hear her apologies.

'Let me get them,' he said shortly.

She was too dazed to protest, rather just watched him gather the pages that had come loose from the clipboard. His hands were as she remembered, strong and well-shaped, and she forced back the memories of how skilfully they had played her body. There was no wedding band, although that didn't necessarily mean anything—she'd learned that painful lesson.

He handed over the clipboard and the papers and she took them, not attempting to sort them into any kind of order, just opening the clip and shoving them haphazardly under it.

'Th-thank you,' she stuttered.

His gaze was intent. 'You're packing boxes these days? What happened to the career in international hotels you planned?'

He remembered her dream. Not surprisingly, perhaps, when it had stood in the way of the life he'd dreamed of. Their dreams had collided.

She looked up at him. 'I had it. I did it. Now I'm doing this. People Who Pack is my own business.'

She was in partnership with her friend Kitty Clements, although Kitty had been more an investor than an active partner since she'd fallen in love with their client Sir Sebastian Delfont and married him three months ago in February.

'We're very successful and I like being my own boss,' Claudia said, struggling to suppress the note of defensiveness in her voice.

When he spoke, his voice sounded forced…indifferent. 'Still, I'm surprised. That career meant everything to you.'

More than he had meant to her.

Or that was what he'd said, his voice reverberating with pain and anger, when they'd broken up. She'd been nineteen, he twenty when they'd met on vacation in Santorini. A holiday romance that had quickly deepened into something more intense. But everything she'd wanted for her future hadn't been centred around Athens. She'd wanted him, all right—she'd thought she could never have had enough of him. But at the age of nineteen she had seen the possibilities for her life stretching far on the horizon, while Stefanos's vision had been constricted and defined by his family.

He'd been content to stay in Greece, she had ached to see the world.

Hers had been a dream that ran deep. Her parents had managed a popular, traditional-style pub in a picture-perfect Devon village. It also provided accommodation, and travellers from far and wide had passed through. Even as a small child Claudia had loved being part of it all. She'd asked favourite visitors to send her a postcard from where they lived—be it in Britain, Europe or further afield. A surprising number of people had done so. The wall covered in postcards from around the world had become a feature of the pub. And it had ignited in her a thirst to see as many of those places as she could.

Her father had used to joke that she had hospitality in her veins. It was true. All she'd ever wanted to do was work in hotel management and travel the world.

But in later years her dream career had soured. She'd found limits on her ambition. It hadn't just been the realisation that she would get nowhere in family-run hotels, or that the big international hotels were too anonymous for her taste. Her last role had become more nightmare than dream because of a relationship with a colleague that hadn't ended well.

PWP had signalled a new beginning for her and Kitty, who'd had her name blackened by a vengeful boss.

'What about you?' she said to Stefanos, forcing her voice to show a polite interest with no hint of the raging curiosity she felt. 'I'm surprised to see you living in Bloomsbury rather than Athens.'

They hadn't kept in touch after she'd gone back to England at the end of summer.

'I never want to hear from you again,' he'd said grimly.

She hadn't believed he'd meant it. Not after all they'd shared. But Stefanos had been deadly serious. His social media had been blocked to her, his phone number disconnected, her emails to him had bounced. It had hurt, but eventually she'd come to terms with it. She'd stopped doing internet searches on him a long time ago.

'I've been studying archaeology,' he said.

Her brows lifted in surprise. 'I thought you'd be running the shipping business by now.' Hadn't he said that was his destiny?

'Things changed,' he said gruffly.

So many things had changed since he'd last seen Claudia, Stefanos thought, still shocked almost senseless by the sudden appearance on his doorstep of a red-haired vision from his past.

Claudia herself had changed so much it had taken a moment for him to recognise this woman as the vivacious English teenager who had captivated him from the moment she'd first served him his favourite Greek beer in a bar in Santorini. What hadn't changed was how beautiful he found her.

He was unable to tear his eyes away from her, once so familiar on his boat in a skimpy bikini, in his bed wearing nothing at all. Her waist-length red hair had darkened to a rich auburn, cut to her shoulders in a sleek bob, and the freckles scattered across her nose had faded to an English winter pale. But it was in her eyes where he saw the most change. They were still as blue as the Aegean Sea, but where once they had sparkled with laughter and mischief they now seemed guarded and wary.

Was it because of her surprise at seeing him? Or because she had seen more of life's darker side since they'd parted. Who knew? And why should he care?

'What changed?' she asked.

Should he tell her? Did she have a right to know what had happened since those dark days when she had left him nursing his wounded pride and his broken heart? Mentally he shrugged. He'd put Claudia Eaton behind him long ago. It was of no consequence what she knew about his life.

'My father died when I was twenty-four. My mother and I sold the company.'

'Oh. I'm so sorry.' Her voice, which had seemed stilted and ill at ease, now warmed with genuine sympathy. 'I remember how much you admired him. You must have been devastated.'

Why did she have to be so nice? To immediately think of how the death of his father had affected him personally rather than allude to how much he had inherited— as other women had done? But then Claudia had always been thoughtful and kind, unimpressed by his fortune. It had made the pain of losing her run even deeper. He remembered her own father had died when she was fifteen.

'Devastated about losing my father? Yes.' His powerful, energetic father had been felled by a sudden massive heart attack. Stefanos swallowed hard to contain the burst of grief he still felt at the thought of his loss. 'The company? Not so much.'

She frowned. 'You were the only child…your father's successor.'

She remembered that? Not surprising, perhaps, when the family responsibilities he hadn't been able to evade— hadn't wanted to evade, out of his powerful sense of duty—had skewered any hope of a future with wanderlust-fired Claudia.

Stefanos had grown up knowing his future was running the Adrastos Shipping Group—just as his father himself had taken over from his own father, Stefanos's grandfather. Stefanos had an inbred aptitude for business, but he hadn't expected to step into his father's shoes so soon. His mother—daughter of a shipping magnate herself—had sensed his ambivalence about his role. When they'd had an offer for the company they'd agreed to take it, divesting themselves of their tankers and container ships while keeping the lucrative yacht charter business that reflected his own interests.

'It was what I wanted,' he said.

Silence hung between them for a beat too long.

Claudia cleared her throat. She hugged her clipboard with its out-of-order papers to her chest. 'I'm glad it all worked out for you. Now, I need to get started on your packing job…' She paused and looked up to him, her blue eyes wary. 'Unless it's awkward having me here? If you'd prefer, I could send another packer from the company.'

'Don't do that,' he said—too suddenly.

'Seriously,' she said. 'I have an excellent packer who lives not far from here. She can be here within the hour.'

He shook his head. 'I haven't got an hour to waste. There's a lot to pack before the removal company comes tomorrow.'

No way would he admit, now that Claudia had come back into his life so unexpectedly, that he was reluctant to let her out of it too quickly. He had nursed his bitterness against her for a long time before finally letting it go. But seeing her here, now, brought back old emotions, raw and painful. She'd had such grand plans for her life—so much grander, it had seemed, than a billionaire's son could offer her—and yet here she was, packing boxes like one of the domestic staff at his Athens mansion.

Why?

His mind was churning with unspoken questions. Was she married? She didn't wear a ring… Did she have children? Did she ever regret walking away from everything he'd offered her?

'I'll get started on the packing, then' she said. 'Just point me in the right direction.'

Her tone was brisk and impersonal. If she was as disconcerted as he was by this unexpected meeting, she certainly didn't show it. He would do the same.

CHAPTER TWO

IT WAS ONLY with an enormous effort of will that Claudia was able to mask how shaken she was by this out-of-the-blue encounter with Stefanos. All the casual repartee she usually engaged in with a client deserted her. Because while he was indeed a client—and deserving of her full attention—he was also her first love and he had hurt her badly. That made it terribly awkward. And the way he was glowering at her didn't make it any easier.

She was still desperately trying to get her head around the reality of it. Stefanos. Here in London. The man who had ghosted her so thoroughly but whom she had never forgotten. On occasion she'd fantasised about seeing him again—of course she had. But in her fantasies she had been looking her best, composed and confident, with hair, make-up, everything perfect. Not feeling at a distinct disadvantage in trainers, leggings, and a baggy T-shirt with the hot pink PWP logo emblazoned on it. Her work clothes were comfortable and practical, but hardly the outfit she would have chosen to wear for her first meeting with him in ten years.

She was still outside the door and he stood just inside, looming over her like a gatekeeper, formidable in black jeans and dark olive green linen shirt. She'd forgotten how very black his hair was—his beard too. His eyes were half narrowed, as if he were judging her. Judging her on how she looked…how she had changed. Judging her, too, for her job. He would surely see it as a step down in the world, while she saw having her own business as an act of empowerment.

She didn't want to be judged. Not by him—not by anyone.

Head held high, she stepped forward to cross the threshold of his apartment.

Meticulously polite, Stefanos stood back to allow her through. She was intensely aware of his presence, his scent, the sheer masculinity of him. Her arm brushed against his as she passed by. She had to fight not to jerk it back. Not because she found his touch distasteful, but because of the powerful jolt of awareness ignited by that merest contact.

She caught her breath. *Did he feel it?*

Their relationship had been intensely physical. From the moment she'd met him, she'd wanted him. There'd been something about his good looks, his confidence, the touch of arrogance that had seen him assume—correctly—that she'd felt the same way he did. They'd spent every moment they could making love, their appetite for each other never sated.

Did he remember?

Each evening she had pushed through her summer vacation job in that bar, impatient for the end of her shift so she could throw herself into his arms and spend the rest of her time with him.

He had always been there, waiting for her on the cobblestoned street outside the whitewashed restaurant with its blue-painted furniture, which had overlooked the caldera—the submerged volcanic crater. She'd never questioned why he didn't work…why he had the most amazing yacht for his personal use. She had been well and truly head over heels in love with him before she'd discovered he was the son of one of the wealthiest men in Greece and heir to an immense shipping fortune. It had made no difference. He'd been just her beautiful, wonderful, perfect Stefanos. Until everything had changed.

Now here he was in the middle of London, where she could have passed him on the street, on a bus, and never known he was nearby. And she had never felt more uncomfortable. He seemed none too happy about her surprise presence in his apartment, yet he had refused her offer to get another packer. Should she read anything into that?

Stefanos directed her down a short corridor. It opened into a spectacular living room that had been stripped bare of all extraneous detail and was simply an architectural white space. Furnishings were starkly simple—all white and pale timber—highlighted by Greek archaeological artefacts mounted on marble blocks, an imposing pottery urn that must surely be worthy of pride of place in a museum, and a series of framed antique maps of the ancient world on the walls.

It was so striking she had to stifle a gasp of admiration. But she didn't say anything. First, because it was PWP policy not to comment on a client's possessions. Second, because she didn't know how Stefanos would take it. Did he own the apartment? Had it been designed to his taste? Would he value her opinion? It was safer to stick to her policy of being politely impersonal and show no indication of her inner turmoil.

She glanced at the neatly stacked folded boxes and

packing material placed along one wall and felt reassured by their familiarity. They were what she and Kitty jokingly called the tools of their trade. She could do this. She could be a complete professional. She would not take a step out of place.

'Your people delivered the packing materials yesterday afternoon,' Stefanos said. 'There are more in the other rooms.'

'I'd like to see them,' she said, studiously avoiding catching his eye.

With only the minimum of words, he showed her around the spacious luxury apartment. She couldn't help but admire his back view, which hadn't changed from the days when he'd been clad in a pair of board shorts and nothing else and she'd teased him that he had the best male butt in Greece. Or those times when he'd worn no clothes at all, and he'd only had to look at her for her to melt with desire for him.

She forced her gaze away from his too-well-remembered body and back to the apartment. All the rooms were designed with the same white minimalism. She made appropriate comments about the contents that required packing, while hiding her intense curiosity. Back then he'd been so keen on family, yet she could detect no sign of a female presence here, or of children.

But again she didn't dare comment. There was something forbidding about Stefanos that had not been there when he was twenty. It curbed any thought she might have had of engaging with him. They'd never been short of words and laughter back then—not just with each other, but with the circle of other young people from around the world, lured by the beauty and mystique of the Greek islands. Now it was a struggle to choke out the bare minimum of words required to get her job done.

She followed him back to the living room. 'I understand the furniture and electrical appliances are to remain, but the books and ornaments and personal possessions of the resident are to be packed,' she said, in her best PWP voice. 'Household linens and kitchen equipment also to remain.'

'Correct.'

Could he be more terse if he tried?

'Will you be on hand to answer any questions I might have?'

'I will be in my study. You can pack up that room last.'

She nodded. 'I'll start here in the living room.'

'I'll leave you to it,' he said, turning on his heel.

Claudia was both relieved and disappointed after he left the room. She couldn't have borne it if he'd watched her as she worked, yet the room seemed empty without his commanding presence. She hadn't bitten her fingernails for years, but she had to fight the urge to nibble on her thumbnail at the very least.

How could she deal with this? She decided to pretend she wasn't working for her first love but rather the crusty old scholar she had at first imagined her client Stefanos Adrastos to be. Not tall and handsome and dynamic, but stooped, with a long silver beard and rheumy eyes behind metal-rimmed glasses.

She couldn't help but smile to herself at the thought.

But her smile quickly drooped at the corners and she felt the sting of tears. It was no good. Her thoughts were filled with *her* Stefanos. She had loved him so much. *Adored him.* It had ended with them both hurting each other. But that had been ten years ago. Wasn't it natural for her to want to know what had happened to him in the meantime? To ask how he had ended up studying archaeology in London, seemingly with no wife or family? Perhaps he had a wife and children back in Athens. If he did, she would like to know—it was what he had wanted back then.

Surely they could have a civil conversation that acknowledged that they had a past, even if they hadn't managed a future?

Claudia started to pack a shelf of glossy art and history books. Beautiful, expensive books. She picked up a handsome tome on the treasures of Sutton Hoo, the famous archaeological site in Suffolk. Was Stefanos here to study only British archaeology? There was an important archaeological site in Santorini, but she didn't remember him showing any interest in it at the time they'd met. He'd been too focused on his future in Adrastos Shipping—and, she reminded herself, on her.

She worked quickly and skilfully, concentrating on her work and refusing to think about Stefanos—although surrounded by his possessions that was extremely difficult.

She was taping up the third box when he strode into the room, startling her, making her turn. She couldn't help but stare at him afresh. Was her tongue hanging out? *He was hot.* Even hotter than he'd been when she'd fallen so hard for him. For a moment she wished she didn't have that history with him, that he was a handsome stranger who she could flirt with a little and find out more about.

PWP had had a no-dating-the-clients rule. Kitty had broken that rule in a spectacular manner—now she was Lady Kitty Delfont. Which kind of gave Claudia a pass to do the same if she wanted. So far no client had stirred the slightest interest in her...

'I can't sit in there while you do this work,' Stefanos said tersely, gesturing with his hand at the boxes. 'It's not right.'

Slowly, she put down her packing tape gun, took a step away from the box. 'It's my job, and I'm an expert at packing valuables.'

'It's hard physical work.'

'Which I am totally up for.'

She flexed an arm to show off the muscles she was so proud of. The job kept her fit—although that didn't stop her from going to the gym as well, to keep her strong. A strained back could spell disaster in her business.

'Let me at least help you,' he said, sounding very much as if packing boxes was the last thing he wanted to do.

She shook her head. 'Not a good idea. There's a good chance you'll invalidate your insurance if you do. You have employed me to do this.'

He scowled. 'No. I employed a removal company. They recommended packers. I did not employ you. I would not have—'

'You would not have employed the Claudia assigned to your job if you'd known it was me?'

He looked about to answer but she spoke over him. It would be too painful to hear him say yes.

'That's where we're different—as we always *were* very different. I didn't know you were the client. But even once I suspected it might be the Stefanos Adrastos I used to know, I didn't turn tail and slink away. I thought about it—trust me, I thought about it... But I stayed. And I stayed because I was curious to see what kind of man you'd grown up to be…how you'd lived your life and if…and if you were happy.'

Stefanos met her gaze, it seemed she was still as direct as she'd been back then. Not afraid to be outspoken and state her opinions, even if they differed from his. He'd liked that about her. So different from the girls who'd thought the way to dating a billionaire's son was to echo his opinions, to acquiesce with whatever he wanted.

'Of *course* I'm happy,' he said immediately. He scoffed at the thought that he could be anything other than happy. 'Why wouldn't I be?'

Her eyes widened. 'How could I have known the answer to that?'

Because ten years ago she had made him happy.

The thought struck him like a punch to the gut. He had never been as happy as those weeks with her in Santorini—not before, not since. It had been a vacation fling, he reminded himself, of no real significance. That was all it had been to her, anyway.

He folded his arms tightly in front of his chest, rocked back on his heels. 'Let me assure you my life is in a very good place. I don't want for anything and I'm doing exactly the work I want to do since we sold Adrastos Shipping.'

He had inherited so much money he never needed to work again, although he didn't have it in him to be idle. He'd appointed an excellent manager to the yacht charter business so he'd been able to take a year off to pursue his interest in archaeology with an aim of eventually earning a PhD. And yet…she'd hit a raw nerve.

'What about you?' he said.

'Me? Happy? Of course I am. I love having my own

business, being my own boss.' She paused. Then gave a short brittle laugh that surprised him. 'We've both talked about work. Is that all we need to make us happy?'

'Satisfaction with work is important. But of course there is more. Family. Friends.' Family was so very important—which was why her attitude ten years ago had stunned him.

'Of course,' she echoed. 'Are you married?'

He should have expected that question but still it side-swiped him.

'Not now.'

She frowned. 'What do you mean "not now"?'

'Just that. I was married. Now I'm divorced. Single.'

'I'm sorry,' she said.

'I'm not sorry,' he said. 'It's a great relief.'

'Still, it's sad when a marriage ends...they generally start with expectations of happiness.'

'My last marriage was all about lies and deception.' He spoke through gritted teeth.

She put her hand up in a halt sign. 'Hold that. You just said your *last* marriage?'

Inwardly he cursed his misstep.

'There have been more than one?'

'I have been divorced twice.'

Divorced twice by the age of thirty. Not something he liked to boast about.

'Oh...' Claudia said.

'Why do you say "oh"?'

She shrugged. 'I don't know, really. Just to buy time. I'm gobsmacked that you've been married and divorced twice. And you've only just turned thirty.'

She'd remembered that his birthday was in March.

Hers was in November—a date it seemed he'd been unable to forget.

'Both marriages were mistakes,' he said. *Massive mistakes.* The second an even worse mistake than the first. 'There are good reasons why they ended in divorce.'

Claudia looked at him expectantly. There was an unspoken question in her eyes, dancing around the corners of her pretty mouth: *Tell me those good reasons. C'mon. Spill.* He remembered she'd used to do that. She was a master of the silent question. Even after ten years, he remembered. Back then he had answered all her questions—had known she wouldn't give up teasing and wheedling and probing until he had. He had no intention of doing so today.

'Not reasons I care to disclose.'

'Right. Of course not,' she said. She paused before she launched into her next question. 'Any children?'

Of course she would ask that.

'No.' He kept his voice studiously neutral.

'That's a blessing, then.'

He stared at her. 'Surely you must realise I don't see it that way.'

He had wanted children, but neither marriage had brought them. Now it seemed likely he would never have a child. His two ugly marriages had made him vow never to marry again.

She flushed high on her cheekbones. 'I meant it must have been easier to divorce if there wasn't custody to battle over.'

'I take it you're not divorced?'

'Yes. I mean, no. I'm not divorced.'

'Because you haven't married?'

'Right first time.' She slipped off the protective work glove from her left hand and waggled her bare fingers. 'See?'

'So you haven't softened your stance on marriage since we last met?' He wasn't the only man who hadn't managed to put a ring on her finger. For some perverse reason that pleased him.

'No. Perhaps a little bit… For other people. Not for me.'

'You wouldn't marry me to give our baby a name.'

He hadn't meant to blurt that out. But the memories of what had happened back then had forced their way through the barriers he had put up against her ten years ago and spilled out in words.

The flush deepened to scarlet, staining her fair skin. 'But it turned out there was no baby, didn't it?'

He could sense the effort required to keep her voice on an even keel.

Towards the end of their second month together in Santorini Claudia had become uncharacteristically anxious and edgy. At first he'd assumed it was because she was worried—as he was—about what would happen after her vacation came to an end. Finally, clearly terrified of what his reaction would be, she'd told him her period was ten days late and she feared she might be pregnant.

Stefanos had immediately offered to marry her. Not out of honour, or because it had been the right thing to do, but because he had been desperately in love with her. He'd known he'd found 'The One'. He'd been dreading her going back to university in England. Now she wouldn't have to. She would stay in Greece with him. He'd been twenty—not too young to take on the responsibility. He'd wanted her...wanted the baby. He'd known he could give her everything she'd need.

She'd panicked. He still remembered her words, searing through his declaration of love and commitment, kicking it back in his teeth. *I don't want to be a teen-aged mum. I don't want to get married.*

'A false alarm,' was all he said now. He'd been so naïve—believing that because he loved someone, she'd love him back with the same intensity. He'd had everything to offer her, but it hadn't been enough. *He* hadn't been enough.

'Yes,' she said.

Her period had come just as he'd thought he was making progress in convincing her of his love and sincerity, telling her how her life would be as the wife of the heir to billions. Her relief at what she'd called 'a lucky escape' had been palpable—in fact she'd done a little dance of joy on the deck of his yacht...the beautiful vintage racing yacht the *Daphne*, which his grandparents had gifted him for his eighteenth birthday. She'd expected he'd be as relieved as she was, and had been genuinely surprised when he'd expressed disappointment that there wouldn't be a baby.

He'd tried to convince her that even without a pregnancy he wanted to marry her. It hadn't been an option for her.

'Can't you see we're too young, Stefanos?'

She'd wanted to finish her degree, to have a career and see the world. He'd been obliged to prove himself in the family business, with working alongside his father all he'd been able to see on his horizon.

'Marriage, babies—all that would erase the future I want for myself.'

He'd felt erased. It had been a deep, abiding hurt that had prompted him to wipe away all contact with her. He'd vowed he would never again let a woman hurt him like that.

And here they were in the future. Having met only by chance. With not a lot to say to each other. Maybe what he'd taken for love had been about sex. Hot, passionate, exhilarating sex. They'd thought they'd discovered a secret no one else could possibly have discovered before them, revelling in the pleasures their bodies could give each other. He'd been in a constant state of arousal around her, crazy with want and a fierce desire to make her his.

In a cheap, white cotton dress—supposedly Greek, but actually made in India—that had showed off her long, elegant legs, and with a straw hat jammed on top of her salt-tangled bright hair she'd been sexy in a subtle, enticing way. She was just as desirable now—he couldn't deny it. That awful baggy T-shirt and leggings couldn't mask her slender figure, its curves subtle but more than enough to tantalise him. She had grown even more womanly and beautiful, though he preferred her hair long, tumbling down to her waist in a glorious copper fall.

Nothing had been the same after the pregnancy scare. They'd held themselves apart from each other. She'd been planning to stay with him in Santorini for as long as possible into September, before she had to return to Birmingham for the start of her second year at university. Instead, she'd lasted for just a few days of the awkwardness that had sprung up between them before she'd told him she'd changed her flight home.

Now she picked up the chunky tape dispenser, put it down on top of a box that was still only half sealed. Stefanos knew she was doing it to avoid his scrutiny. He realised his arms were still folded across his chest. He unfolded them and shoved his hands into the pockets of his trousers.

Finally she took a step towards him. 'Why did you ghost me? Cut off any means of getting in touch with you?'

'I told you that if we couldn't be together that was the end of it. I was—still am—an all-or-nothing guy.'

He'd been determined to protect himself against further hurt from her. Besides, he had never known a vacation romance that had lasted longer than the summer. She hadn't wanted to marry him—why drag out the pain?

'We talked about staying friends,' she said.

He shook his head. '*You* talked about staying friends. You didn't listen to what I was saying.'

'I didn't want to hear what you were saying. It…it was so hurtful.'

He'd been hurt too. He'd driven her to the small airport at Santorini in silence. Their farewell had been cool and stilted. When he'd got back to the boat he'd noticed that the straw hat she had worn all summer had slipped to the floor of the car and she'd left it behind. For a long time he'd held it close, and had felt as though his heart was being ripped out of his chest.

Now the dregs of past emotion choked his voice and he had to clear his throat to speak. 'I thought I'd made it very clear I wanted you as my lover, as my wife, as the mother of my children. Being a "friend" wouldn't have been enough for me.'

'We could have tried long-distance dating. I thought—'

'*All or nothing.* Where would you have seen the *all* in

you living in England and me in Greece? You'd already knocked back the idea of a future with me.'

'Not a future. Just marriage. And children.'

'The things that were important to me.'

'I was left with the *nothing* and it was terrible.'

She clutched her right hand—still in its work glove—to her chest. He wondered if she realised she was doing it.

Her voice hitched. 'That awful drive to the airport…as if we were strangers. I cried all the way through check-in and onto the plane. I cried until I didn't have a tear left. But I thought I'd at least be able to text you. Or talk to you on social media. But you blocked me every which way and all I had was that great big *nothing*.'

She drew in her breath with a big, anguished gulp that tore straight to his heart.

'It was the way it had to be,' he said.

For his own sanity if nothing else. Although seeing her distress now, still real after all this time, he realised he could have done it better. It had been immature—cruel, even—to handle it the way he had. He should at least have told her he intended to wipe her. But that was the way he'd been aged twenty.

'But you got over it?' she asked, her voice shaky.

'Eventually. Inevitably.'

She didn't meet his eyes. 'I… I did too.'

By the time he'd turned twenty-two he'd been married to Arina.

CHAPTER THREE

FOR SO LONG Claudia had suppressed the pain of losing Stefanos. Now being with him was bringing it back, and it was burning into her heart like drops of acid. She realised she was pushing against her own chest, as if to contain the agony of it, and she dropped her hand to her side.

She'd thought it would be nice—healing, even—to talk to him about the past, about where they both were now. Adult to adult. Laughing a little, perhaps, as they reminisced about their time together in Santorini. No pain. No anguish. Just a string of *Do you remembers?*

It wasn't working out like that. Since Kitty's wedding in February Claudia had found herself questioning the choices she'd made, the way she'd hedged her life in with constraints. The way she now found herself on her own and heading for thirty.

For the first time in years she'd thought about Stefanos and wondered if she had made the wrong decision back then. And now here he was. Unlocking the hurtful memories she'd fought so hard to block. And his memories of her were so obviously underscored with bitterness.

Who had hurt who the most?

She looked up to find his eyes on her, brown with intriguing flecks of green, filled not with accusation but with something she couldn't read. It made her feel even more self-conscious. The full force of her attraction to him hit her. Not to him then, but to him *now*. He was even more handsome as a man, that darker edge to him adding to his appeal.

At nineteen, in the depths of her anger at his inflexibility, she'd wanted to believe what her friends had told her: she shouldn't take it so badly…she'd meet another man…there were many more gorgeous guy pebbles on the beach. She *had* met other men, but no one had ever stirred her body and her heart the way Stefanos had.

Rehashing their painful parting with him, knowing how dismal her love-life had been ever since, realising she might have made a very big mistake ten years ago, was just too distressing. But it wasn't possible to go backwards in life. Here, now, ripping open wounds she'd thought had healed to barely discernible scars was too much to endure.

She couldn't do this.

'This isn't working out,' she said abruptly—too abruptly. But she was struggling to maintain her composure. She stripped off her other work glove. She wouldn't be needing it now. 'I'll call my other packer. Actually, I'll book two packers, to make up for the time I've wasted. Of course I won't charge for the extra person.'

'Good idea,' he said.

His instant agreement stung. Perversely, she'd wanted him to protest at her leaving. Her redhead's temperament sometimes made her speak before she'd fully thought things through. This time, though, she'd had little choice. She couldn't be put through the emotional wringer over events long past by a man who, it seemed, still had power to hurt her.

She picked up her mobile phone from where she'd put it down on the sleek cube of a coffee table. It was an effort to force her voice to sound businesslike and not reveal she was teetering on the edge of tears.

Thankfully, her two preferred packers were available to start ASAP.

She put down the phone and turned to Stefanos. 'I'll stay until I can confirm they're on their way.' Damn that note of shakiness in her voice. 'Then I'll be gone.'

He frowned. 'Gone where?'

'Back home. To another job. Just…gone.' She could hardly choke out the words.

Anywhere but here with him.

Her eyes darted around the room—to the ancient maps on the wall, that incredible urn…anywhere but at Stefanos.

He stepped towards her. 'Don't go, Claudia. Stay. Stay with me.'

Was she hearing things?

She was too shocked to reply.

'Let your people come in and finish the packing. But I'd like to spend some time with you. Talk about where life has taken you.'

'You mean fill in the ten-year gap?'

'As best we can.'

'Like…not exactly like friends, but…but friendly acquaintances?'

'Friendly acquaintances?' He was very serious. 'Something like that. Surely we've met by chance for a reason. We should take advantage of that. I think we'd both regret it if we let that chance slip by. It's unlikely we'll ever see each other again.'

'Perhaps... I... I never told you why I was so against—'

He put up his hand. 'No need for that. I can see that talking about the past upsets you.'

'There was hurt on both sides. Perhaps I didn't understand that at the time.'

'I can see I could have done things differently.'

She hesitated. Then, 'Yes. I'd like to take the chance to catch up.' She felt both relief and just the faintest stirring of excitement.

'Good,' he said. And he smiled. For the first time that morning he smiled.

That hadn't changed at all: his perfect white teeth—she'd used to tease him that he could model in a toothpaste commercial—the way his smile lit his eyes. It brought memories of *her* Stefanos flooding back and she couldn't stop looking at him, taking in every change and everything that remained the same.

He'd been such fun, but at the same time somehow more grown-up than her, even though there was only a year between them. Now he was quite the commanding presence. She'd used to tease him and laugh with him—now she didn't know that she would dare.

She indicated the room with a sweep of her hand. 'When my packers get here it won't be private.'

The last thing she wanted was her staff to overhear her personal conversation. Especially with a man as outstandingly handsome as Stefanos. She could only imagine the gossip swirling around the ranks of full-time staff and into the casuals who worked when they could fit it in around family obligations. She'd learned the hard way to keep her personal life private.

'We won't be here,' he said, the smile still lingering in his eyes. 'I don't know about you, but I'm in need of coffee.'

She smiled. 'Me too.'

He'd taught her to appreciate Greek coffee, *glykos*, which was strong and very sweet. She hadn't drunk it for ten years, but she had definitely become something of a caffeine addict.

'How long did you live here?' she asked.

'For a year.'

'Then I'm sure you know a good place for coffee.'

She could do this.

'I'm staying in a hotel nearby after the apartment is packed up,' he said. 'I fly to Athens tomorrow.'

Tomorrow he'd be gone. Claudia felt powered by a sudden sense of urgency—a kind of greed. She had to grab this chance to spend time with him, even if it stirred up old hurts. As he'd said, so matter-of-factly, there might never be another.

'Sensible idea,' she said. 'People often stay elsewhere during the disruption of packing for a move.'

'I could take you to the hotel for coffee.'

'I would like that,' she said.

He told her where the hotel was, and she realised it was an ornate nineteenth-century hotel, famous in Bloomsbury. She would have loved to see it. It was very posh. But not in trainers and leggings.

She looked down at her clothes in dismay. 'I'll have to change,' she said.

'You could get away with what you've got on,' he said wryly. 'No one seems to care what people wear.'

'*I* care,' she said firmly. Fortunately she had a change of clothes with her, as she had plans to catch up with Kitty after work. 'I can get changed before we go.'

'How long do we need to wait for your packers?'

'If you're happy for them to work without you being here we don't need to wait. Everything is straightforward. These two women are completely trustworthy. Your possessions will be in safe hands. And they can call me if they have any queries.'

'They're women?'

'Yes. That's the whole idea behind PWP. We—my partner Kitty and I—found people appreciated having women taking care of packing their possessions when moving house.' She put up her hand to forestall the comment she often got. 'That's not to say men can't do a brilliant job too. It's just we've built our business around helping people who prefer the female touch.'

'Yet you're called People Who Pack?'

'We originally called the business Ladies Who Pack, but we were criticised for being sexist.' She laughed. 'We worked freelance before we started the business, and we were always referred to as "those ladies who pack". But now we do have some very good men working for us as part of the team.'

'You're successful?'

'Yes. We were fortunate to get some good recommendations, and the publicity around my business partner Kitty marrying Sir Sebastian Delfont—who was our client—certainly gave us a boost. As a matter of fact...' She stopped herself.

'Yes?' he said.

She made a dismissive wave of her hand. 'You don't want to hear about it.'

'But I do. I'm intrigued.'

'I don't want to bore you.'

'From my memories of you, Claudia, you could never be boring,' he said.

His slow smile and narrowed eyes brought a new blush to her cheeks.

'We've had an approach from an investor who wants to talk about franchising opportunities,' she said.

'Are you interested?'

'We haven't had time to give it much thought. I like being in control...keeping standards high. But Kitty can't be as involved as she once was. She's become heavily involved in a charitable trust set up by Sebastian's grandmother. We might have to look at other options.'

'It's always wise to look for new opportunities.'

'Even when they might be a bit scary?' she said.

'Especially when they might be a bit scary,' he said. 'Accepting new challenges is how you grow.'

'You sound like quite the businessman, dispensing words of wisdom,' she said.

'It's in the blood—there's no escaping it,' he said with a wry smile.

Funny, she'd known him as the son of a billionaire, the grandson of a billionaire. Now he was undoubtedly a billionaire himself. And yet he'd always been just Stefanos to her, and that didn't seem to have changed.

'Give me a moment to get out of these clothes,' she said, immediately wishing she hadn't said that. When they'd been together that would have signalled something altogether different from going out for coffee. 'I mean, get changed...you know...put on different—'

Damn, why did that slow, lazy grin make her blush even hotter?

'I know exactly what you mean,' he said, and she felt his gaze follow her out of the room.

While Claudia was getting changed in the main bathroom, Stefanos gave the apartment a silent farewell. He had inherited it from his grandfather on his mother's side, and it had been both an investment and a family *pied-à-terre* for business trips to London. He'd often stayed here as a child, when he'd been taken to London on vacation to work on perfecting his English.

He'd had it gutted and refurbished to his own taste and moved in a year ago, for a year of living *by* himself and *for* himself, escaping from the trauma of his second marriage and finally being able to follow his interests in archaeology.

Now he had got everything he needed from his time here, and it was time for him to go back home. He would let the apartment. There was no point in having it sitting empty when it could be earning revenue.

All thoughts of the apartment or anything else flew away when Claudia walked back into the living room on a wafting scent of something sweet and feminine. She was wearing a multi-pleated skirt in an abstract print like large leopard spots, cinched around her narrow waist with a wide black belt, and a scoop-neck black top that emphasised her long neck and the curve of her breasts. She had a light black coat flung around her shoulders. Her hair was sleek and smooth, subtle make-up emphasised the blueness of her eyes, and her generous mouth was slicked with a soft red. She wore sheer black stockings, spiky heeled black shoes, and carried a large black tote bag.

He swallowed hard. 'You look…sensational,' he managed to choke out.

She was stylish, sophisticated, sexy…with the subtle sensuality that was as attractive now as it had been back then. So grown up—and yet he could still see the girl he'd loved in the woman she'd become. He had to force himself not to stare hungrily and take in every detail.

'Thank you,' she said. 'After wearing my work uniform so many hours of the week, I like to dress a little better when I'm not on duty.' She laughed. 'I'm not dressed like this to go home on the Tube. I'm meeting my friend and business partner Kitty for a drink this evening.'

She was going out to a bar… What man would be hitting on her there tonight? Every guy in the place, most likely. Surprised at the surge of unwarranted jealousy, he had to remind himself that Claudia was well and truly in his past. Such thoughts were quite out of order for a 'friendly acquaintance'.

A phone sounded from the small black handbag she had slung over her shoulder and she reached for it.

'The packers have texted to say they're on their way.'

'We should be on our way too,' he said.

The sooner he had her to himself, the better. This time he wanted to say goodbye to her on better terms than he had ten years ago.

CHAPTER FOUR

As CLAUDIA WALKED side by side with Stefanos into the elaborate Victorian era hotel on Russell Square, with its multiple arches and turrets, she had a feeling she was entering an entirely different world—Stefanos's billionaire world of extreme wealth and privilege.

She was no stranger to luxury hotels—but as a member of staff not as a well-heeled guest. She knew from the attitude of the attentive staff who greeted them that she was in the company of a valued and generous client. She straightened her shoulders and stood a little taller, enjoying their discreet glances at her, knowing she looked good in her new skirt—a designer sale bargain.

The lobby was nothing short of magnificent, with mosaic floors, columns and ornate ceilings. Victorian excess at its finest with a modern update. She had to smile at the contrast to Stefanos's minimalist white apartment. Not the kind of hotel she'd thought he might choose to stay after his possessions had been packed. But it was nearby, and she remembered he had always been a practical kind of person.

They were ushered into the hotel café and seated at a small round table, inviting in its intimacy, overlooking Russell Square Gardens. Claudia passed on the offer of a pastry, delicious as they looked. Her stomach was too tied up in knots to handle anything other than a black coffee. It was just too surreal for words that she was sitting in a London hotel across a table from Stefanos and that the waiters obviously thought they were a couple.

Wrong, she wanted to tell them. We're just friendly acquaintances. Of course it wasn't true. She could pretend that was the case for the sake of civil conversation with Stefanos, but they were ex-lovers and she couldn't forget that—not even for a second. Because all she could think about was what it would be like to be in his arms again.

'I noticed you were inspecting the hotel with a critical eye,' he said. 'What's your verdict?'

'Was I that obvious?' she said. 'I thought I was being very discreet.'

'I could see,' he said.

He'd always said she wasn't good at hiding her feelings. Perhaps that was because he had known her so well he'd been able to read her face. They'd used to marvel that they felt as if they'd known each other for ever almost as soon as they'd met. But that was something too personal for her to remind him of—or for her to dwell on.

'My verdict is that they've done a great job bringing the splendidly ornate heritage of the hotel up to date,' she said. 'It's welcoming, not intimidating. And the staff are attentive and well trained—that's really important.'

'I stayed here while the apartment was being remodelled and thought it excellent. I'm pleased you agree.' He paused to take a sip of his coffee. 'Tell me where your hotel career took you. I remember you wanted to see the world.'

That was safe ground—as long as she avoided any mention of the last hotel where she'd worked. A romance with a colleague had backfired in the worst possible way, with her being accused of *his* fraudulent misdemeanours.

'After graduation, I started an internship in London. London credentials are good to have on the résumé.'

'I can believe that,' he said.

'Next was a stint in a wonderful hotel in Paris—my dream job in many ways as I'm fluent in French.'

'You have a flair for languages. I remember you picked up Greek very quickly.'

'Purely conversational,' she said, pleased that he'd remembered. 'I never got the hang of the alphabet.'

'You were only there a few months.'

'Yes,' she said.

She felt the air was thick with flashes of memory of that time—most of them highly sensual. No wonder she'd never had time to learn the Greek alphabet. She'd been too busy making love with Stefanos. She had to press her knees together at the memory of the pleasure he had aroused in her.

Did he remember?

Was he feeling the same shivers of desire she did when she looked at him and thought about how perfect they'd been together?

'Did you ever work at a Greek hotel?' he asked.

Their eyes caught for a moment too long. 'No. I've never been back to Greece. Not after… Well, not after what happened with…with us.'

It would have been way, way too painful to be back in his country without him. For the rest of her life Greece would be associated with Stefanos and the hurt of their parting; she doubted she would ever visit Greece again.

'I see,' he said.

Did he really?

'My brother had moved to Australia. I went to Sydney to see him and meet his Aussie wife and kids and try my chances there. Sydney became my base—not just for working within Australia, but also New Zealand and Bali. I loved Sydney. At one stage I even thought of settling there.'

Until betrayal had sent her fleeing home to the UK.

She'd thought she'd met the second great love of her life, until she had discovered she'd been scammed. He was a good-looking Aussie, who had been her manager at a five-star city hotel and her lover—who had never told her he was married.

'Home is always a drawcard,' Stefanos said.

He was right. Home was a refuge. She missed her mother and the twin sisters who had wreaked such havoc in her teenage life. Her mother could be flighty, and overly dependent on a man, but Claudia knew she would always be there for her.

'Your turn now. Why two divorces?'

She was aching with curiosity. And couldn't help a stab of jealousy at the thought of him being with any woman other than her. One—two—he had loved enough to marry. Unreasonable and irrational, she knew, as she hadn't wanted to marry him. But it was impossible not to feel it.

His dark eyebrows rose. 'Even after ten years I think you know I won't be discussing that with you.'

'C'mon. Just a line or two,' she urged. 'You can't deny me that. Not after telling me you're divorced twice by age thirty.'

'As persistent as ever, I see.'

'Some things don't change.'

Was she flirting with him? She certainly didn't mean

to. What would happen if she did? If she leaned across the table and took his hand. Whispered that she still wanted him.

Another shiver of desire ran through her.

'I'll tell you what you could easily find by looking me up on the internet,' he said. 'I married the daughter of a family friend when I was twenty-two.'

'That…that was not long after—'

'Classic rebound. That was what some said when we separated on our six-month wedding anniversary.'

'Oh, my gosh, I'm sorry,' she said, not sure what else she could say.

'We weren't suited,' he said, thin-lipped and dismissive.

'I hardly dare ask about the second.'

'Then don't. Here's a one-word answer—*liar*.'

'That sounds bad.'

'It was,' he said grimly. 'Please don't ask me for further details because they will not be forthcoming.' He put up his hand. 'And don't say sorry again.'

'Sorry—I mean, sorry for saying sorry. I won't say it again.'

'Good,' he said with a twitch of his lips, obviously failing in an effort not to smile. Somehow the half-smile was even sexier than his full-on smile.

She picked up her coffee and put it down again without drinking. 'Before you ask, I have nothing of any interest to impart about my personal life. The only thing of significance is that I fancied myself in love with someone and he turned out to be married. Needless to say it didn't end well.'

She forced her tone to be light-hearted, as if it were of no consequence, but of course it had been. Brad had implicated her in a fraud involving inflated contracts for supplies from companies owned by his wife's family that included kickbacks for him. She was still bruised from the fallout. And she was still paying off her legal fees.

'Now it's my turn to say—how did you put it?—no further details will be forthcoming.'

'And my turn not to say sorry?'

She laughed, and after a moment he joined in.

Her heart nearly stopped at the sight of Stefanos laughing, his head thrown back. She heard the deep rumbling sound of it that she'd always found so infectious. It brought everything rushing back: their first kiss while watching the famous sunset at Oia, over the waters of the Santorini caldera. The first time they'd made love, later that night on the mahogany deck of his beautiful white-sailed yacht. And so many times after that, each time better than the last.

Had their lovemaking been as spectacular as she remembered? Another rush of desire ran through her. She couldn't meet Stefanos's eye in case he guessed—in that way he had—what she was thinking.

Two cups of coffee on top of what he'd already had for breakfast was all Stefanos could manage or he would be wired. But he wanted to prolong his time with Claudia. So he ordered a third. If he could keep her here a little longer he could suggest an early lunch. He wasn't ready for her to leave.

Claudia pushed her half-drunk coffee away from her. 'That's enough for me,' she said. 'Even though it's very good coffee.'

'I don't really want this third cup either,' he admitted. He didn't know why he was so reluctant to say goodbye to her. Throughout those two cups of coffee he'd been trying not to think about how awesome he and this beautiful, sexy woman had been together in bed. How much he'd like to take her by the hand and lead her up to his room right now to see if it was still as good.

But it was about more than sex. He could only put it down to feeling so relaxed in her company. More relaxed than he'd felt with any woman in recent times. He and Claudia had known each other a long time ago—in a different life—and, while the relationship had run its course to a bitter ending, it had been good while it lasted. But it was long over. Now there were no expectations for anything else. There was just the undeniable pleasure of being with her.

He'd forgotten how the simplest things she said could make him laugh—not necessarily the words, but the way she delivered them. He wondered if she felt in any way the same, because her eyes had lost some of that haunted look. There hadn't been a lot of laughter in his life in recent years…perhaps it had been the same for her.

She pushed her chair back from the table, inadvertently brushing his legs with hers as she did so. She didn't seem to notice, whereas to him the slight contact was like a jolt of electricity.

He wanted her.

'I'm not used to sitting for long these days,' she said. 'I'd really like to have a look around the hotel. You're a guest here—what if you gave me a guided tour?'

'I don't know about a guided tour, but I can certainly walk around with you. I lived here for a few weeks, so I know it fairly well.'

He would have to be very careful to maintain a distance between them. And keep his eyes off the swell of her breasts revealed by the low neckline of her top.

There were some splendid public areas of the hotel, and as they walked through them together he noted her professional enthusiasm. She seemed to know her stuff when it came to hotels. So why was she packing boxes when her earlier life had been spent in the pursuit of a career in hospitality? He still hadn't got a satisfactory answer.

As they made their way to one of the informal sitting rooms they encountered a large catering trolley, blocking the turn of the corridor. The staff member apologised and started to pull the trolley backwards, away from them.

'No, no, it's okay,' Claudia said, no doubt feeling empathy for the guy as former hotel staff herself, or just because she was well-mannered and considerate. 'We can squeeze by—can't we, Stefanos?' She looked up at him.

He looked at the tight space. Did she realise just how tight it was? Only if they squeezed themselves up against each other could the trolley get by.

'Of course,' he said, not able to hide his anticipation.

He found himself hard up against her, her hips against his, her breasts against his chest, their arms tight by their sides. It was the closest he had been to her in ten years.

It seemed a very long moment as the trolley trundled by them. Claudia looked up at him, cheeks flushed, her pupils so huge they virtually eclipsed the blue of her eyes. He could feel her nipples pebble…no doubt she could feel his arousal. Her breathing was coming a little harder and he fought to control his.

They stood close for a moment too long before she pulled away from him. She pushed her hair back from her face when she didn't really need to do so, and he remembered it was something she did when she was nervous.

'Er... I'd love to see that sitting room—the one with the palm trees you mentioned. That you thought I'd like.' She spoke way too fast and didn't meet his eyes.

When they got to the room she made too many observations, praised it too lavishly. Made sure she kept a non-touching distance away from him. Then she spluttered to a stop. At last she looked up at him. Took a deep breath that made her breasts rise enticingly.

'I'd love to see inside the bedrooms,' she said. 'Would it be pushing our friendly acquaintanceship too far to ask to see yours?'

Her blue eyes were innocent of guile, yet he could not say the same of himself. *Claudia. His bedroom.* He wasn't thinking about the furnishings.

He nodded, cleared his throat. 'I'm staying in the penthouse.'

She smiled a slow smile. He wasn't sure what to make of it—which made it all the more exciting.

'Of course you are,' she said. 'Are you sure you don't mind? I wouldn't be invading your privacy?'

'I don't mind at all.'

Inwardly he groaned. He hoped he was reading her right.

Claudia in his bedroom.

If he hadn't read her right it would be a huge effort of will to keep his mind on anything but how utterly desirable he still found her.

CHAPTER FIVE

CLAUDIA DIDN'T REGISTER much about the penthouse suite except the enormous, contemporary-style four-poster bed. She didn't give a flying fig about what the room looked like—how elegantly it was furnished, the panelling on the walls. She tossed her coat on a chair and didn't notice when it slid to the thickly carpeted floor. All her senses were taken up with Stefanos and how much she had wanted him back then...

How much she wanted him now.

He'd opened the door to usher her through ahead of him. Now he stood facing her, with the closed door behind him, framing him. So big, so tall, so damned *sexy.* He didn't say a word. He didn't have to. Everything he might need to say was in his eyes, and she was sure he saw the same message in hers.

He took a step towards her.

At the same time she took two steps towards him.

Then she was in his arms.

At last.

She suppressed a sob of relief that he seemed to want this too.

He felt the same as he had the last time they'd been this close in an embrace, yet not quite the same. His chest was broader, more muscular, and his arms around her were more powerful. He hadn't worked out back then—he hadn't needed to. He'd got all the exercise he needed from working on the *Daphne*, swimming, and bedroom athletics with her.

She breathed in the familiar scent of him. It wasn't a cologne or a shampoo—it was *him*, and it hadn't changed at all. With his scent came a flood of memories, intoxicating and arousing. She looked up at him, intently taking in his face, so familiar and yet so unfamiliar. Was that tiny scar above his thick black eyebrow new? Or had she forgotten it over the space of ten years?

She rose on tiptoe at the same time as he dipped his head and their lips met in a kiss. The kiss was uncertain at first—a kiss between strangers who had once been intimate and were now tentative with each other. It was exciting, for sure, but part of her held back, analysing how she was feeling about this first kiss after such a long time. There was something different from all the countless kisses they'd shared before. The beard. That was what it was. Back then he'd been clean-shaven. She liked the difference. The brush of his beard on her skin was like an erotic tickle—an extra dimension of sensation.

The analysis lasted for mere seconds before their kiss quickly escalated to become hungry, urgent, demanding. Her heart raced, her breath came short, and a sudden rush of desire overwhelmed her. He pulled her tighter and pressed her body to his, breasts to solid chest, hips to the hardness of his thighs. He slid his hands down the side of her breasts, her waist. She realised he was remembering her body—her shape, her skin, her reactions. His hands felt good—they always had. Her nipples were so hard they ached, and when he reached down to cup her bottom she gasped in surprise, pleasure and arousal.

Impatiently she tugged his shirt from his trousers, so she could slide her hands up to splay them across the warmth and strength of his chest. In response, he walked her backwards towards the bed, each of them frantically attempting to divest the other of clothing. She got as far as unbuckling his belt, and he removed her wide belt, before they fell onto the bed, facing each other. He pushed up her top to caress her breasts until she thought she would come just from the sheer pleasure of it. Her body remembered his, all right. He slid his hands up under her skirt to tug down her stockings, pull her lacy panties to one side. His intimate touch with skilled, knowing fingers was sheer ecstasy. He had always known exactly how to arouse her.

As they lay there, facing each other on the bed, he broke away from the kiss, took his hand from her. 'Is this what you want?' His voice was hoarse, his breath coming in great, ragged gulps. 'If not, say so now.'

'Yes…' she managed to get out in a suddenly husky voice. 'Yes. Don't stop. I want it. I want *you*.' She pulled him back to her. *'Now.'*

Hands unsteady with haste, she unzipped his trousers and pushed them down past his hips over strong thighs, following them with his boxers. She circled his erection with her hand. *That* hadn't changed, she thought, as she trembled in anticipation of the pleasure she knew he could give her.

He bunched her skirt up above her hips, yanked down her stockings to her ankles, tore her lacy panties in his haste to remove them. No need to undress further. She bucked her hips towards him, writhing with impatience.

'Protection,' he said hoarsely, and he broke away to reach for a small satchel on the nightstand.

Thank heavens he'd remembered, she thought. She was so on fire for him, so desperate for him to enter her, she might not have thought about protection, and that would have undone ten years of caution against her fear of pregnancy.

Protection in place, she pulled him down to her. 'I'm ready for you. *Please.*'

There was a distinct whimper in her voice. She didn't care if she sounded as if she was begging. She *was* begging. She wanted him—*needed* him. And it had been so long. She couldn't wait a second more.

When he pushed inside her, filling her, thrusting, she moaned in her intense pleasure and then almost immediately convulsed around him in a mind-blowing orgasm that had her crying out his name. *'Stefanos!'* No one had ever made her feel the way he did—that intensity of sensation, that power.

As she came down from the heights he held her close. Then he continued his steady, rhythmical possession of her body until she came again, in an intense rush of pleasure, accompanied by his great shout of release. They'd practised their timing back then—who knew a simultaneous orgasm would still be so effortless for them now?

She fell back onto the bed, exhilarated, laughing, face flushed. She looked down at her skirt, all bunched up above her waist, her top rucked up above her bra—heck, she still had her shoes on. But then so did he...

She looked up at him. His eyes were dilated, his expression unreadable. He had closed his eyes at the moment of climax. Back then in Santorini they had always looked into each other's eyes—trying, he'd said, to see inside each other's soul.

'That was fast and furious,' she said. She reached up and stroked her fingers down his cheek. Her voice hitched. 'And utterly wonderful. Thank you.'

He caught her hand and kissed her fingers one by one. 'I haven't finished with you yet,' he said, in a deep, determined voice that sent more shivers of anticipation down her spine.

'I like the sound of that,' she murmured.

Slowly he divested her of her top, then her bra, and pinned her hands above her head with one hand while kissing her breasts, tonguing one nipple while he rolled the other between thumb and finger. The pleasure was almost painful.

Just as she was about to implore him to stop—it was simply too pleasurable to bear—he moved down, kissing a path to the top of her skirt, the soft brush of his beard adding to her rising excitement. He found the zipper and soon she was only in her torn black lace panties. He took the remnants of those in his teeth and smoothed them down over her thighs, kissing every inch of her along the way, bringing her yet again almost to the point of orgasm.

'I like these shoes,' he said. 'You look very sexy in them and nothing else. But I'd prefer the nothing else.'

He took off her spike heel slingbacks, caressing her toes and the arch of each foot as he did so until, squirming with ticklish laughter, she had to pull them away. It was silly that amid all this thrilling pleasure she felt glad she'd had a pedicure only two days before and that her legs were waxed.

She sat up and pushed him by his shoulders, down onto his back. 'This is a little one-sided, isn't it?' she said, kneeling over him, dominating him. 'We have to remedy that. Now it's my turn to torture you.'

It was an old game between them—one she hadn't given thought to for years. But here he was again, under her sensual control, and she thrilled to the power of it. She loved the way he narrowed his eyes in anticipation as he raised his arms in surrender to her wishes.

Claudia unbuttoned his shirt and stripped it off him, tossing it dramatically to the floor. Memories of what had pleased him back then flooded her. Would she still please him now? Teasingly, she kissed him all over his face—on his eyelids, on his nose, on the corners of his mouth. But she wouldn't let him capture her mouth in a kiss—that was part of the torture.

She kissed behind his ears, the hollows of his throat, the tops of his arms—which seemed to particularly please him—and across his chest. She kissed, nibbled and sucked a pathway down his belly, loving the way his muscles went rigid and he groaned at her teasing touch. She flirted briefly with his bold erection—until he asked her to stop unless she wanted the game to end right there and then. So she moved down his legs to take off his shoes and tug off his trousers.

She surveyed his gloriously naked body, the smooth olive skin with a dusting of dark hair in all the right places. His defined musculature was like a statue of one of the most perfect Greek gods from ancient times.

'Impressive,' she sighed, aroused just by the sight of him. 'Although I'm not sure about the socks-only look... They really have to go.'

He laughed and pulled her into his arms. This time their lovemaking was slow and sensual and even more satisfying—for him as much for her, she hoped.

Sated, she drowsed, wrapped in his arms. Although as she drifted off the thought persisted: again, he hadn't looked into her eyes as he climaxed. Maybe that lack of intimate communication was the difference between two people deeply in love—as they had once been—and two friendly acquaintances slaking their sexual appetites with each other.

Stefanos, propped on one elbow, watched Claudia as she slept. The late-morning May sunshine filtered through the curtains, illuminating the tumble of her auburn hair with copper glints where it spread against the white of the bed linen.

Her darkened eyelashes fluttered—was she dreaming? Dreaming of *him*?

He could see the delicate bluish-green veins under the translucent skin around her closed eyes. One long, slender leg rested over his. Her skin was strikingly pale against his with its darker olive tone. Her colouring made her look fragile, but he knew she had a strength that belied her appearance. Her body was toned, with sleek muscles. And there was nothing fragile about her sensual responses. Just like in their long-ago past, she matched him for sexual appetite.

Inwardly, he sighed. After they'd broken up he had never again experienced sex such as he'd shared with her. He'd grown to realise how very rare that level of connection was. Today their bodies had read other's wants as if ten years had never passed.

But great sex wasn't enough.

She smiled in her sleep—just a faint upturning of her lovely mouth, swollen from his kisses. Definitely dreaming of him, he thought.

Back then, he had often watched her like this as she slept, scarcely able to believe that she was his. His hadn't been an adolescent love. He had loved her with a man's heart and soul, and had known with a passionate certainty that he wanted to spend his life with her. He had wanted a child with her, to make a family with her, to share his wealth, his heart, *everything* with her.

Her rejection of him had hardened his heart against her and led him to two disastrous marriages. But right now, in the afterglow of great sex, he was inclined to think more kindly of her. After all, she'd only been nineteen. Now, in spite of their obvious physical compatibility, it was too late for them to try again. Their time with each other had come and gone. He was a different person now: distrustful, wary, and cynical when it came to women and their motives.

He'd been in so much pain over his loss of Claudia it had made him vulnerable—too ready to prove she wasn't the only woman he could love. Along had come his mother's goddaughter Arina, from another megawealthy Greek shipping family, newly graduated with a degree in marketing and doing an internship at Adrastos Shipping. Their match had been actively encouraged by both sets of parents. In fact there'd been an ongoing family joke that they, born six months apart, had been betrothed at birth.

Arina had grown into a beauty—petite, black-haired, with soulful brown eyes. The complete opposite, in fact, to Claudia. She was smart, sweet and kind. If anything, something of a people-pleaser—but that hadn't mattered when he was the person she was pleasing.

In his heart, Stefanos had known he hadn't felt for her

what he'd felt for Claudia. But that kind of love only led to heartbreak and loss.

Their families had been delighted when he'd proposed after three months of dating, having convinced himself that Arina was exactly what he needed, and they'd had a big wedding in the cathedral in Athens, both aged twenty-two. Later, he'd realised that had been the happiest day of their entire marriage.

Their wedding night hadn't been a great success. She'd been a nervous virgin and shrunk away from him. And by the time their six-month wedding anniversary had rolled around the marriage had become sexless. That had been the day when Arina, in her kindest, sweetest voice, had told him she was leaving him.

She had fallen in love with someone else—had been in love with her for years, in fact, but unable to admit it. The chief bridesmaid at their wedding. Arina had been unable to deny her sexuality any longer—although she had tried to, for her conservative family's sake. She had apologised to Stefanos over and over. She cared about him, but she simply wasn't sexually attracted to him. He had told her there was nothing to forgive. That she had to stop pleasing other people instead of herself.

Their divorce hadn't stopped him liking her, and they had since maintained a genuine if somewhat distant friendship, but he admitted, if only to himself, how battered and bruised he had been by the experience of his one-sided marriage. Not so much because he had been rejected in favour of a woman—which had struck deeply at his masculinity and his pride as a Greek male even though he knew he shouldn't have let it—but rather it was her dishonesty and deception that had wounded him. She had lied to him from the start.

He'd been happy for Arina that she had found true love. But he'd been too scarred to look for it himself. How could he trust another woman to be what she said she was? Why hadn't he realised?

He had maintained that distrust but somehow, five years later, Tiana had sneaked under his defences. Perhaps it had been because at first she'd reminded him a little of Claudia—although her red hair had been dyed and her forthrightness had been fake too. But she'd been glamorous, exciting, not looking for anything from him but a good time and a supply of expensive gifts of jewellery with which he had obliged her. There was no emotional investment required in a diamond bracelet.

However non-stop fun had palled after a while. Tiana had cleverly read his mood and quietly confessed that all she really wanted was to settle down and have a family. He'd been charmed by her 'honesty'. Although the truth was that he'd been suckered by a mistress of the art.

Now, Claudia stirred in her sleep and opened her eyes, smiling when she saw him. She was so beautiful—everything he'd once wanted in a woman. But it was too late for him and her.

Too late, too late.

The refrain ran through his head as he forced a smile in return.

CHAPTER SIX

CLAUDIA OPENED HER eyes to see Stefanos lying beside her. Naked. She was naked too. In a hotel bed, in the late morning, in central London.

So it hadn't been a dream.

Surprisingly, she didn't feel awkward. What had happened between them had been entirely consensual and very, very good. Nevertheless, she pulled the linen sheet up above her breasts to cover her nakedness, and in doing so covered his.

He smiled at her, but the smile didn't quite reach his eyes. That was okay. He probably felt awkward. It was a potentially awkward situation. Who knew? Perhaps he expected her to hop out of bed, thank him and leave. They weren't really 'friendly acquaintances'—more like strangers. And she didn't have any expectations that there would be any more than this between them. They were very different people from those they'd been back then.

Back on the *Daphne* in Santorini, even after she'd found out what the surname Adrastos stood for in Greece, they'd been equals. Her in a swimsuit, he in board shorts, in the blue waters that had belonged to everyone. Now they moved in very different worlds, and faced those worlds from very different perspectives.

His apartment, for instance, was no doubt just one dwelling in a portfolio of luxury properties. Whereas she was living in a rented maisonette in Hammersmith, building up her savings so she could buy a place of her own. What made for great communication in bed didn't necessarily translate to the world outside the bedroom.

'The sex was…unexpected,' she said.

He raised a dark eyebrow. 'Was it really? I was thinking about sex from the moment I first saw you.'

That sensual edge to his voice made her quiver every time.

'Perhaps I was too,' she admitted. 'When I first saw you, I mean.' Standing there in the doorway…his hostility adding an extra edge to his dark good looks.

He grinned, and there was a flash of the carefree young Stefanos she had loved.

'This…our lovemaking…completes things for me,' she said.

'You mean climax-wise?' he said with a lazy smile.

She smiled back. 'That too. But that was always good with you. What I meant was, we never had a "last time" together before I left Santorini.'

'We didn't,' he said.

In fact they'd scarcely been speaking.

'The pregnancy scare changed everything, didn't it? We didn't make love again after I…confessed my fears. Later I tried to remember when exactly we'd last been together and I couldn't.'

She'd been inexplicably saddened by that.

'Now you have closure?' he said. 'Is that what you mean?'

She frowned. 'Yes… No. I'm not sure if that's it, exactly. But closure is near enough.'

What she was trying to say was that she'd been left with a deeply buried unresolved longing for him. And now that had been resolved.

'Good,' he said.

She sat up to lean against the lavishly padded headboard. She found it difficult to meet his eye.

'Talking about back then—and before we say goodbye again—I... I want to tell you why I behaved the way I did when we...when we broke up.'

He sat up too, the sheets rucked around his hips. 'I thought we weren't going to go over the past.'

'I think I need to—for the closure thing, I mean.'

'I don't need closure,' he said. 'It was a long time ago. It's not possible to step twice into the same river, as we say in Greece.'

'Like we say water under the bridge—I get it. But can you humour me?'

To his credit, he didn't show any sign of impatience. 'If it's that important to you,' he said.

She realised she was clutching the sheet between her fingers and released her grip. 'You must have thought it unusual that I was so anti-marriage and anti-babies when most people hope for that sometime in their futures.'

'Yes,' he said. 'I'm an only child. I always knew I wanted one day to have a family with more than one child.'

And he'd made that so very clear to her at the time. It wasn't just that he'd been trying to be honourable, she realised, even at the age of twenty he had been ready to start a family. She hadn't.

'Do you remember I told you my father died when I was fifteen?' she said.

He nodded. 'I remember feeling sad for you. And now

I've lost my own father I can appreciate even more how you must have felt.'

Even now, after all this time, she felt tears threaten when she thought about her beloved dad.

'He and my mother managed a pub—had done for many years. He died in an accident. A careless truck driver hadn't properly secured a load of wooden barrels of beer he was delivering. My father went to help unload and…and was hit when they suddenly rolled off the truck.'

Stefanos swore under his breath in Greek. 'A terrible accident.'

'Both terrible and tragic. His death triggered massive change in my life. For one thing we lived "above the shop", and we lost our home when the chain who owned the pub put in new managers. It was a huge wrench for me. I loved the pub…the visitors from around the world. I offered to step up and manage it myself, but of course they laughed at me.'

Stefanos smiled. 'You were fifteen.'

She managed a watery smile. 'I know… But I still think I could have done it. I'd tagged along after my father since I was a child.'

'Apart from the fact you were underage and not even allowed to drink at a licensed premises let alone run it.'

'All that,' she said with a sigh. 'My mother wasn't trained to take over the pub's management and nor did she want to. She'd been very happy to support Dad in everything he wanted to do, but her work at the pub was mainly behind the bar and in the restaurant—not management.'

'And she was a mother.'

'Yes. To me and my half-brother, who's five years

older than me. He's from Dad's first marriage. His wife died when Mark was only a toddler. Mum was a good mother—still is. But most of all she was a wife. She went to pieces when Dad died. And I... I didn't know how to help her.'

'That must have tough for you.'

'It was. I was dealing with my own grief. It was a bad age to lose him.'

'Any age is a bad age to lose your father,' he said.

She put out her hand and laid it over his. 'I know. You must still be grieving. And your mother, too.'

Wordlessly, he nodded. She took away her hand. Even though they'd shared every intimacy a man and woman could share in the last few hours, she didn't want to appear presumptuous.

'My mum didn't seem to be able to function without a man in her life,' she said.

'What about your brother?'

'He was ready to help as much as he could, but there wasn't much he could do. Mum had been well-compensated by the pub company, as Dad had died while at work due to negligence, but we moved in with my grandparents—his parents—who didn't live far away. My mum was lost without a man in her life. Six months after Dad died she started dating a man who'd used to stay at the pub on business trips. He'd been friendly with both her and Dad.'

'That seems quick...'

'I thought so too. I resented the heck out of him. And you can imagine what my grandparents—Dad's parents—thought.'

'What was he like?'

'Nice enough. But he wasn't my dad. My dad had

adored my mother. He would have been horrified that she found someone to replace him so quickly.'

'Or glad she'd found someone to care for her?' Stefanos said slowly. 'My mother is very lonely as a widow, despite her friends and family.'

'There is that...' Claudia said, somewhat grudgingly, not wanting to admit she might have been wrong about something so fundamental. 'I don't know how serious it was, or whether they were planning to get married. But they'd been together for less than six months when my mother fell pregnant.'

Stefanos's dark eyebrows rose. 'That must have been a shock. How did you feel about that?'

'Can you imagine how embarrassing it was for a sixteen-year-old to have a pregnant forty-year-old mother?'

'Had they planned it?'

She shuddered in remembered distaste. 'I thought it was kind of icky that she was having sex at her age, so I didn't ask. But Mum said it was an accident, that she'd believed she was too old to get pregnant.'

'Did you believe that?'

'I did. She'd finally gone back to the career she'd had before she gave it up to work with Dad. She'd been a veterinary nurse and had always told us how much she loved it and missed it. After Dad died she updated her qualifications and resumed her career—only to have to give it up again.'

'And the father?'

'He married her.' She paused. 'I rather think he thought he'd been trapped. Mum was fun and outgoing—always good for a laugh. I don't think he counted on a baby coming along to deflect her focus from him.

It got even more complicated when they discovered she was having twins.'

'I remember you said you had twin sisters. You were very fond of them.'

'I was. I am. I love them. Trouble was, my stepfather was in IT and travelled a lot for work. He was often away when the twins were babies. And they were a lot of work. Mum couldn't handle them on her own. She certainly couldn't work in the career she'd finally returned to.'

'I'm beginning to see what you're getting at.'

Could anyone really imagine what it had been like? They'd have had to be there in that small house they'd all moved into as 'a family'.

'Yep, those babies really restricted my mother's life at a time when she hadn't expected that. And good old big sister was the live-in babysitter. Can you imagine studying for exams while looking after two babies? Or having to say no to a date with your first crush? I loved the twins, and I loved my mother—of course I did. But I sometimes felt I was going through a kind of teenage mum hell. It made me realise how much worse it would be if you actually were a teenage mum and unable to hand them back, like I did when my babysitting shifts were done.'

'What about their father?'

'I was too resentful of him for trying to take my father's place and for putting us all in that position by getting my mum pregnant to think too much about him. He simply wasn't significant for me. But when the twins got a little older and could call him Dadda he seemed to bond with them. He got a new job that kept him off the road and he moved his little family to Swindon, where they still live. I stayed with my grandparents in Devon to finish school. By the time I met you I'd finished my first year of uni. I was living away from home and felt as if I had been let off the leash.'

Stefanos slowly shook his head. 'Why didn't you tell me all this back then?'

'I didn't want to talk to anyone about all that—even you. I didn't want to be someone's daughter or stepdaughter or even half-sister. I was totally intent on forging my own identity. But perhaps I should have told you. Because then you might have seen why I was so horrified at the prospect of not only being a teenage mum, but of being dependent on a man and losing the career I so desperately wanted.'

He was silent for a long beat. 'It might have helped me understand why you reacted so vehemently against marriage to me...baby or no baby.'

'In hindsight, I should have told you. But then you might have wondered why I had kept it from you—given you an edited version of my life in the UK. Somehow in Santorini I wanted to leave all that behind. Not to talk to anyone about my family situation. To just be me—Claudia—with my past behind me and the future I'd planned for myself ahead.'

'I see,' he said.

Did he? Could he? Because, looking back, even she found it difficult to understand. Why, when she'd been so in love with him, hadn't she shared such an important part of her life?

There wasn't really any more to tell. Perhaps there were questions Stefanos might have asked...answers she might have given him. Perhaps she might have had the opportunity to tell him that she hadn't changed her stance on marriage since then. But Room Service were at the door.

'While you were asleep I ordered us some lunch,' he said. 'I thought we might be hungry.'

'After all that exercise, you mean?' she said.

The smile in his eyes told her he knew exactly the kind of exercise she meant.

He'd been right—she was hungry. Claudia sat opposite Stefanos at the round table in the dining area of his suite. They were both dressed in the lush black robes supplied by the hotel. He looked so good in black, with his dark hair and that green glint in his eyes, his sensual mouth... Even hotter than he'd been at twenty and just as energetic, she thought, with a secret, satisfied smile.

He'd ordered four separate meals to give her a choice. Such extravagance—yet he didn't seem to think it was an unusual thing to do. The room service waiter certainly hadn't blinked as he'd explained all four dishes.

'I remember you like healthy food,' Stefanos said.

Oddly, for someone who'd wanted a career in hospitality back then, she didn't remember what he'd liked to eat. She'd loved the traditional Greek meals they'd shared—not just in the town restaurants but in the out-of-the-way tavernas he'd taken her to on the *Daphne*, where the vegetables on the menu had been grown in the garden behind and the cheese had been made with milk from the owner's goats. Surely, as a billionaire's son, he had had grander tastes than that.

Now, she chose poached chicken with a tarragon yogurt sauce and salad; he went for salmon. He ate with gusto, but her appetite deserted her after a few mouthfuls and she put down her fork. This was beginning to feel awkward. Too much like a date when it wasn't that at all. She almost wished she would be saved by a phone call, but she'd turned off her phone after a quick text to Kitty asking her to look after her clients for that afternoon. Kitty would no doubt call the two packers now working in Stefanos's apartment to check all was well. She would be aching with curiosity about the reason Claudia had asked them to take over.

'Shall we meet here for lunch the next time I'm in London?' Stefanos said.

Next time? Claudia was so shocked to hear him mention a 'next time' she couldn't find the words to answer. She had assumed this would be the only time she shared with him before they went their separate ways.

'Th-that would be nice,' she finally managed to stutter. She looked up at him. 'I mean to have lunch in the restaurant…not in your bedroom.'

Wonderful as this reunion had been, she had no intention of being his booty call in London.

His eyes met hers, clear and direct. 'That's what I meant too,' he said.

'Not that I haven't loved every minute with you. But…'

'We've both found closure,' he said smoothly.

Neither of them had voiced it, but she sensed his bitterness about her refusing to marry him still lingered— might always linger. Might he even, deep down, blame her for his two marriages that had ended in divorce? He'd used to tell her that vengeance was a big thing in Greece because of all the vengeful Greek gods of mythology. There was definitely now a darker edge to that beautiful, sunny-natured boy she'd loved that long-ago summer.

'Today was perfect. I wouldn't want to risk ruining it by…by repeating it,' she said.

Spending this time with him had reminded her of just how good they'd been together in bed, but it had been about sex, not love. And sex without love had never been on her personal agenda.

'My thoughts precisely,' he said. 'You can't go backwards in life.'

'Or step in the same river twice, as you said.'

'Exactly.'

'We often did think the same thing,' she said, with a short, forced laugh.

Except about the really important issues, like marriage and children. But who could have blamed her for not having them at the front of mind at the age of nineteen?

'There's just one thing I'd like to ask you.'

'Go ahead,' he said.

'You're not cheating on anyone with me today?'

His shocked expression gave her his answer even before he replied. 'I told you I was single and I meant that I was single—no ties.' He paused. 'I've had more than my share of entanglement since we last met…' The mouth that had so recently been kissing her was set in a grim line. 'But I'm not looking for marriage number three—which means no relationships that might give a woman the wrong idea, or any kind of expectations.'

'I see,' she said. That no doubt included her. 'I ask because I… I think I told you I had a bad experience with someone who didn't tell me he was married. I inadvertently hurt his wife and I… I was distressed about that.'

The expression on Stefanos's face flitted from surprise, to exasperation, to a quickly masked fondness and back to exasperation. 'Why do you have to be so damn *nice*, Claudia?'

'Am I? I try to do the right thing by people, but I've never thought of myself as being particularly *nice*.'

'Well, you were back then, and it appears you still are now.'

Had he really thought that? She remembered that grim journey to the airport…the way he had ghosted her. The way she hadn't told him the full story about why she didn't want marriage because she'd been so determined to preserve the image of herself she had created.

'I'm glad you think so,' she said. She took a deep breath. 'I'm glad we met inadvertently, and I'm glad about…about that.'

She waved her hand in the direction of the bedroom… the bed with its tangle of linen, the scent of their love-making. His scent was still on her, and she was in no rush to wash it off. She'd shower when she got home.

'Me too,' he said.

'Do you plan to come to London often?'

'Occasionally. I've had a year in London and now there are things in Athens that need my attention. But there are archaeologists here I want to keep in touch with. I'll be sure to look you up when I visit.'

His words were perfectly pleasant—matter-of-fact, almost. As if they really were friendly acquaintances, not a man and a woman who had made passionate love all morning, intimately explored each other's bodies, and brought each other to the pinnacle of pleasure. She swallowed hard against a pang of hurt that he didn't appear to have seen anything special in the gloriously sensual time they'd spent together.

'I'd like that.'

She pushed her chair away from the table, took a deep breath. She couldn't let him see that at that moment she yearned for something more.

'It won't be easy to say goodbye, so I'm not going to drag it out. I'll find my clothes and go.'

'You don't want to finish your lunch?'

She shook her head. There was no point in prolonging this. If she didn't go she just might be silly and ask if he was sure the grown-up Stefanos and Claudia couldn't have a casual relationship…a friendship, even. She couldn't risk it. Because it wouldn't work. Not for her and nor, she suspected, for him. He was a self-confessed all-or-nothing guy—she was a woman who had never entertained the emotional risk of casual sex. Especially with a man who had the potential to shatter her heart. Again.

She found her clothes where he'd flung them, on the floor next to the bed, and her shoes heels-up at the end. The torn panties were wrapped up in the sheets. She tucked them in her tote bag. Somehow she couldn't bring herself to put them in the wastepaper bin. It was awful for hotel staff to have to clear up after guests' sexual shenanigans—and, besides, it was kind of sexy the way Stefanos had torn them off her. Quite one of the highlights of the morning.

Dressed, she peered in the mirror. Hair dishevelled, mascara smeared around her eyes, lips swollen with the lipstick all kissed off, beard rash around her neck… She looked like a woman who had spent the morning in bed with her lover. Not her lover, she reminded herself. Her *former* lover, a *long-ago* lover, who still knew how to press her buttons and with whom she had managed to put some old hurts to rest. She couldn't forget that.

My God, he was gorgeous, though, and she had

to stamp, crush, pound into the ground any lingering thoughts of *what if?* There would only be this morning for them, and she had to disengage with any wishful imaginings that there might be more.

She picked up her tote bag. She couldn't catch the tube looking like this. She would splurge on a taxi home and repair the damage before her catch-up with Kitty.

Stefanos was still sitting at the table, his meal unfinished. He had obviously not eaten a bite since she'd left the room. Seeing her, he immediately got up from the chair.

'You're ready,' he said slowly.

'Yes.' She covered the few steps between them. 'Stefanos,' she said. 'Thank you.'

'It is I who should be thanking you.'

'Let's thank each other, then,' she said.

He pulled her to him in a hug. The time for passionate kisses had passed. For what seemed like a long time she stood in the circle of his arms, with her head nestled against his shoulder. How secure and safe she felt there. But it was an illusion. She suspected this encounter with her first love would soon begin to seem like a dream.

She pulled back and looked up into his face. His eyes were dark and unreadable. 'I said I was curious about what kind of a man you'd grown up to be. I… I'm glad to see you're such a wonderful man. I hope everything works out for you when you get home.' She paused, drinking in his dark good looks for the last time. Then, 'Goodbye, Stefanos, *yiasou.*'

'*Yiasou,* Claudia,' he echoed, his voice hoarse.

She planted a kiss on his cheek, turned on her heel, picked up her tote bag and headed to the door without turning back. She could not let him see that her eyes were smarting with tears.

CHAPTER SEVEN

CLAUDIA HAD PLENTY of time to hail a taxi and get home to her maisonette in Hammersmith, shower, change, and then meet her friend at the Chelsea mansion on Cheyne Walk, overlooking the Thames, that Lady Kitty now called home. Sebastian was out of town on business, and they'd planned a girls night in.

Kitty greeted her with a hug. 'You look…glowing,' she said. 'What's responsible for that?' She narrowed her eyes. 'Or *who*? Has this got anything to do with the client at the Bloomsbury apartment? The one you mysteriously bailed on?'

'Oh, Kitty, it has everything to do with Stefanos,' Claudia said. 'He's a man from my past. Do you remember me telling you about my first love? The guy in Santorini?'

'*Him?* The billionaire that got away?'

'The very one. Stefanos Adrastos.'

Kitty's eyes widened. 'I can't believe it. Did he plan it? Or was it an amazing coincidence? Come and sit down. I'll pour you some wine and you can tell me all about it.'

Kitty led her to Sebastian's grandmother's private sitting room, which Kitty had appropriated for her own, and sat her down on the sofa next to her. No sooner had she poured Claudia some wine than she pounced on her for details of why she'd so suddenly left the packing job—something she'd never done before.

Her friend was enthralled by Claudia's story of her first, long-lost love showing up in London as a client of PWP, and what had happened after she'd gone to his hotel for coffee.

'Break-up sex postponed for ten years?' Kitty said. 'That's powerful stuff.'

Kitty had nailed it, Claudia thought. Of course that was all it had been. Really good sex between people who hadn't forgotten how to please each other in bed. They certainly hadn't made any promises to each other—not even a nominal stab at being friends. And yet it had been so perfect. *He* had been so perfect.

'Stefanos is indeed very powerful,' Claudia said with a laugh. 'And he is *so* sexy.'

'So what are you doing here with me?' Kitty asked. 'Why aren't you with him right now? Are you going to see him again?'

Claudia sipped her wine. 'We did talk about seeing each other again next time he's in London. But I'm not sure it will happen again—going to bed with him, I mean.'

'Do you want it to happen again?'

'In terms of sheer physical pleasure, yes. But it's complicated. And I mean *really* complicated. He's been married and divorced twice.'

'Perhaps he never really got over you?'

'I suspect he could still be bitter. Remember I refused his proposal and left him.'

'So he's bitter and twisted?'

'Not twisted—perhaps bitter. Heaven knows what

caused his divorces. He wouldn't tell me. That said, he's every bit as gorgeous as he was ten years ago.' She knew she wasn't keeping the longing from her voice. 'Even more handsome, and super self-assured and confident.'

'Seems he finds you gorgeous too.'

'There is that… But you know I've never been one for casual hook-ups.'

'You haven't actually dated anyone since you got back to the UK.'

Claudia had met Kitty at a public relations function at a hotel years ago, when Kitty had been a baby PR person and Claudia in her first job. They'd stayed friends during all the years Claudia had been out of the country.

'PWP takes up all my time and energy,' Claudia said, aware of the defensive note to her voice.

She knew that wasn't quite true. The episode in Sydney with Brad had made her deeply distrustful—too distrustful to consider using dating apps—and she hadn't met anyone who interested her at a bar or a party or any other likely places. She'd been too distrustful, in fact, to spend time with any man. Until Stefanos had opened the door of that apartment in Bloomsbury and there he'd stood. The only man she had ever truly loved.

'I think you could find the time and certainly the energy if the person was right,' said Kitty carefully.

Claudia picked up her glass. 'That's it… I can't help feeling that Stefanos is the right person— always was the right person. But I lost my chance with him ten years ago. And that chance won't come again. Stefanos even has a saying about it in Greek: you can't step in the same river twice.'

'That sounds grim. And very definite.'

'Even if I wanted to see him, the ball is very firmly

in his court. We both hurt each other in the past, and I'm not sure he would want to tear old scars open again. I'd be wary too.'

'It's a real case of *what if?*, isn't it?' said Kitty.

'It is.' Claudia took a sip from her wine and put the glass back on the coffee table. 'What if I'd stayed with Stefanos in Greece when I was nineteen? Dropped out of uni and never gone home?'

'You would have grown to resent him,' Kitty said firmly.

'Would I?'

'Yes. You would have always been asking yourself what if you'd followed your dream career instead of being a teenage bride.'

'What if I'd *liked* being a teenage bride? Plenty of girls do.'

Simply being with Stefanos might have been enough.

'Maybe you would have—who knows?' said Kitty. 'Maybe you'd have had four children by now.'

'I don't think so.'

She thought about how much Stefanos had wanted a baby back then. Would he have wanted four kids? It seemed odd that he was now thirty and didn't have children.

'You would certainly have had enough money never to worry about how many kids you had,' Kitty said.

'It was never about his money with Stefanos and me. I thought he was just a guy working on some rich person's yacht for the summer when I first met him. I would have felt the same about him if that had been the truth.'

'It has never been an issue with me and Sebastian either.'

Sebastian was a self-made millionaire, but had also

inherited billions. He'd been Kitty's boss before he had been her husband.

'Turned out Stefanos *was* the rich person who owned the yacht. I wonder if he still has it? We never got around to talking about stuff like that.'

'Too busy getting down and dirty in his hotel room?' Kitty teased.

'It wasn't dirty! Well, maybe just a little…and decidedly delicious,' Claudia said, with a small smile of remembered pleasure.

It had been so delicious she wanted to close her eyes and relive those moments. It was good to talk with Kitty about it. She certainly couldn't talk to anyone else.

'You'll never know if you made the right or wrong decision back then. It's that "sliding doors" thing, isn't it?' Kitty said. 'But, as your friend, I'd say you did make the right decision. You've had a good career doing what you loved, you've seen the world, and now you have a successful business. If you hadn't made that decision back then in Santorini we wouldn't be friends, and I'd be sad about that.'

'Only you wouldn't know I existed, so how could you be sad?'

Kitty laughed. 'True.'

Claudia paused. 'One part of me wants to hop on a plane and land at his door in Athens, ask if there could be a second chance for us. We were so good before— could we not be good again? We're older, I've got travel out of my system.'

'And the other part of you?'

Claudia sighed. 'The other part knows I wouldn't dare. Today was perfect. I should leave it as it is. We talked about stuff we should have talked about ten years ago.

Perhaps he doesn't feel so bitter towards me now. And we had the break-up sex we didn't have back then.'

'Which has left you wanting more,' said Kitty.

'But what if it was so good *because* it was so unexpected and *because* it brought closure of a kind? It mightn't be like that again.' Although it had always been good with Stefanos, even after a ten-year break. 'The truth of it is, I don't know if I can trust him. Is he really single? He might be twice divorced and never want to get married again, but that doesn't stop him having a girlfriend. Imagine if she opened the door to me when I went knocking? He broke my heart ten years ago. I don't want to risk getting my heart broken again. It's best to leave things as they are. Looking back, I can see it took me years to get over him.'

'Did you ever really get over him?' Kitty asked gently.

'Of course I did.'

Kitty raised her eyebrows. 'If you say so.'

'He did say he'd be back in London and we'd meet for lunch. That is if he doesn't ghost me again.'

'Do you really think he'd do that?'

'Who knows what he might do?'

CHAPTER EIGHT

To Claudia's utter relief, Stefanos didn't ghost her after their unexpected reunion. In fact he texted her almost as soon as he'd returned to Athens. She'd picked up her phone with unsteady hands, heart pumping, mouth dry. Only to be plunged into the depths of disappointment when she'd read his words, saying how nice it had been to meet her in such an unexpected way.

A few friendly yet equally impersonal texts had followed. So that was all it would be. She'd given up checking her messages with any degree of anticipation. Yes, it was a little hurtful that he didn't appear to have seen anything memorable and remarkable in the morning they'd spent together in bed. But he'd made no promises of anything more—and neither, in fact, had she, as she had to remind herself.

On the other hand, she found her memories of that day became more special: the incredible coincidence of their reunion, their glorious lovemaking. It wasn't going to happen again, but she hoped there would be a chance to catch up with him. There was so much more she wanted to know about what had happened to him in the ten years between their meetings. She would have to be content with that.

Claudia threw herself into her work like never before—taking extra bookings, doing extra marketing calls. She doubled her sessions at the gym and binge-watched too much television in the evenings. Anything to take her mind off Stefanos. Not that she thought of him all the time. But he popped up in her thoughts more often than she liked, and it was disconcerting.

Six weeks after he'd gone back to Athens, she began to wonder if she was overdoing it. She was more fatigued than she could ever remember being. She was too tired to eat much, and when she did she felt nauseous. In fact the nausea and fatigue increased so much she cut back on her long hours and the exercise. But she still didn't feel well—although the nausea came and went.

It was so frustrating when she was used to enjoying perfect health and energy around the clock. A virus? She must have succumbed to a virus. But a test proved negative. Some kind of food allergy? But she hadn't changed her diet.

A few weeks later, when she had time she went for an appointment with her GP.

'Have you done a pregnancy test?' the doctor asked, as soon as Claudia had recited her symptoms.

Claudia stared at her. 'I'm not pregnant,' she said immediately.

She couldn't possibly be pregnant.

And yet when the doctor asked the date of her last period it seemed she might have missed one. But a lot of exercise and stress could cause that, couldn't it?

'It's a good idea to rule pregnancy out,' the doctor said.

She handed Claudia a pregnancy test and told her where the bathroom was.

Pregnant? From one morning with Stefanos? One morning when they'd been careful with contraception? She simply couldn't be.

Panic seized her, making her feel shaky and anxious. She nearly dropped the test stick into the loo.

Get a grip, Claudia, she told herself. *The doctor said the test is to rule pregnancy out.*

It was a very long three minutes while she waited for the result.

But it didn't rule it out.

The test showed a resounding positive result. Two blue lines said she was pregnant.

She stared at it for a long time, willing the result to go away. The last thing she'd expected to be at this stage of her life was unmarried and pregnant.

'How accurate is this test?' she asked the doctor, once again sitting across the desk from her in her consulting room.

'Very accurate,' the doctor said. 'Are you okay with being pregnant, Claudia?'

'I... I'll have to get used to the idea,' she said. 'It wasn't planned.'

Had she been in denial about what the nausea and fatigue had meant? Kidded herself that it was the push-ups at the gym that had made her breasts a size larger? Or had she simply not recognised the implications.

'I'll need to examine you,' the doctor said.

Claudia lay on the examination table, her thoughts racing. *Pregnant.* How was she going to manage this? Stefanos! Would she tell him? *Should* she tell him? Did he have a right to know? What would he think? What did it mean for PWP?

'You're definitely pregnant,' the doctor said. 'I'd estimate about eight weeks along.'

'I can tell you the exact day I conceived,' Claudia said.

'You can be that sure?'

'Absolutely. It was the only time I'd had sex in a long time.'

'And the father?'

'Not around,' she said. 'We're not in a relationship and he lives in another country. I'm in this on my own.'

'Do you want to keep the baby?' the doctor said.

Claudia was surprised at the sudden burst of possessiveness she felt towards her baby. She put her hand on her stomach. *Her baby.* How quickly she'd come to think that way.

'Absolutely I'm keeping this baby,' she said. She even managed a laugh. 'You know, I've never seen myself as a mother. But suddenly I know that I really want this baby.' She paused. 'It feels right.'

Excitement began to stir. Her life was about to change irrevocably.

The doctor smiled. 'That's wonderful.'

Claudia felt dazed. This had happened so quickly. 'It *is* wonderful, isn't it?'

'There's a lot of help available for sole parents—including financial help,' the doctor said.

'I'll be okay,' Claudia said. 'I have my own business. I can manage.'

'Do you know much about the father?'

'He…he's actually an old acquaintance. But as I said it was a…a one-off thing.'

'The reason I ask is that there will be screening tests available throughout your pregnancy that, among other things, look for the possibility of inherited conditions. It's helpful if the father takes part in some of those tests.'

'To be honest, I don't know if he will want to be involved, and if so to what extent.'

'One thing you might ask him is what his blood type is. You are Rh-negative. If you conceive an Rh-positive baby, there can be consequences. Have you had any previous pregnancies or miscarriages?'

'No,' Claudia said. 'I thought I was pregnant once, but it was a false alarm.'

'A false alarm can be an early miscarriage. It would be a good thing to find out the father's blood group if you can. It's important.'

Now she had no choice. She would have to tell Stefanos she was pregnant and she dreaded it.

She stumbled out of the doctor's surgery, clutching a handful of pregnancy information leaflets, unable to think of anything else but what Stefanos's reaction might be. In doing so, she passed a mother wheeling a pram with a young baby in it. She couldn't help but look, and was swept by a surge of unexpected emotion at the sight of its sweet little face and the unblinking eyes looking up at her.

She was not the kind of woman who gushed over strange babies in prams. Until now.

'Your baby is beautiful,' she said, unable to take her eyes off the baby. Those tiny starfish hands. That fine, wispy hair. The little rosebud mouth. The sheer adorableness of this little one.

'He is, isn't he? Thank you,' the mother said, smiling, looking lovingly into the pram. She looked at the leaflets. 'Are you expecting?'

'Yes—yes, I am,' Claudia said. 'Due some time in January.'

'Congratulations,' the other woman said. She looked fondly down at her baby. 'Best thing I ever did was to have this little man.'

Claudia was swept by a sudden wave of joy and she couldn't stop smiling.

She was going to be a mother. And she couldn't be happier about it.

Claudia sat on her news for the next two days. She simply couldn't find the strength to get in touch with Stefanos. He had sent her a text to say he had plans to visit London soon, and hoped they'd be able to catch up, but had given no definite date. She hadn't yet replied.

She couldn't ask him about his blood group by text. It would have to be a phone call—and that terrified her. She was not the procrastinating type, and yet she kept putting the call off. But the doctor had stressed how important it was to get the father's information.

She knew she'd delayed as long as she could. She sat down in the living room, took a deep breath, and picked up her phone. She would start by chatting about his forthcoming visit, and then ease into a query about his blood group.

Athens was two hours ahead of London. It was just before lunch his time. With thumbs that seemed suddenly clumsy, she keyed in his number.

She'd startled him—that was obvious when he answered—and she wondered if there had been a moment when he had thought about not answering...when he'd seen the caller ID on his phone had shown *Claudia*

Eaton. Calling him out of the blue hadn't really been part of their deal.

'Is this a good time?' she asked tentatively.

'An excellent time. I'm at home.'

At the sound of his voice, so deep and manly, still with that charming trace of accent when he spoke in English, she felt her prepared speech fly out of her mind. Instead, she dived in headlong.

'Er... I... I need to ask you about your blood group. I don't have a clue what it is. Of all the things we talked about, we never talked about that. Well...well, why would we?'

This was so difficult.

'My blood group?'

She could hear the puzzled frown in his voice. She hadn't meant to hit him with it like that.

'Why would you want to know that?'

'Tell me and I'll tell you.'

That had not been the right thing to say—she knew it as soon as the words escaped her lips. It would make him suspicious. She wanted to disconnect the call and pretend it never happened.

'No one has ever asked me that before,' he said, and indeed his voice was underscored with suspicion.

Would he put two and two together? She'd been surprised at how little any of the few people she'd told about her pregnancy knew about potential rhesus factor complications.'

'Please just tell me,' she said.

Had he picked up the anxiety in her voice? Because now he answered immediately.

'O negative.'

'Oh,' she said.

'Why, *"oh"*?'

'Relief. That's good news.' No matter how she said it, this was not going to be easy. 'I… I'm Rh negative and…and…' her words spilled out in a rush '…it turns out I'm pregnant and it could be a problem if the father is Rh positive. But he isn't—he's negative. That is…*you're* negative.'

At his end there was silence for a moment. Then, 'You're pregnant? By me?'

She nodded, then realised he couldn't see her. 'Yes. There's no doubt. There…there wasn't anyone for a long time before you and…and there hasn't been anyone since.'

Another silence told her that if some part of her had hoped he would be pleased at the news that wasn't the case. She felt sick. Not sick with the morning sickness that she hadn't recognised as an early sign of her pregnancy, but sick with trepidation at his reaction.

'This is…a shock,' he said. 'We were careful.'

'Not careful enough, it seems.' She paused, but he didn't fill the silence. 'I'm not asking anything of you, Stefanos,' she said. 'Please be reassured of that. But I needed to know your blood group. This might be a second pregnancy for me with you as the father. I might have had a miscarriage before. It can be dangerous if the baby is found to be Rh positive, inherited from the father.'

'A second pregnancy? But—'

'My doctor said a ten-days-late period can be a very early miscarriage.' This was so difficult to explain on the phone, where she couldn't read his face. 'If it was an actual pregnancy back then, my body might have set up antibodies against an Rh positive baby—which could harm it. That's why I had to ask you. But if you're negative, and I'm negative, no dangerous sensitivity can develop and we're okay. Well, the baby is okay. Thankfully.'

Another pause. Then, 'When were you going to tell me you're pregnant?'

Claudia didn't know the answer to that herself. 'I... I don't know. It's early days yet. I didn't want a repeat of last time.'

How could she possibly have called him, told him she was pregnant, and then found out she was just late and history had repeated itself when her period came? She'd had to be certain. If she hadn't had to ask him about his blood group she would have waited until twelve weeks, which people said was a safer time to let people know.

'You're definitely pregnant?'

'There's no doubt. The doctor has confirmed it. Eight weeks.'

There was silence. Was he counting back the days to their time in that hotel in Bloomsbury?

'What do you feel about the pregnancy?' he asked.

Was he asking her, in a roundabout way, whether she intended to continue with the pregnancy? She couldn't blame him. She had made it clear, even at their recent meeting, that marriage and children weren't on her life plan.

'Shock. Disbelief. Acceptance. And finally...joy. Yes, joy. It might surprise you, considering what I've said to you before, but I... I want this baby very much. I'm not nineteen this time. The prospect of a baby from the perspective of being twenty-nine with my own business, is very different from the prospect as a nineteen-year-old student.'

'That's quite a turnaround,' he said.

He was choosing his words carefully, she thought.

'Back then…as we've both said…it was a different world. *I'm* different now. At a different stage of life.'

'What role do you expect me to play?'

No instant proposal of marriage this time.

'Whatever we sort out. Between us. You can have as much access as you want.'

She had adored her father, and would do all she could to make sure Stefanos played a role in their child's life.

Another pause. Then, 'I need to think about this,' he said. 'It's quite a shock.'

Her voice caught. 'It was for me too.'

'Are you all right? Health-wise, I mean?'

'Feeling a little fragile, to be honest. But it's early days yet. I'm taking it easy…having some time off work and not packing boxes or doing heavy work. The doctor said it will get better.'

Claudia hoped she was right. She'd been prepared for morning sickness, but recently it had intensified—morning, noon and night sickness had come as quite a shock.

'Make sure you look after yourself,' Stefanos said.

His words sounded so impersonal—but what had she expected? She'd made such a big deal of telling him how independent she was, and how she didn't need a man in her life. Only just a few kind words would make a difference. She hadn't realised how vulnerable being pregnant would make her feel.

'I will,' she said. 'I'll put my feet up and read through the pile of "what to expect" books I've had delivered. And I need to call the doctor's surgery to tell them about your blood group.' She paused. 'Thank you, Stefanos.'

Why had she felt the need to thank him? For not being Rh positive? For being an involuntary sperm donor? For not berating her for getting pregnant in an effort to trap herself a billionaire?

She knew he wouldn't believe that of her.

Or would he?

Stefanos put down his phone on the table where he sat near the swimming pool at his Athens mansion—his favourite spot to have lunch, overlooking the harbour. For a long time he simply stared into the aqua blue waters of the pool, sparkling in the sunshine.

Claudia was pregnant with his baby. He didn't doubt the truth of that. What he wasn't sure was how he felt about it. His two divorces had done a lot to kill his long-held desire to have children. If you had a child with a woman you were tied to her, whether you wanted to be or not. He shuddered at the thought of being tied to a person like Tiana for life.

If he didn't have such a painful history with Claudia... if he didn't have those two disastrous marriages behind him...he would ask Claudia to marry him. It would be expected of him. It would be the right thing to do. He was still attracted to her—there was no doubt about that. *Man, was he still attracted to her...* But he didn't actually know her any more.

She'd done a good job of hiding her family history and her motivations back in Santorini. Who was to say there weren't other secrets she was hiding? And he still wasn't sure if theirs had been a relationship based only on sex, and that wouldn't weather everyday life together.

And yet there was a child on the way—*his* child.

The news was something that years ago he would have rejoiced at and celebrated with vintage champagne. But that had been then. Now he had become so mired in distrust he'd given up on the idea of a family. But the more he thought about Claudia being pregnant, the more those long-buried feelings about holding his child in his arms and a future with his son or daughter, infiltrated the barriers he had erected around his emotions.

Yes, he wanted a child very much. But he did not want any attachment to its mother.

No way would he let himself be trapped in a loveless marriage for a third time—baby or no baby. He'd made grave misjudgements about the women he'd married—especially with Tiana. He was not going to tread that path again.

Tiana had pretended to be something she was not. It had only been after he'd married her that he'd discovered she was older than she'd claimed to be, and already had a child with another man. She had never stopped taking the contraceptive pill.

What kind of woman hid her child from the man she'd married because she'd had an eye on that man's money? And what kind of blindly trusting man didn't pick up on the discrepancies in her story? That man no longer existed. He would never take a woman at face value again. If a woman like Tiana had called out of the blue to tell him she was pregnant his first call would be to his lawyer.

But deep in his gut Stefanos knew Claudia wasn't like Tiana. A person surely didn't change her intrinsic nature that much even after ten years.

For one thing, she had never displayed the slightest sign of greed when it came to his considerable fortune. Back in Bloomsbury she had insisted on paying her share for the coffee in the hotel and their room service lunch. That had come as quite a novelty to him. Even his friends expected him to pick up the tab—it came with the billionaire turf.

But he'd been shocked by her revelations about her family and the reasons why she'd been so anti-marriage—something so important and yet she'd withheld that from him.

Still, he was worried about her. She'd obviously been making an effort to sound chipper, but he'd heard the weariness underlying her voice.

She was pregnant with his child.

She did a strenuous, physical job.

She might have miscarried before. Wouldn't that make her vulnerable to miscarriage again?

Now he had accepted the idea of this baby, he discovered he didn't want to lose it.

His mother had suffered miscarriage after miscarriage, both before and after having him. It had been the heartbreak of his parents' lives. Somehow he'd thought he had to make it up to them, as the only child upon whom all their hopes and expectations were centred. That was why he'd agreed to put aside his interest in history and archaeology to go into the family business—even though it wasn't what he'd have chosen. And that was why he'd known from a young age that he wanted a family of his own—why he'd offered to marry Claudia back then.

He wanted this baby with a fierce yearning. A baby was a gift. He didn't have to marry Claudia—that was assuming she'd even entertained thoughts of marrying him. But he had to look after her. And their child. The sooner the better.

CHAPTER NINE

THE NEXT MORNING, busy brushing her teeth in the bathroom of her maisonette in Hammersmith, Claudia didn't at first hear the repeated buzzing of the doorbell downstairs. The maisonette, in a converted period house, comprised a small entry hall on ground level, with a coat rack—and maybe enough room for a pram—and a set of narrow stairs leading up to a reception room, the kitchen, the bathroom and two bedrooms—the smaller one used as her home office.

'Urgh…' she muttered to herself as she brushed her teeth—again—and washed out her mouth. This morning sickness was really getting out of hand.

'Don't fight the nausea in the morning, give in to it,' her mother had advised. 'Then try a dry cracker when your tummy settles.'

That was all very well—until the next bout of nausea hit.

She kept checking the books, reading about the developmental stages of the baby, worrying that he or she wasn't getting enough nourishment because 'the mother'—*her*…she was still getting used to that idea!—wasn't keeping enough food down.

Claudia secured her long kimono-style wrap around

her waist and headed to the door. She wasn't expecting a parcel. It was too early to start buying baby things, and she didn't want to jinx the pregnancy until she was past twelve weeks and had had her first dating scan. But what else could it be?

She looked through the intercom camera. A tall, broad-shouldered man filled the steps outside. *Not the postman.* She felt what little colour she'd had left in her face drain away. She opened the door with a shaky hand.

'Stefanos. What are you doing here?'

'I've come to see how you are. You didn't sound well when we spoke yesterday.'

'But how…?'

'Very early flight,' he said.

Did Stefanos get even more handsome each time she saw him? His hair was slightly longer, his beard shorter, and he was wearing charcoal trousers, a white linen shirt with the sleeves rolled up to show tanned forearms, and black sneakers with thick white soles. He looked as if he'd stepped off the page of a glossy men's fashion magazine. He wore dark sunglasses, but took them off as he spoke.

'Kalimera,' he said cheerfully—*good morning* in Greek.

'Uh…*kalimera,'* Claudia mumbled.

She was suddenly aware of how dishevelled she must seem to him—hair a mess, no make-up, still not dressed. She prided herself on looking well groomed. She even ironed her leggings and T-shirts for work and polished her trainers. But she simply didn't have the energy to care about how she looked now.

She clutched the neckline of her silky wrap—at least

it was clean—to close it tighter. 'Come in. The living room is up the stairs.'

The tiny entrance hall seemed suddenly filled with tall, powerful Greek male. She almost danced around him to avoid contact. He gestured to her to go first up the stairs. She was utterly aware of him—his height, his strength, his scent. Even in her weakened state, he still made her shaky at the knees.

'Nice apartment,' Stefanos said, looking around him as he got to the top of the stairs.

The room was light and airy, with windows that faced south. The landlord had painted the apartment an off-white before she'd moved in, and the bathroom and kitchen were fairly new. She'd kept the furnishings neutral, with cushions and throws in beautiful Batik fabrics from Bali, and other souvenirs of her travels. With a baby on the way, she'd have to shelve plans to buy her own place. She would need all her savings.

'I like it, and the rent is reasonable for this area,' she said.

Why did she feel she had to explain?

He frowned. 'You don't own your place?'

'I'm working on it,' she said. *Welcome to the world of everyday folk*, she thought, but didn't dare say. Her entire maisonette would fit into the living room of his Bloomsbury apartment with room to spare.

'Can I get you a coffee?' she asked without thinking, simply from force of habit when a guest arrived.

'Yes, I—'

But just the mention of coffee, the thought of the smell of coffee, had made the nausea rise again.

'Excuse me, I—'

That was all she could manage before she made a

dash to the bathroom and slammed the door behind her. More retching, more teeth-brushing, more splashing of cold water on her face.

Why did Stefanos have to visit right now?

She emerged to find Stefanos looking out of the window, which looked over to the small garden below that she shared with the other two maisonettes in the building.

He spun around to face her. 'You look terrible,' he said bluntly.

She managed a watery smile. 'I guess I do. Nice of you to say so.'

'I didn't mean to insult you. I was speaking the truth. You're obviously not well.'

'Morning sickness is a normal part of pregnancy,' she said.

'But to be this ill? You look like you've lost weight, not gained it.'

'It is worse than I thought it would be,' she admitted. 'But the doctor says the sickness will pass.' So did all the pregnancy books she'd read.

'How are you managing with your job?' he asked.

'I'm not,' she said. 'I don't want to take any chances with lifting and heavy work. I'm just doing admin at home. We've been training a very good woman to take over most of Kitty's duties. She's able to step in for me too.'

Even the paperwork was an effort with her constant nausea and tiredness. She wasn't sleeping well. Truth was, she felt dreadful—but she didn't want to admit it to him.

'What about eating?'

She knew her smile was on the wan side. 'That's not such an issue as I'm too nauseous to eat much.'

He strode back and forth the length of her living room. 'Is anyone helping you?'

'I don't need help. I can manage on my own—plenty of women do. And my mum is on the phone any time I need her. She's ecstatic at the prospect of being a grandma. She's never actually seen the Australian grandchildren. And the twins are looking forward to being aunties.'

'That's all very well, but how long since you've actually had a vacation?'

'I went to my family in Swindon for Christmas.'

He frowned. 'I mean a proper break?'

She thought about it. 'Not since we started the business, nearly three years ago. There's been no time for holidays for either Kitty or me. Besides, the recent world situation has made it difficult to travel.'

Stefanos made an exclamation of dismay. 'You obviously need rest and proper nourishment. For both your sake and...and the baby's.'

It was the first time he'd mentioned the baby.

'Kitty sends me yummy care packages whipped up by her cook.' She couldn't tell Kitty that the gourmet food usually didn't stay down. 'I do my best,' she said.

'But is it enough?'

'I'm sure I can manage. I was very healthy before I got pregnant.' She paused. 'That... I mean me getting pregnant... I... I was as shocked as you. I thought I had food poisoning, or an allergy. I can assure you that you are the father, but I won't be offended if...if you want a DNA test. Apparently a test can be done with no risk of harm to the baby while I'm pregnant, or it can be done after the baby is born.'

For some reason just talking about it made her feel tearful. She'd been up-and-down emotional for weeks—

apparently due to the fluctuating hormones of pregnancy. But having to explain to people that the baby's father was out of the picture, that she didn't know his blood group, and that she intended to be a lone parent was stressful. Asking about DNA tests at a local centre had been embarrassing. She was sure the receptionist had automatically assumed she was uncertain who the father was and needed to clarify which of a number of men it could be. Although Claudia would rather they believed that than know that the billionaire father of her baby would want a DNA test in case she was a gold-digger making a false claim to his fortune.

'I don't need a DNA test,' Stefanos said.

'But I—'

'I don't believe you would lie about something so important.'

She looked up at him, unable to stop her eyes from misting with tears. 'Thank you, Stefanos, that means a lot. I… I…can't tell you how much it means.' Frantically she scrubbed at her eyes with her fists. 'I'm not crying. I'm really not. It's just that I feel so unwell, and I'm so tired, and I'm overwhelmed, and…and I'm terrified.'

Despite her every effort to suppress them, she burst into full-on sobs.

Stefanos immediately drew her into a hug. He had broad, accommodating shoulders and he wrapped his arms around her and let her cry.

Finally, she sobbed herself out. Her breathing evened out except for the odd gulp and the occasional sniffle. She stilled, wishing she could stay there for ever and not have to face him after making such an exhibition of herself.

That had been one of her grandmother's expressions

when Claudia had lost her temper or started to cry—or, as a teenager, had had too much to drink. Grandma Eaton had had quite a lot to do with her and Mark's upbringing while her parents had been busy at the pub. And apparently Claudia, as a child, had quite often made 'an exhibition of herself' and had to be reprimanded. No wonder she'd grown up tamping down on strong emotions, determined to present the best possible view of herself to others.

Finally, she reluctantly pulled away from Stefanos, feeling as if she was leaving a safe haven. She looked up at him and was relieved to see kindness, not criticism, in his eyes.

'I'm sorry. I didn't mean—' she started.

'Do you remember what I said about not saying sorry? You have absolutely nothing to be sorry about.' He wiped a damp strand of hair away from her face in a gesture that was surprisingly tender.

'Your shirt! Oh, no, there are wet patches.' Ineffectually, she tried to dab them away with the sleeve of her wrap. 'Luckily I wasn't wearing make-up, so no mascara stains at least.'

'Just salty tears,' he said, sounding more than a touch amused. 'They'll dry.'

'But…but that nice linen fabric could be rumpled. Let me iron your shirt—it's the least I can do.'

'There is absolutely no need for you to do that, Claudia.'

'If you're sure…but it's no trouble. And—'

'What I want you to do is tell me why you're so terrified of having a baby.'

Stefanos led Claudia to her sofa—a fragile Claudia who didn't look pregnant except for the notable swelling of her breasts. She seemed thinner than when he had last held her in his arms. That couldn't be right if she was eight weeks along.

'Come and sit down,' he said. 'Can I get you a drink?'

'That…that would be nice. There's some fizzy mineral water in the fridge. I… I seem to be able to keep that down.'

He headed towards the refrigerator in her compact kitchen.

'Help yourself to any drink you like,' she said. 'Although I… I'd ask you not to make coffee. Even the smell of it makes me nauseous.'

He carried two glasses of chilled mineral water to the coffee table near the sofa. 'Nothing to eat?'

'Please, no,' she said, wiping her hand across her forehead. Her eyes were reddened and her hair straggled across her face. It made her seem vulnerable, and yet somehow did not detract from how attractive he found her.

She slowly took a few sips of cold water, closed her eyes, and sat back in the sofa.

'Better?' he asked. He angled himself so that, while he stayed at a distance, he could still clearly see her face.

She nodded. 'Thank you.'

'So tell me why you're terrified.'

She sniffed. 'Can I start with why I'm feeling overwhelmed?'

'It's a good enough place to start.'

'First of all—as you know—I had no plans for starting a family. Not within marriage, and certainly not outside it.'

He started to say something, but she put up her hand in a halt sign.

'Not that there is anything wrong with having a baby when you're not married. Lots of women do it and are wonderful mothers. As I will be, of course.'

His very conservative family would definitely think it was a problem. A major problem. But he had no intention of telling his mother anything about Claudia. He loved his *mitera*, but he still hadn't quite forgiven her for encouraging his marriage to Arina when she'd known full well that Arina's mother had suspected her daughter was gay. And he would not be forced into marriage with the mother of his child simply because not marrying her would be socially unacceptable.

'Of course,' he said.

'But a baby is a lot of work—as I know only too well. How I'll manage motherhood and running my own business is concerning me. Again, lots of women do it, and I'm sure I'll manage, but everything I'll have to put in place is a tad overwhelming.'

Stefanos didn't want to offer help at this stage. Not until he'd really got his mind around the fact that he was going to be a father but not under the circumstances he'd dreamed of. He would definitely offer financial help. Lifelong support for his child was a given. And who knew? If Claudia decided she really couldn't manage a baby he would ask for custody and she could have visitation rights, rather than the other way around. But, again, it was too soon to bring that up. He didn't know how she would take it.

It was less than twenty-four hours since Claudia had dropped the baby bombshell on him. He needed to speak to a lawyer before he committed to anything. He'd learned that lesson from his dealings with Tiana.

'And the terror?' he asked.

'Does it sound cowardly to admit that I'm actually scared of childbirth? One of the ladies who packs for us had a baby last year and she said it was literally like passing a watermelon. The birth videos I've watched online are nothing short of horrific. Do you ever watch that television show about midwives?'

'Er…no. Why would I?' He couldn't imagine anything worse.

'Don't.' She shuddered. 'It's quite scary. Admittedly, it's all lovely at the end, with the mums having forgotten the ordeal they've been through once they have their babies in their arms.'

'But can it be that bad if so many women have babies? More than one baby?'

'Rationally, yes, you'd think not. The human race continues to thrive. But my fear is irrational. Maybe because my mother had such a difficult time with the twins. And…er… I shouldn't admit to it, but I'm not sure I like the idea of breastfeeding—even if it's the best thing for the baby.' She paused to take a deep breath. 'There's another thing I worry about. Mum told me she had bad morning sickness because she was having twins. What if *I'm* having twins? The doctor says there's a chance, if a small one.' She took another cautious sip of water. 'Remember I told you what it was like for my family?'

He knew he'd have to tread carefully here. 'It would be different if you were their mother.'

'It would still be as much work, and with no sixteen-year-old daughter to help me like my mum had. Would I be able to cope?'

Stefanos had to stop himself from saying that of course he would pay for a nanny. Two nannies if she needed them. As many nannies as she wanted. The time wasn't right for that yet.

'I understand your fears, but surely in London there are good doctors and midwives to help you?'

'Of course there are. I'm probably worrying too much. I've only been on leave since Monday—yesterday, that is. Two days into the week and I've probably already spent too much time on my own, worrying and…and brooding.'

An idea that had been formulating in his mind since he'd first seen her downstairs and been shocked at how frail she looked suddenly crystallised. 'I have the answer to some of your problems. You need a holiday and you need to be looked after. I have a villa on the privately owned Greek island of Kosmimo.'

Her eyes widened. 'Kosmimo? That fabulous resort Pevezzo Athina—isn't that on Kosmimo?'

He nodded. 'It most certainly is. It's owned by my cousin Alex and his wife Dell.'

'Wait…that's meant to be the most amazing resort. One of the most acclaimed in Europe. I've dreamed of visiting it. That is…'

'If you could ever bring yourself to visit Greece again?'

'Yes.'

'Can you overcome your reluctance to go to Greece and stay with me on Kosmimo?'

'I… I don't know what to say.'

'Just say yes. It could be just what you need. Pevezzo Athina is a very upscale health resort, as well as a six-star hotel. Good food, relaxation…medical help not far away if you need it.'

She couldn't meet his gaze. 'Go with you? As…as what?'

'I could say you can pretend to be my fiancée, but I won't. There has been too much deception in my life. If you agree, we'll say you're a former girlfriend, that we met again by chance recently, renewed our friendship and…and perhaps weren't as careful about contraception as we should have been.'

'I don't know that we'll need to go into that much detail. We *were* careful. No contraception is one hundred percent effective—but heaven knows what went wrong that morning.'

He could only remember what had gone absolutely *right* that morning. Sex with beautiful, sensuous Claudia. Memories of her had rarely been out of his mind since. But he was still not sure about letting his former lover back into his life. Her pregnancy had brought them together in a way he had never envisaged.

'Agreed. But Dell has a way of getting confidences out of people, so be warned.'

'So, quite simply, what you're saying is that we tell the truth.'

What a relief it was for him to hear her say that. *The truth.* 'Yes.'

'And about…about the accommodation…?'

'I have a villa on the island, which is used by guests when I'm not in residence. It's very private, with its own swimming pool. But you can also use the facilities of the hotel. It's a beautiful island. I think you'll like it.'

Again, she couldn't meet his gaze. 'And the…er…bedroom situation?'

'Two separate suites. You in one—me in the other.'

'What about the airfare?'

'There is no need for you to worry about airfares or any other expense.'

'But I can't allow that. I—'

'You are giving me a child, Claudia. Please allow me to look after you.'

She paused for a long moment, and he could see her debating her independence against her need for help. Then, 'Thank you. I have to say it sounds absolutely wonderful. When do we go?'

'Right now—as soon as you can pack your bags.'

CHAPTER TEN

IF STEFANOS HADN'T caught her when she'd been feeling at such an impossibly low ebb, no way would Claudia have agreed to let him whisk her away to a luxury resort where she wouldn't know a soul. But he'd caught her at a super-vulnerable moment and had been unexpectedly kind, rather than acting the domineering Greek male.

No wonder she'd gone to mush. It had made absolute sense to go with him. Even though she knew she needed to confront him about what he'd meant by his words, *'You're giving me a child.'*

Because she most definitely was *not* giving him her child. She was offering to share her child with him, for the child's sake.

The huge discrepancy between her wealth and power and his was beginning to scare her into thinking he might intend to make a claim on the baby. In some ways she regretted telling him she had never wanted to get married or have a family. Or opened up on her worries about childbirth and how she was going to manage being both sole parent and a businesswoman. Could he use that information against her if a custody battle eventuated?

She knew she would have to talk with him about their expectations concerning the baby they had conceived

that unexpected and exciting day in Bloomsbury eight
weeks ago. But she would have to stay wary and pick
her moment.

And now, a few hours later, with the large backpack
that had seen her through her travels hastily packed with
summer clothes, she was boarding a private jet with
him. The 'very early flight' he'd caught to Heathrow
had clearly been waiting for his return and they were
heading to Athens.

She had never flown in a private plane before, although she tried to act cool, as if it wasn't something out
of her experience. The jet was just like in the movies—
all leather seats and luxury and a very attentive crew.
She was glad she'd dressed in grape-coloured narrow
linen trousers, a stylish cream silk knit top and a light
linen jacket, so she didn't look out of place. Her right
wrist jangled with the copper bangles she'd been told
staved off morning sickness, but they didn't seem to be
having any effect.

It was a shame she was unable to eat anything for fear
of feeling nauseous, because the food on offer looked
delicious.

The flight was smooth and trouble-free and she slept
for most of it. Stefanos told her a little about his cousin
Alex and his wife Dell. Alex was Greek-Australian, born
in Sydney, and Claudia soon realised she knew of him.

Alex Mikhalis was considered a legend on the Sydney hospitality scene. He was a nightclub and restaurant
mogul whose fiancée had been killed in a hostage situation at one of his restaurants. A broken man, he'd returned to the village of his ancestors to find peace. He'd
bought the island of Kosmimo, which had once belonged
to his family, from its Russian owner and founded a ho-

listic resort which had been a success from the start. He'd also found happiness with Dell.

After landing in Athens, Claudia and Stefanos transferred to the helicopter that would take them to Kosmimo in the Ionian Sea, to the east of the island of Lefkada. Claudia had only once flown in a helicopter, on a holiday in New Zealand. It seemed surreal to fly by private jet and then by helicopter. But for Stefanos they seemed to be everyday modes of transport, scarcely worthy of mention.

The hour-long helicopter ride to Kosmimo was quite different from the smooth jet. The helicopter flew with a swooping motion, and either jerked sidewards or dropped suddenly if it encountered turbulence. And then there was the vibration…

Claudia battled nausea from the second she smelled the fumes of the fuel as they boarded. She and Stefanos wore headsets, to block the racket of the blades and to communicate with each other, but that made it only marginally better.

The only thing that took her mind off the nausea was her first sight of the small green island that looked like an emerald set in the multi-hued azure waters of the Ionian Sea. It was utterly beautiful. As the helicopter hovered above a helipad, preparing to land, she could see what looked like cleared farmland and, as they got closer still, white marble buildings interspersed with the aqua rectangles of swimming pools.

She couldn't help but feel a buzz of excitement. Pevezzo Athina was a luxury resort—the kind she had once dreamed of working at. She'd come close when she'd worked at a superb resort in Bali, but Pevezzo Athina had won so many international awards it was in a class of its own. How could she ever have imagined she would see it under these circumstances? And as a guest, not a member of staff?

'That's Alex and Dell down there, near the four-by-four, come to meet us,' Stefanos said through the headset. 'You'll like Dell. She's Australian, a foodie, and very warm and welcoming. She and Alex have two children—a little boy and a little girl.'

'I… I'm sure I will—like her, that is,' Claudia managed to force out through gritted teeth. She could scarcely talk, all her energy taken up with trying not to retch.

Her stomach lurched as the helicopter started its descent, flattening all the grasses and shrubs around it. And instead of arriving in style, meeting Stefanos's cousin and his wife with a confident smile, she had to be helped off the helicopter, taking care to stay out of reach of the blades.

Immediately she rushed to the cover of a bush, where she dry-retched until she could retch no more. She was left shaking and weak. Making an exhibition of herself again, she thought, as the helicopter took off.

'This…this is so humiliating,' she choked out to Stefanos, when she staggered back towards him from behind the bush. 'How can I face your cousin and his wife?'

'Not humiliating,' he said calmly. 'Natural for a pregnant woman, I believe.'

Her voice rose. 'I can't face them. Not like this.'

'Not much choice, I'm afraid. It's quite a walk to my villa from the helipad.' He paused. 'No one will think any less of you. In fact, knowing my cousin and his wife, you will be bombarded with kindness. They're good people.'

She groaned. Without a word, he handed her a bottle of cool water to rinse her mouth and splash her face.

'Feeling better?' he said.

She nodded. 'Marginally. Thank you.'

The air smelt fresh and pure, with a hint of herbs and the tang of salt. She took a few deep breaths until the shakiness went away. But she was still grateful when Stefanos held her elbow as he steered her towards the car where Alex and Dell were waiting to greet them.

Dark good looks certainly ran in Stefanos's family—that was immediately apparent. And Alex was not only handsome, but charming in his greeting to her.

'*Kalosorizo*…welcome,' he said, with a big smile that had something of Stefanos in it.

Claudia liked him instantly.

Dell rushed to her side. Sweet-faced, auburn-haired, with kind olive green eyes. 'You poor thing—you must be feeling ghastly. I had morning sickness when I was pregnant with both my kids, and I remember only too well what it was like. But it doesn't last for ever. One day I woke up and felt fine—something to do with oestrogen levels, apparently. You'll see.'

'I certainly hope so,' Claudia said, attempting a weak smile.

'And it will be so worth it when you hold your baby in your arms.'

'I'm looking forward to that.'

Every time she thought of her baby it was with a rush of fierce, possessive love.

As Stefanos and Alex put Claudia's backpack in the car, Dell tucked her arm through hers.

'Stefanos did the right thing, bringing you here. Fresh air, healthy food—that is, when you can face food. The whole place is designed for guests to relax and revive. I'll personally devise a tempting pregnancy menu for you.'

'You're very kind,' Claudia murmured.

Again there was that sudden smarting of tears at Dell's thoughtfulness. Pregnancy was definitely an up-and-down journey.

Stefanos joined them. 'Straight to my villa for Claudia, I think,' he said.

Claudia was relieved. She was so exhausted that she didn't mind Stefanos taking over. In fact there was a certain comfort to it. 'I'm sorry,' she said. 'I know pregnancy isn't an illness, but after the helicopter flight I really don't feel wonderful.'

'Of course you don't,' said Dell. 'As soon as Stefanos called I had your suite in his villa made up with fresh linen, and left a selection of organic crackers, fruit, and some ginger tea—which is very helpful for nausea,' Dell said. 'Your suite is ready too, of course, Stefanos. Later, you can both have dinner with us at our house, if you're up for it, or just order room service.'

Claudia was grateful for Dell's understanding. By emphasising the separate suites Dell was making it clear that she knew about the somewhat unusual situation with Claudia and her husband's cousin. She was grateful, too, to Stefanos. He had obviously told them the truth. She knew she couldn't have gone through the charade of pretending to be his fiancée or a long-time girlfriend.

The resort was a short drive from the heliport. Dell thoughtfully sat Claudia in the front seat of the car, with the window open and the breeze on her face. As they passed through the grounds Dell and Alex explained that they had always planned for Pevezzo Athina to be as self-sufficient as it could. They grew much of the fruit and vegetables for the resort, cultivated olives for olive oil, made cheeses, and had restocked the surrounding waters with fish. Renewable energy too.

'I'd love to know more,' Claudia said. 'I'm really interested.'

'Stefanos told us you had a background in hotels and hospitality?'

'That's true,' she said. 'But it's behind me now.'

For the first time she felt a real pang of sadness at the loss of her career.

She wondered what else Stefanos had told them about her?

Stefanos's villa was a white marble pavilion-style building, set around a courtyard with a swimming pool and an outdoor entertaining area shaded by a pergola covered with fresh green grapevines. A hot pink bougainvillea grew across the whitewashed wall in startling contrast.

'This is fabulous, Stefanos. What can I say?' she said as they stood by the pool after Alex and Dell had dropped them off.

'I can imagine you'll be spending some time lying in the shade around the pool and relaxing,' he said. 'Or I hope you will.'

She looked up at him. 'I'm not sick, you know. Just… hormonally incapacitated.'

He smiled. 'I realise that—but tell me you don't need a break.'

'I do need a break. You're right about that. And… and I'm grateful to you for bringing me to this heavenly place.'

Even though she wasn't quite sure how she would be spending her time here—and knew that she needed to keep on her guard against him.

'My mother used to say to my father and I that on vacation we needed to wind down from stress and relax to the point of boredom.'

She smiled. 'I bet that didn't last long.'

'You're right. My father wasn't one for sitting around. He was energetic. We'd soon enough be sailing or hiking or skiing. Mama would more often than not come with us.'

'Energetic like you used to be?' she said. Then flushed as she remembered how very energetic they'd been together both back then and more recently. 'Er...can we go inside?'

The two main bedroom suites were set on either side of the courtyard. Between was a central kitchen, expansive living and dining areas, and a further two bedrooms with en suite bathrooms at the back. They were for extra guests, or if he wanted to bring his own staff, Stefanos explained.

His own staff. Again, she was struck by the differences in their worlds.

'Let me show you to your room,' he said. 'There are dark circles under your eyes.'

'Stop right there,' she said in mock command. 'I appreciate your concern, but you've already told me I look dreadful once today. It's not great for a girl's ego.'

He smiled. 'Even tired and nauseous you still look beautiful,' he said.

'That's better,' she said with a smile.

He might not mean it, but it sounded nice. She felt swept by an urge to hug him. Not with anything sexual in mind, but just because he was being kind. She hadn't expected he would want to please her—after all they meant nothing to each other now.

But ten years ago, in those passionate few months when they'd been together, he'd been not only her lover but her best friend—her *everything*. She had never imagined she would feel that way for a boy. She had never allowed herself to wonder how it might have ended if it hadn't been for that pregnancy scare and the awkward issues it had raised. That would have been far too painful. Although his ghosting had hurt, at the age of nineteen she had thought there would be other men like him— perhaps even better than him—in her future. How very wrong she'd been.

'Oh, my gosh, this is palatial—there's no other way to describe it,' she said, looking around her in delight.

The villa was all on one floor. All white, with white walls and marble floors, white linen and leather. Large windows with white shutters displayed views to the sea, which had white sails traversing across it, and out to the green hills behind the resort.

'It's so beautiful and peaceful,' she said.

'*Pevezzo* means safe haven in the local dialect,' he said.

'And Athina for the goddess Athina?'

'Or for Athens.'

'I think I'll go with the goddess rather than the city,' she said.

'It's also in honour of Alex's family's Taverna Athina, on a nearby island, and his grandfather's Athina restaurant in Sydney.'

'That's quite a link,' she said.

Stefanos showed her to her suite—a spacious bedroom, living area, bathroom and a small kitchen. The bed was enormous and looked very inviting, with a note of blue introduced into the white bed linens.

'If I can't rest and relax in here, I don't know where I could,' she said.

Images of what exactly she and Stefanos had done the last time they'd got within touching distance of a super-king-sized bed flashed before her. Thank heaven he had turned away from her and didn't see her blush.

'My suite is the mirror image of yours,' he said. 'I'll show you later.'

She felt an immeasurable relief. She looked up at him. 'Thank you, Stefanos, for bringing me here. I can't imagine a more perfect place.'

'I think so too,' he said. He looked pleased.

'But how…how are we going to handle this? I mean, I don't expect you to hang out with me all the time. Are you actually going to stay here? Or will you go back to Athens?'

'I'm taking a vacation too. It's my favourite time of the year.'

It had been June when they'd first met in Santorini.

'It's a perfect time,' she said, unable to keep the wistfulness from her voice. This time around, life in June had become so much more complicated.

'As for how much time I spend with you—that's entirely your call,' he said. 'I can stay out of your way, if that's what you prefer.'

'No! I mean, I don't want you out of the way…'

But she had to play this carefully. There was a baby at stake here—*her* baby. And he was an all-or-nothing guy.

'Can we play it by ear?' she asked.

'Perhaps we could start with me showing you around tomorrow. There's something here in particular I think you'd like to see.'

Why did her mind stray to parts of *him* she'd like to

see? It seemed that just because she was pregnant it didn't make her stop desiring him. But that was just sex, nothing else, she had to remind herself.

'Er...that would be lovely,' she said.

'In the meantime, you should really eat something. Dell has left lots of stuff for you in the kitchen.'

'I'll shower first, and change,' she said.

'I'll be in the living room.'

Although she had the very best of intentions to join him, after a shower in the fabulous bathroom, surrounded by jets from all sides, Claudia changed into the thoughtfully provided white cotton pyjamas with the Pevezzo Athina logo in blue on the pocket and lay down on the bed...just for a minute. She closed her eyes...just for a minute.

When she woke it was well past dark, and she was alone in her beautiful room. A sheet was draped over her and she had vague memories of a deep, masculine voice as she was tucked in, a hand smoothing the damp hair from her forehead.

She must have imagined that he'd murmured, 'Goodnight, *koukla mou*.' Because that was the name he'd used to call her—a Greek endearment literally meaning *my doll*. But he would never call her that. He had never called her *koukla* again after she had refused his proposal. There was absolutely no way he would use that endearment now. It must have been a dream.

She got up and went in search of dry crackers.

CHAPTER ELEVEN

NEXT MORNING, CLAUDIA WOKE to the sound of soft splashing from the pool area and sun streaming through the shutters of her white bedroom in Stefanos's villa. She felt an immediate lifting of her spirits. Stefanos had brought her to a dream resort, and she was looking forward to exploring.

There was the familiar stirring of nausea, but thanks to Dell's supplies she was prepared. She sat up in bed and nibbled on the crackers she'd placed on the nightstand when she'd gone back to bed last night after a nocturnal snack. They were delicious—full of seeds and nuts. Would organic Greek crackers work better than the regular kind from a supermarket? She was prepared to believe it.

Feeling way better than she had when she'd arrived the previous afternoon, Claudia slipped into a simple white, embroidery-trimmed dress she'd bought in Bali, slid into leather flip-flops and headed out to the pool.

Stefanos was swimming. She stood in the shade of a grapevine and watched him as he streaked up and down the pool, his body as strong and true as an arrow, his even, rhythmical stroke barely breaking the surface of the water.

Her heart caught in her throat, arrested there by memories. She remembered all the times they'd swum together, diving with squeals of laughter from the deck of his boat into the aquamarine waters of the Aegean around Santorini. She hadn't been a confident swimmer when she'd first met him. Swimming in a chlorinated indoor pool for school lessons had never much appealed, although she'd enjoyed splashing around at the beaches in Devon. But, thanks to twenty-year-old Stefanos's help and encouragement, she'd soon been joyously swimming in the open sea with him, her lover.

She'd swum since on the Great Barrier Reef in Australia, among green turtles and baby sharks, in Bali among glorious coral and brilliant fish, and in New Zealand's Bay of Islands. She'd swum in so many different waters she should have forgotten where she'd learned to love open water swimming and who had taught her. But she never had forgotten. Never quite forgotten *him*.

He raised his head from the pool, his black hair wet to his head, droplets of water glistening on his tanned skin in the sunlight. He smiled that magnificent white smile and waved. She caught her breath as her heart tripped into overdrive. No other man had ever had the same effect on her. To be on holiday with him—yet not *really* be with him—was disconcerting, and it made her thoughts travel down pathways long blocked.

How could his appeal still be so strong? Back then it had surely been a fleeting first love—infatuation and sex and fun all wrapped into one all-encompassing emotion. It would have faded if it had run its course. What did she feel for him now? For the father of her baby? There was certainly something. Lust? Yes…oh, yes. Residual friendship? Who knew? Affection? Did she know this new Stefanos enough even to contemplate growing fond of him? But he continued to surprise her in good ways. His kindness was unexpected, and yet she shouldn't be surprised. Even back then he'd been way more thoughtful than the usual twenty-year-old male she'd encountered. When she'd told her university boyfriend she'd be away in Greece for a summer vacation he'd bluntly told her he wouldn't wait for her—typical behaviour for him.

But with Stefanos now, had that new dark layer of bitterness she'd identified in him smothered his essential nature? Would he be capable of ruthlessly taking her baby from her? A shiver of dread ran through her. She would never let that happen.

'Are you coming in?' he called.

She shook her head. 'Not right now.'

With a few powerful strokes he was by the edge of the pool, looking up at her. 'Perhaps you'd rather swim in the sea?'

'That's a tempting offer,' she said.

'Shall we take a boat out before it gets too hot?'

'I would love that. Thank you.'

Effortlessly, he pulled himself up and out of the pool. His muscles rippled as he moved—they actually rippled—and she was struck speechless by the force of her attraction to him. An attraction she had to keep at bay. He had been wounded by his experiences with women since he'd known her. A wounded man could be dangerous...a man who could hurt her. Not physically—she didn't believe that of Stefanos for one moment. But he could hurt her emotionally. Especially when they had a child to bind them. Long gone was her naive belief that things in life would work out just because she really wanted them to.

Yet he was so impossibly hot, and she had to force

herself not to stare at six foot two of virile, powerfully built Greek male, wearing nothing but brief swim-shorts, standing before her seemingly totally unaware of the effect he had on her. Being pregnant did not stop her from wanting him.

Thankfully he flung a towel around himself and her heartrate slowed back to normal.

'Dell sent over some food she thought might tempt you,' he said. 'She said she was able to keep down plain bread and cheese when she had morning sickness. She also suggests finely sliced peach and watermelon.'

'That's very thoughtful of her.' Claudia paused, looked up at him. 'Why is she being so nice to me?'

She had to remain on the alert. Did Stefanos have an ulterior motive in bringing her here? Was he manipulating her? If so, were Dell and Alex in on it?

'First of all because she seems to have taken to you...'

'And second?'

'You know the kind of married people who'd like to see everyone else paired off too? That's Dell and Alex.'

'But surely you've made it clear to them you're not interested in getting married? Er...getting married again, I mean.'

'Repeatedly. But they want to see me happy. Maybe they don't realise how unhappy a person can be within a marriage—or they've forgotten; Dell was married before.'

Back came the scowl that darkened his face when he mentioned marriage.

'They do know we scarcely know each other, don't they?' Claudia said.

What had he told them about her?

'They do. But they like you. And they didn't approve of my ex-wives.'

She needed to think about that one. He'd been so grim when he'd mentioned his matrimonial history before. 'When are you going to tell me about them? The ex-wives, I mean, who've made you so bitter,' Claudia said.

His jaw tightened. 'Don't you remember I told you I had no intention of discussing either of them?'

'I remember. But that was back then.'

He frowned. 'Why would that change?'

'Come on, it's kind of unfair to keep me in the dark when everyone else knows. It could get awkward. Imagine if I have lunch with Dell and she mentions one of them but I know nothing.'

A reluctant grin lifted the stern line of his mouth. 'You haven't changed at all, have you? If I don't spill you'll stage a relentless campaign until I do, won't you?'

'Maybe…' she said.

She needed to know so much more about this man who was the father of her child. She wanted to be able to trust him. Right now, she wasn't at all certain she could, in spite of this unexpected trip to this fabulous place—or perhaps because of it.

He raised his eyebrows. 'Perhaps we can talk about them on the boat.'

'Sounds like a plan.'

Even more importantly, they needed to talk about how they would share their baby and how it would work.

'I'll think about it,' he said. He looked up at the perfect blue sky, which had just a few white clouds scudding across it. 'Conditions are perfect for sailing now, but there could be a storm later this afternoon. I know you want to see the resort, but I suggest we get out on the water first, then come back to the hotel for lunch. That is if Dell hasn't exhausted her supply of crackers.'

Claudia laughed. 'It's not fair to tease a pregnant woman. I might suddenly turn green on you.'

'Point taken,' he said, his grin still lingering. 'The resort is built on the top of a cliff. There's a road down to the dock but it's quite steep. Are you okay to walk or should I pick up a buggy?' Stefanos asked.

'I can walk. Just tell me they don't have donkeys here, like they use in Santorini for transporting tourists up the steep hill from the harbour.'

'No one here would countenance that, I can assure you.'

'Good,' she said. 'I'll go inside and get ready now.'

He went one way to his suite and she went the other to hers. She changed into gauzy white trousers and a cool, loose white shirt with boat shoes. Then she jammed on the white folding hat she always kept in her bag. As a redhead, she was always aware of striking a balance between enjoying the outdoors and protecting her skin from the sun. She managed to nibble on some bread and cheese, and packed up the rest to take on the boat.

The day before, Stefanos had told Claudia there was something he thought she might like to see. But he hadn't expected her to burst into tears at the sight of the *Daphne*, with her graceful lines and white sails, moored by the dock.

'You still have her after all this time! Your beautiful yacht!'

'She was a gift from my grandparents, named after my grandmother. I would never sell her,' he said. Even though, as an increasingly rare vintage model from a renowned designer, she was worth multiple millions.

Claudia fanned her face with her hand to excuse her tears. 'I'm sorry. Emotional...'

'Hormone disruption?' he said.

'Not just that, but it's that too, I suppose. It's just...it's like stepping through a portal into the past. I... I never thought I would see the *Daphne* again. Or you, for that matter. It...it brings back so many memories.'

'Not bad memories, I hope?' he said. Although he suspected he had left her with some bad memories.

'The very best of memories,' she said. 'Until...until right at the end.'

'We won't fast-forward to the end,' he said.

He had been so hot-headed, so stubborn, so determined to get his own way. And she had concealed information that might have made him less harsh towards her. Perhaps their ending could have been different. Or perhaps their passion for each other might have dwindled away with time, with distance, with other people... But knocking on the closed-off wall of his mind came a reminder about how quickly their passion had been reignited in London. He had to tread carefully.

She looked up at him, her blue eyes still misted with tears. 'I don't know if I can bear to get on board.'

'You don't have to if you don't want to,' he said. Although he was disappointed at her reaction. Back then, she had loved the *Daphne*.

'I do want to. Or maybe I don't. I don't know... *Why?*' She gesticulated with her hands. 'Why are we back here together like this? How did it happen?'

'Fate, perhaps?'

'Fate?' she scoffed. 'You mean we had nothing to do with it?'

'The Ancient Greeks believed so strongly that fate governed our lives that we had not just one but three goddesses of fate.'

'Three?' she said.

'Sisters. Clotho, who spun each person's life thread, Lachesis, who measured how long that thread would be to give them their destiny, and Atropos, who cut the thread of life with her shears at the time of the person's death.'

'And you honestly believe that fate rules our lives?'

He shrugged. 'I can't discount it. Of all the people in London, why was it *you* who came to pack up my flat?'

'Coincidence?' she said.

'Why did you conceive, even though we used contraception?'

'Carelessness on our part? A fault in the manufacture?'

'All possibilities,' he said. 'Or I could choose to believe that you were fated to bear my child.'

Her eyes widened. 'That makes me sound like some kind of…of incubator. I don't know whether to be amused or offended.'

'Please don't be offended. I didn't mean it like that. I was just trying to answer your question of *why*. Don't think I haven't thought about why we've found ourselves in this situation.'

He'd thought of it constantly during the eight weeks they'd been apart after that day in Bloomsbury. He'd thought it might be fun to keep seeing her when he visited London, on a no-strings basis. He hadn't wanted anything serious, but he'd had too much respect for her to offer a pick-her-up-and-put-her-down kind of arrangement. And there had been a growing feeling that perhaps he shouldn't let her go. He didn't want marriage—neither did she. Perhaps they could have made something work...

But then she had called to inform him she was pregnant and everything had changed.

'Does there have to be a reason?' she said now. 'Couldn't it be coincidence?'

'Or luck?' he said.

'Luck?'

'Good luck that you came so unexpectedly back into my life,' he said. 'Good luck that you're pregnant with my baby when I had given up on any thought that I would be a father.'

'Good luck that I'm to be a mother when I hadn't chosen to be one? Good luck that I am deliriously happy about it?'

She paused, and he could read the emotions shadowing her face. She looked up to meet his gaze directly.

'I'm scared that you might try and take my baby from me,' she said. 'Would you do that, Stefanos?'

CHAPTER TWELVE

SHE HAD STUNNED him into silence. As Claudia looked up at Stefanos, where he stood opposite her on the board-walk, his brow creased in what looked like sheer disbelief. Had she said the wrong thing? Had she wounded his feelings? But it had needed to be said.

'What do you mean?' he said slowly. 'You think I would take your baby?'

She gritted her teeth. 'I would hope not. But it's a possibility. You're so wealthy and I… I'm so not. I don't believe it's unheard-of for wealthy men to use their power to enforce sole custody. To not return children home from visits, to abduct them and…and take them to another country where the mother has no rights.'

'That might be true, and it's horrific,' he said gruffly. 'But I am not—would *never* be—one of those men.'

'I… I'd like to believe that, but—'

Stefanos put both his hands on her shoulders and looked deep into her eyes. 'Claudia, please believe me, I would never take your baby from you. A child needs its mother.'

'I'm glad you think that.'

He seemed so sincere but who could know? She remembered how coldly he'd ghosted her...how cruel it had seemed.

'However, a child also needs its father,' he said seriously. 'I want to be a father to our child in any way I can.'

She narrowed her eyes. 'On whose terms would that be?'

'Terms? I was fortunate to have two good parents—as were you. I would hope for the same for our child. Visitation rights. Shared custody, if it comes to that. Financial support. Security. We need to sort out an agreement that's satisfactory to us both, in the child's best interests. It's early days. I only found out you were pregnant two days ago. You've had more time to get used to the idea of becoming a parent.'

He dropped his hands from her shoulders and stepped back. She missed his warmth, the connection. Even the most casual of contacts with him send awareness zinging through her. By confronting him, had she damaged the trust they'd seemed to be developing?

'What you've said is very reassuring,' she said.

She was glad she'd brought the subject up. It had been nagging at her. Now it seemed her fears as to his intentions might have been completely off the mark. But there was still that doubt.

'And it's the truth,' he said.

'Stefanos, I want to believe you... I really do.'

He turned on his heel away from her, took a few steps and then came back. 'Do you honestly think I would abduct our baby and spirit him or her off to another country? Deny you your child?' He slowly shook his head. 'I look at the *Daphne* now and think of the two people we were then and wonder. How are we so very different?'

She swallowed hard against his anguish. 'The trouble

is, we don't really know each other any more, do we?' she said. 'We had that glorious time together when I was a teenager, but we've known each other for only a few days since.'

'You're right. And in seven months' time we are going to be parents—independent of each other but joint in our care for our child. We each have to do our best for this baby who was—'

She put up her hand in a halt sign. 'Please don't call our baby an accident. That's a terrible label to give a child.'

'I was going to say unplanned—not an accident.'

'Good. Sorry. I'm glad. My twin sisters were never allowed to think they were in this world by accident. In fact they turned out to bring joy to all our lives.'

'We also have to do our best for each other, so we can be our best as parents,' he said. 'It's uncharted territory for us.'

He'd always had that grown-up side to him. Now, at thirty, he really was worldly wise. What he said made complete sense. Yet she felt an underlying sadness that two people who had conceived a child not in love, but in passion and respect, should be making such businesslike arrangements for their child's upbringing and their separate participation in it. However—overwhelmingly—she was glad Stefanos wanted to be a part of her baby's life. That had turned out beyond her expectations. There were, she knew, many men who would deny all responsibility, all care, for a baby conceived from a one-day fling.

'Perhaps the best thing we can do is get to know each other all over again,' she said. 'As the people we are now...not the people we were back then.' She waved her hand towards the *Daphne*, symbol of their carefree past selves.

'Agreed,' he said, more quickly than she had expected him to. 'We have the next ten days to really get to know each other. A fresh start.' He held out his hand to shake. 'Deal?' he asked.

She shook his hand. 'Deal,' she said.

Long moments passed as she looked up at him, warmed by his smile and smiling back. This was a better outcome than she could have dreamed of.

'Now, do you remember how to help me cast off lines so we can set sail?'

'Remind me, and I'm sure it will all come back,' she said, still smiling.

Stefanos motored directly out in front of the resort. Claudia gazed back in admiration at the architecturally splendid white structures on the top of the cliff that formed the main part of the hotel. There were a series of other white buildings at the back. One of those larger buildings, set well away from the main complex, he explained, was the house Alex and Dell had built for their family. And quite a distance from everything else was a small white church.

'The views must be sensational from the front rooms of the hotel,' she said. 'No wonder it became so well known, so quickly.'

'Every room is sensational in its own way. Pevezzo Athina is magnificent at any time of the year. One year there was a family party here during the winter, and all the guests got snowed in for days. The island was cut off by rough seas and violent skies. I think they all enjoyed it.'

'It gets that cold here in the winter?'

'It doesn't snow every year—but, yes, it gets cold.'

'I think of the Greek islands as being eternally summer.' Like the eternal summer of her time with Stefanos, she thought wistfully.

Claudia helped him to raise the sails so he could navigate the *Daphne* around the island. With him at the helm, wearing white shorts and T-shirt—surely not the same shorts and T-shirt from ten years ago?—it was as if she'd stepped back in time to when she'd first been on his boat with him. Back then, she'd declared he'd had the best butt in Greece. She wouldn't say anything different now.

Only this time *he* was very different, *she* was very different, and the landscape around them was nothing like the volcanic ruggedness of Santorini and the smaller islands in the caldera.

Most of Kosmimo was heavily forested. Glorious waves of aquamarine and deepest blue lapped onto white sand beaches beneath white limestone cliffs, and the sun sparkled off the surface of the water. While the main beach formed part of the resort, there were smaller beaches along the coastline that were only accessible by boat.

'The hotel had been half constructed and then abandoned when Alex bought the island,' Stefanos explained. 'He finished it and added new buildings, working with architects from Athens.'

'What a project—and what a success,' she said. 'I can't wait to find out more about it…from a professional point of view, I mean.'

'Would you ever go back to your hotel career?' he asked.

'Never say never,' she said.

But her experience in Sydney had scarred her. Not just the duplicitous behaviour of the man she'd trusted, who had eroded her faith in other men, but her realisation that she might have been chasing a dream—a dream fuelled by her memories of her parents' pub in Devon, not the reality of working for multinational hotel operators. But she didn't regret it, and she'd loved having a job that let her travel.

'When did you buy your villa?' she asked.

'After my father died and I inherited,' he said. 'Alex was looking for investors, and he approached the family first. He's a few years older than me—we're related on my father's side through one of his sisters.'

'I wondered…there is a resemblance.'

Although, to her eye, Stefanos was the more handsome.

Not for the first time, she wondered what her baby would look like. Could she share that kind of discussion with Stefanos? He'd probably want to have some input into naming the baby. When would be too soon to discuss that?

She would have to be careful that such discussions didn't cross the line into a couples-type of intimacy that wasn't part of the arrangement. They might be going to be parents, but they weren't anything more than former lovers— although perhaps at the end of this holiday they might have formed a kind of friendship.

A pain as sharp as a stiletto pierced her heart at the thought of what they'd been to each other and how they had lost it. How would she explain to her child that he or she had both a mummy and a daddy, but Daddy lived in a different country and Mummy and Daddy didn't love each other?

'Alex and I became friends as adults, not as children,' Stefanos said.

'You were an only child—weren't you close to your cousins growing up?'

'Alex was older than me, and he lived in Australia. There were other cousins and family friends nearer to me in age, so I didn't lack companionship.'

She wondered why his mouth had tightened on the words *family friends*.

She dared to risk a question she'd wanted to hear answered since they'd first met again, back in his apartment in Bloomsbury. 'Tell me why you sold the shipping business. I remember, even after all this time, you telling me it was your destiny.'

'I did say that. It was. And in some ways I felt like I'd let my father and my late grandfather down by selling the business that was their hearts' blood. But it wasn't mine—never had been mine.'

'So why…?'

He looked straight ahead, his hands on the wheel. 'I wasn't always an only child. I had a brother—older than me by two years. He died when he was five years old of a childhood cancer. I remember him… I was his little shadow, my mama says.'

'Oh, no. I'm so sorry, Stefanos. For your brother, for you, for your parents. Such a loss.'

'I sometimes dream of him as he might have been grown up. When I wake up, I feel the loss over again.'

'I'm sorry,' she said again, feeling how inadequate her words were. To lose a child—a sibling—would be an unimaginable grief. She'd have to remain vigilant that, in spite of his reassurances, Stefanos didn't renege and take her baby away.

'Not only did I lose my big brother, I had to step up into the gap he'd left in the family. He would have been groomed for the business. I could have followed my own interests. I was always fascinated by the ancient history of my country.'

'How could you not be, growing up in Athens?'

'Not everyone shared my passion. And I wasn't destined to be an academic. How could I refuse to take on the mantle of heir to Adrastos Shipping? There were no other children to take it. My mother had suffered repeated miscarriages.'

Claudia gasped, and put her hand on her still-flat belly in an automatic reaction of protection. In her ninth week of pregnancy, she was still at the vulnerable stage.

'You can see why I want so much to take care of you,' he said.

'Yes, and I appreciate it even more now I know that,' she said. 'Fingers crossed my doctor will tell me everything is as it should be for a healthy pregnancy.'

Already, here in this beautiful place, on this glorious sea, she felt the tension, the stress and the worry starting to dissipate. Surprisingly, she wasn't feeling seasick—but then she had never been seasick, even in the roughest of seas.

Stefanos continued. 'There was always an obligation—unspoken, but very much there—for me to make up to my parents for the son they'd lost...for the babies that were never born. I had to be everything to them.'

'Did that seem like a burden?'

'Sometimes.'

She sensed a wealth of feeling behind that single word.

'Did you ever tell them you didn't want to go into the business?'

'I was too dutiful to rebel. And there was a lot at stake. My father had me working in some capacity in the office from when I was twelve years old—first in school vacations and then university. I liked that. Believed I was part of something. I felt grown-up and important, even if I was only doing minor clerical jobs. I was told that all work was vital to the company. At that age I wasn't aware of the scope of the wealth Adrastos Shipping generated. But I knew it had my name on it and would one day be mine.'

'That was clever of your father.'

'I was indoctrinated at an early age,' he said wryly. 'The summer I met you, I'd rebelled. I'd had enough of working in my vacations. I wanted the summer off. I took the *Daphne* to Santorini to party with my friends.'

'Which you did,' she said. 'And you partied with me too. Those were good times.' *The best of times.*

'There was another reason I chose Santorini for my vacation…'

'You mean apart from the fact it's one of the most desirable destinations in the Mediterranean?'

'I also wanted to visit the archaeological dig at Akrotiri. It's the remains of a sixteenth-century BC city, incredibly well preserved in volcanic ash. So much is still there of the life the Minoan people lived before the volcano blew out the centre of their island. They had drainage systems, and they traded using pottery to hold oils and wine, just like we use today, painted incredible frescoes… I'm fascinated by it as a record of an advanced civilisation at a time when much of the world was in the Stone Age.'

'When did you visit Akrotiri?' she asked, curious that he had never mentioned this when they'd been together.

'Before I met you at the bar. And again when you were at work.'

'You never told me about your interest in archaeology. Or your work at the shipping company and your rebellion that year.'

'The archaeology had become a hidden passion I didn't talk about. And when it came to Adrastos Shipping, I didn't want to identify my job as my life.'

'Seems like we were both wearing masks of some kind that summer,' she said slowly.

CHAPTER THIRTEEN

STEFANOS FOUND IT almost impossible to stop admiring Claudia in her swimsuit. It was a modest one-piece, a serious swimmer's suit, in a swirl of blues that complemented her fair skin and bright hair, showed off long, slender legs.

Her body had changed. Her stomach was still flat, but her breasts definitely looked larger. For all their civilised talk of custody and support, he felt the raw truth hit him. The miracle of it. Inside her body she was growing their baby—a *person*. Someone who would become a child, a teenager, an adult—a member of his family. *An Adrastos*. He didn't want to miss out on any of that. Hell, he didn't want to miss out on seeing her body changing and growing. A fierce surge of possessiveness hit him. Not just for his baby, for *her*.

'Yes, my breasts have grown,' she said teasingly.

'You weren't meant to notice me looking,' he said, disconcerted at being caught out and by the fact that she'd called him on it.

'I'm quite impressed myself,' she said. 'They've never been on the generous side.'

Her breasts were perfect. Everything about her was perfect. *She* was perfect. As perfect as an imperfect human being could be. But could he trust his own judgement any more on what was perfect and what wasn't? What if he got it wrong again?

Claudia fitted her goggles. 'Are you coming in?'

He had anchored the *Daphne* within easy swimming distance of a small, postcard-pretty beach with a curve of white sand and a limestone cliff towering behind.

'Yep,' he said, picking up his own goggles.

She moved to dive from the edge of the boat, as he'd seen her do so many times in the past. But he covered the distance between them in two quick steps and grabbed her by the arm. 'Wait,' he said. 'Should you be diving from a height straight into the water? You know…because you're pregnant?'

Claudia started, shocked. 'I… I probably shouldn't.' She tore off her goggles. 'How stupid of me. I didn't give it a thought.'

Tears misted her eyes. He thought the hormones must be playing up again, but didn't dare say so.

'Not stupid. And I thought about it in time to stop you. So no need to worry.'

'I want to do everything right for the baby.'

'You *are* doing everything right,' he reassured her.

'But I didn't even think about diving.' Her voice rose, then broke. 'I… I've got a library of pregnancy books. I must have flicked over the chapter about swimming because at the time there wasn't any possibility I'd be in a Greek paradise, diving off the side of a yacht.'

She seemed to crumple, and he realised again how vulnerable she was. He took her into his arms in a hug. And realised it was exactly where he wanted her to be.

'It's understandable. When your bump gets bigger you

probably won't even think about diving. Besides, there's two of us here to think about such things.'

'It's sweet of you to say so, but I know you're only trying to make me feel better.'

Her voice came muffled, from against his shoulder, and he felt a shudder that might have been a poorly disguised sob.

'Is it working?' he asked.

'It is.' She sniffed. 'I do feel better. Not only just now…since you helped me pack my bag and spirited me away from London. Since you made me feel better about staggering off a helicopter and retching in front of people I didn't know. The fact I'm here at all is because you're looking after me. I… I don't feel so alone. Thank you.'

Stefanos tightened his arms around her. There was only the thin fabric of her swimsuit between them. He was bare-chested, in just swim-shorts. He didn't want to let her go. She felt so good there—as if she were reclaiming her place by his side from before, when they'd been together.

As the water slapped gently against the side of the boat, black-headed gulls wheeled above them, and silvery fish rose to the surface, he held her close. He felt her heart beating against his chest, marvelling that another little life was there too. *His child.* When were you able to hear the baby's heartbeat? Would Claudia let him come with her to her doctor's appointments? Would she trust him enough?

She pulled away and leaned back against the circle of his arms so she could look up into his face. Their gazes met and he looked into her eyes for a long moment. He didn't know what he was searching for, but he had an overwhelming feeling that one day he would find it there.

She smiled, a slow, tremulous smile, and as he dipped his head to kiss her mouth she reached up to meet him. Her lips parted under his, warm and pliant and welcoming. It wasn't a passionate kiss—not yet. Although the potential was always there when he was this close to Claudia. It was tender, affirmative, acknowledging something he could no longer deny.

'You know I haven't ever stopped being attracted to you?' she murmured against his mouth, her voice not quite steady.

'Nor me you,' he said. 'I can't imagine I would ever stop being attracted to you. Even if I fought it.'

She kissed him again—slowly, tenderly, almost pretty.

'I have fought it and it wouldn't go away,' she said. 'I've never felt for anyone the way I felt for you. It made me angry with myself—that I'd let a teenage crush hold me back, stop me from giving other people a chance. Eventually I talked myself out of it. Or thought I did. Then, when I saw you again in Bloomsbury… Well… you know what happened.'

'It was the same for me. Instant. All-encompassing. Only this time there are consequences. Something that could spin us apart. Or focus us together.'

'Is talking like this part of us getting to know each other again?' she said.

'I believe it could be,' he said.

'Almost…almost like dating?'

'We didn't date as such in Santorini,' he said. 'There was nothing gradual about it back then. We fell straight into a relationship.'

A relationship he'd thought would be for life.

'We went from hello to head-on with nothing in between,' she said.

How exhilarating that had been. No feeling had ever come close to the crazy tumble of falling in love with her. And his attempts to find it again had ended in unmitigated disaster. Perhaps because he was fated not to be with anyone else but Claudia?

He didn't put forward that idea, anticipating a scathing reaction from her. He was not too sure how he felt about it himself—it could be a trap he fell into.

'Shall we start dating now?' she said.

'Ten years after I spotted a gorgeous, laughing redhead in that bar in Santorini?'

'Why not?' she said.

'For our first date, would you care to join me for a swim? Followed by a snack of dry bread?'

She laughed. 'I couldn't think of anything better.'

From the ladder at the side of the *Daphne*, Claudia pushed herself safely into the unbelievably clear aquamarine sea. The water embraced her and refreshed her, the perfect temperature. She turned around to watch Stefanos execute a perfect dive into the water and emerge next to her.

'This is heaven,' she said. 'Absolute heaven.'

She duck-dived below the surface, marvelling at the light coming down in shafts through the different tones of turquoise, illuminating the white sand, the water plants waving in the current, the small brighty coloured fish darting between the rocks, and a red starfish. She would like to snorkel here. Did the resort stock snorkelling gear? she wondered. Stefanos had taught her to snorkel in Santorini.

She emerged to swim parallel to the beach, Stefanos keeping pace beside her.

'There must have been good beaches in Sydney,' he said, when they paused to tread water and look around.

'There were amazing beaches. But I was always a bit nervous in the water…about sharks and stinging things.'

'No sharks here,' he said. 'But keep an eye out for the occasional jellyfish. And when we get close to shore don't step on any sea urchins.'

She'd forgotten how protective he could be. Not possessive, but nurturing and encouraging. For the first time she let herself imagine what kind of father Stefanos would be. And then lost the thought when he challenged her to a race to the beach.

Once she'd dried off in the warm mid-morning sun, Claudia decamped to the shade of a group of small fresh-scented pine trees growing at the edge of the sand. Stefanos joined her. She sat with her arms wrapped around her knees. He picked up a stick and doodled circles with it in the sand.

'Please tell me we can swim here every day,' she said. 'I absolutely love it.'

'Here, or one of the other beautiful beaches of Kosmimo. If you like, we can sail to the other islands, or to Nidri for its shops and restaurants. There are some family-run tavernas on the smaller islands accessible only by boat.'

'Like the ones we went to in Santorini?'

'The same. Do you remember that taverna on the water, where you fed all your barbecued sardines to the stray cats?'

She laughed. 'And you pretended to be cranky, but kindly let me share your lunch.'

'I wasn't pretending to be cranky.'

'Yes, you were. I noticed you feeding some of your

sardines to the poor, hungry little cats too. You just wouldn't admit it.'

'I will neither confirm nor deny the truth of that,' he said very sternly, although a grin played at the corners of his mouth.

'But I remember the truth,' she said.

'I'm surprised you remember so much about those times.'

'You do too,' she said.

'Yes,' he said.

But did he remember it like she did? How they'd spent so much time making love? How they'd laughed at the same things?

'But can you not mention sardines again? My lurking nausea doesn't like the idea of them. Urgh...'

He laughed. 'Forget I ever said that word.'

A long silence fell between them. An iridescent dragonfly landed on her foot and she held her breath until it flew away. Wasn't a visit from a dragonfly a portent of transformation and change? If you believed in such things, of course.

She turned to him. 'What happened with your ex-wives?'

He groaned. 'I might have known you wouldn't let go of that.'

'You knew I wouldn't,' she said, with a laugh.

But she was very serious. What had happened in the last ten years to make him so bitter, so anti-marriage, when back then he'd been so keen on it? She hadn't changed *her* views on marriage—not after having held on to her independence for so long.

She shuddered when she remembered how she had weakened in her long-held stance of not letting a man come before her career and allowed Brad to dominate and manipulate her. Perhaps she'd been so vulnerable to him because she'd been lonely in Sydney. Whatever the reason, she'd been blind to the fact he was a con man of the first order. But if she'd married a man like that, not knowing what he was, she would have been trapped. Of course there had been no chance of that with Brad because, unbeknownst to her, he'd already been married.

No, she was no more open to marriage than she had been at nineteen. And even if she had changed her mind, was a man with two ex-wives a good bet as a husband? But he was the father of her child. She needed to know what had made him the man he was now.

'If it was a real first date surely you wouldn't ask me about my ex-wives,' he said.

'Technically, I asked you before we went on this date.'

He sighed a deep, heartfelt sigh that almost made her feel sorry for him. *Almost*.

'Start with wife number one,' she suggested.

'Right. Wife number one,' he said, and snapped the stick he'd been doodling with in half. He looked at the two broken pieces but didn't say anything further.

'Her name?' she prompted.

She needed to hear what had happened to him, but at the same time she felt a sick dread. Because she could not bear the thought of him with any other woman but her. Even though she had initiated this conversation, she wanted to put her hands over her ears.

'Arina,' he said. 'She was my mother's goddaughter, a family friend, a childhood playmate.'

So that was why that shadow had darkened his eyes at the words 'family friends'.

'So you'd known her all her life?'

'That's right—although I hadn't seen her for some years while she was away at university. Then she started an internship at an Adrastos Shipping supplier and we were thrown together again. I was devastated by losing my English girlfriend—'

'Me?'

'Who else?' he replied curtly, with an edge to his voice that cut. He tossed the broken sticks away from him down the sand. 'Little did I know Arina was suffering heartache of her own. Also, both sets of parents, for reasons of their own, were pushing us together. Arina was—is—a sweet person. Whether she was saying what she thought I wanted to hear, or genuinely believed it, she told me that above all she wanted a family. Her words were a balm to my wounded pride after your rejection. Before I knew it we were married. We were both twenty-two. It was a disaster for both of us. I got a wife who seemed to see the marital bed as a duty to be endured or evaded.'

Now Claudia really did want to cover her ears.

'And she got a husband who couldn't be what she wanted.'

'Why was that?' Claudia asked, not sure she really wanted to hear the answer.

'Because, to put it bluntly, I was the wrong sex. She'd been in love with her best friend—her chief bridesmaid at our wedding—since they were at school. But her family was ultra-conservative.'

'So she couldn't come out as her true self. Poor Arina. That's very sad. I wonder if her parents hoped marriage to you would "cure" her.'

'Something like that. Her story has a happy ending. Six months after our wedding she left me for her friend, who felt the same way about her. They're very happy. I went to their wedding. Arina and I are friends now—of a sort.'

'But you hold a grudge?'

'Because of the dishonesty. I was lied to by her, by her family, even by my own mother—who was hoping marriage would be the best thing for Arina—and by my father because he saw it as a strategic marriage between the heirs to two major shipping companies.'

'That was a lot to bear on your shoulders.'

And she'd bet it had been a blow to his masculinity—to be left for a woman.

'I didn't want there to be lies about the reason for the break-up, and neither did Arina and her wife. We told the truth and eventually the wave of scandal ebbed away.'

'And left you lying shattered on the shore?'

'That's one way of putting it,' he said. He took a deep breath. 'Both the marriage and its aftermath were hell. How could I ever trust again?'

'I'm sorry it turned out so rotten for you. But it's nothing you can be blamed for.'

No wonder he was wary.

'Marriage number two was even worse.' He cradled his head in his hands in a gesture of despair. 'I really don't want to relive that time. It was brutal.'

'Then don't,' Claudia said, alarmed. She reached out a hand to rub his back in silent comfort. 'Please. Forget I asked.'

He raised his head to face her and she dropped her hand. 'You'll only ask me again later, now your curiosity's aroused.'

'Of course I won't. Not if it upsets you.' She paused. 'Maybe I will ask you again. But you don't have to tell me now.'

He groaned in mock surrender. 'Now I've started, I might as well finish.'

'Only if you feel comfortable. Seriously. It was obviously very painful for you.'

'This is for the last time, okay? We won't speak of it again.'

'Okay.' She felt guilty that she was stirring up bad memories. But she had to know. His marriage mistakes could impact on her child's future. And she also wanted to know for her own sake. She'd be lying if she denied that.

His face set in grim lines. 'I met Tiana at a big annual yacht show in the South of France when I was twenty-seven. It's an international trade show for superyachts.'

'Wait. You were twenty-seven? Hadn't you sold the shipping company by then?'

'All but the yacht charter division, which is lucrative and has always interested me. I've doubled the business since.'

He might be an archaeologist in his heart but he was a billionaire in his blood, Claudia thought.

'So you met her at the yacht show…' Another indication of his elite world, inhabited by the richest of the rich.

'I should have known better. There are people there from all around the world. Not everyone is who they say they are at such an event.'

'And she wasn't?'

Again, she felt uncomfortable to think about him with another woman. But it was in his past, the experience had shaped him, and he had already flagged that it hadn't ended well. She had to grit her teeth and listen. After all, she'd asked him.

'She was glamorous, fun, just what I needed at that

time. I didn't expect her to end up in Athens, but she did on some believable pretext. What I didn't realise was that she'd targeted me, researched me and hunted me down.'

'Surely not?'

Yet he was a billionaire, and quite a prize for the kind of person who went after such a trophy. Again, she began to see why he might be bitter and reluctant ever to commit again.

'My mother had a name for her: *chrysothíras*, which translates as gold-digger. But of course I didn't believe her.'

'And was she? Tiana, I mean? A gold-digger?'

'A gold-digger extraordinaire. She knew exactly how to play me. I was snared before I knew it. I thought I was marrying a caring woman who wanted a family as much as I did. But by accident I found out she was older than she'd said, and had a child hidden away with her parents—who she'd told me were dead—and no interest in having more children. Everything was a lie.'

'Stefanos, I can't believe it… Why would she do that?'

'Money.' His voice was blunt with betrayal.

'I hope she didn't get any.'

'Enough to get her out of my life for ever.'

'I'm so sorry you had to go through that. You do know, though, don't you, that you are worth so much more than money? You're handsome, intelligent, kind—'

He brushed her words away. 'And a terrible judge of women. I will never, ever take that risk again. There won't be a marriage number three. Thanks to you, I will have a child in my life, but I don't want a wife.'

She couldn't blame him for being so vehement.

'Those two divorces were hardly typical,' she said.

'You've had very bad luck. Many of us make our mistakes without actually marrying them.'

'Like you did?'

She paused. 'If you want to hear my unedifying story, I suppose I'll have to share. It's not pretty. You might think less of me when you hear it.'

'I very much doubt that. Let's hear it. On the proviso that we never talk about past mistakes again.'

'Agreed,' she said wholeheartedly. 'I was a real mug. Do you know that expression?'

'Someone who's deceived, made a fool of?'

'That was me. I was made to look a real sucker by Brad.' She gritted her teeth. 'I still cringe when I remember how it panned out. I can't bear to think about how blinkered I was.'

Now it was Stefanos's turn to lay a comforting hand on her shoulder. 'It's not a good feeling.'

'Here goes,' she said, putting her hand over his. 'I was working in a hotel in Sydney. It was in a fabulous spot—right on the harbour. Brad was my boss. Usually I wouldn't go out with someone I worked with, but I only knew a few people there and he was very persuasive. He soon had me hooked. I didn't know he was getting my signature on documents that were contracts for supplies from companies owned by members of his wife's family. Yes, his wife—who I didn't know existed. Turned out she had no idea I existed either, and she wasn't aware of the deals Brad was doing with her brothers. She reported him and me for fraud. It got nasty. The press picked up on the "love triangle", which was further humiliation. I had to fight to clear my name—which I eventually did, at considerable expense and anguish. The shine was already wearing off the hotel business for me, and that completely tarnished it. That's when I went back home to the UK, with a firm resolve that I would never let myself get caught like that again.'

'You weren't dealt a fair hand.'

'No. But I ended up with my own business, so perhaps it wasn't such a bad hand. I don't have to answer to a man for anything.'

'And that business led you back to me...'

'And now I'm having a baby—which is happy news for both of us.' She took a deep breath. 'Stefanos, I'm sorry I couldn't be what you needed back then. But I'm glad that in an unconventional, roundabout way you're getting something of what you wished for—a child.'

'And you still say you don't believe in fate?' he said.

CHAPTER FOURTEEN

Stefanos relaxed back into his chair at the table in the hotel restaurant where, after their swim, he and Claudia had met Alex and Dell for lunch. He marvelled at how instantly Claudia had got on with his cousin and his wife, with her warm laugh and easy, informed conversation. She fitted in as no other woman he'd introduced to them ever had.

She talked all the talk—about hotels and hospitality, travel around Asia, her thoughts on Sydney, Alex and Dell's hometown, as well as on babies and children. Not only that, she talked the talk in Greek *and* English. As they'd sat down at the table she'd announced she wanted to practise and get her language skills back. She was doing well—soon she'd be back to the fluency that had seen her bantering back and forth with the customers in that Santorini bar so long ago. He felt inordinately proud of her.

He contributed to the conversation when required. Of course he had to tell the story of how Claudia had suddenly appeared from his past, to pack up his apartment for his move back to Athens. How they'd reconnected. How—obviously—they'd got on very well indeed. How they were taking it day by day in terms of a renewed friendship.

'Did all the old attraction come rushing back when you first saw her?' Dell asked.

'Yes,' he said.

That was the polite response, but it was also the truthful one. That old attraction was churned up with bitterness and blame, but it was still there, strong as it had ever been. Thoughts of how their morning together had been an echo of earlier times, when they'd been everything to each other, kept intruding. But he didn't want to get married, and neither did she. How could they make that work to result in something mutually beneficial?

When he'd got back to Athens he had texted her, suggesting a meeting in London, intending to have the same kind of conversation he'd had with her on the *Daphne* this morning—to suggest they get to know each other again with no pressure for commitment on either side. The baby had put an entirely different slant on it. Others seemed to be putting an urgency on the nine-month countdown that he and Claudia did not.

Dell was obviously dying to know the details of what had happened in London, and he wondered if Claudia would share them with her. He hoped not. Their encounter might have been what some would call a 'one-morning stand', but making love with Claudia had always been special and private to him, and that time together had been no different. Dell wouldn't be getting the details from *him*, that was for sure.

Alex and Dell had not got on with either of his ex-wives. Arina had been awkward with Alex—Dell hadn't been on the scene then—in the way of someone hiding a deep secret. And after he'd split with Tiana, Dell had made no bones about how much she'd disliked and distrusted his glamorous older wife.

'Frankly, she was the kind of person where you'd count the silver after she'd been in the room,' Dell had said.

That had only made him feel worse about his massive error of judgement in marrying Tiana. He'd beaten himself up about it ever since. But he felt better about those disastrous marriages now, after his conversation with Claudia on the beach. He'd had very bad luck, she'd said, putting a different and more forgiving slant on it. He'd married his mistakes, she'd said.

Maybe it wasn't such an irrevocably shameful thing to be twice divorced before thirty when you looked at it that way. But it still made him dead against marrying another 'mistake'. And he was being not so subtly pushed towards marriage by his cousin and his wife. They'd made their approval of Claudia very obvious.

'She already seems like part of the family,' Dell joked, but narrowed her eyes to see his reaction.

When his mother found out about Claudia's pregnancy the pressure would really be on. But Claudia also had reasons to resist marriage—she had made that very clear. These days, pregnancy was no reason to get married. He was determined he and she would sort out access and time spent together without interference from his family, no matter how well-meaning.

He noticed that Claudia was eating very little. 'You okay?' he asked quietly.

She nodded. 'Just being careful. I'm actually feeling much better.'

'The swim did you good,' he said.

She leaned towards him to murmur in his ear, so that only he could hear. 'So did being with you.'

She then turned away to talk to Dell, and he was left wondering if he had misheard her.

After the meal, he headed back to the villa to make some calls while Dell gave Claudia a grand tour of the resort. He was surprised at how empty his villa seemed without her, though she hadn't spent even twenty-four hours there. Her presence was there in the flip-flops left outside the door, the linen jacket draped on the back of a chair, a hint of her floral perfume in the air. Oh, and those dry crackers and the scent of ginger tea.

He was in the living area, talking on his phone, when Claudia got back, flushed and excited after her tour of the resort. Stefanos immediately ended the call to greet her.

She was bubbling. 'Stefanos, this place is even more wonderful than I had imagined! It has to be the best resort I've seen. Better even than that heavenly place in Bali. Better than Bay Breeze, my favourite place near Sydney—which, it turns out, is owned by Alex's friends the Morgan brothers. Dell helped put it on the map when she was a food writer. Pevezzo Athina just excels in every way. Of course the location is superlative, and the views priceless, but the white marble buildings, the luxury of the fit-outs, the grounds, the holistic approach, the level of service—everything. This place deserves every accolade and award it's been given.'

She flung herself on the sofa beside him.

'Thank you, thank you, thank you for bringing me here.' She planted a kiss on his cheek before kicking off her boat shoes and throwing herself back against the sofa. 'Trouble is, I'll never want to leave.'

Why did she have to? She could live here. Help his

cousin run the resort if that was what would please her. He was sure it would please them. Surely that would beat packing boxes? And it would be so much easier for him to visit his child here than it would be to go from Athens to London. It seemed a perfect solution. But it was early days yet to mention it to Claudia.

'I'm glad you like it so much.'

'You were smart to invest,' she told him.

'Yes,' he said.

His father had also made an initial investment, as had Alex's other cousin Cristos. It had indeed proved to be a smart move.

'But my feet are killing me,' she went on. 'I didn't realise they would swell in the heat. Dell said it happened to her when she was pregnant too.' She wiggled her toes and rotated her ankles.

'Here, let me,' he said, taking her pale, slender feet in his hands. He massaged her ankles, her feet, between her toes.

'Oh, that's so much better,' she said, closing her eyes, sighing her appreciation. 'Oh, yes. Harder. That's lovely. Mmm... Don't stop.'

She was making the same moans of pleasure as she did when they made love...

Claudia lay back against the sofa and gave herself over to the bliss of Stefanos massaging her feet with his big, strong hands. He had a magic touch. It felt so good. Mmm...

Perhaps too good.

Abruptly she sat up and swung her feet over the edge of the sofa. 'Thank you, that really helped.' She wiggled her feet. 'Much better.'

'I don't have to stop.'

His voice was deep and husky and she knew exactly what he meant. Because her thoughts had run along exactly the same sexy track.

'Yes. You do. If you don't stop, the next thing we'll be making love on the sofa.'

He grinned a lazy grin that chipped away at her resolve. 'Would that be such a bad thing?'

'Not a bad thing—of course not a *bad* thing. But...but an unwise thing. We might only have one chance to get this shared parenting thing right. Making love raises the stakes...makes it more difficult for me to think straight. I know it's different for men, but for me sex is more than just physical, it's emotional. And the more invested I am, the more...well, the more vulnerable I am.'

The more in danger she was of falling in love with him all over again. The more in danger of being hurt when they went back to their separate lives.

'What makes you think it's different for men?'

She shrugged, as if no explanation was required. 'Well... Men.'

He frowned. 'That's an unfair generalisation. Some men, perhaps. Not this man.'

'I'm sorry if I got that wrong.' She remembered how he had worshipped her, looked into her eyes while they made love.

'You're forgiven,' he said.

But had he forgiven her for how she'd hurt him ten years ago?

'The idea of us "dating" is that we get to know each other slowly,' she said.

'In Santorini we went to bed together that first night.'

'My point precisely. And then we realised we didn't

know each other as well as we thought we did. Perhaps didn't know each other as well as we needed to when we hit a barrier.' She paused, planted a quick, fierce kiss on his mouth. 'That doesn't mean I don't want you. Because I do. Badly.'

He groaned and sat back further away from her on the sofa. 'Don't say that. Knowing you want me as much as I want you only makes it worse.'

'It does for me too—believe me. But we don't have just us to consider now. There's our baby. And the better the relationship is between us, the better it will be for him or her.'

'How can I argue with that?' he said.

'Talking about the baby…can I ask you something?'

'As long as it's not to stop wanting you, because I can't,' he growled.

She laughed. 'No. Not that. Would you like to be involved in my pregnancy? Come along with me to my first scan, for example? It's done at around twelve weeks and it's called "the dating scan". It's to check that everything is developing okay and to confirm how far along I am in the pregnancy so they can calculate the due date.'

'I would very much like to be there,' he said.

He sounded pleased—that was a first step. She was glad. She genuinely wanted him to be there. There was also another motive—if she involved him, showed him what a meticulously caring mother she intended to be, that would be a defence against any later attempt by him to undermine her. Not that she really thought that might happen, but she had to consider it.

'Of course I know exactly the day this baby was conceived, because it was only the once with you. I mean it wasn't just the once—it was more than once…more than twice—but the one day…you remember.'

'Oh, yes, I remember,' he said.

'Being pregnant and single isn't…well, it isn't as easy as I thought. Medical people keep asking about the father and I don't know all the answers—like I didn't know your blood group and it was important. It's all so exciting, but it's a bit lonely. There are some things I want to share.'

'Give me notice and I'll be there. I'll come from Athens. Thank you for not locking me out.'

She was surprised he might have felt locked out. But perhaps she had been so fearful of him taking her child that that was exactly what she had done.

'Do you have any questions?' she asked.

'When can we hear the baby's heartbeat? That will be a reassuring thing to hear.'

'I think we'll hear it at the ultrasound scan.'

'Are you aware of it now?'

'Not at all,' she said. 'I'm looking forward to hearing a heartbeat too.'

He got up from the sofa. 'I've got more questions—but first can I get you a drink or some more crackers? By the way, are your feet still hurting? If so, why not put them up on some cushions? I'll stack them for you.'

'The cushions are a good idea—why don't I stack them while you get us that drink.'

Had he been this thoughtful when he'd been twenty? Looking back, she thought he probably had. Only she had taken it for granted. Perhaps she needed to trust him now.

'*Entaxei,*' he said. Okay.

Comfortable on the sofa, her feet elevated on a stack of cushions and a Greek lemon drink recommended by Dell in her hand, Claudia returned to their conversation.

'What other questions do you have?'

'When can they tell you the sex of the baby?'

'I haven't asked because I don't want to know. Old-fashioned of me, I suppose, but I'd like it to be a surprise.'

'I'm good with that,' he said. 'I don't care what the sex is, as long as it's healthy.'

'As long as it's healthy,' she said at the same time, and they laughed. 'That said, if tests need to be done that reveal the sex, I couldn't bear for the medical staff to know and not us.'

'Agreed,' he said.

'I wonder what our baby will look like?' she mused.

'With you a fair-skinned redhead and me with black hair and olive skin, who knows?'

'I reckon your colouring will dominate. Your hair is so very black.'

'It might. But there are some blondes in my family. And some green eyes.'

'Another surprise for us,' she said. 'Have you thought about names? I believe there's a lot of naming traditions in Greek families.'

These were all the things she'd wanted to discuss with him but hadn't dared.

'Traditionally, a first son is named after the father's father, and the first daughter after the father's mother. Then the second son is named after the mother's father and the second daughter after her mother.'

'As we're not married, would that be expected?' she said.

'I don't see why,' he said. 'Sometimes a grandparent's name is used as a second name.'

'Were you named after your grandfather?'

'Yes.'

'What are your parents' names?'

How little she really knew about him.

'My mother's name is Dimitra and my father is Vasileios.'

'Dimitra is pretty, but I'm not so sure about your father's name.'

'I like it because I loved my father. But we don't have to stick with any of those traditions. After all, we're not following convention, and of course you're not Greek. Perhaps our child deserves its own name.'

'I'll think about it at another time,' she said, taking the ball back into her own court.

'Do you want our baby to be bilingual?' he asked.

'Absolutely. I'll talk to him or her in both languages. For one thing, when he or she goes to visit you in Greece, they'll need to be able to speak Greek.'

Claudia was beginning to find this subject painful— their separateness, their child going back and forth between them. A future with Stefanos in it only at designated times and meeting places. Good for the child, but not so good for her to hear it put in such matter-of-fact terms.

Because so many times today she'd been reminded of just why she had fallen so deeply in love with Stefanos.

CHAPTER FIFTEEN

STEFANOS COULDN'T IMAGINE a moment more perfect than this: swimming with Claudia around one of the small uninhabited islands near Kosmimo. The *Daphne* was anchored on the other side of the island in perfectly calm seas as they swam the island's perimeter. There was no other boat or person in sight. Just him and Claudia together in the warm, buoyant sea under the most perfect blue summer morning sky.

He was a strong swimmer, but she matched him, her stroke graceful, her body sleek and strong, as they speared through water that ranged from midnight-blue to sparkling turquoise. Shafts of sunlight illuminated the white sand of the sea floor, shoals of tiny fish darted around them, and small ghostly white jellyfish pulsed away with their stinging tentacles wafting behind them.

Claudia tapped him on the arm. 'Look up on the cliff-side.'

She trod water, drops of salt water glistening on her shoulders like crystals, and Stefanos looked up to see five small, shaggy wild goats defying gravity as they effortlessly scaled the sheer vertical surface.

'Never fails to amaze,' he said.

'How on earth do they get up there without falling off?'

'Their hooves are very hard on the outside, so they can dig into the tiniest of ledges, and they have soft, cushiony pads below, which mould to the wall like a natural climbing shoe. Those goats are sturdy and agile. They have been a part of this landscape for a very long time, and their ancestors played an important role in Greek mythology.' He stopped. 'You probably don't want a lecture on that.'

'But I do—it's fascinating. Tell me more.'

'Zeus, the king of the gods, was hidden as a baby from his father Cronus, who wanted to destroy him because he would eventually dethrone him. He was given shelter by a goat named Amaltheia, who nourished him as a foster mother. Her horn became the cornucopia—the horn of plenty. There are other myths about goats going back thousands of years. And they're depicted on a lot of ancient art.'

Claudia looked up at the goats with something akin to reverence. 'It's a privilege to see them.' She waved her arms around her. 'In fact it's a privilege for us to be here on these beautiful islands, this perfect sea. I love it.'

She plunged back into the water and swam ahead of him, her pale limbs ethereal in the translucent water. He stayed a few strokes behind her so he could enjoy watching her swim.

He had never shared moments like this with either of his dreaded ex-wives. In fact he'd never shared moments so perfect and harmonious with anyone else—only that vibrant nineteen-year-old, so long ago in the waters of Santorini.

Now, as then, Claudia got the same enjoyment as he did from nature, good music, simple food well cooked and the company of friends. She even seemed to enjoy his tales of Ancient Greece. He reckoned she'd got more pleasure from the sight of a small pod of dolphins swimming alongside the *Daphne*, leaping out of the water, than ex-wife number two had got from yet another of the diamond bracelets she had demanded.

That wasn't to deny his privilege in swimming around a private island and never having to worry about money. Or the fact that, elegantly dressed, Claudia might very well like a diamond bracelet. In fact he would get one made for her to celebrate the birth of his child. Hell, why not get one to celebrate her pregnancy? But all his money hadn't bought him harmony such as he shared today with Claudia.

Back then, he had initiated Claudia into the joys of swimming in Greek waters, and he couldn't help thinking of what fun it would be to teach their child. Together. Perhaps more than one child…

He pinpointed just why he was enjoying her company so much—it was because they had so much in common, liked doing the same things. That had not been the case with his ex-wives. Could there be a chance that marriage would work for him after two such dreadful mistakes? A marriage that would secure the company of his child not just at weekends and school holidays but every day?

He took a few powerful strokes to take him ahead of Claudia, then slowed down so she would ease up too and the swim would take longer. He didn't want this perfect time to end. Not just the swim but her time on the island. She'd been, here with him on Kosmimo for a week now. He only had three more days left with her. It was going too fast. This magical time was ebbing away too rapidly. All too soon, real life would intervene. The life she would live in London and he in Athens, with too much distance between them.

He realised he was beginning to trust her. Perhaps there could be another way forward. He didn't want to let her go.

The *Daphne* was anchored at one of the small islands that inhabited the seas near Kosmimo. It seemed to Claudia like a particularly lovely part of Ionian paradise. In fact it was utter bliss—not least because of the company. This morning she and Stefanos had swum right around the island. They'd been entertained by the wild goats clambering up clifftops.

They'd planned a whole day exploring away from Pevezzo Athina—just the two of them. Stefanos intended to sail to a taverna on another island, accessible only by sea, for lunch, then go elsewhere for the afternoon—perhaps for a spot of snorkelling.

Now, she lay on a deck chair in the shade on the mahogany deck of the *Daphne* and watched Stefanos as he polished some of the yacht's metalwork. She was sure he must have people he paid to maintain the boat—after all, he owned a fleet of luxury charter yachts, moored all around the Mediterranean—but he'd told her he liked to do the work himself. The *Daphne* had been a gift from grandparents who had both passed away, and he cherished it.

The boat was special to her too, for all the memories it held of that summer she'd spent with him. And now she was making new memories.

She'd never been happier—or not since the time she'd spent on board the *Daphne* with Stefanos ten years ago. Each day had been an opportunity to explore Kosmimo and the surrounding islands, to relax in the luxury of the resort, to share meals with Alex and Dell, who had so quickly become good friends.

But in three more days, on Friday, the helicopter would come to take them back to Athens, where Stefanos would stay while she flew back to London. She dreaded the thought of the helicopter, although her morning sickness was more under control now. More than that, she dreaded the thought of not seeing Stefanos again until her twelve-week scan.

That was if he could make it. If he didn't change his mind about getting involved in the nitty-gritty of pregnancy. If business didn't get in the way. If he didn't meet a woman in the meantime—someone who wouldn't want him to have anything to do with a pregnant former lover in London.

Claudia batted the thoughts away as if they were a swarm of sandflies. She had to trust him. If she didn't she would drive herself crazy.

She got up from the chair to get a drink. As she did so, her white hat was caught by a sudden gust of wind and flew off her head and into the water.

'My hat!' She started to pull off the shirt she wore over her swimsuit. 'I'll go in and get it.'

'Wait! I'll grab it with the boat hook.' Stefanos reached over the side of the boat with the pole. 'Got it.' He dropped the sodden hat on the deck.

'Thank you. That's a useful hat. I won't be able to wear it until it dries, though.'

'There are other hats on board,' he said. 'Look in the closet in the galley.'

The interior of the *Daphne* was like a luxuriously appointed apartment. The kitchen might be called a galley, but it was full-sized. She found the closet and several hats inside, stacked on a shelf. They seemed to be men's hats, too big for her, but right at the back, almost as if it had been hidden, was a straw hat that looked smaller.

As she pulled it out, she gasped.

Her hat.

The battered straw hat she'd worn all that summer, bought at a market stall the first day she'd arrived, all fresh and eager for her job at the bar. Her initials were marked on the label, and a single long strand of auburn hair was caught in the weave. She'd left it behind somewhere in Santorini. When she'd got back home it hadn't been in her luggage, and she hadn't been able to remember where she'd last worn it. For a long time she'd mourned the loss of that hat.

Now she straightened the edges, put it on her head. It still fitted perfectly. Her favourite hat. She got some drinks from the refrigerator and headed back to the bow.

As she approached him, Stefanos stopped what he was doing to stare at her. 'You found your hat. I should have realised—'

'Realised what?'

'That you would find it where I'd hidden it.'

'Hidden it? Why would you do that? I assume I left it here on the boat ten years ago and you shoved it in the closet.'

He put down the polishing cloth he'd been using. 'You didn't leave it on the boat. The last time you wore it was that day when you got into my car and I took you to the airport. After you'd gone, I found it on the floor of the car. I picked it up and…and I held it close. The scent of your shampoo still lingered on the straw.'

She felt the smart of tears. 'Oh, Stefanos, that's so sad.

To think at the same time I was crying my heart out and making an exhibition of myself in the airport. Remember I told you?'

'Yes,' he said.

'I cried until I didn't have a tear left. I wish I'd known you had my hat.'

'I took it home to Athens with me. Kept it in my bedroom for a long time until I got engaged to Arina. It didn't seem fair to her for me to hang on to something that had belonged to my first love, the English girl who had let me down so badly, but I couldn't bring myself to throw it out. The next time I came to the boat I put it in that closet, right at the very back. It was your hat. I didn't want anyone else wearing it.'

'And it's been there for all these years?'

'I'd forgotten all about it until just now, when I suggested you look in there for a hat. I hoped you wouldn't find it...or that if you did you wouldn't recognise it.'

She frowned. 'Why?'

He shrugged broad shoulders. 'I didn't want you to think me stupidly sentimental.'

'I don't think it's stupid at all—what you did was beautiful. If I'd known, perhaps it would have given me some comfort to know I'd meant more to you than your thorough ghosting of me indicated.'

He reached out and touched the brim of the hat. 'Only now, seeing you wear this hat again, do I realise just how much you meant to me. How much I threw away by breaking off all contact with you. How stubborn I was—how arrogant to think there was only my way of doing things.'

'Stefanos, we were young, and it was so long ago, but

knowing you kept this hat for ten years means a lot. It…
it goes a long way to healing old wounds.'

She took the few steps across the deck to him. She put
her hands on his shoulders and kissed him. He tasted of
salt and lemon, memories and possibilities, his beard soft
against her face. How many kisses had they shared on
this boat? How many more would they share? She was
leaving—going back to everyday life in London. This
'dating' time had made her realise she already knew everything she needed to know about Stefanos. And their
time together was running out.

He took off her hat—that so-important hat. 'Please
don't let it fly into the sea,' she said.

'Never,' he said, and he folded her hat and shoved it
in the pocket of his shorts. It really wasn't meant to be
folded, but it had been done so many times before, ten
years ago.

He brushed his fingers through her hair and she sighed
at the pleasure of it.

He wore only his shorts, his chest bare, strong and
muscular and tanned. His skin was warm from the sun,
smooth over hard muscle. He pulled her close…so close
she could sense the hammering of his heart, feel his
arousal. She bucked her hips against him in reply and
kissed him again, hard and hungry and urgent.

He broke the kiss and pulled away. 'We have to stop,'
he said, his voice hoarse, his breath ragged.

'Why?'

'Because you said—'

'I've changed my mind,' she said.

'You're sure?'

'Absolutely sure.'

They strained against each other as their kiss grew in

intensity. He slid her shirt up and off her, until she was left in just her swimsuit. He slid the straps down off her shoulders to free her breasts.

'Definitely bigger…' he breathed.

And more sensitive. Desire throbbed though her as he caressed her, his hands sliding down to cup her bottom. All she could think of was Stefanos and how much she wanted him…how much she had wanted him from the moment she'd first seen him…how much she would always want him. Was she fated only ever to want this one man with this all-consuming passion?

'Shall we take this inside?' he said. 'Although we didn't always.'

Many times they had made love out on the deck, their naked bodies silvered by moonlight.

'Inside might be more private than the deck if boats or helicopters come by,' she said, scarcely able to catch her breath. 'A cabin, maybe?'

'A cabin it is,' said Stefanos, and he swept her up into his arms as if she were weightless and carried her inside.

They didn't make it past the saloon—the living area. Once he started touching her she was gone. He made pulling down her swimsuit into a caress, sliding his hands over her body exactly as she liked it. And as she stepped out of the swimsuit he took the opportunity to kiss her intimately, using his tongue and lips to bring her to a peak of arousal.

'I want *you*,' she said, as she tugged off his shorts, her hands clumsy with haste, and pulled him down onto the sofa with her.

She loved him. She had loved him from the moment she'd first met him. She had never stopped loving him. The reason she had never loved another was because no one was him. She couldn't bear the thought of life without him. How had it taken her so long to realise that?

'Is it safe?' he asked. 'For the baby, I mean.'

'Perfectly safe. The doctor assured me.'

Stefanos didn't give in to her demands to take her fast and furiously—rather he teased and tormented her with his clever fingers, before finally pushing gently into her, stroking slow and even, until they both caught the same rhythm of extreme pleasure. He knew just the right moment when she was on the edge to increase the pace. They climaxed together, and as Claudia looked up into his face, as she cried out his name, he was looking down, his eyes searching hers.

She let herself hope against hope that he might love her like she loved him.

She tried to stay awake. She wanted more lovemaking…wanted to talk to him about what had just happened between them…but she slid into sleep.

She woke to find Stefanos sitting on the edge of the sofa and gazing down into her face. He was wearing a towel around his hips. He was so handsome… She could never have enough of seeing his face so close. The flecks in his eyes seemed very green. She looked up at him and smiled a slow, lazy smile of completion and satisfaction. She reached her arms above her head and stretched like a cat.

He brushed her tousled hair away from her face. She caught his hand and kissed it.

'We always got that right, didn't we?' she said. 'The sex, I mean.'

'Always,' he said.

'Perhaps that's why we never talked much—we were too busy making love at any opportunity.' She stretched again. 'How long have I been asleep? I must have been tired out from the swim.'

And the wonderful, wonderful sex.

'Not long. You were smiling in your sleep. I think you were dreaming of good things.'

'I was dreaming of us swimming in a beautiful aquamarine sea like this one. We were naked and heading towards a happy place… I don't know where.'

'Sounds perfect to me,' he said.

'There was a baby mermaid swimming between us.'

'A mermaid? That must mean a little Dimitra is on her way to us.'

'Maybe not a mermaid. You can't really tell with a merbaby. This one had short baby hair floating around its head—black, by the way, so it could have been a merboy.'

'I guess we'll have to wait and see.' He smiled—indulgently, she thought.

'Am I making sense?' she asked.

'Kind of. I believe in fate; you believe in mermaids.'

'I… I want to believe that dreams can come true,' she said.

He dropped a kiss on the corner of her mouth, then looked back into her face. 'I think we should get married.'

Claudia stared at him. She sat bolt-upright, clutching the cotton throw from the sofa to cover her. 'That came from nowhere,' she said, not certain whether his tone of voice should lead her to feel excited or otherwise.

'I've thought about it a lot since we've been on the island. It seems the right thing to do.'

His tone was very serious. Not proposing-to-the-woman-he-loved serious, but business-proposal serious.

'The best thing for the baby. And for us. We get on so well with each other. We're great in bed.'

He might as well have summed up the pros of his proposal in point form. Which made her think about the cons.

Claudia swallowed a hit of intense disappointment. She hadn't expected or wanted a proposal—especially this kind of pragmatic proposal. But she had hoped for words of love.

While they'd been making love she'd desperately wanted to tell him how much she loved him, that for her first love was true love, but she'd known it wasn't the right time. Thank heaven she hadn't gasped out those words when he didn't appear to be thinking the same way. That would really have been making an exhibition of herself. She'd been fooled by the way he had looked into her eyes when they came together. Fooled into thinking that he might feel the same. Seemed she had misread him—big-time.

'What do you mean "the right thing to do"?'

'It makes sense. We're having this baby together so we should be together. You being in London and me in Athens doesn't make sense.'

No, no, no. This wasn't how it was meant to be. He was supposed to say he loved her and couldn't live without her. *She couldn't settle for less.*

'Our current situation makes sense to me,' she said. 'We can legalise the arrangements we've discussed if you'd feel better doing that. You don't have to marry me to be a father to our child.'

She realised she was holding her shoulders up near her ears and forced herself to relax them.

'But surely it would be better for the child and easier for us to be married?' he said.

'I don't agree,' she said.

Couldn't he see he was offering marriage for all the wrong reasons? A proposal that was all about what would make life *easier* with the baby and nothing about *her*. He was offering her a loveless marriage. What made him think she'd even contemplate such a trap?

'Why not?' he said, dark brows drawn together. 'You love it here. You'll love my house in Athens. You could even work with Alex and Dell on the resort if you wanted to—I'm sure they'd like to have your input.'

All that would be wonderful if it was in the context of a loving marriage, rather than a convenient arrangement between two people who were compatible in bed. Worse, he assumed she'd move to Greece without even asking her thoughts on such a move.

'I actually have my own business in London, thank you,' she said, trying desperately to keep her voice without a wobble.

'Didn't you say you'd had an offer to franchise it?'

'An offer that we may or may not consider.'

'You wouldn't need to work at all if we were married.'

Never had he sounded more arrogant. He must be very used to getting his own way. Was she seeing *that* Stefanos, born to privilege and wealth, here on Kosmimo? A Stefanos who would charm her into doing what was most convenient for him—that was put her life on hold to suit him and ever so conveniently have his child close by. The child she suspected he wanted to possess for himself.

'I have never wanted to not work,' she said. She spoke through gritted teeth, but he didn't seem to notice her tension. 'I think you know that.'

'You might feel differently after you've had the baby.'

He looked shocked that she hadn't immediately jumped on his proposal. He really thought he was doing the right thing. But he couldn't offer her love. And marriage without love, no matter how convenient, could not be considered.

'And I might not.'

'Dell and Alex really like you, and I know they'd want you to be part of the family.'

'My child will be part of your family by blood. I assume I might have some status in it as his or her mother, married or not.'

'It would be better for our child to have a mother and father married and living together.'

'Didn't you yourself point out how unhappy a person can be within a marriage? How good would it be for a child to have unhappily married parents?'

'Have you been unhappy with me this week?'

His question tore at her heart. She had never been happier. She was in love with a man who seemed dedicated to pleasing her and it had been heaven. But it seemed his dedication to her pleasure had been simply a means to an end.

'On the contrary, I've been very happy. But this is a holiday. It comes to an end on Friday.' She was finding it more and more difficult to speak calmly and give rational, reasoned answers.

'So why don't you want to marry me?' he said.

Claudia stared at him in total and utter disbelief. 'I don't get it,' she said. 'I really don't get it. Why this sudden turnaround from being a man who has repeatedly told me how ghastly his ex-wives are, how terribly they wounded him and how he never wants to get married again. Why are you messing with me like this, Stefanos?'

He looked genuinely bewildered, but she was too furious to care.

'I'm not messing with you,' he protested. 'If that's what—'

'What about *me*?' she said, glaring at him. 'What about what I want? My needs? Me being someone more than a sex partner and the mother of your child? Not once in all your talk of marriage have you asked how I see *my* future.'

She got up from the sofa, hastily tucked the throw around her, and stalked up and down the length of the saloon as she tried to gather her thoughts through a red mist of anger.

He stood up to face her. 'I'd hoped you'd see your future with me,' he said. 'Me and our child. Perhaps more children if we are blessed that way.'

She gritted her teeth. 'You really don't get it, do you? Is this an elaborate plot to get your hands on our baby just for yourself? Are you going to kick me out of the way in a third divorce and keep the baby?'

He went very still. Her words had obviously hurt him, and that pained her, but she had to get through to him.

'You know that's not true,' he said.

'*How* do I know? I don't know anything of what you're feeling apart from your wanting marriage as a practical transaction for the two of us. I'm puzzled why you would propose to me like that and expect me to be overjoyed. I don't think it's a language barrier. It's…it's more an emotional barrier you don't even know is there.'

'I don't know what the hell you're talking about,' he said, jaw clenched.

Claudia knew she couldn't keep this up any longer. She couldn't—*wouldn't*—let herself burst into tears of disappointment and misery.

'I'm sorry, Stefanos. I don't want to get married. I didn't ten years ago and I don't now. I appreciate that you want to do what you think is best for our baby, and I thank you. But let's keep the arrangement as it currently stands.'

He frowned. 'I don't understand… We're back where we were ten years ago.'

'Actually, the circumstances are very different,' she said, barely able to keep her voice even. 'I… I think you'll come to see that.'

In the meantime, she was trapped with him on his boat. If they'd been nearer to Kosmimo she'd have swum back to the resort. Where she'd be trapped with him in his villa. How had she got herself into this? How would she get back to London? She wouldn't be able to ask Alex or Dell. And she didn't want to embarrass herself or Stefanos.

She walked towards the smallest of the cabins. 'I'm not feeling well and I'm going to lie down. I'm sorry, you'll have to count me out for lunch and for snorkelling. Can you please take me back to the resort?'

She couldn't keep her voice steady enough for speech for a moment longer.

'Of course,' he said, tight-lipped.

As she walked past Stefanos, trying desperately not to show how upset she was that she had fallen back in love with him when he wasn't in love with her, she noticed she had thrown his shorts on the ground in her frenzy to get them off him. Her old straw hat had fallen out of his pocket and now lay on the floor.

She felt like kicking it.

CHAPTER SIXTEEN

STEFANOS DID NOT know where he'd gone wrong. Claudia hadn't come out of the cabin until the *Daphne* was back moored in its dock at Pevezzo Athina. Once back on land, she'd walked up to the villa next to him with only the minimum of polite exchanges, her voice completely lacking its usual warmth. Unless he'd said anything she'd lapsed into silence. Once inside the privacy of the villa she had reiterated that she wasn't feeling well, then disappeared into her suite with a supply of those darn crackers. Not once had she met his eyes.

He could hear her now, quietly sobbing in her suite, and it was tearing at his heart. She sounded so utterly miserable, and he had the gut-wrenching feeling it was all his fault. What had he done to offend her so badly? He had overcome all his dread of marriage and asked her to marry him. Why had that been so badly received?

He paced the length of the living room in the villa. Back and forth, back and forth. Maybe she could hear his footsteps and it was scaring her. He cursed under his breath in Greek. Surely she didn't think he'd hurt her? *Never.* He wanted to protect her and never, ever hurt her. Although somehow he seemed to have grossly hurt her feelings.

He gave the pacing a break and headed to his suite to change into fresh white shorts and shirt. When he came back out her door was still closed, although thankfully her sobs had died away. He wasn't good with women's tears—didn't know how to handle them.

He was worried about her. What if she really wasn't well and it wasn't what he'd said that had upset her? Did he need to helicopter her to hospital? He couldn't bear it if anything were to happen to her; he felt overwhelmed by the reality of how important she was to him. It wasn't just about the baby. It was *her*. After these idyllic days together, he could not imagine life without her. Yet she was as uninterested in marrying him as she had been ten years ago, even though she was pregnant with their child.

He stood outside her closed door. Had he given up too easily? Today on the boat, seeing her in her battered old hat, it had been as if those ten years had rolled away and it was like it had been back then, when they were crazy for each other and no other person in the world had existed. It had been him and her, together in their bubble, and he wanted that again. Now he knew for sure it wasn't just about the sex—albeit mind-blowing. He felt more comfortable in her company than with any other woman—hell, with any other person. He wanted to make her his.

But had he lost her?

One thing was for sure: he wouldn't be ghosting her and spending another ten years in the wilderness without her.

He tried to ignore the inconvenient fact that she appeared to be ghosting him.

He looked at his watch. She'd been locked away in her suite for half an hour. He knocked on the door, expecting to have to bang hard. But the door swung open at his touch. She wasn't in the bedroom. The bathroom door was open, but she wasn't in there. Or in the walk-in closet.

Claudia was gone. There was just a lingering trace of her scent on the air, mixed with the tang of ginger. She must have sneaked out when he was in his own suite. She'd run away from him.

The realisation was like a kick in the gut.

But where had she gone? He gathered his senses enough to note that her clothes were in her closet, the swimsuit and white cover-up shirt she'd worn on the boat in the bathroom. She hadn't left the island—she actually *couldn't* leave the island, as it was only accessible by boat or helicopter. Dear heaven, he hoped she hadn't tried to take a boat out by herself. He froze at the thought. Then realised that whatever she might think of him, she wouldn't do anything that might put the baby in danger.

Dell. She had probably gone to Dell. They'd become close in the time he and Claudia had been here. She would certainly seek help from Dell. Although the reason *why* she needed help continued to evade him.

Would she have gone to the hotel? No. She knew Alex and Dell had lunch at home with their young children whenever they could. Claudia would have gone to their house.

When he got there, maybe he pressed too long and too hard on the bell, because Dell looked concerned when she opened the door. 'Stefanos. Are you okay? Is Claudia okay? The baby? Is everything all right with the baby?'

'Claudia isn't here? I thought she'd be here.' He ran his hands through his hair.

'Come in,' Dell said, practically dragging him inside. 'What's going on?'

'I don't actually know,' he said, hating to admit it.

'I saw Claudia out for a walk a little while ago. I asked her if she was okay. She said she was fine, but she didn't look fine to me. She said she just needed some fresh air, but she'd obviously been crying. I tried to coax her into telling me what was wrong but she wouldn't tell me. She's very loyal to you, you know.'

Alex joined them. 'What's the drama?'

'Stefanos is looking for Claudia, but Claudia doesn't seem to want to be found. He thought she'd be here.'

'Why would she be here?' Alex said. 'Weren't you and Claudia meant to be out on the *Daphne* all day?'

'We were—until she wasn't well and wanted to come back,' said Stefanos.

'Why?' said Dell. 'I thought her morning sickness was getting so much better.'

'It was. It is. It wasn't—'

'Wasn't morning sickness?' said Dell.

'No. She…uh…wasn't very happy with me.'

'What's going on, cousin?' asked Alex. 'You and Claudia seemed to be getting on so well.'

'We were hoping for an engagement before you left the island,' said Dell.

'So was I,' said Stefanos.

It had taken him a while to come round to the idea of marrying again, to let down those barriers. But now there was nothing more he wanted than to make Claudia his wife. For life.

'So what went wrong?' said Alex.

'And why is Claudia walking around the gardens crying?'

'I have to go and find her,' Stefanos said.

Dell put her hand on his arm. 'I don't think so. Not

just yet. You need to think about how you're going to make things right with her.'

'What happened? Just tell us straight,' said Alex.

'I asked Claudia to marry me.'

'That's wonderful,' said Dell, beaming.

'I thought so,' he said. 'But it didn't go down well.'

'What do you mean, it didn't go down well?' said Dell.

'Basically, she said no.'

'She said no? I don't believe that,' said Dell. 'She's obviously in love with you. She's having your baby and she said no?'

Claudia was in love with him? Why hadn't she told him?

But she had…in so many ways, when he thought about it. Why hadn't he told her he loved her? That he had always loved her?

'*How* did you ask her to marry you, cousin?' said Alex.

'On bended knee?' asked Dell.

'No,' he said. 'I just said we should get married.'

He wasn't going to tell them he'd been on the sofa with her, having just made love to her. That was his business. His and Claudia's.

'So, no flowery proposal?' said Dell.

'What did she say when you told her you love her?' said Alex.

'I didn't.'

There was silence from his cousin and his wife. 'You didn't tell her you love her?' said Dell in disbelief.

'Have you *ever* told her you love her?' said Alex.

Stefanos nodded. 'Back then. In Santorini.'

'Ten years ago?' said Alex. He put his arm on his cousin's shoulder. 'Do you realise how that sounds?'

'Yep. I'm beginning to.'

What a fool he'd been. So busy protecting himself

from getting hurt he'd opened himself up to worse—losing Claudia.

'You got tricked into marriage the first time, and pretty much tricked into marriage the second time. Your track record for picking Mrs Right isn't great, is it?' Alex put up his hand. 'You don't have to answer that.'

'I will answer it. You're correct,' said Stefanos.

'We know you were hurt,' said Alex, obviously casting himself in the older cousin role.

But he had gone through real tragedy and come through to give his heart to Dell. So Stefanos listened—his advice would be welcome.

'And you were wounded,' said Dell.

'You put up barriers,' said Alex. 'But you've got to get past that now.'

'Is Claudia the genuine Mrs Right for you?' said Dell.

'Yes. She was right for me ten years ago, when I stupidly lost her, and she's right for me now. No one could be more right.'

His words solidified into the absolute truth.

'I'm taking a guess she might think you asked her to marry you because of the baby, not necessarily for her,' said Dell. 'No woman in love wants to hear that. Do you want to lose her, Stefanos?'

'No!' His life would be empty without her in it.

'Then you have to reassure her that you love her and don't want to marry her just to give the baby your name.'

Surely she wouldn't have thought that?

He remembered her last angry words.

He'd got that wrong too.

'Don't let Claudia go,' said Alex. 'You've got to let her know how you really feel. You've made a mess of this, mate. You need to go to her and fix it. Be vulnerable and lay your heart on the line—difficult as that might seem.'

Stefanos didn't consider himself to be a humble type of person. But he knew he had to humble himself in front of Claudia.

'Do you think she'll have me?' he asked. 'After I screwed up the proposal?'

'That's entirely up to you,' said Alex. 'Only you can make this right. I suggest grovelling might be required.'

His cousin grinned. He was enjoying this. There was nothing like a Greek family for support.

'Okay…if required.' Not only would he humble himself, but grovel.

'Seriously, mate, I reckon you and Claudia could be very happy. She's a gorgeous girl in every way. The baby is a bonus.'

Dell's phone rang and she went over to the table to pick it up, turning her head away from the two men.

When she'd terminated the conversation she turned back to them. 'That was Claudia. She told me she's sorry for having worried me, but she's perfectly fine and is back in her suite.'

Stefanos had already turned to leave the room. 'Wish me luck,' he said. 'And thank you.'

This time he knew Claudia was in her suite. He was going in. Armed with a packet of organic crackers and a bottle of cold ginger drink, he knocked on the door.

'Claudia, are you okay?'

Silence.

'I heard you sniff,' he said.

'No, you didn't.'

'Okay, I heard you snore. I was being polite,' he said.

'You must be hearing things because I wasn't asleep.'

'You're awake now. How do you know you didn't drift off to sleep and start snoring?'

'Because I don't snore!' she said.

'Can you be one hundred percent sure of that?'

'Why are you standing there on the other side of the door insulting me?'

'I wouldn't be if you let me in. I have a cold ginger drink for you. And your favourite crackers. It's past lunchtime.'

The door opened and Claudia peered around the door. 'I doubt I will ever eat a cracker again after this.'

Her face was pale, the scattering of freckles across the bridge of her nose and across her cheeks standing out. He had kissed those freckles one by one just this morning. Her eyes were reddened, as if she'd been crying, and her hair was still tousled and full of salt. She looked vulnerable, sad, and he felt a fierce urge to protect her. But he knew he had caused her defences to go up and that she wouldn't welcome him pulling her into his arms.

'Are you going to let me in?' he said.

Without a word, she swung the door wide. He handed over the drink and the crackers and went through. He stepped further into the room. The bed linen was rumpled, as if she'd been lying down. Her laptop was open on the desk, with sheets of the resort notepaper beside it, covered with scribbled notes. She'd been busy since she'd come back from her walk.

'What are you doing?' he said, with a creeping sense of foreboding.

She seemed edgy, distracted, not wanting to meet his eye. 'I'm trying to find a way I can leave here before Friday. By myself.'

Stefanos stared at her, disbelief, pain and anguish roiling through him. 'Why would you do that?'

She picked up a piece of paper from the desk, screwed it up, put it down again. 'Because I don't think I can endure even another few days here. It's too uncomfortable for me, now I've said I won't marry you. And awkward around Alex and Dell, who had such hopes for us.'

'Have you found a way to leave?'

If she had, he would use everything in his considerable power to block it.

She looked down at the laptop. 'Unfortunately, no.' Her voice dropped with despair. 'I don't have the resources for a helicopter, the public ferry to Nidri doesn't stop here, all the charter boats are booked out, and I don't want to involve Dell and Alex. I don't want to embarrass them—or embarrass you in front of your family.'

'I looked for you at their house. Dell said she saw you out walking.'

'So they know I don't want to marry you? They adore you and now they'll think me mean. How embarrassing.'

'Not embarrassing. A friendship based on a first meeting with you retching behind a bush can survive that. They care about you too.'

'Family always comes first,' she said, with a watery smile.

'Not always,' he said. 'You know you can't leave the island?'

She sighed. 'So it seems. But I should be able to leave if I want to. I'm a guest here, not a prisoner.'

'Of course you're not a prisoner—how could you even think that?'

She turned away. Perhaps she could hear the distress in his voice. 'I'm sorry. Of course I know that. I didn't mean it. You've all been very good to me here.'

'I couldn't bear it if you left.'

She didn't meet his eye. 'You'll be seeing me again. In London, remember? At the hospital for my dating scan.'

'You and me as part-time parents…' He reached out, put his hands on her shoulders. 'Haven't the last few days meant anything to you? Didn't this morning mean anything to you?'

'You mean our wonderful romp or your business proposal?'

At the coolness of her tone he dropped his hands. 'I know. I'm sorry. Looking back, I guess that's exactly what it seemed like.'

'I believe you thought it was a proposal of marriage.'

'I *did* ask you to marry me.'

'You talked about how marriage was "the right thing to do" in terms of convenience for you and our child. The fact that we get on appeared to be a bonus.'

Her voice wasn't as steady as she'd obviously hoped it would be.

'You've got it wrong,' he said, aware of the fear searing his voice…the fear that he had lost her.

She took a step back, turned away, and then turned to face him again. 'You know, I've never chased the idea of marriage—but I've never completely dismissed it either,' she said. 'You might have thought you were asking me to marry you. But I never heard one word about love. And to me the only reason to get married is if you're head over heels in love with the other person, and they with you.'

'I wouldn't have asked you to marry me if I didn't love you.'

'You talked about being "attracted" to me. You talked about us having interests in common. You talked about looking after me and the baby. But you never talked about love.'

Last night she'd wheedled him into watching a rom-com on television. She'd sat next to him on the sofa and jabbed him with her elbow every time he'd dozed off. He'd told her he liked action movies, or arthouse films, but she'd kept on swooning over the romance of the movie, the crazy ups and downs of the plot that kept the hero and heroine apart until the end.

Romance.

'I didn't give you romance,' he said.

'Actually, you did. The way you kept my hat was incredibly romantic. But you didn't give me love.'

How to explain to her that he'd been so closed off to love for so long he didn't know how to express it—was deep-down scared to express it. That was the emotional barrier she'd accused him of erecting. But when he really thought about it, when he was with the right person—and she'd always been the right person—it really wasn't so difficult at all.

It was all there in his heart, just waiting to be said. To the only Mrs Right.

Now it was not a case of knowing he had to tell her he loved her if he had any hope of winning her, it was a case of wanting to.

'I love you, Claudia,' he said, looking into her eyes so she couldn't doubt his message. 'I fell in love with you the moment I met you that night at the bar in Santorini. Maybe because we were young...maybe because we were on vacation and you were English and I was Greek...it seemed somehow fleeting, and I didn't fight enough for it. I wanted to marry you, but I let you go. Where was the sense in that? I could have waited for you to be ready.'

'Stefanos—'

'Let me finish. This has been a long time coming.

I've been thinking about it a lot—in fact it's all I've been thinking about since we've been here. That first day here, when you were so unwell on the helicopter, when you fell asleep and I tucked you into bed, I knew I'd brought you home and I never wanted you to leave.'

She took his hand, clasped it in hers. 'I dreamed that you called me *koukla mou*, the way you used to.'

'It was no dream,' he said. 'I don't want to marry you because it's the right thing to do because you're pregnant. Or to give our child my name and an inheritance. Or because it would make parenting easier. I want to marry you because I want to live with you and wake up beside you every day of our lives. Swimming around the island with you this morning, I knew I wanted that.'

She smiled a tender, warm smile. 'You realise you might have had a very different answer from me this morning if that was the way you'd proposed?'

'It was a mistake,' he said ruefully. 'I was subconsciously trying to protect myself, I think. After spending this time with you I've realised the mistakes I've made—the disastrous marriages, the relationships that went nowhere—were made because I was looking for you in other people, seizing upon things that reminded me of you which ended up being fool's gold. I've only ever loved one woman, and she's standing in front of me now, looking at me like I'm crazy.'

'Not crazy at all. Because I've only ever loved one man. First love was true love for me, and no one else could match up to you. I love you, Stefanos, and I've been aching to tell you so.'

'Why didn't you?'

'I wasn't sure you felt the same way.'

'Do you know now? Or do I need to keep on telling you?'

'Yes, to both questions. I do know now, and I couldn't be happier about it. But we need to keep on saying *I love you*. And showing each other too.'

'Will you marry me?' he asked.

Claudia looked up at him, her blue eyes warm with love and happiness and relief. 'Yes, yes, and yes again.' She flung her arms around him. 'I want to marry you not for practical reasons, nor because we're having a baby, but because I love you and I want to spend my life with you. I don't want to blow this second chance we've been given.'

He could not resist. 'Given to us by…?'

'Fate—I know,' she said, with a smile that warmed his heart.

Claudia pulled Stefanos's head down to hers for a kiss. They kissed long and tenderly, and her heart soared to a new level of joy in their togetherness. Tender kisses led to passionate kisses, and then they made slow, exquisite love. And this time when they came to their climaxes she didn't have to guess how he felt, because he whispered words of undying love and she whispered them back.

'Do you ever wish we had stayed together ten years ago? Do you wonder how our lives might have been?' she murmured.

'No. Because we are the people we are now, and this time I know it's going to work for us. I want you by my side when you're an old lady with silver hair.'

'With our children and grandchildren around us,' she said. 'I love the idea.'

She lay nestled into his shoulder, within the protective circle of his arms. She couldn't imagine a place anywhere in the world she'd rather be. She and Stefanos had gone through so much angst and heartache to find their way back to each other. But maybe she'd had to see the world and satisfy her need for independence before she could return to him.

She'd worried back then that she'd lose her sense of self if she committed her life to another. But now she could see that rather than losing herself by being with Stefanos she would gain more, because they were pledging themselves to a life together. Two together and committed were stronger than two apart. Perhaps things had worked out the way they'd been meant to.

'Dell and Alex will be very pleased to hear our news,' he said.

'I think you're right.' She knew Dell would be thrilled to welcome her into the family.

'You know I meant it when I said there would be a role for you here at Pevezzo Athina if you should want it.'

'As it is definitely my favourite resort in the world, I would love that. Being here has made me remember why I enjoyed working in hotels and hospitality.'

'You'll like my house in Athens, too. It's white marble and very modern and overlooks the sea,' he said. 'Although I'm sure you'll want to put your stamp on it. And there's the apartment in Bloomsbury too—although we might want to buy a house outside of London too. It depends on how much time you want to devote to PWP.'

'There's been an interesting development there,' Claudia said.

'The franchise opportunity?'

'Something different and quite out of the blue. We helped a very nice woman move house after an ugly and well-publicised divorce from her wealthy businessman husband. She gave up her career to raise their now grown-up kids, so was left with loads of money and not a lot to do. She moves in the same social circles as Kitty does now, and she discovered that Kitty wanted to devote more of her time to a charitable trust started by Sebastian's grandmother. She told Kitty she liked the way we ran PWP and asked if she could buy into the business—or even buy the business outright if that suited us better. Kitty called me yesterday to run the idea by me, and we've agreed it might be time to move on. The business has been good to us, and tided us over some difficult times, but perhaps we don't need it any more since our lives have changed direction.'

'Remember what I said about new challenges helping you grow?' Stefanos said. 'Now might be a very good time to free yourself to follow different interests.'

'Including motherhood?' she said. 'And being your wife?'

'I couldn't agree more,' he said, drawing her close for another kiss.

'There's one more thing,' she said. 'Can we get married as soon as possible? I have this thing… I don't want to look pregnant in my wedding gown.'

'That can be arranged,' he said. 'Whatever you, *agape mou*, my beloved, want. One final question: would you like a diamond bracelet for a wedding present?'

She shook her head. 'Thank you, but that's not really my thing. Some diamond earrings for the wedding might be nice, though.'

'You can choose whatever you want,' he said.

As she kissed him she thought about the night she'd seen that handsome, black-haired boy across the crowds of people in that popular bar. As their gazes had connected the chatter and buzz of the bar had fallen away. In that moment the world had rearranged itself and her entire life had changed.

Somehow they had found their way back to each other now, so they could live life together as husband and wife. This day was the start of that journey.

CHAPTER SEVENTEEN

CLAUDIA REMEMBERED HER first sighting of the little white church that sat serenely on the clifftop, set apart from Pevezzo Athina. It had been from the deck of the *Daphne*. Who would have thought, just weeks later, she would be getting married to Stefanos in that very same church on the most perfect of summer days? Or that she, who had always said she didn't want to get married, would have flung herself with such enthusiasm into the preparations for her wedding.

She'd become a veritable Bridezilla, as Kitty had teased her.

Her friends in London had marvelled at how quickly she'd decided to get married, but she'd pointed out that Stefanos had first asked her to marry him ten years earlier. It had just taken her an awful long time to say yes, as he liked to explain.

Being a Bridezilla had been so much easier when her billionaire fiancé, with his influence and his bank account, had been able to overcome every hurdle towards holding a wedding in a hurry. It had been no problem for one of Athens' top bridal designers to make not only Claudia's exquisite white gown, but also dresses for her thirteen-year-old twin sisters, Lucy and Lily, for Kitty and Dell, and for the mothers of the bride and groom—both formidable ladies who were still reserving judgement on each other.

Claudia suspected that the battle lines would dissolve once her baby mermaid was born. Tests had shown they were to have a single baby, a daughter, who would be named Dimitra Anne, after both her grandmothers.

The reception had, thankfully, been taken out of her hands. It was to be held in Alex and Dell's beautiful home, catered by the resort's chefs, with wine from their own vineyard. She couldn't have had her wedding celebration in a place she loved more.

Now, on her wedding day, Claudia stood outside the tiny church with her bridesmaids clustered around her like beautiful blue flowers. Her sisters with their long blonde hair so lovely in pale blue… Kitty and Dell in a deeper shade of delphinium-blue. Claudia wore diamonds at her throat and at her ears, to match her solitaire engagement ring, and her attendants wore sapphire pendants and earrings—all gifts from Stefanos. As was Greek custom, she had greeted their guests on the way in, and now they were all waiting inside for her.

The tiny church was packed with friends and family. Inside, Stefanos waited for her, along with his best man Alex, and the Adrastos family priest from Athens, who would perform the traditional ceremony.

Her mother was to give her away.

'Ready, darling?' she said now, taking her daughter's arm. 'All I ever wanted was for you to find the kind of love I was fortunate enough to find twice. And now you're marrying your first love. He's an exceptionally wonderful man and I couldn't be happier for you.' She paused. 'And I promise never to ask again why on earth you didn't snap him up when he was twenty.'

Claudia had come so far she was even able to laugh at that with her mother as she hugged her.

The twins preceded her down the aisle, casting rose petals as they went. Then Kitty and Dell made their graceful way down. At last came the bride's turn. As Claudia walked slowly down the aisle next to her mother, smiling faces from both sides turned towards her. But she only had eyes for one face. The face of the man waiting for her at the simple stone altar—her husband-to-be.

Stefanos was wearing a white linen suit which perfectly suited his dark good looks. He caught sight of her and smiled, his love showing in his eyes. The only man she had ever loved…would ever love. Her heart leapt with joy.

Stefanos had always thought Claudia looked beautiful in white—going right back to the simple cotton peasant dress she'd worn in Santorini ten years before. But today she was breathtaking in her long wedding gown, elegant in its simplicity, made of heavy white lace with cap sleeves, the only colour being her vibrant hair under a lace veil. She carried a simple bunch of white flowers tied with white ribbon.

He could not believe his luck that she was to be his after all these years. Fate had finally smiled on him. First love had grown into for ever love.

The wedding service emphasised the intertwining of two lives through the blessing of rings, the two crowns attached by a single ribbon placed on their heads, and the ceremonial sipping of blessed wine. He welcomed the traditions and the values binding their families together.

Finally they were husband and wife, and the priest even allowed the not-so-traditional custom of kissing the bride.

'I love you,' Stefanos murmured against her mouth. 'I can't tell you enough how much I love you.'

'I love you too,' she said. 'We can never, ever say it too many times.'

'And even more importantly we must show how much we love each other,' he said. 'Until death do us part.'

Holding hands, joyously smiling, they walked back down the aisle, taking their first steps towards the start of their new life together.

* * * * *

THEIR SURPRISE SAFARI REUNION

ELLA HAYES

MILLS & BOON

For Steven and Adeline. Thank you for Madikwe.

CHAPTER ONE

'LINA...? HEY! MS JAMES!'

She jerked awake, heart thumping, trying to locate the strange voice in her head, and then a cream cabin came into focus followed by windows full of blue sky and wispy streaks of cloud. *Of course!* She was airborne, strapped into the tiny, noisy plane that was taking her to Masoka, and the voice in her head wasn't in her head at all, but was coming through the headset she was wearing, or rather, half wearing. Must have slipped while she was sleeping. She straightened it and looked up.

Steve, the pilot, was eyeing her over his shoulder, his aviators glinting. 'Sorry to wake you but we're starting our descent shortly and it could be bumpy. There's a ridge up ahead. The air currents on the other side can be lively.'

'You mean hairy!'

He grinned. 'I prefer lively.'

'Whatever.' She held in a smile. 'Thanks for the heads-up!'

'Anytime!' He turned forwards, flicking a switch on the panel. 'Just don't drop off again, okay? You need to be awake for landing...'

In case of emergencies was what he wasn't saying, but she knew the script. She was a seasoned traveller after all, a seasoned sleeper on planes, and trains, and buses. Sleeping at night, in an actual bed, was the thing she couldn't do. She touched the mic. 'Roger that!'

A chuckle filled her ears followed by an empty hiss. He was speaking to someone else now, probably checking in with the airstrip.

She pulled the cans off and stretched, swallowing a yawn, then looked down at the *bushveld*. Vast. Green. Empty. She felt her heart expanding. It was perfect! Perfect place, perfect time! She wasn't a lucky person—far from it—but she'd felt lucky that morning four months ago when Fran Palmer's email had landed in her in-box...

Lina, I know you're in demand and probably already booked, but we're opening Masoka Safari Lodge at the beginning of February and a write-up on your fantastic blog would really help to put us on the map. If you could fit us in for a week early in the month, we promise to give you plenty to write about: game drives, hot-air ballooning, a night under canvas at our luxury bush camp followed by a river cruise at dawn. But it's not only a ringside seat to the Big Five we're offering! At Masoka you can expect the finest cuisine, the finest rooms and the finest facilities—including our relaxing spa and infinity pool. In short, we are offering the ultimate luxury safari experience. We would love the opportunity to welcome you to our world...

She *had* been booked but reshuffling her plans for Fran Palmer had been a no-brainer, not because she was desperate to see the Big Five, or to cruise along an African river at dawn, but because Masoka Safari Lodge was six thousand miles away from London and being six thousand miles away from London in the week that her scumbag father was being released from jail had suddenly felt like the best idea she'd never had.

And now she was here, flying deeper and deeper into the back of beyond, feeling freer and lighter with every mile. She drew in a slow breath, watching the plane's shadow rippling over the grass, shimmering across a stretch of silver water. Here were hills starting, golden slopes strewn with giant boulders and, winding through them, narrow paths. *Animal tracks?* She chewed the edge of her lip. Kaden would have known. He'd been mad about animals, and wildlife and—

Don't!

But it was too late. He was already shimmering into view, tanned and wet by the lake, his lips twitching with mischief. *'Look, Maddie!'* And then he'd been opening his hands... Only a tadpole, but it had wriggled suddenly, and she'd stumbled backwards, and he'd creased up with laughter, eyes shining into hers like molten copper...

Kaden...

Why couldn't she let the memories go, memories that always sprouted questions. Was he happy? Married? She touched her travel belt, feeling the tug of the phone inside it. Tracking him down on social media would be easy; after all, he was heir to the Barr retail empire! Maybe he was CEO now, although, *no*, he hadn't wanted that, not at seventeen anyway. Back then, he'd had his heart set on becoming a vet. He'd been busy applying to universities when— *Stop!*

Vet... CEO... Starship trooper! It was academic. She couldn't look. She'd promised herself years ago not to. It would only have been a torment. Besides, looking couldn't turn the clock back. She and Kaden were history, had been from the moment her mother had bundled her onto the Eurostar all those years ago. No goodbyes. No contact allowed. *God!* How he must have hated her for leaving like that, for not sending word… She felt her heart twisting. But she'd had to do it…for Mum…because everything had been falling apart, and Mum had been worried about the press and phone hacking. Mum had only been trying to protect her, but knowing it hadn't made it any easier to bear, hadn't stopped her crying her heart out for Kaden every day for months and months…

And then after her father was jailed, it had come to her that she couldn't contact him. Hearing him say that he couldn't be associated with her any more would have crushed her all over again because that's what he would have said. How could he have said anything else? The Barrs were good people with an impeccable business reputation whereas her father, Peter Saint James—treasury minister and so-called pillar of society—had been sent down for corruption and conspiracy to perjure.

She felt her stomach shrivelling. Because of *him* she was tainted. Because of *him* she'd had to disappear, had had to change her name and her appearance so she wouldn't be hounded. She'd had to start a whole new life, and she'd done it, hadn't she, made a life for herself that was hers to control, except… She felt tears prickling, burning behind her lids. She wasn't in control. She was running away again because of *him*, this time because of his bloody book, the memoir he'd written in jail that was somehow already a *Sunday Times* bestseller before either he or it had been released! What was he doing it for: money, notoriety? Didn't he have enough of both already? Didn't he ever stop to think about the effect on her and on Mum, or didn't he care? *God!* If only *she* could make herself not care, could make herself not feel ashamed every waking second of her life!

She leaned her forehead against the window. *Enough!* Self-pity never helped. She needed to focus on the positive. Yes, her father was a sleazebag, but Mum was a rock. And *Destination Heaven* was a success, the number-one luxury travel blog on the circuit, and the blogging life was far more interesting and sustainable than the modelling career she'd had to abandon. Even better, it kept her moving. *Safe...*

As for Kaden... Muss-haired and laughing by the lake, pulling her up again, his eyes all aglow... She blinked the image away. Of course he was in her head, and *yes*, in her heart too, still, but it was probably like that for everyone with their first love. *First lover!* The feeling never left. That feeling of not being able to breathe, of not wanting to be even an inch away... It had felt like that with him. It had felt like for ever. She swallowed hard. But they'd been kids. What had they known about anything? Just because it had felt real didn't mean they'd have necessarily stayed tog—

The plane pitched suddenly, throwing her sideways, then it waltzed, creaking and straining. She pressed herself into her seat, bracing for the next judder. She wasn't scared. If anything, she was glad. The plane had jolted her back to the present, the all-important now. She turned to watch the ground see-sawing closer, the bright green bushes and the red brown earth. The past was dust. Kaden and Maddie were long gone. In the all-important now she was Lina James, award-winning travel writer, and yes, admittedly she was ever so slightly on the run, but she was also about to throw herself headlong into her first ever ultimate luxury safari experience. On balance, maybe it wasn't all bad.

Kaden felt the Jeep slide as he took the bend. *Too fast!* What had his grandmother used to say? *Better to be five minutes late in this world than five minutes too early in the next...* He spun the wheel, straightening, then accelerated hard, squinting through the tangle of grass and bushes, trying to see the airstrip. Grandmother Barr's wisdom was all very well, but it didn't mean that being late was okay, especially when the person you were late for was, according to Fran, the queen of the elite travel scene. *Fran!* His chest went tight. *She* wouldn't have been late. She'd have had it all under control, but he absolutely couldn't think about Fran right now. She was gone, and he was... *Oh, God!* He was in trouble! The Piper was already parked, its doors open. He eased his foot off the accelerator, scouring the tarmac, heart thumping. There was Steve, helping someone out of the plane. Lina James! And she was probably already marking Masoka down for the lack of a welcome party!

Damn!

He refocused on the road and pressed on, feeling a dead weight sinking. If he'd sent Jerry to check on the wild dog pups that morning, instead of going himself, he'd have been here on time. The problem was, when it came to animals, he was useless at delegating. It wasn't sentimentality. Vets couldn't afford to be sentimental! The ten pups wouldn't all survive, he knew that, but knowing it didn't make them any less compelling, and it was compulsion that drove him, a sense of mission. Without that passion, without that compulsion to watch, and monitor, and protect animals, particularly the endangered species like the wild dogs, then he'd have had no business buying Masoka Game Reserve in the first place! No, he wasn't going to beat himself up for putting the animals first. Bottom line, the frilly, romantic, safari side of the business only interested him in so far as it was going to fund his conservation operations and his second-phase plans. But it wasn't going to fund anything without wealthy punters, and here he was, arriving late to pick up the very person who could deliver them!

He barrelled through the entrance, rattling over the cattle grid, then touched the brake. Screeching up in a spray of grit wouldn't do. It would make him seem chaotic, and chaos was not what he was selling at Masoka. He drew in a steadying breath and coasted sedately over to the plane. Two fat leather holdalls squatted under the shade of the wing; Lina's, presumably, but where was she? And where was Steve? He killed the engine and twisted to look back at the small, thatched building that the pilots jokingly called 'the terminal.' Maybe Steve was showing Ms James the facilities!

He parked his shades on the dash and jumped down. Maybe it was better this way, being alone for a few moments. It meant he could catch his breath—*calm the hell down*—and get her bags loaded.

He swung them into the back, leaning in to wedge them so they wouldn't roll. Not that he any intention of driving back like a lunatic! *No!* He was going to take it easy, spin it out, take the opportunity to schmooze—

'Hello there…'

His heart bounced.

'Oh! You've put my bags in already. Thanks so much. Sorry I wasn't here. I had to go and splash my face. It was so warm in the plane…'

He stared down at his hands, heart clanging. The voice was familiar. Achingly familiar. But it couldn't be. *No.* It was surely just the acoustics under the canopy, or his mind playing tricks because he was hot and bothered and overwrought. *Get a grip.* He drew in a breath and turned round.

See! Blond hair. Short. Not dark red and endless like… And mirror shades weren't Maddie's style… His mouth dried. But that nose… His heart bucked. And those lips… His lungs were emptying out, collapsing. He reached for the canopy frame, gripping it hard, trying to make the face he was looking at not fit the memory, but her hand was going to her sunglasses, slowly drawing them down, and his pulse was hammering in his ears, seismic waves rising and falling beneath his feet, and he couldn't skew the pieces out of sync no matter how hard he tried because it was *her* blue eyes fastening on his, *her* luscious mouth falling open. It was absolutely, unequivocally, one hundred percent *her.*

'Oh, my God…' Her eyes were filling. 'Kaden…?'

'Madeleine!' It came out as a mangled whisper, but he couldn't help that. His throat was a desert. Was she really here, the girl he'd once loved more than life itself? He gulped a breath. What to say, how to feel? So much history, so many exploding emotions. There wasn't enough space for it, no way of gathering it together into any kind of order, especially when there was this wave of pure joy rising, engulfing the rest, propelling his legs forwards and then somehow—*how?*—his arms were going around her and she was melting in like she'd used to do a lifetime ago, and for a piece of a second nothing was broken, nothing else mattered, but then her body stiffened and she was pulling away, and just like that the wave collapsed.

'I'm sorry… I'm…' She was breathing in bursts, twisting her fingers into the legs of her sunglasses. 'I wasn't expecting this…' Her eyes came to his. 'I mean, *you*…'

His heart crashed. Of course she hadn't been expecting him. If she'd known he was here she wouldn't have come, would she, not if the past twelve years were anything to go by. And yet…she'd folded into his arms so easily and the warmth he'd felt flowing from her had felt real and deep and familiar. Way to confuse himself, hugging her like that, opening himself up to whatever. He should have resisted the impulse, fought a bit harder instead of caving in a heartbeat. Seemed that old habits did die hard. He'd need to watch himself.

He pushed a hand through his hair, collecting himself. 'I wasn't expecting you either. I was expecting—'

'Lina James.' She seemed to shrink into herself. 'I changed my name a long time ago. Had to, after everything…'

Of course she'd have done that. *Of course!* That was why he'd never managed to find her on social media. All that searching. Friends, friends of friends, every oblique connection. Meanwhile the name she'd devised was a simple distillation: Lina James from Madeleine Saint James. At twenty he might have picked up on it but when Fran had started talking about emailing Lina James regarding a feature on *Destination Heaven*, he hadn't thought a thing about it except that if she could pull it off, then it would extend their reach far beyond the press coverage she'd already lined up. And she *had* pulled it off.

He swallowed hard. But now Fran was gone, and Lina

James was standing in front of him, except that she was really Madeleine—*Maddie*—taking him apart with her eyes, making him feel…what? *Oh, God!* Why couldn't he pin a single feeling down? All he could do was look at her.

There were hollows under her cheekbones now, tiny lines at the corners of her eyes, but the freckles over her nose were the same. They matched her hair, not this hair but the dark red hair he'd loved to fold into his hands and let slip through his fingers, the hair that had bounced and tumbled its way across billboards and television screens for Tresses Organix.

He pressed a finger along his eyebrow chasing an ache. 'You changed your hair too…'

'Yes.' A wan smile ghosted across her lips. 'It was kind of recognisable…'

Famous hair. *Of course!* And then before he could stop them familiar words were lining up on his tongue, flying free on the wings of his famously terrible mid-Atlantic accent. 'Turn their heads with Tresses Organix!'

A smile broke her face apart, switching the light back on and all the lovely radiance he remembered. And then she was giggling, dropping her shoulder, doing the advert. 'Go on…' One flirty eyebrow went up. 'You know you want to!'

He felt laughter vibrating, warmth rushing in. *Maddie. Mads.* Beneath the peroxide she was still there, the same. *Still beautiful.* He smiled. 'You've still got it, you know!'

'Thank you.' Her eyes held him for a moment and then her lips quirked. 'Sadly your voice-over still sucks…'

He felt a pang, a sudden unbearable itch in his fingers, because in the before this would have been his cue. She'd have been giggling, teasing him with her eyes, and he'd have dived for her, making her squeal, catching her wrists, pinning her body with his, and then there'd have been that sublime moment when the tempo changed, that moment when everything softened, and her hands would have wound into his hair, and her lips would have come to his and—

Don't!

He drove his hands into his pockets hard. Sliding backwards was a seriously bad idea. He couldn't go there, couldn't waken all the slumbering details. It was the now that mattered, how to deal with—

'Kaden...?' He blinked her back into focus, felt his heart skip the way it had never skipped for Fran. 'What do we do now?' A shadow lengthened behind her gaze. 'What I mean is, do you want me to stay?'

His chest went tight. Did he? Gut reaction: he didn't want her to go, but could he handle her staying? Could his heart handle it? *Oh, God!* He needed to find his voice before the space between them filled up with hesitation, but the only thing surfacing was a question of his own, somewhat disingenuous, but then hadn't he earned the right to be that at least? He swallowed hard. 'Why wouldn't I want you to stay?'

For a moment her expression was incredulous, and then her lips pressed together, tears mounting from the lower lids of her eyes. 'Because...'

He felt his heart contracting, an unwelcome drop of bitterness expanding. *Because* after the Peter Saint James scandal broke, she'd vanished without a word, even though she was supposed to have loved him. *Because* in twelve whole years she'd never messaged, emailed or sent him so much as a sodding postcard! Because now— *now*—she was having an attack of the guilts!

Stop!

Hadn't he just resolved not to slide backwards, and especially, he couldn't let himself slide into bitter waters, not while the fact of her was still sinking in, while the shock of her was still thrumming through his veins. This wasn't the moment to be sifting through old hurts, letting them twist him even more out of shape than he already was. This was a moment for objectivity. Focus. Purpose. He needed her to write that blog post. Yes, courtesy of Fran's brilliant organisational skills, he had a posse of travel journalists on the case, but the reach of *Destination Heaven* was far greater. A glowing endorsement there was going to put him on track to achieve all the things he wanted to achieve at Masoka.

And Masoka was his life, *ergo* Masoka trumped everything, *ergo* she had to stay.

He took a breath and freed his hands from his pockets. 'Maddie, whatever you're thinking, you need to let it go.'

Wetness flooded her gaze. 'But I just—'

'Please. Don't—' His throat closed. Maybe it was selfish cutting her off, but he couldn't let her unravel. If she did, then he'd start unravelling too and what would be the point of that, of pulling all the pain into the foreground for the sake of, what…an apology? *No.* Staying laser focused on the business was the only way he was going to get through the week, so she needed to know that he wasn't looking for explanations or for anything from her except the thing she'd come to do.

He held up his palms. 'Look, just to be clear, I do want you stay, all right, but what I don't want is to…' The words dried on his tongue. 'What I can't do is…' Why couldn't he say it? Was it because her eyes were gleaming, full of history, tugging his heart out, or was it because what he was trying to say—that he didn't want to get into the past—was only half true after all? *Oh, God!* That was it. He was struggling to get the words out because the words were lies and lying had never been part of their landscape. But how could he possibly open up and tell her that the part of him that wasn't terrified of hearing what she might say was desperate for an explanation, hungry for the closure he'd been denied? Fact was, he couldn't, at least not now. He wasn't nearly strong enough, or level enough. God, right now he could feel the angry ghost of his seventeen-year-old self, rampaging, kicking down the walls in some alternative universe, but in this one, in *this* moment, he needed to find an adult perspective, because whatever he thought he knew, there was so much more that he didn't. He drew her back into focus. It was all there behind her gaze.

And then her gaze was narrowing into his, and her lips were parting. 'You don't want to get into the before, do you? You don't want to go back...' She swallowed. 'Am I getting warm?'

Half warm, half true, but it was a push in the right direction, a way out of the hole he was in.

'Yes, that's exactly what I was failing miserably to say.' He managed a smile and caught an answering warmth in her eyes that bolstered his spirits. 'Look, I'm not trying to be a jerk about it, Mads, but frankly I'm in a state of shock. And so are you, right?' She nodded almost imperceptibly. 'Truth is, I can barely think straight right now so maybe I *am* being a colossal jerk and if that's the case, then I'm sorry.'

'You're not being a jerk. I'm not thinking that at all.' Her hand closed over his forearm for a warm, brief second, and then a light came into her eyes that looked a lot like relief. 'And you're right about the shock.' A corner of her mouth twitched up. 'It's certainly not your average day, is it?'

He felt a smile coming. 'You can say that again.' *One last push.* He ploughed his hands through his hair. 'So, what do you say to us just focusing on the present?'

Her eyebrows flashed. 'Sounds like a plan to me.'

Relief loosened his limbs. It was going to work out. Squaring things away, cleaning off the slate, had been the right move. Now they were on the same page. Now there was a nice safe space for them to move around in.

He slid his hand along the canopy rail. 'Speaking of plans, I hope you're ready to throw yourself into the luxury safari experience.'

'Hmm…' She pressed a finger to her cheek, waggling her eyebrows. 'Sounds tough but, you know, I'll give it my best shot.'

Maddie! Irresistible when she was playing the clown, irresistible full stop, but he was going to have to resist her, not let all his freshly drawn lines blur.

'Seriously though, I do need you to write a cracking piece about us.' And then suddenly he could feel his own inner clown stirring, a familiar mischievous spark igniting, an urge too compelling to resist. He held in a smile. 'That's assuming you can write as well as that Lina James girl…'

Her face stiffened for a beat, and then she was laughing her rich fruity laugh, her eyes shining. 'Oh, I'm *way* better than her.' She parked her sunglasses on her head, and then her eyebrow slid up in that cute way he remembered. 'Actually, between you and me, she's a bit of a fake!'

CHAPTER TWO

SHE WATCHED HIM walking round and getting in. Same easy gait, same tilt of the head. A tingle shimmered through. Was this really happening? Just twenty minutes ago she'd been stepping on to the tarmac wondering why Fran Palmer wasn't there to meet her, and now she was about to take off into the *veld* with the only boy she'd ever loved, except…he wasn't a boy any more. The broad shoulders he'd had at seventeen were fuller now, their muscular curves all too obvious beneath his shirt. His hair was still thick, still deliciously unkempt, but the smattering of stubble around his jaw was new. Its soft rub had grazed her temple when he'd pulled her into his arms, and she'd wanted to slide her hands upwards and touch it, but then she'd remembered that he wasn't hers to touch, and she'd had to pull away quickly before it got too confusing. Not that it seemed to have helped any. She was still fifty shades of confused, everything reeling and thrumming and skittering, and having him sitting barely two feet away wasn't helping one little bit.

His eyes pinned her suddenly. 'You, okay?'

She felt her heart flip and tumble, a sudden ridiculous urge to laugh. She was many things but *okay* definitely wasn't one of them. She moistened her lips. 'Yes. I was just—' Her mind went blank.

His eyebrows drew in. 'Me too.'

'Me too, what…?'

He shrugged, then lifted a pair of Ray-Bans off the dash. 'I don't know, but isn't that the point?' His lips twitched upwards. 'We're basically not fit for purpose right now.'

She felt a smile filling her cheeks. *Kaden!* No one had ever been able to make her smile the way he could, even now when she was in total disarray…

Whatever you're thinking, you need to let it go…

He'd given her a free pass. *Thank God!* Because just before he'd said it, there'd been something in his eyes that had made her think that in spite of the hug, and in spite of laughing over the Tresses advert, he was going to tell her that she couldn't stay, that he couldn't have anything to do with her. She'd felt her father's shame pulsing through, wanting to spill out in tears, apologies, explanations, anything that would fill in the years and make things right. But he'd stopped her, and then his tight words and unfinished sentences had stopped her again, because pushing through would have meant pushing him too much. And then he'd said it. No retracing old steps, no going back. Just the here and now, focusing on the present. A clean slate, a clear plan, a breathing space…

'Earth to Maddie…'

His eyes snapped back into focus, warm burnished copper with those lighter flecks that had used to seem like stars twinkling when he was smiling. She felt her breath catching low down in her throat. 'Yes. Sorry. What?'

'I was just saying that the windscreen's locked down

so you should put your sunglasses on if you don't want bugs in your eyes.' He slipped his own on, then started the engine.

She dropped her shades, heart thumping. The only problem with focusing on the present was that Kaden was very much in it, sitting beside her, stirring memories of a different car, one with a privacy screen and a huge back seat. *Stop!* She needed to focus on something else and fast, something mundane like…the dash. She slid her eyes over it. Black. Dusty. There was a two-way radio with a curly cable dangling, also dusty. She twisted to look at the three rows of seats behind which were higher, to give a better view of the wildlife presumably. The canopy over their heads was beige, tightly sheeted. No windows. No frills. No minibar.

Steve's voice rang out suddenly. 'Hey, Kaden!' He was striding towards them out of the funny little building where she'd gone to freshen up.

'Hi, Steve.' Kaden leaned back, parking a thick, tanned forearm on the door. 'How's it going?'

'Good, thanks. I was just wanting to ask Lina…' His eyes settled on hers. 'Are you okay now?'

Oh, no!

She felt Kaden turning to look at her, could feel his curiosity burning through her skin. The drama of the landing had been so utterly eclipsed by the shock of seeing him again that she'd forgotten all about it. She flicked him a glance, then looked at Steve, feeling heat creeping into her cheeks. 'Yes, I'm fine now, thank you.'

Kaden's attention switched to Steve. 'What are you talking about?'

'Family of wild pigs decided to cut across the runway just as we were touching down. Lina was…'

Pretty please, Steve, don't say freaking out for England!
He licked his lips. 'Lina was concerned.'

'*I'm* concerned!' In one swift movement Kaden
twisted back to look at the airstrip, his whole focus seeming to narrow.

'It's all right, Kade.' Steve's voice was placating.
'They got away unscathed.'

'Thank God!' Kaden swung back, the tension in his
shoulders visibly melting. His dark lenses met hers for a
moment, and then he turned to Steve. 'What's that saying about greased piglets…?'

'I think you mean greased lightening…' Steve was
laughing.

She drew in a short breath. So, Kaden was *still* mad
about animals, manifestly concerned for their welfare…
Made sense. After all, he was here, wasn't he, connected
to Masoka in some way. But how exactly? She watched
him, the way his hands were juggling the air while he
was speaking. That was familiar but there were so many
other things to know, twelve years' worth of things that
suddenly really mattered, like—her heart pulsed—
was he married? Maybe Fran was his wife. *Oh, God!*
Fran's emails had always had a vaguely proprietorial
tone about them. *We can't wait to welcome you…* And
hadn't Kaden used the 'us' word when he'd been talking about her writing the piece? He'd said '*for us.*' Did
that mean for him and Fran? And what about kids? Her
heart clenched. *Kids!* Was there a brood of little Barrs
all freshly scrubbed and lined up waiting to meet her at
the lodge?

She looked down at her hands, trying to breathe herself calm. Of course Kaden was married. *Of course.* A
gorgeous guy like him was bound to have been snapped

up. It was probably the reason why he didn't want to go digging around in the past, because it didn't matter any more. He was shocked to see her, yes, needed to acclimatise, but for him that's as far as it went because he had a life that didn't include her.

She swallowed, letting the thought smooth itself out. If so, it was for the best. It was actually good. *Good.* If Kaden was married, if he had kids, then he must be happy and isn't that what she'd always wanted for him, to have someone who loved him, a person that his family could properly approve of, someone who wasn't a liability—

'So, Lina…' Steve's voice broke into her thoughts. 'I hope you have a good week.' He was backstepping, a smile twitching on his lips. 'Don't let this one feed you to the lions…'

'Shh, *Steve*!' Kaden was stage whispering behind his hand. 'You know I only do that to the *annoying* guests.'

She felt a smile breaking her face apart, warmth filling her chest. How did Kaden keep managing to make her smile even when she was stumbling around inside her own head? She slid her sunglasses down, looking over the top of them. 'If I make it out alive, Steve, I'll see you next week.'

He threw up a hand, laughing, and then Kaden was revving the engine and they were off, passing the little terminal building, rumbling over a cattle grid, turning onto a dirt road.

Kaden leaned in a little, his voice rising over the engine. 'It's about twenty minutes to the lodge so kick back and enjoy the ride.'

Kick back?

Was he saying that he didn't want to talk? She wound

her fingers around her pendant. Whatever *he* wanted, no way she could sit in silence, not when questions were stacking up in her head like Jenga bricks. She flicked him a glance. But how to begin? Which brick to pull out? *So, Kaden, are you married? Is Fran your wife? Do you have kids?* Her chest went tight. No. Personal questions were out, direct ones anyway. It needed to be something more general. Background for the blog piece, maybe. That could work, and if the conversation just happened to spin out…

She shifted, angling herself to face him. 'So, how come you're here? What's your connection to Masoka?'

His chin lifted. 'I own it.'

'You *own* it?'

He spun the wheel, turning them onto a different, bumpier track. 'Is it such a surprise…?'

Not on his own account, no, but his father had always wanted him to go into the family business and just because Kaden hadn't wanted that didn't necessarily mean he'd have got his own way. But alluding to his father's expectations was probably off-limits because those whispered confidences belonged to the past and they weren't supposed to be going there.

She scanned the *veld,* pale gold, and tangling green stretching to an endless sky. It was Kaden's kind of place, all right. One hundred percent. She took a breath and turned back to him. 'No, actually, it isn't. You always loved wide open spaces and wildlife…' She felt a smile coming. 'Did you do veterinary medicine in the end?'

'Yes.' He seemed to falter and then, perceptibly, he stiffened. 'I got into Edinburgh…'

Edinburgh!

For a beat she couldn't breathe. His first choice. Hers

too, for English. She felt a lump thickening in her throat. It's what they'd planned. Being at uni together, living together in some cosy garret on the Royal Mile with a view of Edinburgh Castle. *Stupid!* Everyone knew that the Royal Mile was all short-term lets for tourists, not students, but they'd dreamed it anyway, talked about it, and somehow, God knows how, she must have buried it so deep that it had been nowhere near the front of her mind when she'd asked him about vet school. But now the memory was swelling into the silence like ink on blotting paper, and he was feeling it too, she could tell. It was etched on his face in hard, silent lines.

She clamped her eyes shut, breathing in the smell of dust and sweet grass through the warmth. She couldn't let herself get stuck in this moment. There were things she needed to ask, to know, to protect herself. She couldn't let this silence set hard.

Think!

Maybe… Maybe the way to push through was by sim- ply *pushing through*, pretending she hadn't noticed a thing. Faking it was hardly a stretch. After all, it's what she'd been doing for years, playing a part. She could do this, definitely…

Breathe in. 'Ah… Edinburgh.' *Smile.* 'That's amazing, Kade.' *Draw eyebrows in.* 'Your first choice, wasn't it?'

'Yes.' It sounded curt but then he sighed and flicked her a glance. 'It was a really good course.'

Relief skipped through her veins. Deadlock broken. 'So, you qualified, and then…?'

'Is this an interview because I haven't exactly pre- pared.' He looked over, his eyes pinning her over the top of his shades.

'It's not an interview, no, but I do need some background for my writing. I like to get the vibe of a place, understand the people who make it tick...' Was he buying it? Hard to tell, but at least they weren't log-jammed. She shrugged. 'It's just how I work, okay?'

'Right.' He turned back to the road, rubbing a place just north of his eyebrow—a thing he seemed to do now—and then he blew out a breath. 'So...after I qualified, I came out here with Fran.'

Her heart double thumped. 'Fran Palmer?'

'Yes.' His hand fell back to the wheel. 'Fran was on the same course. We were both keen on wildlife conversation, so we came out together, worked as rangers at Kruger for a while, and then somehow we ended up here, at Masoka, working with Richard Petersen...' His expression clouded. 'About a year after we arrived, Richard's health started to fail. We didn't know it then, but he had cancer. He was getting tired a lot, you know, slowing down, so Fran and I took on more and more, helping him to run the place.' His voice cracked into a frown. 'Finally, we managed to persuade him to get a medical. That's when he was diagnosed. Pancreatic cancer. Stage four.'

His jaw clenched, the grief still there. She felt it aching in her own chest. 'I'm so sorry, Kaden.'

He let out a long, ragged breath. 'Richard was a character. Crusty, irascible, stubborn as hell, but underneath he had a huge heart, cared so much about the world. He didn't have any family, just a younger sister in Cape Town who wasn't interested in running a game reserve. He said she'd likely sell it on after he'd gone, that she wouldn't care what happened to it, so he asked me if I wanted to buy it.'

'You mean you *and* Fran...?'

'No.' He shook his head. 'I was the one with the trust fund. *I* bought it.'

A very definitive 'I.' She felt her brows knitting together. So he'd moved out here with Fran, worked with Fran, for, what…years? And yet Fran wasn't part of the financial picture. For all the talking, she was no nearer to knowing what was waiting for her back at the lodge. As for Kaden plundering his trust fund to buy a piece of southern Africa…

She licked her lips. 'It's a lot of land! The website says it's, what…around six hundred square kilometres?'

'Six hundred and thirty, but actually, it's not enough.' His gaze swung her way. 'There's a parcel of land on the eastern boundary I want to buy.' He shrugged. 'To be honest, it's why we're doing the luxury safari thing, to fund expansion, and to push forward with other projects.'

There it was again, the royal 'we,' but the conversation was tilting in a new direction and all she could do was go with it. 'Other projects such as…?'

'Schools. Clinics. Welfare stuff. Thankfully we don't have a problem with malaria here but there's a lot that's needed, a lot I can help to make better.' A wry smile touched his lips. 'It's funny. You start off thinking about animal conservation, but then you realise that the people here…the economy…' He was shaking his head indulgently. 'It's all meshed so tightly that suddenly you find yourself being sucked into all kinds of community schemes.'

She felt a backwards tug, memories flying in, the way he'd used to rant and rave about animal extinction, man's inhumanity to man, feeling it so deeply, still chewing on it well after everyone else had moved on to lighter fare. And now he was doing something about it, putting his money where his mouth was, expanding his operations into the community, helping others. She felt warmth surging into her chest. 'You do if you're a good person—'

'Steady on.' His glance clipped her. 'I'm making money too.'

She felt a smile coming. 'Kaden, you're making money so you can plough it back in, so there's no point trying to pretend that you're some bad-ass safari tycoon.'

'Some, what…?' And suddenly the boy she'd loved with every fibre of her being was back, laughing into her eyes so hard that his shoulders were shaking. 'Is that even a thing? I mean, I'll bow to your superior knowledge, being the travel queen and all that, but—'

'Travel queen?'

His laughter faded. 'It's what Fran called you…' His gaze drifted frontwards, some new firmness affecting his mouth. 'The queen of the elite travel scene, to be exact.'

'I'll take that…' She felt her own smile slipping, a knot tightening low down in her stomach. Was *this* the moment to ask about Fran? He'd given her a springboard. She might not get another. She moistened her lips. 'I was going to ask about Fran actually. In her last email she said that she'd be the one—'

The two-way blared suddenly, cutting her off.

'Sorry.' Kaden threw her a shrug and unhooked the mic. 'Jerry, what's up?'

Typical! Just when she'd got to her big, burning question. Still, it was halfway out now, so there was no putting it back. She stared at the speaker, trying to make out what Jerry was saying but it was all a scramble, or maybe it was just her nerves scrambling the words. She bit her lips. Kaden seemed to be understanding everything just fine. He was nodding, and laughing, talking into the mic, and then he was looking over, his shades glinting. 'Okay. Okay. Thanks Jerry.' He slotted the mic back. 'Sorry about that. Jerry's one of my rangers. He was just checking in...' He drew an audible breath. 'Anyway, you were asking about Fran...'

'Yes. I was just—'

'She's not here.' He turned back to the road quickly. 'She left a couple of months ago.'

'Oh...' A momentary relief flared. So, Fran wasn't his wife. And odds were there'd be no line of freshly scrubbed offspring waiting at the lodge either. It had just been her all along, conjuring scenarios, imagining the hardest thing to bear so she'd be prepared, but what now? What to say? If only she knew what Fran had been to him, then she'd know where to put her feet. She searched his profile, trying to read his expression. 'I suppose, it *is* a while since her last email...' His jaw tensed fractionally. Not much to go on! She licked the dryness off her lips. 'I'm sorry I won't get to meet her. We had a good rapport going, you know...'

'Yes, well. I'm sorry too.' He was rubbing his eyebrow again, slowing the vehicle right down so that they were barely trundling towards the next bend. 'The thing is, she wanted me to...' He seemed to be debating with himself, struggling with something. 'She wanted...' He glanced over, and then his hand dropped to his lap. 'She wanted a full partnership and sadly I wasn't in a position to offer that.'

Definitely not what she'd been expecting. Hadn't he already intimated that Fran hadn't had the funds to put into Masoka, that *he'd* been the one with the trust fund? What kind of business partnership could Fran possibly have envisaged? It didn't make sense.

He was pushing up his shades. 'It's been tough because she'd pretty much taken on the whole hospitality side of things, oiling the wheels for the launch, securing *you*, but it is what it is… I've had to involve myself a bit and, in spite of that, it's coming together.' A smile ghosted over his lips. 'I started a new manager last week, Chandapiwa. She's great!' He grinned. 'Very enthusiastic as you'll see for yourself when we get to the lodge.'

She felt a smile coming. Whatever the story was with him and Fran, it was good to see the tension leaving his face, the warmth coming back into his eyes. It was good to see him, full stop!

And then he glanced ahead, and it was more than just warmth in his eyes. It was his entire face lighting up. 'Looks like Jerry was bang on with his intel. Look! We've got company.'

She followed his gaze, and her breath stopped. Barely twenty metres away, a herd of elephants was crossing the road, red dust puffing up around their huge feet as they moved. And then suddenly everything around her seemed to be animating, brightening. She was seeing tall grass rippling, long acacia thorns sparkling with sunshine, rust-coloured termite mounds towering. She could hear a cacophony of chirrups and whistles, could feel the breeze riffling through her hair. All this time, driving with Kaden, she'd barely registered the landscape because of the shock of him, the tangle of him, but now it felt as if the world was coming alive just for her. And the elephants were the icing on the cake. Great lumbering things, smaller ones hurrying behind, wrinkly knees bending, feet almost prancing, trunks going, and then a tiny one came scampering out beside its mother, its head bobbing, trunk scoping the air, its little feet scurrying.

She felt her heart filling, tears gathering behind her eyes. 'Oh, my God, Kaden.'

'Isn't it something?' He switched off the engine and sat back, his eyes coming to hers full of light and shine. 'It never grows old, Maddie.'

'I can see that.' She slipped off her sunglasses, suddenly not wanting there to be a barrier between them, wanting only to feel his light warming her face. 'You look like a kid at Christmas.'

'So do you. You look…' The smile in his eyes was softening to a glow, drawing a faster beat from her pulse, pulling at all the old strings, tangling them up all warm and hazy. And then he turned back to the view with a smile in his voice. 'You look as if you've never seen an elephant before.'

She blinked, steadying herself, then refocused on the herd. 'It's probably just that I've never seen one in the wild before.'

'But you're the travel queen! This can't be your first safari…?'

'It is…' She met his gaze, incredulous now, which was easier on the heart than warm and glowing. 'It's just the way things have panned out. I do a lot of spas and island retreats, and exclusive winter resorts. The rest of the time it's city hotels and private villas. The closest I've come to a safari was a cattle drive I did in Arizona…'

A boyish light filled his gaze. 'Like in that movie, *City Slickers*?'

'No. Think polar opposite.' She felt a familiar playfulness starting. She widened her eyes into his. 'I only do luxury travel remember.'

'So, that's, what—' his lips were twitching '—diamond-studded reins and gold saddles?'

'God, no! Far too hard on the bum. We had well-padded saddles and five-star ranch accommodation. No bed rolls, no beans, no Curly.'

'That's tragic.' He was shaking his head. 'Every cattle drive should have a Curly.'

'We had a Ray.'

'Was he gnarly?'

She felt her belly vibrating. 'Not very.' Kaden's eyes were glowing, and she could feel hers glowing too, and it was so good to be glowing and laughing after all the hedging and the weirdness. She parked her sunglasses on her head. 'Don't get me wrong, Ray knew his stuff, but he was more manicured than gnarly.'

Kaden's eyebrows slid up. 'Manicured?'

She smothered a chuckle. 'He was very nice. Let's just leave it at that.'

Kaden looked pointedly at his hands, grimacing, and then he looked up and his expression altered. 'Uh-oh! Here we go.'

'What?' She followed his gaze, and her breath caught. A huge elephant was coming towards them, ears out, tusks gleaming. Her heart thumped. 'Kade...'

'It's okay.' His eyes came to hers. 'It's just the bull.'

'But you said *uh-oh*, as if it was a bad thing.' The animal was coming nearer, its gait disconcertingly purposeful. 'I mean, what's it doing?'

Kaden's focus was fixed forward. 'He's checking us out.'

'And what does that involve, exactly? Goring...? Trampling...?'

'Only if he's in a bad mood.'

'Is he?'

'I'm not sure yet.'

She flicked him glance. 'How can you be so calm?'

'I'm not.' He looked over, the faintest glimmer of a twinkle in his eye. 'I'm just acting calm for your benefit.'

'Thanks. Way to freak me out by the way.'

'Sorry.'

Impossible!

'Look, what's actually going on here, Kade? Are we in trouble or are you just winding me up?'

'We might be in trouble…' He split a grin. 'Then again, I could be messing with you.'

Like he always used to, except this was an elephant not a tadpole.

And then suddenly he was squaring himself to the wheel, starting the engine. Immediately the animal stopped in its tracks, trunk waving.

'What's it doing now?'

'He's wondering whether tangling with a Land Cruiser is worth a try, so we're going to give him a fright.' His eyes came to hers, serious now. 'Don't be scared, Maddie. I'm going to make some noise, spook him a bit.' A smile touched his lips. 'There will be dust!' And then he was revving the engine, inching them forwards towards the rigid bull, lifting his hands from the wheel. '*Get* on!'

She pressed herself back into the seat, heart pounding. The closer they were getting, the bigger the elephant looked, and it didn't seem to be particularly fazed. But Kaden kept going, taking them nearer, waving and revving, telling the animal to 'Get on,' and then suddenly the bull shrank back, protesting and flapping its ears but backing off all the same, backing down. And then it was turning, hastening off the road and into the bush, leaving a swirl of dust behind. She felt limpness taking over, relief pooling in her lungs.

Kaden blew out a long breath, then turned, concern flickering behind his gaze. 'Are you okay?'

Time for a little payback. She touched her chest, fanning her face with her other hand. 'Ask me again when I've emptied a bottle of wine.'

'I wouldn't have let him hurt you, Maddie, you know that, right?' His gaze tightened on hers, a protective glimmer just visible that sent a tingle running through her veins. 'Worst case, I'd have got us out of there, but brazening it out was better.'

'Why?'

'Because I can't have the bulls throwing their weight about, challenging vehicles. When we're at capacity, we'll have five Land Cruisers out at any given time. It's essential that our guests feel safe. Aside from any injury or trauma, which would be horrific in itself, an animal incident could bring us a truckload of bad press. It could ruin us.'

'God, I hadn't even thought about danger...' Because even though her pulse was still fluttering, she hadn't felt unsafe for a single second. She'd trusted him completely, had felt safer facing off an elephant with Kaden by her side than she did moving through the regular world where the threats were far more insidious.

'Why would you?' A playful light filtered through his gaze. 'You're just a pampered guest.'

She ran her finger over the dash and turned it over. 'Hardly!'

'Dust is part of the experience.'

'Alongside the mild peril, you mean?'

His eyebrows flashed warmth.

She bit her lips together. This playfulness was lovely, sweet and familiar, but it was starting to feel confusing.

She needed to disengage a little, find a different, more neutral track.

She swept a hand through her hair feeling the dust powdering her fingers. 'It's so different seeing elephants like this instead of at the zoo.' She fastened her eyes on his. 'Here, you feel everything, don't you, not just the thrill of seeing them but, jokes aside, also the thrill of your own vulnerability… Does that make sense?'

'Yes.' Something warm and steely came into his eyes. 'One hundred percent.' And then his hand went to the gears, and in the next moment they were moving again, jouncing along the track under an endless blue sky. 'Here you're deep in it, Maddie, feeling all the feels. It gets into your blood.' He smiled over. 'I call it living.'

CHAPTER THREE

HE SHOT MADDIE a covert glance, bracing himself for the little shock that happened every time. Was this whole thing feeling surreal to her too, driving through the *veld* together after twelve years of nothing, seeing off a posturing young bull, bantering back and forth about *City Slickers*? Had to be because it *was* surreal. At least the bantering was familiar, and her smile. That throaty laugh. Better than those questions. Background. Vet school. Edinburgh! Of all the things to have asked but maybe it was just him, being oversensitive.

He felt an ache across his knuckles and loosened his grip on the wheel. Jeez! he was tense. Twitchy. His heart kept missing beats, his breath catching halfway in, or out. It was like being seventeen again except… No… At seventeen he'd been far surer of himself than he was now. Back then he'd been sure of everything. Himself. Her. They'd been joined at the hip, heart and soul. The only thing he'd had to worry about was getting good grades at school. Outside of that, life had been one big party because Maddie was the Tresses girl…

It had been clubbing in all the best places, even though they were underage, and riding in limos, limos with wide seats and drivers who were trained to keep the screen shut and the music on, drivers who'd happily take the long way home for a hefty tip... God, that rich leather smell, Maddie scooting across the seat giggling and kicking off her heels, inching up her tiny dress all the way to her tiny lacy G-string, to that sweet tempting triangle, eyes ablaze, hands seeking him out, stroking, teasing, then very slowly unzipping him—

Stop! Why torment himself? The memories were vivid, but the fact was all those promises they'd made, all that heart and soul stuff, hadn't counted for anything in the end, had it, no matter how real it had felt. Real for him. Evidently not real enough for her! *Oh, God!* And now he was sounding like a petulant, slighted teenager. Thinking wasn't doing him any favours. Time to shift focus.

He took the last bend, pointing the vehicle down the slope towards the river that should have been gushing and roaring but wasn't because the rains were late. Nothing to do with climate change, of course...

'Are we driving over *that*?' Maddie was pushing up her shades, staring at the bridge.

'We are.'

'Is it wide enough?'

He felt his lips twitching. 'Well, it was when I drove over it earlier...'

Momentarily a smile lit her eyes, but then she was looking forwards again, biting her lips. 'Seriously, Kade, you need a wider bridge, with actual sides. This is hairy.'

Fran had thought so too. She'd wanted him to have it widened as part of the upgrade, but he liked it just the way it was, the way it had been in Richard's day.

He touched the accelerator, felt the tyres biting into

the planks. 'Maybe so but it means slowing down and when you slow down you see more.' He scanned the riverbank. 'Like there, see...' He flicked her a glance, pointing to the place where hordes of yellow butterflies were congregating in the mud. 'See those butterflies...'

'Ooh.' She rose out of her seat, craning to see. 'What are they doing?'

'Taking in salts and minerals from the mud. That's the theory anyway.' He felt his eyes drifting to her nape, to the little blond wisps curling there, then noticed his thumb moving over his lips. He dropped his hand quickly. 'My theory is that if the bridge was wider, we'd have sailed across without noticing them at all.'

She plonked back down. 'Okay, I concede.' And then she was turning to the riverbank again. 'I'd like to come back and photograph those butterflies. I know safaris are meant to be all about the Big Five, but I like small details, little unexpected things...'

A memory flew in, a tadpole wriggling in his hands, Maddie stumbling backwards into the long grass, shrieking. He held in a smile. 'Well, coming back will be easy. As you're about to see, this place is very close to the lodge.' He drove them off the bridge, accelerating up the steep incline that curved through the trees and onto the wide pale sweep of gravel that fronted the main building.

'Oh, my God!' She was shaking her head. 'You really *are* close to the river!' And then she went quiet for a long moment, taking it in. 'It's beautiful, Kade. Perfect.'

Warmth bloomed in his chest. He could see in her face that she meant it.

He shifted his gaze to the lodge, trying to see it through a first-time lens, but its thick timbers and gently curving thatched roofs were so familiar that all he could see was home, albeit with a few upgrades. The veranda, where he and Richard had used to sit on creaky old chairs drinking sundowners, had been extended, sanded, stained and oiled, and the furniture was all new, square and wicker with wide arms and plump cushions in toning ethnic prints. And there were floor lanterns now, for night-time, and hurricane lanterns dotted about on low coffee tables. It looked inviting. Luxurious. Sophisticated. It was hard to imagine Richard sitting there now.

And then a movement at the entrance brought him back, shooting happy little tingles through him. 'Looks like your welcome party is on its way...'

Maddie turned her head to look at him. 'Welcome party?'

He schooled his voice into a clipped butler tone. 'Of course, Ms. James. I'm only the chauffeur. The real pampering starts now.'

She grinned. 'I like pampering...'

'Good.' He jumped out and went round to open her door. Why was he buzzing? He'd told Fran he wasn't interested in all the frilly bits but suddenly he couldn't wait to show Maddie around. He wanted her to be impressed with Masoka and with his staff—*his family*—and curiously the blog post had nothing to do with it.

He yanked her door open, and no sooner had her feet touched the ground than Precious was coming forward, basket in hand, exactly as they'd rehearsed.

He touched Maddie's elbow. 'Ms James, meet Precious. She's in charge of housekeeping so if you need anything in your suite, just let her know. Precious, this is Ms James.'

The girl's eyes came to his briefly, full of impish light, and then she was smiling, offering the basket to Maddie. 'Hello, ma'am. Hot cloth for you?'

'Thank you.' Maddie took one, unravelling it, lifting it to her face. 'Ooh, it smells lovely. Is it lavender?'

'Yes, ma'am.'

Precious was nailing it, bobbing her head, being supremely courteous. He held in a smile. Behind the masquerade, she was anything but meek. She was deeply mischievous, unswervingly candid.

He shifted his gaze to the man coming forward. 'And this is Tumo. He's going to take your bags to your suite.'

Tumo gave a little nod, smiling. 'Welcome to Masoka Lodge, ma'am.'

'Thank you.' Maddie nodded back. 'I'm very happy to be here.'

'And last but not least—'

'Hello, Ms James.' Chandapiwa rushed forward, radiating joy. 'I'm Chanda, the lodge manager. You are going to have such a wonderful time with us. We have so much planned for you.'

'Thank you, Chanda, thank you, everyone.' Maddie was looking at each of them in turn, her smile brimming. 'You're making me feel very special.' And then her eyes flicked to his, lingering for a long, still moment. 'Like a queen, in fact.'

His heart skipped—*again*—and then it was filling. She seemed so delighted with everything: the elephants, the butterflies, the lodge, the staff. It meant she was bound to write a great piece, so asking her to stay had definitely been the right thing to do…for Masoka. It was just himself he was worried about. If she kept looking at him like this, how on earth was he going to cope?

'Kaden...' She was dropping her cloth into Precious's basket. 'Are we going inside now? I'm dying to see everything!'

'What an incredible room!' She was gliding through the guest lounge, skirt flaring around her ankles, one circled with a fine leather thong that kept drawing his eye. It was hard not to stare at it, hard not inch upwards in his mind, conjuring her calves, and knees and thighs. It was impossible not to remember how those silky smooth, endless legs had felt wrapped around him, skin to skin...

'Earth to Kaden...'

He blinked and her face came into focus, a mischievous light in her eyes. Could she sense where his thoughts had been, thoughts he shouldn't even have been having?

He smiled. 'I'm sorry, what?'

'I was just saying that your décor is totally on point.' She trailed her fingers over a chair back. 'I adore this tribal print. It's subtle, not overdone.' And then she was moving again, heading over to the grand mahogany sideboard that ran along the gable wall. 'And I *love* this rococo lamp base. It's blingy but in a good way.' She turned, her eyes merry. 'It's an inspired visual disruption!'

He looked at the lamp base. It was hefty, a golden mass of curlicues and flourishes that did somehow work against the plain stone and timber wall. His heart thumped. He hadn't had anything to do with choosing it. It had been Fran, working with the designer, putting in the hours, getting the décor *on point*. He drew an uncomfortable breath, felt his smile vanishing before it had quite arrived. 'I'm glad you like it.'

Maddie's eyes narrowed slightly, and then her gaze shifted. 'Oh, and just look at that fabulous sunset abstract.'

Sunset?

She was walking to the opposite wall, shaking her head. 'It's wonderful…'

His heart thumped again, right up in his throat. It *was* a wonderful painting, a hazy blaze of orange bleeding into a sea of rich browns with splashes of gold and green. Fran had picked that too. She'd said she was going to hang it so it would catch the last of the afternoon light, but it hadn't clicked that the huge smudge was actually a sunset itself. Until now. Until this very moment.

'Is it by a local artist?' Maddie was looking back at him over her shoulder. 'Because if it is, I could mention it in my piece, to give him or her a boost…'

He felt a band tightening around his chest. 'I'm not sure…' Why wasn't he sure? And why hadn't he known that the painting was a sunset? He swallowed hard. 'I could find out.'

From whom, Kaden, Fran?

Maddie was coming nearer, frowning a little. 'That would be great…' She was trying to read him, he could tell, but she was only fuelling the guilt that was suddenly spreading through him like glue.

He broke away from her gaze, looking around the room, *really* looking. Chairs, lamps, art. Ethnic touches. All Fran's work. Each detail lovingly chosen. *Oh, God!* How could he have been so blind? She'd thought she was building a for ever home with him. And he'd been, what, asleep, thinking that the safe, dependable relationship he'd fallen into wouldn't make any demands of him, wouldn't need him to engage more, do more, *be* more? His mouth dried. All this time he'd been cruising, nice steady altitude, no bumps, no bruises, zero likelihood of a sudden vanishing, but he hadn't *seen* Fran, hadn't seen that she was nesting. He felt a drab ache spreading. He hadn't seen her at all outside their mutual passions: the wild, and Masoka. And then she'd spoken, dropped the bomb.

Maddie's voice filtered in. 'But it was just a thought...'

He turned, meeting her gaze, felt his pathetic heart missing for the umpteenth time.

She smiled. 'You know, desirable, not essential.'

She was trying to ease off, but it was too late. He was in tatters.

He forced some words out. 'It's a good thought. I'll look into it.'

'Cool.' Her eyes held him for an interminable moment and then she turned her attention to an art book that was lying on one of the occasional tables. 'Wow! This is nice...'

He swallowed past the dry edge in his mouth. He hadn't seen Fran, but he was seeing Maddie, all right. The rise of her small breasts under her vest, that luscious bottom lip she was busy chewing, the sweet little blond hairs nestling at her nape. He felt a tug, then a raw, tearing ache. He wanted to plant his lips right into that warm hollow, wanted to breathe her in, lose himself in her the way he'd used to. *Maddie!* She looked so different but the ache building and building inside was the same. He'd never ached for Fran like this, and that must have been a sign, a sign that his feelings weren't right, but he hadn't heeded it. He'd convinced himself that second love wasn't meant to torch your soul, that it was supposed to be calmer, and that calmer was better. He'd told himself it was all fine, but then Fran had laid out what she wanted, and everything had come crashing down. If he could have, he'd have scooped her up and offered her the for ever she wanted, but how could he make himself feel what he wasn't feeling? His stomach roiled. Poor Fran. Did she know how much he hated himself? Had she seen it in his eyes as she'd been leaving? He hated himself so much that he hadn't been able to tell Maddie the truth. He'd tried but the words had got stuck, twisted out into some nonsense about Fran wanting a business partnership. He'd caught the glitch in Maddie's response, but he'd ploughed on.

Ploughing.

It's what he'd been doing for weeks, turning things over and over, trying to figure out why Fran couldn't be enough for him, and now, suddenly, the answer was standing right here.

Maddie...

Gone but still there after all, deep inside.

Maddie...

Bent over the book, all smooth tanned shoulders and graceful arms, pendant swinging, a large drop of amber on a fine gold chain. Had someone given it to her, an old lover or—his breath caught—a current one? He felt his heart shrivelling, taking his gut with it. Why was that such a hard thing to think about, Maddie, with someone else, those legs wrapped around someone else…? He dug his fingertips into his forehead hard. Because he'd wanted to be her last as well as her first. He'd wanted to be her only one. Her everything. Her hero!

That terrible day in her back garden he'd been going out of his mind with it, hammering on the door until finally her mum had drawn him inside, furious, lashing out that Maddie was safe in Paris and that he needed to leave, forget about her. As if! Instead, he'd raced to St Pancras and jumped on the Eurostar, faith firing on all cylinders, believing utterly that love would somehow lead him to her, that if he was where she was, he'd find her. He'd believed it for days, combing those streets, searching, and searching, until his father had appeared and dragged him home.

He closed his eyes for a beat, pushing it all down. That's how much he'd loved her. He'd loved her stupid and now she was here, improbable as a snowflake in June, illuminating the space that Fran had made, the space that Fran had filled with hopes and dreams, and he was drowning in guilt, and yearning, misery and joy, and the worst of it was that she was sensing it, he could tell, mulling it over between the pages of the book. He couldn't stand to watch her slender fingers turning the pages for another second, fingers that had used to trail warm paths over his skin. He needed to go.

He dragged his hands through his hair. 'Maddie, I'm sorry but I've got some stuff to do so I'm going to hand you over to Chandapiwa for the rest of the show-around…'

'Oh.' Her hands stilled and then she looked up, something retreating in her gaze. 'Of course, yes. That's absolutely fine.'

His heart clenched. It wasn't fine. She was hurt. *Damn it!* He wasn't trying to hurt her; he was simply trying to stop his head from exploding.

She lifted her chin a little. 'And you don't have to apologise. I know you must have lots to do all the time…' Her sweet mouth quirked into a not-quite smile. 'Like training the bad elephants…'

His heart clenched again. Now she was trying to make

light of it, pretending she was okay when she wasn't. He drew in a slow breath. He'd make it up to her somehow, but right now there was nothing he could do. He needed to be alone, needed to sort out the tangle inside.

He held out his arm, motioning for her to walk, doing his best to sound bright. 'It's not only the elephants, as you'll see tomorrow when you go on your first game drive…'

Chandapiwa was smiling. 'Now remember, if you need anything, just dial one for Reception…'

'Thanks.' She forced out a smile, hoping it didn't look as limp as it felt. What she needed was to be left alone, but even though Chandapiwa was standing tantalisingly close to the door, she seemed not to be in a hurry, any more than she had during the show-around. Through the bar, the dining room, the spa and all around the swimming pool, Chanda had taken her time, talking her through what was on offer, and then she'd strolled her around the numerous verandas that flowed seamlessly around the entire lodge. High ones, built right into the canopy of the trees that crowded the riverbank, some small, for intimate dining, and some that were bigger, furnished with sofas and low tables for taking coffee or enjoying sundowners. The low wide veranda at the front of the lodge, the one she'd seen as she'd arrived, faced out over the golden expanse of the *bushveld*. Chanda had dallied there too, talking about the different species of birds, then showing her the unit where the binoculars were stored, in case she was partial to birdwatching.

Then they'd come along the quiet winding path to her private lodge, Chanda explaining as they walked that Kaden's focus at Masoka was on exclusivity, so he'd spaced out the individual guest lodges, making sure that none of them overlooked each other. *That* kind of privacy was her ideal, and she'd have been lapping it right up if she hadn't been churning away over Kaden's sudden change of mood in the guest lounge.

When Chanda had opened the door and handed her the key card, she'd thought—*hoped*—that she was going to be left to her own devices, but no, the older woman had smilingly insisted on showing her everything: the small kitchen where the private chef would prepare her meals if she decided to use that service, the sitting room with its huge sofa, open fire and a neat mahogany desk—'*for your computer*'—the luxurious bathroom with its sunken bath and glowing copper fittings and finally the spacious elegant bedroom. All of the rooms opened onto the wide veranda that wrapped around the lodge. Beyond its rustic rails on one side was the *veld*...acacia trees and golden grass stretching into the distance, and on the other side, a cluster of trees with a canopy so dense that it was impossible to see the river below. Now they were back in the entrance lobby.

Chanda's eyes suddenly widened. 'Oh! I almost forgot. We serve afternoon tea on the main veranda at four. If you're not feeling too tired after your journey, you should come, meet our other guests.'

Her heart sank. Making small talk with strangers was the last thing she felt like doing. She mustered a smile. 'It sounds lovely but actually I *am* a little tired.'

'In that case, we'll bring afternoon tea to you!' Chanda beamed, and then finally—*finally*—she was leaving, closing the door softly behind her.

For a moment she stood listening to the older woman's retreating footsteps, and then she blew out a long breath and made for the bedroom, throwing herself onto the vast canopied bed. The pale thatch above was showering sweetness into the air, and she breathed it in, listening to the silence. If only her mind could be as quiet. She'd take that all day long over the drumbeat that wouldn't stop, his name pounding through her head, questions pulsing through her veins. *Kaden, Kaden, Kaden...* Did he really want her here? He'd said he did, but it hadn't felt like it in the guest lounge. All of a sudden, he'd seemed to step inside himself. *Why?* All she'd said was that she loved the sunset painting, and bam! That had been it!

She felt a throb starting in her chest, a hot tingle behind her eyes. Just when everything had seemed to be going well, when they'd been interacting *in the present* as per the plan, having fun even. For pity's sake, what could have been more *in the present* than focusing on the décor, all those gorgeous finishing touches? She'd been in the zone, in work mode, paying attention to the small stuff, because that's the way she rolled. Those small things she pulled into the light added texture to her writing, gave her pieces that extra something that had won her blog so many accolades. She'd been doing *exactly* what Kaden had said he wanted her to do, but for some reason, he'd closed himself off.

She squeezed her eyes shut, bearing down. It had stung. So much. The distance that had vanished while they were watching the elephants and laughing about *City Slickers* had come funnelling back with a vengeance. Thank God for that art book! Page after page, feeling him retreating, feeling tears prickling, because he'd never dropped the shutters down on her before, *ever*! They'd used to fit, hand in glove, but staring down blindly at that book, it had come to her that distance was their biggest part now. And yet, he'd hugged her, hadn't he, and it had felt warm, close, genuine. The opposite of distant. And within moments of meeting hadn't they'd fallen into their old groove, laughing over the Tresses advert? She felt a smile tugging at her lips, tears welling behind her lids. He'd never got that mid-Atlantic accent but hearing him again, hearing him mangling it like before, had felt so good because for a moment she'd been sixteen again, a whole person, a person with a past that went all the way back to an actual beginning.

She bit her lips together hard. How she missed that, sharing a memory with someone who'd known her before, someone she felt safe with. No pretending. No having to be guarded. Nothing short of blissful after years and years of always wondering if the seemingly decent person she was talking to in a hotel lobby or on the deck of a boat was really a journalist sniffing around.

She gulped a ragged breath. The only person she could ever be herself with was Mum, but they didn't talk about the past because her father was stitched through it and neither of them could bear it. But with Kaden, she had a warm hub of memories that were theirs alone. Pristine, untainted memories. Loving, intimate memories. And yes, maybe at first they had been a bit stiff with each other, him not wanting to talk about the past, and her, wound tight over Fran, wondering how Fran fitted, how she'd stopped fitting—that whole *full partnership* thing that still didn't make sense—but in spite of all that, she'd felt the old threads pulling, unravelling, all loose, and easy.

She swept her hands over her face, wiping away her tears. Or maybe she'd only been imagining that warm connection, grasping at old threads because she was lonely, because she'd never found intimacy with anyone else, hadn't even dared to try. Maybe without realising it, she'd latched onto the warmth in Kaden's gaze, latched onto a fanciful notion that he might still have feelings for her, so that when he'd changed, when the light had left his eyes, she'd felt small, and stupid, and stung. She'd tried to hide it, but she'd heard the brittle edge on her own voice. Had he noticed? She got to her feet. Probably not! Too busy moving her along, handing her over to Chandapiwa, making good his escape!

Escape...

She looked at the two holdalls neatly stowed on the luggage rack. Escaping was an option. If Kaden was going to be blowing hot and cold, making her feel like this, then maybe it was the answer. Her stomach knotted. Except it wasn't an answer at all, not when he was counting on her for the blog post. Whatever was jumbling her up inside, leaving Kaden in the lurch wasn't an option. She'd been forced to do it once and wouldn't do it again. *Couldn't!* But being around him was going to be hard. When he was smiling it was impossible not to feel the tug of their old connection, but leaning into it, letting it kindle all the old feelings, was a mistake, a mistake she couldn't afford to make again. No. If she was staying, seeing this thing through for Kaden's sake, then she needed to keep her emotions tied down and not read between lines that weren't even written.

She went to the veranda doors and slid them back, inhaling the warm damp breath of the river. Of course, keeping her emotions tied down was all very well, but she couldn't switch off her brain, couldn't make herself not wonder why Kaden's mood had turned one-eighty when she'd started asking him about the painting. Had she touched a nerve, invoked some hidden provenance? She sighed. That was the problem. Almost everything she knew about Kaden was in their past and twelve years' worth of water had flowed under the bridge since then. Plenty of time for joys and hurts she knew nothing about to have accrued, and now that she was right here where he was instead of a million miles away, she could feel her curiosity itching. She wanted to scratch, wanted to know everything about the man he was now, his hopes and dreams, but what right did she have to ask him anything personal? An ache sawed through her chest. None, because she'd disappeared from his life, hadn't she, decided to sever contact, and yes, she'd had her reasons but looking at things from his point of view, he owed her nothing, least of all his trust. *Oh, God!* How on earth was she going to get through the week?

A sudden bright knock made her jump, then a girl's voice came lilting through the door. 'Tea for you, Ms James.'

She opened up, found Precious standing with a laden tray. 'Shall I take it onto the veranda, ma'am?'

The girl's smile was warm as sunshine and, in spite of herself, she felt her own lips curving up in reply. 'That would be lovely, thank you.'

Precious went ahead, setting the tray on the veranda table, and then her eyes snapped up, a bit mischievous. 'There's a note for you.' She lifted an envelope into view, handing it over with another smile. 'It's from Mr Barr.'

Kaden!

She felt a little wrench inside. Sending each other notes was what they'd used to do at school. It had been a game, sliding notes into each other's bags without the other one knowing, or slipping them, unseen, into one another's lockers. A lump thickened in her throat. This wasn't just a note. It was a message.

'Enjoy your tea, ma'am.' Precious bobbed a little curt-sey, a smile still playing on her lips, and then she was disappearing through the French doors. A moment later, the main door thumped shut.

She stared at the envelope in her hands. His writing hadn't changed. She bit her cheek. What was he doing? He'd said he didn't want to revisit the past but what was this if not pulling the past right into the present? Or was she reading too much into it?

For heaven's sake!

She took a deep breath and ripped it open, shaking out the note.

Mads,
Sorry for running out on you earlier. I know it's
not what you were expecting. If you'll have dinner
with me tonight, I'll do my best to explain.
Yours hopefully,
Kaden

She felt her heart buckling, tears wanting to come. So, he *had* been aware of her feelings, *had* heard the torn edge on her voice. And now he was holding out an olive branch. She sucked in a breath. She was taking it, no question, but dinner with Kade in the most romantic setting imaginable was fat-to-fire stuff. She was going to have to keep her head screwed on tight, and her heart tied down!

CHAPTER FOUR

KADEN SHOOK THE ice around in his glass and looked over at the veranda doors. Still no sign of Maddie, but of course he was too early, not by Grandma Barr's five minutes, but by a ridiculous twenty. He downed a mouthful of water, feeling its chill lodging at the base of his throat. *Dope!* Talk about overcompensating. But he hadn't wanted to risk Maddie getting here first and being the one sitting alone in the candlelight, not when he'd been late to the airstrip, then abandoned her half-way through the show-around. This dinner was about smoothing things over, hopefully making things better, not worse.

He slid his eyes over the tall lanterns marking the edges of the deck. Would she like this? Outdoor dining, lamplight, all the sounds of the African night? He lifted his gaze, watching a bat darting and turning. Had she minded him sending the note? He had thought twice about it because it was breaking the rules, invoking the past, but what were the alternatives? Calling her room? Showing up at her lodge door? Either would have put her on the spot, made her feel awkward or, worse, made her feel impelled to say yes to dinner and that was the last thing he wanted. A note had seemed like the gentlest way of asking her without piling on the pressure, so he'd risked it and, miracle of miracles, she'd sent a note back accepting, same loopy writing, same bump to the heart when he saw it.

He set his glass down. The Note Game. Hiding notes for each other to find. Flirty, funny, sexy. Some had been downright dirty. It was why they'd had their burn-after-reading rule, because the thought of her father reading any of that stuff... His stomach coiled. Ironic, all that worrying about Peter discovering that he and Maddie were having sex when the scummy louse had been busy shafting everyone! He ground his jaw. But he didn't want to be thinking about Peter Saint James. Not worth it. It was Maddie he needed to think about, the breathless shock of her, that unexpected realisation that he hadn't let her go after all.

He stared into the lamp flame. He thought he had, thought he'd left her behind, but he must have just pushed her in so deep that he couldn't feel her any more. Not a job of seconds. It had taken years. Years of waiting for something, *anything*, to say that she was thinking of him, that she *loved* him, that she'd be back. After Peter was jailed, he'd thought she'd come back for sure. That was a hopeful time. His belief recharged itself. Belief in *her*, belief in the two of them. He'd thought, no way could she be gone for good, not after everything they'd been to each other, not without a single word. Bright hope attached itself to moments of sunlit hair. He'd chase after her, heart soaring, then have to apologise.

Three years into uni he stopped chasing glimpses and threw himself into pointless sexual encounters that left him empty and aching. Two years on the fantasies stopped: Maddie at the door; Maddie appearing at his table in a café. *Hello, Kaden*. Probably that had some-thing to do with Fran. In their fifth year they did a clini-cal practice stint together at Edinburgh Zoo. Dark-haired and brown-eyed, petite and blushingly shy, it took a few days for him to discover that behind the careful reserve, Fran was as passionate about wildlife conservation and as hungry for adventure as he was. By the time uni fin-ished they were good friends with a plan in place. Africa. And it was perfect, not only because it offered every-thing he'd ever wanted professionally, but because it had no Maddie associations.

Until today.

And now here she was, exploding everything, scat-tering his pieces, making him see things in a new light, things about himself, and about Fran. That awful mo-ment in the guest lounge, guilt rinsing through him like acid rain. He'd had to escape, do his unravelling in pri-vate, but he'd carried the look on Maddie's face with him all the way back to his office, that hurt in her eyes, the way her lovely mouth had folded in on itself. He'd never seen hurt in her eyes before, not on account of something he'd done. Pain had never been a part of their landscape, so he *had* to explain, to take the hurt away. That's why he'd sent the note…

But telling Maddie about Fran was a bittersweet pros-pect. It meant opening himself out, talking, leaning into that closeness they'd always shared, and how would that feel? What was it going to do to his poor heart, the heart that on the quiet had seemingly never let her go? *Oh, God!* The coping strategy he'd devised at the airstrip—boxing them into the present—had seemed sound in the moment, but the box was falling apart already.

He slugged back another mouthful of water. Maybe

it had been a vain hope all along. He and Maddie had always been talkers, right from that very first moment when she'd put her stiletto through his foot at Rory Fraser-Hamilton's sixteenth. Even the excruciating pain hadn't dented the chemistry. They'd sparked. Crackled. Started talking. God, how they'd talked. Walking—*limping*—and talking and flirting their way through the gardens, and it had felt so easy, so natural. And they'd gone on like that always telling each other everything. Deepest fears. Highest hopes. She'd been his safe house, and she'd said she couldn't talk to anyone the way she could talk to him. They'd kept each other's secrets, secrets like how it weighed on him wanting to be a vet when he knew that his dad had really wanted him to go into the family business, and like how Maddie loved modelling but hated the contempt she attracted from snide hacks who claimed, wrongly, that she'd only got the Tresses gig because she was Peter Saint James's daughter.

He looked down into his glass. And now here he was again, about to let Maddie in so he could clear away the hurt and confusion he'd caused, but it couldn't be two-way traffic. He wasn't ready to ask her about herself or her life, nothing beyond the superficial anyway. He'd only be opening himself up to hearing explanations too painful to bear, or to the possibility of getting attached all over again, and what would be the point of that? She was a rolling stone, here for one week only. He hooked an ice cube out of his glass. Maybe she was in his heart, still, but he needed to lead from the head. He needed to be open and friendly, but also sensible and neutral, like Switzerland.

'Kaden...'

The ice slipped from his fingers. A goddess was gliding through the doors towards him, hair swept up from her forehead, the wide legs of her dark jumpsuit rippling around her ankles.

'Maddie.' He scrambled to his feet, searching his lungs for breath. 'You look—'

'A bit fancy?' Her lovely breaking smile stole his breath again. 'I thought I'd make an effort because I hardly ever get asked out for dinner.'

So there was no boyfriend, no significant other attached to the amber pendant? He felt his heart lifting and contracting at the same time. Who wouldn't want to have dinner with her? She was gorgeous, and clever, and she smelt exotic and orangey, like…what was that shrub Grandma Barr had used to like so much? Philadelphus. That was it. *Stop, idiot.* Why the hell was he thinking about shrubs? He needed to be saying something, something complimentary but also neutral.

He stepped round to pull out her chair. 'I find that hard to believe.'

'Well, it's true.'

For the love of God. Her back was bare, a tempting bow tied at her nape, that sweet, sweet nape. He felt heat pulsing into his groin and gripped the chair back hard, glad that she couldn't see, glad that she was talking away.

'I eat out a lot because I have to write up the food in the places I'm reviewing, but that's work.'

He took a quick breath and tucked her in. 'And this isn't?'

Her face tilted up sharply and instantly his heart froze. He hadn't meant for it to come out like that, implying that she was reading more into this dinner than there was, implying that she was mistakenly seeing it as a date. He was just in a spin because she was dressed to the nines, and she smelt lovely, and he was busy noticing all that when he was supposed to be Switzerland.

He swallowed. 'What I mean is, I'm flattered that you don't consider having dinner with me to be work.'

Her gaze softened a little. 'Well, it never used to be…'

He felt his breath catching low down in his throat. How on earth could he stay neutral when she was looking at him like this, alluding to their old carpet picnics, and everything that had used to follow, because no mistake that's what she was talking about. All he could do was go with it.

He went to take his seat. 'Well, that's because it was usually pizza out of the box.' He aimed a wry nod at the cutlery. 'We're at the grown-up table now.'

'What!' Her mouth stretched and then she was doing the fake double-take thing that had always cracked him up. 'You mean we've got knives *and* forks?'

He chuckled. 'And spoons…'

She screwed her face up into a look of cartoon dismay. 'And here was I thinking that this was going to be a cinch.'

Maddie Madcap! How long would they be able to keep this going? He felt a tug of nostalgia. For ever, because that's what they'd been like, rolling a lame joke along, on and on, until the kissing started. His ribs tightened. But there'd be no kissing now, or ever again. Just talking, explaining.

He laced his fingers together. 'It will be. For you anyway. You were always good with your hands.'

Her eyebrows slid up.

Oh, no. He hadn't meant it like that but now there was no way of recovering without drawing attention to the fact that it had sounded one hundred percent like a double entendre. *Move on!*

He smiled. 'How about a drink?'

'Sounds good.' She glanced at the ice bucket. 'What have you have got chilling?'

'Sauvignon Blanc.' Because she'd always preferred white to red and because champagne would have been too confusing.

'Lovely.' A look came into her eyes. She was onto him, knew that he'd remembered.

He freed the bottle and poured, going slowly to catch his breath. Why was it so hard to stop chinks of the past glinting through? Pizza, and now the wine. Everything seemed freighted, or maybe he was just nervous because of all the Fran stuff, all the explaining he still had to do.

Breathe...

He looked up and his heart boomeranged. The occasion surely demanded a toast, but what?

Lovely to see you?

After twelve silent years.

Here's to us?

What us?

To unexpected reunions?

Because obviously they both relished being thrown into awkward situations like this.

Maybe it was time to pass the buck.

He picked up his glass. 'What shall we drink to?'

'Oh, that's easy.' Her cheeks dimpled into a heart-stopping smile. 'I think we should drink to this being our very first legal drink together.'

The perfect balance of past and present. She was a genius as well as a goddess.

He touched his glass to hers, feeling a sudden overwhelming rush of warmth. 'To our very first legal drink together.' And then, somehow, more words were coming out. 'It's so good to see you, Maddie…'

A momentary confusion scurried through her gaze and then a warm glow kindled, deepening, holding him fast. 'It's good to see you too, Kade.' She smiled. 'So good.'

His mouth dried. What was he doing? It *was* good to see her—incredibly good—but saying it out loud like that, not just saying it but sounding all wistful about it, was breaching the Swiss border by a million miles. He sipped without tasting, slipped a finger to his collar imagining a tie that wasn't there. That look in her eyes, all warm and deep. He felt sweat prickling along his hairline. But first there'd been confusion, caused by him. He took another sip. Hefty. He couldn't let himself to be like this, confusing her, confusing himself. Whatever happened to leading from the head?

'Nice wine.' Maddie was putting her glass down and then her eyes came to his, her gaze level now. 'So, anyway, there was something you wanted to say, to explain?'

He felt his heart rate slowing to a treacly bump. The explaining. Exactly the bucket of cold water he needed.

He drew in a slow breath. 'I hear you. You want me to get on with it, right?'

She smiled what she hoped was an encouraging smile. 'I think so.' Otherwise dinner was going to be purgatory. Whatever was on Kaden's mind, he needed to offload it because he was like a cat on a hot tin roof and it was contagious, making her own pulse hop, or maybe her pulse was hopping simply because it was him, *really* him, sitting right there, looking better than heaven.

He put his glass down. 'Okay, first, I want to apologise for bailing on you earlier.' His eyes held her, a gentle light filtering through. 'I know you were upset.'

Her heart contracted. When was the last time she'd heard anyone say *I know you* anything? *I know you* prefer white to red. *I know you* were upset. She felt a burn starting behind her lids. *I know you* were the three words she most dreaded hearing, the words she'd primed herself to kick into the long grass but, coming from Kaden's mouth, they were freighted with everything, everything they'd ever been, every small thing they'd shared, and it felt like being scoured out and filled up at the same time.

She drew in a breath, trying to sound level. 'I wasn't upset. I was confused, that's all.'

His shoulders lifted slightly. 'Well, either way, I need to explain because it's going to bug me otherwise.' He sighed out a breath. 'Maddie, I couldn't finish showing you around because you were noticing all the things that Fran chose. The textiles. The painting...' He pinched his lips together and she felt a cold weight sinking. He was about to tell her what she already knew, deep down. Those waves of unease coming off him every time he'd mentioned Fran, the business partnership stuff that had sounded so odd, the look on his face when she'd asked him about the painting.

'You're saying that you and Fran were together.'

He nodded slowly. 'Yes.'

She felt a frown coming. 'Why didn't you just say?'

'I don't know...' He shook his head and then suddenly his gaze opened out. 'I think mostly it's because I feel bloody terrible about what happened, and there's no way of explaining it that doesn't make me look bad. And...' Something raw came into his eyes that made her heart hurt. 'I suppose I didn't want to seem bad to you, not when we'd only just met again.'

She wanted to say that he could never look bad in her eyes, that he didn't have a bad bone in his body, but badness was in the eye of the beholder, wasn't it, and her eyes were still those of a besotted sixteen-year-old. Fran would undoubtedly have a different take on things and without knowing more…

'So, what happened?'

'She wanted us to get married, start a family. Normal stuff, but the moment she said it I realised that I wasn't feeling it. Suddenly I knew that I'd drifted onto the wrong track with Fran.' He blinked, swallowed. 'I wasted her time, Maddie, and the only defence I've got is that I didn't realise…' His voice was cracking, leaking disbelief. 'How lame is that? Wouldn't stand up in court, would it? "Sorry, m'lord. I made a terrible mistake, but you've got to let me off because, you see, I didn't realise."' And then, as if he couldn't bear to hold her gaze, he looked away, staring into the blackness beyond the lanterns.

She felt an ache tearing through. This wasn't Kaden. Kaden had always been in touch with his emotions, known his own mind. He wasn't a drifter, a wrong-road-taker. He knew what passion was, what it felt like, because it's what they'd had together. But she couldn't say that. *Opening old wounds.* She looked at his face, felt her heart flowing out. He wasn't hers any more, but he'd sent her the note asking her to come so he could explain. Maybe as much as anything he needed to offload, talk to someone who knew him well. A friend. She sipped her wine and set her glass down. She could be a friend. It was the least she could do now that she was here.

'What didn't you realise, Kade, that you didn't love her?'

He swung back. 'No, I *did* love her. Just not in the right way, not like—' She held her breath, catching something steely filtering through his gaze, and then he blinked. 'Just not in the right way.' His hands went to his glass, twisting it. 'As I said before, we were uni friends, came out here as friends. It was after Richard died that...' He was shaking his head and then his eyes fastened on hers. 'I can't believe how badly Richard's death affected me, Mads, the stupid things I was feeling, like that he'd abandoned me, as if it was all about me. I mean, God, the poor old stick had terminal cancer! He didn't want to die. He didn't die on purpose, and yet, at his funeral there I was, feeling heartsick, for sure, but also feeling angry.'

Is that how he'd felt when she'd left, heartsick, angry? Easy to imagine all that passion inside him running high, kicking down walls. Had Richard's death dredged it all back up for him or was she misreading herself into his pain?

'I was in a state.' More head shaking. 'I didn't know what to do with myself and then Fran...'

The rest shuttled between them silently. Fran had stepped in, and he'd folded.

He suddenly stopped twisting his glass and picked it up. 'With hindsight, I think that maybe I took Richard's death so hard because he totally got me, one hundred percent.' The anguish in his eyes shaded into a frown. 'You know how I always felt that Dad was disappointed that I wanted to be a vet?'

Was he really reaching back into the past, pulling her along with him when he'd expressly said he didn't want to do that? It was hard to keep up. She lifted her glass, taking a quick sip. 'He was disappointed that you didn't want to go into the family business. It's a different thing.'

He pressed his lips tight and shrugged. 'Maybe, but you know how it used to make me feel, Mads, like I was doing the wrong thing, making some catastrophic career decision?'

'I remember.' Everything had used to run so deep with him, emotions, feelings, even the misguided ones, which is why it was hard to fathom the Fran thing.

'Richard made me feel the opposite, and it wasn't just because we shared the same passion. He made me feel sound, made me feel that what I was doing was right, important!' He took a sip from his glass and set it down, a smile ghosting over his lips. 'It was like he was proud of me, and it meant something, you know. I wasn't looking for a father, but I suppose I came to think of him that way.' His focus drifted and then his gaze sharpened. 'It's why I won't get rid of the old bridge. Richard put it in when he first came here, and I don't want to change it. We've changed so much, adding all these verandas, extending the front so it looks nothing like it did before. Don't get me wrong, I'm pleased with everything, but at the same time it just makes the bridge feel, I don't know, all the more sacred.'

'I get that…' But the conversation was going walkabout. It was hard keeping her place and it didn't help that his eyes were suddenly filling with fond light.

'I'm going on a bit, aren't I?' A corner of his mouth ticked up. 'I know that's what you're thinking.'

Kaden! She felt warmth blooming, a smile arriving. It was such a sweet feeling being *known*, being read by someone who she knew for certain wasn't a threat. She pinched her thumb and index finger at him. 'You are going on just a smidge, but it's okay. Sometimes it's good to let everything out. I think they call it therapy.'

'Therapy!' He chuckled and then his smile faded, but his eyes held on, holding her fast. She felt her pulse gathering. What was he seeing? Was he seeing how much she wanted to talk…about herself, her feelings, just explaining, just letting everything out? He had to be seeing it because she could feel her layers peeling off under his gaze, everything showing through, and she could see something surfacing in his eyes, a small movement on his lips as if he was going to say something, but then suddenly his lips zipped together and he was leaning back in his chair, going for his glass.

'So rewinding to earlier, I suppose what I'm trying to explain is that I fell into a relationship with Fran, and I hurt her, badly.' A moist gleam came into his eyes. 'And then you were looking around, noticing all the things she'd put in place, and it hit me that I must have been sleepwalking all this time because I hadn't noticed any of it, not properly. God, I didn't even know the painting was a sunset, and there you were, seeing it all, asking me about the artist, and all I could think was, how could I have been so blind? How couldn't I have seen that Fran wasn't furnishing the lodge so much as—'

'Making a home?'

'Yes.' He dragged his hands down his face, misery personified. But something didn't feel right. Something didn't fit. He sighed again. 'I didn't think I could feel any worse about Fran than I was feeling already but then seeing your—' he faltered '—your confusion made it ten times worse because I couldn't unpack it all right there and then, couldn't find the words. It's why I had to go, Mads.' He pressed his palm to his forehead, sighing. 'I'm sorry.'

'It's okay.' She tried to load her gaze, so he'd know she really meant it. 'It's not like you planned to have a meltdown, and if it makes you feel any better, Chanda was an excellent deputy.' She felt her lips twitching. 'Her tour was comprehensive and thorough.'

A smile dented his cheeks. 'Talked your ears off, did she?'

'Yep, but in a very informative way.'

'That's Chanda.' He was reaching for the bottle, smiling widely now, looking more relaxed. 'How about a top-up?'

'Good idea.' She watched the wine splashing into her glass.

For all his explaining, the sleepwalking bit still didn't make sense. Hadn't he and Fran ever talked about their feelings, or about the future, not even after their first night together, because that's when everything fell into the light, wasn't it? It's how it had been with them after their first time—the very first time for both of them. She felt a tug inside, an ache ebbing through her veins. They hadn't been able to stop touching, and kissing, looking at each other, saying, *I love you*, over and over again, and oh, how they'd talked, whispering through the night, making plans. Uni in Edinburgh, sharing a cosy garret, picturing themselves together. Naïve probably, but still, if it hadn't felt like that with Fran, then Kaden should have known, and Fran should have known too, because how couldn't she have known that his heart wasn't in it, and if she *had* known and settled anyway, then what had she been thinking? Impossible to know, but it meant that it wasn't all Kaden's fault.

'Earth to Maddie...'

His face came back into focus, his dear face, warm eyes narrowing, slightly quizzical. She felt a pang, something building inside. He'd called himself bad, but he wasn't. He was a good person. Principled. Driven. Fiery. And she'd kept herself away from him, made choices that had seemed right at the time... *Stop.* There wasn't space for that kind of thinking, not now. In this moment, more than anything, she wanted to soften all the blows: her own, Fran's, Richard's. She wanted to make things better, and if that meant spelling it out to him...

She took a breath. 'Can I say something about you and Fran?'

He pushed his lips out. 'Sure.'

'I don't think it's all on you.'

'How?' His eyebrows flickered. 'What do you mean?'

She felt her pulse ramping, drumming in her ears. 'I mean that if two people are together and one of them isn't fully invested, then the other one is going to know it, aren't they, surely...?' She caught something unfolding in his gaze and swallowed past the sudden dryness in her throat. 'I mean, I would...'

His eyes narrowed into hers, and then he looked down, grinding his jaw, his mouth working. 'So you're saying—'

She cut in, suddenly desperate to draw a line under what she'd started. 'I'm saying that if *you* were sleepwalking, then Fran must have been too, so she's as much to blame as you.'

He let out a sharp breath, then seemed to stop breathing altogether. For an endless pulsing moment he stared at the table, and then suddenly his eyes came back to hers, a chink of wry light just visible. He shrugged. 'I don't know if that makes me feel better or worse, but thanks for the insight.'

She felt a held breath trickling out, relief spinning through her veins. He was okay, didn't hate her for meddling. Now she just needed to bring his smile back.

She pressed her lips together. 'You're welcome. Shall I mail you the invoice?'

'Funny!'

But he wasn't laughing. Instead, he was looking at her, his eyes full of comings and goings, and then a familiar glow was kindling, deepening, a glow that in the past would have started a conflagration.

She looked down, tingling, catching the red gleam of her nails and the flowery scent of her own perfume, and suddenly, her stomach clenched. What had she been thinking, getting all dressed up like this, putting on the jumpsuit she'd bought on a whim because it had reminded her of her modelling days, but which she'd never actually worn for fear of attracting the wrong kind of attention? Was it just that she'd wanted to feel like her old glamorous self again, or was it because what she'd said to Kaden before was the God's honest truth: that she *never* got asked out for dinner and she'd wanted to enjoy it, the freedom of being with him, all dressed up on a private veranda, private dining? Or was it that she'd hoped to elicit exactly that glow in his eyes that was now freaking her out? *Gah!* He'd been so right back at the airstrip. They weren't fit for purpose. He was having a Fran crisis, and she was losing the plot, and to top it all she was ravenous.

'Mads...?'

She snatched a breath and looked up.

He was holding menus, his eyes twinkling. 'Since you

have it in writing that I promised you dinner as well as an
explanation, we should probably take a look at these…'

She felt a smile coming, warmth rushing in. Maybe
they weren't fit for purpose, but somehow, they were
here, together again, and it was so incredibly good to
see him.

Maddie was conducting the air. 'So you've got six guest
lodges here, four tented suites at Kgabu Bush Camp, and
just the one tented suite at Tlou?'

'That's right…' Her perfume was coming at him in
orangey bursts with every wave of her hands. It was dis-
tracting, and so were her smooth bare shoulders, but he
had his finger on the pulse now. No more breaching bor-
ders, no more confusion. He caught her eye. 'Going with
low guest numbers works across the board. It means we
can charge premium rates for exclusivity and that means
more money for expansion, more ranger jobs for the lo-
cals and better wages for everyone, all with minimum
impact on the wildlife.'

'Sounds like a win-win!' She smiled, then looked
ahead. 'I'm assuming you're going for the honeymoon
market at Tlou?'

'Absolutely. One hundred percent…' This was nice,
walking and talking, sticking to safe subjects. Not that
talking about Fran hadn't felt cathartic, but he'd opened
up more than he'd meant to, going off on tangents because talking to Maddie had always felt as natural as
breathing. Then she'd said that thing about how if he'd
been sleepwalking with Fran, it followed that if Fran
hadn't twigged, then she must have been sleepwalking
too, and suddenly somehow, it had started feeling as if

she was trying to remind him of the way they'd been together, holding it up as some sort of gold standard.

That had been hard to take given that she'd left him behind. He'd come close to unravelling, had had to ride it out by pretending to be slow on the uptake, but then she'd made her invoice quip and he'd started unravelling from the other end, remembering how funny she could be, how much he'd loved that about her, how much he'd loved the way she could lighten him with a single quirk of her eyebrow. And maybe she'd read it in him and felt awkward because suddenly she'd been looking away, then he'd felt awkward. Thankfully he'd noticed the menus. Ordering dinner had reset things. Since then, apart from getting himself all steamed up about climate change, he'd managed to keep the conversation rolling on narrow tracks, like this one.

He dodged a noisy, low-flying beetle and looked over. 'At Tlou we're unashamedly milking the whole *Out of Africa* vibe, except there's a luxury shower instead of a water jug.'

'Hang on a minute!' She was giving him the side-eye, mock scowling. 'You can't not provide your honeymooners with a jug. I mean, seriously, *that* scene: Robert Redford washing Meryl's hair, reciting poetry, that blissful look on her face…' She clasped her hands together, clowning a dreamy smile. 'Who wouldn't want to replicate that? I know I would.' And then her smile paled, and she was touching her hair, pulling the short lengths about. 'Not that it would be much of a job these days.'

He felt his heart contracting. Did she miss her long hair? He wanted to know, wanted to know so many things, but he couldn't ask. Oh, she wanted him to, all right. He wasn't blind. No doubt she'd find it cathartic, offloading to him like he'd offloaded to her, but the difference was that he couldn't bear to hear her truths: that she'd thrown him away because she'd stopped loving him, because she'd fallen for someone new in Paris. Because what other reason could she possibly have had for *never* contacting him again after she left? Maybe it was weak of him, but he wasn't up for riding a fresh tide of pain with a grown-up smile strapped to his face, and if she was wondering why he was keeping to his own corner, then it was just too bad.

He looked ahead. But keeping to his own corner didn't make him immune, didn't make him not care. He could still feel her, sense her shadows, same as he always could. The problem was, showing it could cost him more than he had left. He pressed his lips together. But not showing it at all would make him seem cold, which he wasn't. He was the opposite, which was why he was churning away like this. God, there had to be a way through this, surely.

He flicked her a glance. She was walking head down, chewing her lips, little blond hairs sitting sweetly in the hollow of her nape. Such a different look but, actually, it suited her really well, made more of her delicate cheekbones, and it made her eyes seem bigger and bluer. Could she see those things when she looked in the mirror, or could she only see what she'd lost? His heart contracted again. She'd got all dressed up for dinner, and he'd been so busy gawping and gasping that he'd never actually told her how stunning she looked and maybe it was time to do that, let himself off the leash a little bit, so she'd know she wasn't lost on him. He just needed to think of a subtle way in…

He considered for a moment, then nudged her shoulder gently, the way he'd used to when they passed in the corridor at school. 'Hair that's a breeze to wash must be liberating though…'

For a moment she looked surprised and then her shoulders lifted into a little shrug. 'As a matter of fact, it is.' Her fingers went to her pendant. 'I did cry the day I had it cut but it went to charity, you know, for wigs, which meant I got to feel a little bit noble at least.'

'Well done you, for donating it.'

'Oh, lots of people do it.' She was shrugging off his words, but he could see from her face that his approval meant something. 'Anyway, it worked out for the best. I wouldn't want to be toting waist-length hair around now, shampooing it, conditioning it, all that brushing and combing. Such a faff!' Her lips quirked up. 'Unless you've got Robert Redford on standby, of course.'

She was smiling again but it had to be at least partly bravado. Maybe he could fix that.

He took a breath. 'Well, for what it's worth, I think you look great!'

She stopped walking, which meant he had to stop too, and then she was turning, looking up at him. 'You do? Really?' Tears were mounting at the corners of her eyes. 'You're not just saying it?'

He felt a pang in his chest. She looked so vulnerable, so stupidly grateful. Didn't anyone ever tell her how lovely she was? Hard to imagine that, like it was hard to imagine that she never got asked out for dinner. Still, it left a gap for him to fill, a chance to balance the books after forcing her to endure his pathetic ramblings over dinner.

'Come on, Mads, this is me. You know I don't just say things. You're stunning—' in for a penny '—seems that some things never change.'

Her mouth ticked inwards and then suddenly her gaze was opening out, filling with such a landscape of light that for a beat he couldn't breathe. God, she was lovely, maybe even lovelier than before. Freckles over her nose that he'd used to kiss one by one, eyes blue as a high summer sky and those lips, sweet and full, parting softly. He swallowed hard. One small step would put him close enough to cup her nape and pull her in. Would it feel like the first time? Spark. Tug. Searing ache. Would she taste the same? His belly pulsed. Would she kiss him back? Her eyes were moving over his face, going to his lips. He felt a familiar heat rising. Oh, God, she totally would kiss him back. But why? What for? Old times' sake? His veins went cold. Enough. He'd drifted onto the wrong track with Fran, and he wasn't letting it happen with Maddie. There was too much at stake. Too much history. Too much hurt. He had to put himself back in his corner right now. *Right now!*

He tore his eyes away from hers and looked along the path, vision pulsing. Her lodge wasn't far. All he had to do was get her to the door, say goodnight and then he could escape, no harm done. He drew in a breath, groping for something to say, but she was already walking, going faster than before. Two strides brought him level with her again.

'Thanks for the compliment, Kaden. It means a lot coming from you.' He felt a shrinking sensation in the pit of his stomach. Whatever she'd detected in him had wounded her and now she was trying to hide it, twisting her face away, rooting in a pocket at her hip. 'What I mean is, apart from Mum, you're the only person I know who's seen me with long and short hair, the only one who can make a comparison.' She produced her key card, then glanced ahead. 'Oh, look! We're here.'

His heart seized. She wasn't meeting his eye, wasn't giving him room to speak. How was this even happening? He'd only been trying to give her a boost and now everything was curdling. How to fix it? He swallowed hard, looking past her, catching a movement by her lodge door. *Gecko...* The small brown creature was darting up and down, hunting. He felt his pulse tingling, an idea taking shape.

He jerked his head towards it. 'I see your doorman's waiting...'

'What?' She turned, following his gaze, and then suddenly, *miraculously*, she was smiling. 'Ahh, yes. That's James. He keeps an eye on the place for me.'

Relief rinsed through him. Did this mean she was okay, that *they* were okay? He needed to be sure. He ploughed a hand through his hair. 'I'm glad to hear it since that's what I pay him to do.'

'About that...' Her gaze came to his squarely, a trace of mischief behind it. 'He was saying that a pay rise wouldn't go amiss.' She cocked an eyebrow. 'Just passing it on, you know, FYI.'

He felt a smile coming. 'I'll mention it to HR.' She *was* okay. She wouldn't be spinning this out otherwise.

'Anyway.' She was toying with the amber drop between her breasts. 'It was a lovely dinner, Kaden. Thank you.'

'My pleasure.' A kiss on the cheek wouldn't be inappropriate, might even smooth things out more, but if he let himself get that close... No. Best stay put. He shot her a smile. 'I look forward to reading your review!'

'Oh, it'll be good, don't worry.' Her eyes held him

for a long moment and then she was backstepping towards the door. 'I'd better get to bed. Dawn game drive tomorrow, right?'

'That's right.' But not for him. He didn't routinely lead the game drives, but even if he had been scheduled to take her, he'd have swapped with one of the other guides because being around her was too confusing. He waited while she sprang the lock and then he stepped back. 'Sleep well, Maddie.'

CHAPTER FIVE

The pre-dawn wake-up call feels brutal, but a steaming cup of freshly ground coffee softens the blow, as does the smiling face of our knowledgeable guide, Jerry, who's there to greet us when we venture outside...

SHE LICKED HER bottom lip. It was okay. Stoic but upbeat, with a nice bright ring of adventure about it. She attacked the keyboard again...

The game drive information pack—a must-read—advises wearing a warm layer for the dawn outings and it is sound advice. I'm certainly glad of my fleecy top as we clamber into the open vehicle and take off into the chilly darkness...

What to say next? She wiggled her fingers, staring at the screen. She had nothing. Zilch. There was nothing beyond that chilly darkness.

Gah!

She pushed up out of her chair and threw herself onto the sofa. This wasn't *her*. Usually ideas came faster than she could get them down. But now? She pulled her arms over her face, feeling the tightness starting in her chest. The problem was that she was trying to concoct a vibe instead of writing from the heart, writing what she'd actually experienced. But how could she write that Jerry's smile had sent a shock of disappointment hurtling through her synapses because she'd been expecting Kaden to be the one guiding her first game drive. And how could she write that when Jerry had introduced her to her two game drive companions, Birgitte Sommer from the *Cologne News*, and Gerhardus Du Plessis from the *Johannesburg Gazette*, she'd felt a crushing pang of utter dismay.

Stupid Madeleine!

If she'd left off mithering about her father's release for one single second and thought things through when Fran's invitation had landed in her inbox, it would have come to her straight away that Fran was going to be courting journalists alongside the eminent Lina James. Fran was soliciting publicity. She'd had no way of knowing that Lina James was terrified of journalists, that Lina James would sooner chew off her own leg than spend two hours with them jouncing through the *bushveld* in a Land Cruiser!

She'd endured, thrown up the usual defences, keeping herself to herself, obsessing with her camera, but she'd caught the perplexed expression on Jerry's face more than once when he'd turned his bright friendly smile on her, and as for the journos, they must have thought she was seriously weird. She felt her heart contracting. She wasn't weird, she was just scared, scared of being recognised, scared of being challenged about her father, confronted by questions she couldn't answer. The fear was ingrained now, always there. And yet somehow, maybe because of the privacy and tranquillity here, its grip must have come a little loose because that morning she'd felt it tightening back up so hard and fast that she'd almost had an attack.

How had she even got it into her head that Kaden would be guiding the game drive, that it would be just the two of them? It's not as if he'd said it. Last night, he hadn't said, *See you in the morning*, had he? She'd said something like, 'Dawn game drive tomorrow, right?' and he'd said, 'That's right.'

She sat up cross-legged, looking out through the open French doors to the glinting green of the tree canopy beyond the deck. *That's right.* Two words she'd got all wrong. But if she was getting things wrong, getting confused, was it any wonder? Dinner last night had felt like being on a merry-go-round, one moment sinking into pockets that had felt deep and warm and familiar, the next moment rising into an alien landscape of careful conversation. Up and down, round and round, until she was dizzy. And then he'd insisted on walking her back which had seemed sweet and protective, and yes, maybe stupidly she'd leaned into that feeling of being cared for, allowing herself to enjoy the prettily lit path and the warm breeze and the crazy high-pitched trilling of the cicadas, the feeling of him being there right by her side where he'd used to be. It had felt nice. Harmless.

But then they'd started talking about *Out of Africa*, *that* scene, and it had made her think about her hair, and the past, and all the things she'd lost, and she'd felt him sensing it in her like he'd always been able to do. And then he'd said he liked her hair like this, not just said it but said it with that same melting look in his eyes that had always turned her inside out, and she'd felt her heart opening out, a desperate ache starting inside, and for a sublime stretched-out moment it had felt mutual, like something could happen, but then he'd looked away and it had seemed that he was judging the distance to her lodge, as if he couldn't wait to escape. She'd walked on, trying to hide the sting of it, talking away as if she was fine, but she couldn't meet his eye, and then... Then he'd made the doorman joke and she'd remembered that this was Kaden—*Kaden*—who'd never done anything to hurt her, ever.

Her heart clenched. But she'd hurt *him*, hadn't she, disappearing the way she did? Must have. And even if he still found her attractive, even if the desire in his eyes had been real, he'd have quickly remembered what she'd done, wouldn't he? How could he not? No wonder he'd broken the moment to pieces. Kaden was way too smart to put his hand in the fire twice.

She felt tears scalding, a livid heat swelling. It was so bloody unfair. The choices she'd made weren't hers. She'd never have made them if it hadn't been for Daddy. She bit the inside of her cheek hard. *Daddy dearest!* Up to his scummy neck in tar, smothering her in it too, so that it would have rubbed off on everyone and everything if she'd let it, especially Kaden and his impeccable family, pulling them down, tarnishing them by association. That's why she'd stayed away. To save them from that, and—she felt her tears sliding free, trickling down her cheeks—to save herself too, from seeing the open rejection in their eyes, from having to listen to all the polite excuses. Easier removing herself than being removed, than watching their backs turning one by one. Kaden. His family. Her friends.

A sob filled her throat. She hadn't meant to hurt anyone, least of all Kaden, but back at the airstrip, when she'd tried to explain, he'd cut her off, said that he didn't want to get into all that, and she'd got it. In that moment she'd got it one hundred percent. She'd agreed, felt relieved even, but now...

She wiped her face with her hands, then drew up her legs, parking her chin on her knees. Now it wouldn't do. She wanted to explain, had to, so he'd know that hurting him was the last thing she'd ever wanted, and then maybe, once he knew... Her heart bucked. What...? She felt her pulse gathering, drumming in her throat. What was she hoping for? A blissful reunion? A happy ending, now, after all these years? She felt her heart twisting, a cry wanting to come out. *Yes!* It's exactly what she wanted.

Seeing him again, being with him again, was lighting a torch inside, bringing back all the feelings she'd been forced to push down. She'd stayed away because she had to, and then because she'd been too scared to face him, to brave his reaction, but fate had somehow taken that decision for her, and now she was here, seeing that same old glimmer in his eyes, feeling all the old feelings. Now there was a chance to explain, make amends, and if she could do that, then maybe, just maybe, they could start again.

Except...

Her heart pulsed. What if he didn't want to hear her explanations? She swallowed hard. True, last night she'd seen the old warmth coming into his gaze over and over again, and yes, there'd been that brief eternal moment on the path when it had felt like he was going to kiss her, but he had broken the moment, hadn't he? And although he'd said she looked stunning, he hadn't so much as kissed her cheek at the door. And yes, he had opened up about Fran, purportedly because he thought he'd upset her, but he must have known that she'd find out anyway, from Chanda or Precious.

She felt her veins shrinking. And he hadn't asked her a single thing about herself, had he? There'd been ripe moments ready for him to pick, but somehow he'd always seemed to go off on a tangent, monologuing about climate change, the way it was impacting wildlife habitat, and then he'd talked about his plans for expansion, and that had led him onto how Masoka was carbon neutral, aside from the flights required to bring in the clients which he felt bad about but was trying to offset with his community projects, and it had been so good to see his eyes dancing, to see the familiar fire burning inside him that she hadn't minded. But thinking about it now…

She got up and poured herself a glass of water, sipping slowly. Thinking about it now, it all felt rather too deliberate. That feverish light in his eyes, the way he'd never let the conversation stall, filling it up so there was no room for her. Her stomach clenched. Maybe she was getting everything wrong, just like she'd got the wrong idea about the game drive. Maybe Kaden was simply being nice to her because he wanted her to write, what had he called it, *'a cracking piece.'* Her heart froze. Last night, hadn't he even mentioned her reviewing the dinner? She felt a lump thickening in her throat. Oh, it was all falling into place now. He was all about the blog post, wanting to pull in clients so he could do the things he wanted to do. Everything he'd said last night was a sales pitch: emphasising Masoka's green credentials, conjuring the romance of Redford and Streep for the honeymoon bush camp. All things he wanted her to write about.

And what had she been doing? Reading too much into the warm moments, reading too much into his gaze, because warmth and desire were what she'd wanted to see.

She felt tears sliding down her cheeks, a fresh well opening up inside. And that was all because she was lonely, so, so lonely. She bit her lips hard, feeling her heart buckling and twisting. She'd tried not to be. She'd tried dating but it had always felt like a minefield. All those questions: Where did you grow up? Where did you go to school? What do your parents do? *Impossible!* She couldn't let anyone in, couldn't trust anyone with her history, never mind her body. Celibacy had been her only option, loneliness the only way she'd been able to keep herself safe, and then she'd landed here, where Kaden was, safe, warm, gorgeous Kaden.

She shuddered out a breath and put her glass down, rubbing the wetness off her face. Kaden was here, and yes, he was all of those things. His smile still made her heart hurt and the glow in his eyes still made her blood sing, but it was time to face facts. He was only interested in the blog post she'd come to write, not her. At dinner he'd said that it was good to see her, and maybe in the moment he'd meant it, or maybe he'd just meant it in a friendly way.

She pushed her fingers through her hair, slow breathing, letting everything settle. That had to be it, because if he'd been interested in her in the old way, he'd totally have taken her on her first ever game drive. If he'd been interested in her in the old way, his curious, smart brain would have got the better of him by now and he'd have been asking questions. She flicked a glance at her watch. Three o'clock! No word from him all day. The writing was on the wall.

She drew in another slow breath. At least she knew the shape of things now. Knowing the shape of things always helped. She went over to the sideboard and picked up the hospitality folder. There was a private chef service on offer, and obviously, Kaden would want her to try it, so that she could write a review! She flipped through and pulled out the menu. Having dinner by herself on her own balcony would kill two birds with one stone. It would save her from accidentally bumping into Birgitte and Gerhardus up at the lodge and it would save her from any more of Kaden's warm, confusing looks across the table, assuming he was even intending to ask her to join him for dinner again!

Kaden struck out along the path, heart thumping. Last night, with the solar lamps glowing through the thick darkness and the scent of Maddie's perfume winding through the air, walking this way had felt very different, except that his heart had been thumping just as hard, maybe even harder. That moment when she'd looked up at him with the past in her eyes. His stomach dipped. He'd come this close to pulling her in for a kiss, but then he'd come to his senses. *Thank God!* If he'd kissed her heaven knows where he'd be now. On the road to heartache probably. Not a road he wanted to travel twice.

He strode on, scanning the trees for a flash of avian colour, anything to distract, but there was nothing, just the low afternoon sun spangling through the leaves and the relentless drumming in his chest. So much for well-laid plans. He'd intended to keep right out of Maddie's way today so that any lingering confusion about last night had time to fizzle out. He'd checked on the wild dog pups first thing, then checked the state of the watering holes—worryingly dry—then he'd taken a leisurely drive along the eastern boundary, dropping in on one of the local communities to see how the construction of the new school building he was funding was progressing.

He'd only got back ten minutes ago and the moment he'd set foot in his office, Jerry had appeared, minus his usual happy smile. Ms James seemed not to have enjoyed the game drive, he said, and he didn't understand why. They'd seen giraffes, and impala, elephant and rhino, and although she'd been busy with her camera the whole time, she hadn't seemed at all happy. When they'd stopped for coffee and pastries, she'd taken hers to the other side of the vehicle, away from him and the other two guests. He'd gone to make sure she was all right, he said, and she'd smiled at him and said she was fine, but she didn't seem fine. And Jerry was worried that it was something he'd done, or said and, 'Really, Kade, you need to go see her because I don't know what I did wrong. I've never had an unhappy client before…'

And so now, contrary to intention, here he was, heading to her suite with a hammering heart and an ache bouncing between his temples.

Maddie not enjoying the game drive didn't make sense. Her face had been a picture when they'd stopped to watch the elephants on the way back from the airstrip, so how on earth couldn't she have loved seeing rhino, and impala, and giraffes? Unless it really was something Jerry had done or said. *Impossible!* Jerry was a brilliant guide, his best, which is why he'd asked Chanda to put Maddie on Jerry's drive in the first place.

At Maddie's lodge, he went straight to the door and knocked before his nerves could interfere. Within moments there was movement, the sound of feet padding, drawing nearer, and then the door opened and she was there, perfect in a white sleeveless shirt and old jeans, and…that pendant.

'Kaden!' Her eyes lit for an instant and then her face stiffened.

His heart seized. Jerry was right. Something was definitely wrong.

'Hi, Mads.' He swallowed quickly. 'Sorry to spring this on you but can I talk to you for a moment?'

A frown ghosted over her features and then she smiled a smile that didn't quite reach her eyes. 'Of course, yes. Do you want to come in?'

He faltered. Going in hadn't been the plan, but whatever was wrong was beginning to look bigger than a doorstep conversation. He nodded. 'If you don't mind.'

'Why would I mind?' She spun round in one swift movement, heading for the sitting room, trailing a scent of soap and exotic orange.

He snatched a breath and followed, trying—and failing—not to watch the movement of her hips and her cute rear as she walked. Her jeans were old, worn through in places, showing skin. They looked familiar, red tab, button fly. He felt a tingle starting. God, how he'd used to love unbuttoning her, hearing her breath hitch— *Stop!* What was he doing? Those days were gone. Right now, he had a problem to fix.

He forced his gaze into the wider room taking in all her small clues: her phone lying on the open welcome pack; a green garment draped on the sofa arm; the half-empty jug of water on the sideboard; a pair of sandals abandoned on the rug. Her laptop was on, connected to her camera, and images were flashing onto the screen in quick succession. Jerry said she'd been busy with her camera. Maybe he could start there, break the ice.

He nodded towards it. 'Did you get some good pictures today?'

'Well, I took lots.' She gave a little shrug. 'Whether they're any good or not remains to be seen. I'm just downloading them now. I haven't actually looked yet...' Her fingers went to her pendant, then fell away again. 'I'm sorry, can I get you a drink or something or is it too early?'

He tried a smile. 'It's always five o'clock somewhere right, but no, I won't have anything, thanks.'

'Okay.' Her expression warmed a little and then she bent to pick up a glass from a side table. 'I'm having water.'

'Nice.' He felt a pang in his chest. This wasn't them. Staccato rhythm. Trip-wires. They were smooth flow, nice and easy, or at least they had been. *Don't!* Thinking about the past wasn't going to help. Right now, he had a problem. Maddie was unhappy and he needed to fix that. He swallowed hard, catching her lifting gaze. 'So, not to beat about the bush, I'm here because Jerry has just told me that you didn't seem to enjoy the game drive this morning.'

'Oh.' For a piece of a second a door seemed to open behind her eyes, and then it closed again. 'Well, it was fine.'

Fine?

'And Jerry was very good.'

Good?

She lifted her chin a little, her gaze edging towards the ceramic. 'You needn't worry, Kaden. I've been writing it up and it'll be favourable.'

As if a good review was the only thing he cared about!
He felt a stab of hurt, then a sudden hot lick of anger.
He didn't like the cold look she was giving him, and he
definitely didn't like the snarky way she'd said his name.
He didn't deserve this!

He drew in a careful breath. 'If you've got something
to say, just say it. Don't wrap it in a riddle.'

Shock stiffened her face and then suddenly she was
blinking, her mouth wobbling, folding in on itself.

His felt his heart collapsing. *Oh, God!* He hadn't
meant to upset her. Yes, he was cross, but he thought
he'd tamed it well enough, but now, now it looked as if
she was about to cry. He took a step towards her. 'Maddie, I'm sorry.'

'No… It's…' She turned her head away sharply,
knuckles white around her glass.

A vision flew in, the glass shattering, blood every-
where. He moved in, easing it out of her hands, keeping his voice gentle. 'What's going on, Mads? Tell me
so I can fix it.'

She stayed rigid for two interminable seconds and her
eyes came to his, wet at the edges, bright with anguish.
'Jerry was right. I didn't enjoy the game drive. I hated
every second of it.'

'Why?' What the hell had happened out there? Had
Jerry missed something? He licked his lips. 'I don't understand. Jerry said you saw stacks of wildlife.'

'We did. The wildlife wasn't the problem. It was…'
She faltered, throat working. 'It was the company.'

'What?'

'Journalists, Kaden.' Her eyes pinned him hard, welling again. 'Of all people, you sent me on a game drive
with journalists!'

Journalists! *Of course.* She'd never cared for them, their nastiness, their sideswiping. It's why she'd always used to dive from the nightclub doors straight into the limo on their nights out, because the paparazzi were always waiting.

'How about a picture, Maddie?'

'C'mon, Maddie, strike a pose.'

She'd been sweetly obliging at first but then she'd found that no picture was ever published without some snide accompanying caption. It's why her mother had sent her away after Peter's arrest, to save her from all that, and worse. And he'd tasted it for himself, hadn't he? Press camped outside his own house and at the school gates, lobbing questions like stones, lenses primed.

'Kaden, where's Maddie?'

'What does she think about her father?'

'Is your family worried about the scandal, Kaden?'

It had meant weeks of slipping out the back, weeks of being driven to school behind tinted glass, weeks of seeing his father tense, tight-lipped.

'Don't say anything, Kaden. We absolutely cannot be associated with that family...'

He inhaled a slow breath, steadying himself. But it was a long time ago, water under the bridge. Except—he brought Maddie's face back into focus—maybe it wasn't, for her. His heart thumped. She'd changed her appearance because of the media, but she was still blonde, still cropped, wasn't she? And what about her blog? His ribs went tight. When Fran had shown it to him it had struck him as odd that there was no smiling picture of Lina James, only oblique fragments indicating a presence: a hand around a lens; a pair of feet in the sand; a skewed reflection in a bistro window. He'd taken it for artiness but now?

He ran his eyes over her face. Sweet lips pinched tight, something hollow behind the steel in her eyes. His heart thumped again, pieces starting to fit. Those mirror shades that hadn't seemed like her kind of thing. Short hair. Fake name. Faceless blog. He searched her gaze. Was she still scared, even now, still hiding, after all this time? *Oh, Maddie.* He felt his heart opening, flowing out towards her. He could keep her safe, shield her...

Stop.

What was he doing, firing up the old noble instincts? There was no role here for his inner hero. The cold hard truth was that if Maddie had ever wanted him to save her, protect her, she'd have reached out a long time ago.

He broke away from her gaze and went to put her glass down. Even so, it wasn't healthy for her to be living under a perpetual cloud of paranoia. Twelve years on, who the hell was going to be interested? That juice was well and truly extracted. Could he at least help her see it, help her get past it? He felt his stomaching dipping. It would be ideal if he could, given the circumstances...

He turned back to face her. 'Look, Maddie I'm really sorry that you didn't enjoy the game drive. I know that journalists aren't your favourite people, but the thing is, I didn't *send* you out with them because I was being insensitive. It's just that, well, the way Fran pulled things together...' He felt his stomach tightening. This news was going to go down like a lead balloon. 'The fact of the matter is that all of our guests this week are journalists.'

'What?' Her face bleached. 'All of them?'

'Yes, but they're travel writers, not gossip columnists.

They're not paparazzi.' He went to stand in front of her so he could measure the effect of his words. 'They're interested in good food, and lovely views, and spa treatments. That's what they're paid to write about, that's what they're focusing on.'

Her gaze was locked on, listening, but it was still loud, still panicked. Why? It didn't make sense. These people weren't a threat, except to him maybe… He felt a tingle. Now there was an idea, a way to take the weight onto his own shoulders so that hers could feel lighter. It was worth a try. He took a breath, venturing a smile. 'If you think about it, it's me who should be worrying. If Masoka doesn't pass muster, then I've got a huge problem.'

Her face softened a little. 'Masoka more than passes muster, as well you know.'

'Thanks for the vote of confidence but until the reviews are in…' He shrugged, catching a glimmer of warmth in her eyes, but behind it the shadows were still there.

He rubbed his eyebrow. What else could he do? What more could he say, except more of the same? He fastened his eyes on hers, loading his voice with everything. 'Look, seriously, these journalists aren't a threat. Not to you. Surely you can see it?'

A wet gleam was filling her eyes again, and suddenly he couldn't stand it, couldn't not touch her. He took her shoulders into his hands. Maybe he could pump faith into her somehow through his palms, bring the light back with one last ditch attempt. 'Do you remember the story of the Japanese soldier who stayed in the jungle for years and years because he didn't know the war had ended?' She was blinking, opening her mouth to speak, but he couldn't let her interrupt. He had to finish, *had* to free her. 'Can't you see? The war's over. You can come out of the jungle.'

Her heart gave. Kaden's gaze was so warm. So earnest. So achingly dear and familiar. And that touch... She could feel her shoulders throbbing around his hands, awareness tingling though her veins. How long was it since she'd felt the warmth of a hand on her shoulder, let alone two? How long since she'd bathed in such clear light? Copper light, flecked with concern, copper light intent on putting her mind at rest, and it had nothing to do with reviews and write-ups, she could see it now. *Oh, God!* How could she have even thought that? She'd wound herself tight for nothing because she was always on the defensive, primed for slight. But this was Kaden. *Kaden!* Who'd never hurt her, ever!

'Jerry has just told me...' And he'd come straight away, hadn't he, to make sure she was all right. No note. No calling ahead. Just there at the door, breathless, as if he'd been hurrying. Warmth came surging into her chest. The writing was on the wall. On some level he must still care but he wasn't up to speed, didn't understand the whole situation.

She felt her ribs tightening. She'd wanted to talk to him, hadn't she, wanted to open up, but starting with this...? She felt a cold weight sinking. This was the place where her dread lived. Right now, his gaze was loaded with kindness, but would disdain filter in when he knew? Would he step back, rub his head in that new way he did? Her heart thumped a heavy beat. Whatever, there was no avoiding it now, witnessing his reaction. She inhaled, willing her lungs to keep working. Maybe it was for the best, facing it, finally. At least she'd know the shape of things.

She put her hands over his, squeezing them for a moment so he'd know she appreciated his warmth, and then she lifted them away from her shoulders. 'The war isn't over.'

His gaze sharpened. 'What do you mean?'

Her throat closed over. Why was this so hard? She was innocent. Why couldn't she seem to throw off the weight of this shame? *Come on, Madeleine.* She swallowed hard, trying to keep her voice level. 'Dad's getting out.'

A frown flitted across his face, but there was no disdain, no sudden detachment. That was something.

She pushed on. 'It's happening this week. I don't know the exact day.'

'Okay.' He pressed his lips tight and shrugged. 'I suppose it had to happen sooner or later...' And then suddenly panic flared in his eyes. 'God, I'm sorry. I'm assuming you don't, but maybe you do...' His eyes were reaching in, narrowing. 'Do you see him, visit? Are you...? Do you still—?'

'No!' She could feel bile rising into her throat. How could he even imagine that she had any affection for her father? She locked her eyes on his. 'I hate him, Kade. You've no idea how much. No. Idea.' She could feel her neck prickling, the back of her nose, her eyelids, a torrent starting. 'He was supposed to do good in the world! He was supposed to be a good man!' She could hear her voice cracking, breaking in two. 'He was supposed to love me, but instead he stole my life!'

'Oh, Maddie.' He was shaking his head, his gaze softening into hers, and then suddenly his arms were around her, pulling her close, and it felt like falling over a finish

line, collapsing to the ground with euphoria pounding.
She felt a sob coming, expanding with all the hate inside.
It was too much, this sweet, sweet feeling of being held
against him warm and tight. *This* was what she'd lost,
exactly *this*, and feeling it again was hurting, hurting
so much that it was almost unbearable, but the thought
of moving was unbearable too because he was stroking
her hair, talking softly. 'Shh. It's all right. It's all right.'

She screwed her eyes shut, pressing her face into his
shirt, feeling her tears seeping out, seeping, and seeping. 'It isn't though.'

His hand stilled. 'Look, your dad's getting out. So
what? Who cares? He's a footnote.'

If only!

She dragged in a breath, wiping her face, easing herself out of his arms. 'He isn't a footnote. He's headline
news.'

'How?' Kaden's eyes were suddenly wary. 'Why?'

'Because he's written a memoir.' Kaden's face stiffened, his gaze cooling. Was this the nail in the coffin
for him, the bridge too far? She felt her gorge rising, a
sudden pang of nausea. Might as well finish. She swallowed hard. 'It's coming out this week, to coincide with
his release.'

Silence. And then…

'You have *got* to be joking!' Kaden was turning
circles, dragging his hands through his hair, and then
suddenly his eyes locked back on, blazing. 'I mean, seriously, Mads, who the hell's going to buy it?'

She felt her soul shrivelling, her voice shrinking. 'Everyone. It's already a bestseller, pre-release.'

'God almighty!' His throat was working as if he
couldn't get enough air and then he exploded. 'The

world's gone mad! The planet's burning, habitats are being destroyed, animal species are being wiped out, and people are putting money into the pockets of an utter shit-bag like your father! People actually want to read what he has to say…like it could possibly count for anything?'

She closed her eyes. Bad enough hearing it inside her own head all the time but hearing Kaden blasting it out was somehow making it worse. 'I know.' She pressed her fingers into her eyes, trying to staunch a fresh spill of tears. 'You've no idea how proud I am to be his daughter.'

'Oh, Madeleine.' Kaden's hands slapped to his sides, his voice suddenly softening into gentleness. 'I'm so, so sorry.'

She looked at him. Kindness in his eyes. Sorrow. Empathy. Her heart lifted. He didn't despise her. She was still here, still standing, wilting a little admittedly, but it was over. Telling him about her father had been an ordeal but she was on the other side of it now, seeing warmth coming into his eyes, not distaste.

He sighed a deep sigh. 'So I get it now, why you found the game drive so tough.' He shrugged. 'For what it's worth, I still think you're safe here, but…' He paused, seeming to weigh a thought, then he carried on. 'But if you're going to be uncomfortable around the other journalists, then I feel duty bound to offer an alternative arrangement…' There was a smile hiding at the corners of his mouth, a spark of mischief gaining ground in his gaze that was giving her tingles.

'What kind of alternative arrangement?'

His eyes crinkled. 'It's more of a one-to-one service, really. Very exclusive, although the drive guide's a bit of a maverick.'

Her heart skipped. 'You mean *you*?'

He nodded, breaking into a smile. 'I'm not nearly as good as Jerry but I'm at your service for the rest of the week if you want me?' His eyebrows flashed. 'What do you reckon?'

Was he mad? How could she not want him?

She felt a smile flying through her veins, exploding in her cheeks. 'Honestly, I reckon it's the best offer I've had all day.'

CHAPTER SIX

'THEY'RE ADORABLE, KADE…' Maddie was watching the wild dog pups through the long lens of her camera, elbows propped on the Land Cruiser door. Her voice was low, mindful of their proximity to the animals, but there was excitement in it. Delight.

He smiled inside. Delight was good. Watching her now, glowing the way she'd used to, it was hard to believe that just yesterday she'd been vibrating with pain and anger and hate. She was cut so deep, courtesy of her scumbag father, but the worst of it was that the depth of her pain had shocked him, and it shouldn't have. He felt guilt curling, flaking off into his veins. It absolutely shouldn't have because he knew how much she'd loved Peter, how proud she'd been of him.

He rubbed his eyebrow. It had seemed to cost her so much to tell him about Peter's release and about the book. Why? None of it was her fault. It wasn't like him, with Fran. Guilt was the reason he hadn't come clean to Maddie about Fran straight away, but the book thing, he just didn't get. Then again, had he ever really tried to *get* Maddie's situation, ever truly let his imagination roam into her reality? He licked his bottom lip. No. He'd been too self-absorbed, hadn't he, too ensnared in his own hurt and loss to think about how it must have felt *being* her. Somehow, in his bruised juvenile mind, she'd always been the one with agency, the one who'd spirited herself away to a life she was happy to lead—without him—but then being fair to himself, what was he supposed to have thought because the fact was, even if leaving hadn't been her choice, she'd never come back, had she? She'd left him dangling, hurting, wondering. Had she ever stretched her imagination to that, to *his*, reality?

Stop! Why was he tangling himself up like this? The only reality that counted was this one, the present, this soft dawn moment in the *veld*, Maddie clicking away on her camera, smiling all the way to her cheeks. This was a moment worth staying in.

He lengthened his gaze to the dogs. 'They *are* adorable. I love watching them.'

One of the pups stilled, sniffing the air, and Maddie pressed the shutter. 'It's so sad that most of them will die.' She looked over. 'Aren't you ever tempted to do something?'

'Er… *Hello?* I think running a game reserve counts as doing something.'

Her eyebrows flickered. 'Well, yes, obviously, there's that.' She turned back to her camera. 'I just meant that aren't you ever tempted to, you know, save one, take it home?'

'At the level of the heart, yes, but that would be meddling, and mankind's done quite enough—'

Wait a minute. Her shoulders were shaking and there was something very suspicious about the way she was pulling the camera closer to her face. Was she teasing him, provoking one of his ranting monologues to see how long he'd go on before realising?

He felt a playful spark igniting, a smile loosening in his cheeks. 'Very funny, Ms James.'

Dancing eyes flicked to his, wicked, glinting.

His pulse jumped. Her body language was one hundred percent invitation. He could feel his fingers itching. Did he dare? *Hell, yes!* He lunged at her, going for her ticklish spot, and she exploded, giggling hard, twisting away from him, camera up.

'Pax! Pax! Mind the camera. Kaden, *mind* the camera!'

She was panting, her body a warm curve, smooth shoulders turned, vest straps slipping, gold chain against her golden nape, that sweet hollow. He felt heat pulsing, a vibration starting in his belly. 'You should have thought about that before.'

Her body curled tighter. 'No, Kade. No.' But she was giggling, eyeing him over her shoulder, beaming out another challenge.

He went in again, laughing, catching her on the turn, pursuing her just enough to generate another fit of giggling, but then suddenly she was twisting back sharply to face him, lips parted, breath coming in short bursts.

'Listen.' Wide eyes gripped his, blue as cornflowers. 'Let me go. We're disturbing the pups.'

'Listen... Dad's coming... Can't you hear him...? Kade, I'm serious! Let me go.'

Which had never meant let her go at all. It had meant the opposite, adding a frisson of danger, heightening the tension, stretching out that sweet moment of surrender. And he could feel it now, danger thrumming, the thrill of the tangle, the warm scent of her filling his nostrils, a blur closing in at the edge of his vision, closing in so that all he could see was her face, her eyes, her lips—

'Listen!' Her voice jerked him back and then he heard it, the high-pitched rippling chatter of the dogs, the excited whining and squealing. She was wriggling, impatient now. 'What's going on?'

He blinked. What *was* going on? What was he doing? He released her, heart pounding, lifting his gaze to the commotion at the den. 'The hunters are back. You should watch.'

'Oh, look at their tails going.' Her voice was husky, breaking a little. 'They look so happy to see each other.'

'They are.' Patchiness in his own voice too. 'They're family.' He swallowed hard. Had that tantalising closeness really just happened? Had he gone too far? It didn't feel like it. It had felt like old times, her teasing, him diving. He flicked her a glance. She seemed fine, settling back behind her camera. But why had she started it?

He felt his stomach roiling, then shrinking. What was happening here? What was he getting himself into? He'd offered to be her guide for the week because she'd been crying in his arms, warm and soft and broken, and he couldn't stand her pain. All he'd been thinking…all he'd wanted, was to give her some peace of mind, save her from having to worry about the other journalists, but what about his own peace of mind? Suddenly that peace was feeling very fragile. Was spending time with her like this a good idea? Barely two hours into the day and he was already falling off the wagon, succumbing. His heart clenched. The problem was how not to when every smile, every teasing glance, made his skin start to beat.

Fran had never used to make his pulse race and tumble like this. Petite, brunette, hardworking, Fran was a serious type, not given to teasing. She was like him. It's why he'd related to her, why they became friends. *Why they'd plodded along.* But there was no plodding with Maddie. It wasn't only that she was still the best thing he'd ever seen, it was that he liked her, and he liked the person he was when he was with her. They'd used to be so good together, comfortable enough to be wild, comfortable enough to be open. Not being open was an effort, not asking things was an effort, things like where she'd got her pendant, why it was always there around her neck. So many questions all leading to the biggest, scariest one of all: why she hadn't come back to him.

His ribs went tight. He wasn't ready for that one. And he was going to have to stop himself from falling into rose-tinted alleys as well, because rose-tinted alleys led to tickling, and tickling led to confusion, and God help him, wasn't he confused enough already?

'Ugh! Gross!'

Maddie's voice snapped him back. She was rearing away from her camera, grimacing. He switched focus to the pack. *Ah!* No wonder she was grimacing. The hunters were regurgitating red gobbets of meat onto the ground. It wasn't the prettiest sight, but it meant they'd made a kill.

He met her eye, holding in a chuckle. No one grimaced quite like she did. 'Look, they have to bring it back somehow. They don't have shopping baskets.'

'Pity, because *that* would be a great picture, whereas this—' she waved her hand towards the pack '—is definitely not luxury travel blog material.' She settled the camera on her lap and then she looked up. 'So, while they're busy doing the hoofing-up thing, maybe you can tell me all about them...'

There was that glimmer of mischief again. More teasing, but he wasn't falling for it this time. 'That could be a very long monologue and I know how much you enjoy those.'

She smiled an acknowledging smile and then a soft light came into her gaze. 'Okay, so instead, tell me why you love the dogs so much.'

'Is it that obvious?'

'It is to me.'

To me. Was she deliberately invoking their old connection or was he getting paranoid?

'You couldn't wait to get here, and you were smiling all the way. You're like a proud father.'

She had him, although the dogs weren't the only reason why he'd been smiling all the way here.

His heart pulsed. That thought had slid in on the sly, hadn't it? Smiling because of the pups, and—*admit it*—because of her, because he liked being with her, because setting off into the pale dawn with her had felt amazing.

He licked his lips. 'I am a proud father. And I think I love the wild dogs because they know how to live.' He could feel his blood stirring, the passion rising. 'They help each other, Mads. They look after each other. The dogs we saw with the pups at the start aren't the parents. They're babysitters.' He flicked a glance at the pack. 'If you look now, you'll see that the babysitters get a share of the kill, even though they weren't on the hunt.'

She turned to watch, then her eyes came back to his, glowing. 'That's wonderful.'

'It is.' He felt a familiar grey pall descending. 'In many respects I think that wild dogs are better than humans. Humans don't share any more, they just take.'

A shadow flitted across her face.

Oh, God! Way to put his foot right in it! He hadn't been thinking of her father, just humans in general. He swallowed quickly. 'Hey, here are some factoids for your blog. Each animal has its own unique coat pattern, and, unlike other dogs, they only have four toes.'

'Four toes?' Her eyes narrowed a little and then a slow smile curved on her lips. 'You once told me that you only had four toes.'

What? And then it came rushing back. 'You remember that?'

Something flickered behind her gaze. 'Yes, I remember.'

Unbelievable. Just two days ago he'd been thinking about it as well, not the part about toes, but about Rory Fraser-Hamilton's sixteenth, colliding with Maddie. *Falling hook, line and sinker.* He felt his mouth drying. Sharing the memory would be opening a box, and she knew it. That's why she was looking at him so carefully. He felt his pulse gathering. Did he want to open that box? Did he have a choice? Because if he didn't, it would be tantamount to stonewalling her, and that would spoil the mood, the day, everything. He inhaled a slow breath. What harm could it do? It had been fourteen years ago. Just two kids at a party. One of them with only four toes. Apparently.

He licked his lips. 'I didn't say that. You're not remembering it right.'

Her eyebrows ticked up. 'I think I am…'

He felt a smile straining at his cheeks. 'No. What happened was that we were dancing with our different friend groups, then you twirled, lost your balance and put your stiletto through my big toe.'

Her mouth froze. 'That's a gross exaggeration.'

He dipped his chin at her. 'And—' this was fun, watching her eyebrows climbing to maximum elevation

'—then you said you were sorry, and I said, *"It's fine, I can walk with four toes—"*'

'"*But my dancing days are over!*"' She was laughing, clapping her hands together softly. 'You're right. That's exactly what happened. And then we went outside...'

'To see if I could still walk...'

'Which you could, but then it was me, remember, struggling on the gravel path because of my shoes...'

The dusk closing in, pipistrelles darting above the darkening trees, the pink remnants of the sunset clinging to the horizon, the circular fountain plashing white water, the beat of the music thumping across the wide sweep of lawn and *her,* hair longer than the dress she had on, and those ridiculous, lethal shoes. It was locked in.

He nodded. 'I do. You took them off at the fountain and got in.'

'Not just me. You did too.'

Because he hadn't wanted to be even an inch away.

Her eyes were filling with dismay. 'Your poor toe. Black and blue. I felt so bad.'

He pressed his lips tight. 'To be honest it's never been the same.' He winced for effect. 'It still twinges sometimes.'

Her eyes narrowed into his. 'Very funny!'

He felt warmth blooming in his chest. That had been fun, and not scary at all, but it would probably be a good idea to quit while he was ahead.

He shot her a smile, going for the ignition. 'Right, I think it's time to find a suitable place for breakfast.'

'Here we are.' Kaden switched off the engine.

It wasn't the most inspiring breakfast spot. A flat hardpan, bald save for a few small boulders and sparse tufts of pale green grass. Where the dust ran out, a low monotony of scrubby acacia started, interrupted only by the occasional stricken remains of a dead tree. In the far distance, hazy in the early morning light, low hills rose, similarly clad in low green scrub.

She shot him a glance. If it weren't for him—hearing him laugh, feeling the warmth coming through his smile—she'd have been feeling a little disappointed, but as it was, she was fine. Simply being with him was enough. A joy. *And* they were talking, peeling corners off memories, having fun. So much fun. Crazy how simply being herself, her real self, could be so intoxicating. No one watching, no one overhearing, no burdensome sleazeball of a father weighing her down. This was freedom—living—and even if Kaden's perfect breakfast spot looked a bit like an empty car park, it was still a slice of heaven, a slice of heaven that, for some reason, he was scrutinising with great care.

She caught his eye. 'What are you looking for?'

'Buffalo.' His gaze moved on again, combing the terrain. 'They're unpredictable, AKA dangerous.' He motioned right. 'About five hundred metres that way there's a river—more of a trickle right now because the rains are late—but it's a draw, which means there could be buffalo about. I'm not letting you out of the vehicle until I'm sure we're alone.'

Now the choice of location made sense. No animal would be able break cover without them seeing it. She felt a little rush of warmth. He was keeping her safe, protecting her, and yes, thinking about it, Jerry had parked in a similar spot yesterday, a dust bowl with clear views all around, so obviously it was standard practice, but still, something about the way Kaden was being so intensely forensic was making her feel special.

'Right!' He turned finally. 'We're good to get out, but no wandering off, okay?'

'Like I'd even consider it now that you've thumped the buffalo drum.' And then suddenly, because he was looking so serious, it was impossible to resist a little mischief. She looked at the scrub and frowned a nice deep frown. 'In fact, actually, I think maybe I'll stay right here.'

His eyes narrowed momentarily and then he nodded. 'Okay.'

She pressed her lips together, willing herself not to crack. He was on the hook, settling himself in for the game just like he'd used to, that mirthful spark just visible in his eyes.

He opened his door. 'Sadly there's no in-vehicle steward service but obviously it's up to you. If you'd rather stay here while I sit on the fender stuffing my face, then it's absolutely your call.' He dipped his chin, giving her a long look that contained the tangible gleam of victory. 'After all, at Masoka, what the guest wants the guest gets.'

She felt her belly vibrating, laughter spilling out. 'Oh, you're good.'

His eyebrows flashed—up, down...up, down.

'Stop it.' He was too funny, too breathtakingly handsome. 'I'm conceding, okay? You win.'

'Yes!' He punched the air and then he was chuckling, pinning her with an irresistible copper gaze. 'Who's the daddy?'

She felt her breath catching. 'That would be you.'

His eyes held on for an endless second and then he was moving, jumping out. 'Coffee, madam?'

'Sounds good.' She cracked her door, heart drumming. Had that felt like a moment because it *was* a moment, or was she just high on life, high on Kaden essence? Whatever, she was tingling all over, feeling giddy. Was he?

She slithered out, going round. 'Is it the same great coffee Jerry had?'

'It is.' He'd already got enamel mugs and a picnic box set out on the folding bumper grid and he was busy pouring. 'Do you still take milk?'

A pang caught her in the chest. She'd given up milky coffee in Paris. The small bitter espressos had felt like a better fit for her bitter black moods, but she didn't want to get into that with him. Not now. Yes, they were talking, breaching some walls, but rushing fences when they were still finding their feet didn't seem like a good idea.

She smiled. 'You remember.'

'Not the hardest thing.' He put a steaming mug into her hands. 'We spent a lot of time at Book Stop...'

...after school, at their special table on the mezzanine. The bookshop café had always been quieter than the mainstream places, and warmer, with that nice new-book smell. They'd sometimes started on homework, but mostly they'd held hands, whispering and flirting and, when no was looking, kissing.

'Croissant?' He was holding out a box, a smile hanging on his lips.

The pastries smelt divine, looked authentic. She wanted to say so but that would only lead her to back to Paris. Into the dark.

'Thanks.' She took one and turned to look across the *veld*. So empty and yet the air was alive with squawks and whistles and clicks. The word *teeming* came to mind. That was how it felt here—that you were just one creature among many, no more important than the rest but alive to the tips of your senses. What had Kaden said?

'Here you're deep in it, Maddie, feeling all the feels. It gets into your blood.'

Her spine quivered. He was right. She was feeling all the feels, a strange and wonderful elation stirring, because of this place and—she turned back to him—because of him. The combination of Kaden and this place was close to overwhelming.

'You okay?' He was rubbing crumbs off his hands. 'More of anything? Coffee?'

She lifted up her mug and croissant. 'I'm still going, thanks.'

'Slowcoach.' His eyes crinkled and then he turned to freshen his own cup.

She felt the hairs on her arms standing to attention. He looked so good. Irresistibly tousle haired. Irresistible full stop. His blue shirt was laundered soft, the sleeves rolled up, showing tanned forearms that had never used to be so thick. He'd grown into his man's skin, filled out in all the right places, but his hips were still slim and, if the contours inside the seat of his cargos were anything to go by, his tush was still firm as an apple. She felt a low-down ache starting. Hot. Tugging. Raw. Yesterday, crying in his arms, it had felt as if there was still something warm and real between them. The way he'd stroked her hair, so gently, like she was a precious thing, the way it had felt so right, so perfect…

But torturing herself with fanciful notions was foolish. He might have been warm, yes, and sweet, but the wall of the past was still there, the past he didn't want to revisit. Maybe, by degrees, bits were crumbling off but the memories they were sharing were safe ones: Rory's party, Book Stop. They'd still been kids then. Fourteen and fifteen. They hadn't made their promises yet, hadn't made love yet. Recalling those things was a world away from the messy part, the going-to-Paris part, and the afterwards part, the hard-to-explain part when insecurity had taken her prisoner. A knot balled tight in her stomach. Would they ever get to that and, if they did, would anything she said make sense, because, increasingly, all the things she'd thought were beginning to seem incomprehensible even to her.

She bit her lips together. But she couldn't think about that now. She needed to stay in this moment, keep things rolling along all light and airy. Neutral. Also, she needed to be thinking about the blog piece at least a little bit.

She finished her croissant and swallowed a mouthful of coffee. 'So, Kade, what are we actually hearing? I mean, I can't see anything but there's all this noise.'

'What are we hearing?' His head tilted, listening, and then suddenly he was levering himself up onto the hood, holding out his hand. 'Come sit and I'll tell you.'

That face. Those eyes. Setting off shivers.

She parked her cup on the bumper and put her hand into his. Warm. Dry. Familiar. Strong! The bonnet felt warm too, and there was his arm, so close that she could feel heat radiating through his shirtsleeve. She flicked him a glance. Was he feeling it, this tingling awareness? If he was, he was hiding it well. He seemed intent on the business of listening.

His eyes clipped her suddenly. 'So, this one—' a low, grating vibration was starting, getting louder and more raucous '—is guinea fowl.' He scoured the *veld* and then his hand shot out, pointing. 'There! See...'

She caught a low hastening movement in the long

grass close to the scrub line. 'Yes. I see them.' Plump and black, white-spotted. Vaguely comical. She felt a smile coming. 'I like those.'

'They're ubiquitous.' He leaned away a little, smiling into her eyes. 'It's adorable that you're so thrilled.'

Her heart skipped. 'Ubiquitous doesn't stop them from being appealing.'

'True.' His gaze held her for another sweet moment and then he turned back to the view. 'The constant trilling sound is cicada, and *this*...' His finger went up as a *tock* sound rose into the air, then repeated, going faster, escalating into a sort of a hiccup: *tock-tock, tock-tock, tock-tock*. His teeth caught on his lip. 'That's the southern yellow-billed hornbill, otherwise known as the flying banana.' He leaned forward, combing the landscape. 'If I can just locate it...' And then his hand shot out again, pointing. 'On the bare branch over there...'

She followed his gaze. 'Yes, I see it!' A biggish bird, with a pale grey breast, black mottled wings and huge yellow beak that did look exactly like a banana. 'He's rather handsome. I should get my camera.'

'Will you get a good enough shot from here?' He was shifting back, the swell of his arm pressing against hers.

Warm. Firm. Heavenly. Suddenly the thought of moving was beyond unappealing. She looked at him. 'You've got a point. Closer would be better.'

Which had an unfortunate ring of double entendre to it, or maybe it was just her.

He smiled. 'I'll keep an eye out when we head off. We're bound to catch one close to the track at some point.' His eyes held hers for a long still moment and then they narrowed a little. 'I'm curious. What's with the pendant? You're holding on to it as if it's a lifeline.'

Her heart clenched. She *was* holding it, hadn't even noticed, and now he was asking, and it was Paris again, erupting, inescapable. Paris. So close to the raw spot, so close to all the hurt. But he didn't know that, did he? He was looking at her, his eyes all warm and curious. No hidden layers. *Oh, God!* He had no idea he was pushing them into the messy part. Her heart was drumming now, thumping in her throat and in her ears. Maybe talking about it would be a good thing but were they ready? Her mouth dried. No. But lying about the pendant wasn't an option. She'd never lied to Kaden, and she wasn't about to start.

She drew in a breath, then leant to pick up her cup from the bumper. 'That's because it *is* a lifeline, kind of...' She took a quick sip, then met his gaze. 'It was given to me by a friend of Mum's... Renée Colbert...' She swallowed hard. 'In Paris...'

A dark light flickered through his gaze.

'Paris is...' Her throat was thumping hard. 'Paris is where I went when Dad was arrested.'

He seemed to falter, and then he blinked. 'I know.'

'What?' Her heart pulsed. This couldn't be right, surely, and yet his eyes weren't lying. She searched her mouth for moisture. 'How?'

'Your mum told me.'

Mum...

'When?' Mum had never said anything about any such conversation with Kaden.

'The day your dad got arrested. You weren't at school. You weren't answering your phone, so I went to your house. I wanted to see you...' His eyes flickered. 'Didn't she tell you?'

'No. She never said a word.' Not then, not since.

His mouth tightened. 'That figures.'

'How?' Nothing was figuring. Nothing was making sense. 'Please, tell me, what happened?'

He gave a little shrug. 'It was lunchbreak. When I got to your house the press was camped outside so I went round the back and over the wall.'

Ten feet high and planted with a dense yew hedge on the garden side. How on earth had he even done that?

'I knew your mum was inside, but I had to bang on door for ages before she finally opened up. She told me to leave. She was distraught, obviously, but I wanted to know where you were.' He was shaking his head. 'I wouldn't go. I was loud, and stubborn, and then she got angry, exasperated. She said that you were safe in Paris and that for everyone's sake I should go back to school and forget about you.'

Her heart seized. And he'd have gone back to school, of course, but he hadn't forgotten her, had he? He knew she took milk in coffee—or had—and he remembered Rory Fraser-Hamilton's party, and Book Stop, and the stupid Tresses catchphrase. Why hadn't Mum said anything?

She looked into his face. Remnants were glistening in his eyes, tugging at her heart, but what was worth saying now? As for Mum… She felt her fingers tightening around her cup. Maybe it was just as he said: Mum not telling her figured. Knowing he'd been at the house ranting and raving would only have made her cry harder, miss him more. Mum wouldn't have wanted to inflict that on her. And anyway, Mum had had her hands full, playing dutiful wife to the scumbag, keeping her famous daughter safe. To Mum, her teenage romance with Kaden must have seemed like a trivial sideshow next to her husband's scandalous extravaganza. And later, when she might have mentioned it, she'd probably decided that it wasn't worth rattling loose, not when Lina James was all moved on, making a success of things. No. She bit her lips together. There was no one to blame here, except her father. *Daddy!* Only him.

She drew Kaden back into focus, feeling warmth surging into her chest. 'I don't know what to say except… thank you.'

He shrugged. 'For what?'

'For scaling a wall. Breaching a yew hedge. For caring about where I was.'

His eyes clouded, then turned steely. 'Did you think I wouldn't?'

She felt a pang inside. 'No, of course not…' The doubts had crept in afterwards, hadn't they, the fear taking root, growing firm and strong, pushing out everything else. But telling him that when he was looking at her like this was impossible. Rather, he needed to hear something good from her, something equal, so he'd know that she'd been confounded too.

She tipped the dregs of her coffee into the dirt, then fastened her eyes on his. 'When they came for Dad, Mum confiscated my phone. That's why you couldn't reach me, but in any case, she'd made me promise not to contact friends, or the agency, and especially not you.' He was opening his mouth to speak but she knew the question that was coming. 'She was worried about my phone being hacked. She was worried about your family being associated, being brought down in some way through us.'

A shadow lengthened behind his eyes, and then he nodded an acknowledgement.

She felt relief unwinding, tears prickling. His understanding meant the world. 'Mum was so strong, Kade. She had all Dad's crap to cope with, but she was set on protecting me, set on limiting the damage. I had no choice. I had to do what she said, even though I didn't want to, because I knew that whatever I was feeling, however stunned, and angry, and heartbroken I was, it was a million times worse for her.'

'I'm sure.' His eyebrows flickered and then his gaze shifted past her, disappearing to some inner place.

I'm sure.

She put her cup down. What did that mean? It seemed inadequate, somehow, but then again, what was she expecting? *It must have been awful for you all, Maddie. I understand completely. Of course you had to disappear. And it's fine that you didn't message, or call, ever. I'm cool with that.*

Her heart thumped a dull beat. He was rigid. Staring at nothing. So close and yet so far. She felt her insides twisting. What a mess. What a total, utter mess. Her heart thumped, then missed. She could feel absence expanding, her throat starting to close.

Oh, no.

The familiar darkness was coming, threading through her veins, drawing the tightness in. She gasped, trying to breathe, trying to stay calm, but the spots were starting, dancing before her eyes, and her lungs were locking.

Please no.

She went for the pendant, gripping it hard, pushing back.

Focus! Smooth. Smooth. Smooth. You are alive. You are here. You are fine.

She went to swallow but her throat wouldn't work.

Come on! Breathe! Breathe!

'Hey...' A warm hand closed around her arm. 'Are you okay?'

Kaden's eyes swam into focus, wide, full of concern, then blurred.

Breathe!

'Maddie...' His voice was low, urgent, bending towards panic.

Her heart jarred. She couldn't have him panicking too. It was bad enough that she was having an attack. She dragged in air through her nose, felt her lungs sticking, then opening, taking it in, letting it out, settling, everything settling, heart, pulse, head, stars. She swallowed, breathing. Just breathing. The cicadas were trilling again, and Kaden's eyes were reaching in, and there was a delicious sensation of warm fingers at her nape, stroking, sending tingles shooting through her veins.

You are alive. You are here. You are fine.

'Maddie?' Copper light, blazing. 'Maddie, talk to me.'

She blinked, swallowing again. 'I'm fine.'

'Are you?'

His head was so close to hers she could feel his hair tickling.

'Yes.' She inhaled again, pushing air into every recess. 'It just happens sometimes.'

'Panic attack?'

'Yes.' It felt so good, letting it out. 'It's what I was about to tell you about the pendant—'

'Being a lifeline?' His fingers stilled for a beat and then they were travelling downwards from her nape, palming slow lulling circles.

'Yes...' She could feel her focus sliding, her eyes wanting to close. 'The attacks started coming after I moved to Paris. At first, I didn't know what was happening. I'd be out walking or sitting in a café and then suddenly I'd be gasping for air, paralysed, terrified. It got that I was too scared to go out.' Renée's face filtered in, kind, careworn. 'Then one day Renée came home with the pendant. She said I should try to use it as an anchor.'

Kaden let her arm go and took the amber drop into his hand, weighing it. 'It's certainly hefty.'

She felt a smile coming. 'It needs to be. It has to do a lot of work. When I start feeling out of whack, if I can make it my centre, then it pulls me back.'

'So if I see you grappling for this, then I should pay attention?'

His hand was so close to her breasts that she could feel its heat, could feel her nipples responding.

'Yes. No.' *Focus.* 'Not always. Not now. I think a lot of the time I touch it because it's there. I hardly know I'm doing it.'

He smiled. 'Well, just in case, I'm going to be keeping my eye on you.' He released it gently, and then he was on the move, vaulting off the hood.

She watched him packing away their cups. *Kaden...* He'd scaled a ridiculously high wall and battled through a yew hedge in his school uniform just to see her. He'd been meticulous about checking for danger before allowing her out of the vehicle, and now he was on panic attack watch. And he hadn't seemed to care about her dad's release, or about his stupid book either, at least not in any way that related to her personally. Her heart contracted. He was the same, the same as he'd always been. Noble, kind, passionate. Perfect.

She felt a burn starting behind her lids and turned away, staring across the *veld*. Had she got everything wrong, built herself a jungle to hide in, staying away when all this time—she felt a sob filling her chest—all this time she could have been by his side, giving him love, being loved—

'Maddie!' The urgency in his voice spun her around. He was in the vehicle holding the two-way, his face bleached. 'A bull elephant just charged Jerry's vehicle. No one's hurt, thank God, but I've got to get back right now.'

'Oh, my God!' The sob in her chest died, adrenalin taking over. She scrambled down and ran round to the passenger seat, clambering in. 'What are you going to do?'

'I'm going to find the elephant.' He started the engine and then they were pulling away fast. 'Posturing is one thing, like the bull we encountered, but this seems to have been spontaneous aggression. Unprovoked. It points to the animal being in pain.'

She gripped the door top hard as he threw the vehicle round a bend. 'But how are you going to find it?'

'The rangers have got the drones up already. By the time we get back, hopefully they'll have got the location down.'

She scanned the *veld*. Expansive, dense with acacia. The dust trails weren't exactly autobahns but at least the going was clear. Driving through the vegetation would surely be far too arduous. She licked the dust off her lips. 'And then what? I mean, how are you going to get to it?'

'In the chopper.'

She felt her eyebrows shooting up. 'You've got a chopper?'

'Of course.' A smile lit his eyes momentarily. 'It's essential out here, the only way to get anywhere quickly. Mostly, I use it for veterinary work.' They slewed around another bend stirring dust. 'So, once I know where this elephant is, I'll dart it from the helicopter, then examine it. With a bit of luck, I'll find something wrong, something I can fix.'

'But you'll have someone with you, right?' She was thinking of the buffalo, how careful he'd been before he'd let her out of the vehicle. In the thick of the *bush-veld*, there could be all kinds of danger lurking: buffalo, lions, leopards. Stinging things, biting things. *Snakes!*

'Step away from the pendant, Mads.'

She felt it between her fingers and let it go quickly.

He was laughing, his eyes pouring out copper light. 'I always go with a team. You don't have to worry.'

Easier said than done. It was great that he was so well set up for getting to the elephant and treating it, but even so, she was going to be counting the seconds till he got back.

CHAPTER SEVEN

'WELL, WELL, WELL. If it isn't the flying vet!' Maddie was smiling, looking fresh and completely lovely in a long brown skirt and vest. 'I heard you found the elephant. Did it go okay?'

'Yes.' He felt a smile coming, partly because of the elephant, but mostly because the sparkle in her eyes was contagious.

'So don't just stand there. Come in.' Her hand was on his arm, tugging gently. 'I want to hear all about it.'

His pulse quivered. Just her hand but the contact was sending lightning bolts through his veins. *Again.* He'd felt them that morning too when she'd been trying to escape his tickling fingers, and again when she'd been sitting next to him on the hood of the Land Cruiser, her warmth seeping through his shirtsleeve. Unforgivably perhaps, he'd even felt a tingle when she'd been having her panic attack, well, not during the actual attack itself—at that point he'd been on the verge of panicking too—but just after, when she'd been calming down, and he'd been stroking that sweet spot at the back of her neck. Truth was, he couldn't stop tingling around her. Never could.

He stepped inside, following her into the sitting room. Same exotic orange scent trailing in her wake as last time, but this time he wasn't dropping in unannounced. This time he was invited. Her note had been waiting for him when he got back. Dinner at her lodge, courtesy of the private chef, an excellent service, she'd said, which he really ought to try for himself. He wasn't going to argue.

'So what would you like to drink?' She was opening the doors of the minibar, giggling a little. 'As you can see, I have everything.'

'Or do you mean you've *had* everything?' He felt a smile tugging at his lips. 'You seem sort of high.'

Her eyes caught his. 'I am high, but it's got nothing to do with alcohol.' And then her expression changed, growing serious. 'I'm just glad you're back, that's all, in one piece.'

He felt his breath going still. The pendant in her fingers as they'd been driving back.

'But you'll have someone with you, right?'

That drop of amber wasn't only a focal point she used to pull herself back from the edge. It was a tell, the thing she touched whenever she was unsure of herself. She was touching it now, lightly. His heart thumped. Because she was telling him, in a roundabout way, that she cared about him, and it was making her nervous. And yet if she still cared, then why had she left him high and dry? He got that her mother had taken her phone away, got why she'd made Maddie promise not to contact him. With the wisdom of maturity, he could understand all that, but what he didn't understand, still, was why she'd stayed away. He felt his stomach tightening. Why had she done that if she cared? He wanted to know, wanted to ask, but Kristopher was coming in, his chef's whites almost as dazzling as his smile.

'Good evening, Mr Barr. Ms James.'

'Good evening, Kristopher.' Was there a second, secret smile going on behind Kristopher's eyes? It felt like it.

Kristopher's gaze shifted to Maddie. 'Just checking that you still want—'

'Yes! Absolutely.' There was a firmness in Maddie's tone, a smile hiding at the corners of her mouth. 'Everything we agreed before, okay?'

Kristopher flicked him a glance, then nodded to Maddie. 'Very good.'

'And we're going to be having a drink first, so we'll be ready to eat in about twenty minutes...' Her eyes came to his. 'Or longer? What do you think?'

'I'm easy.' He could feel a chuckle sitting high in his chest in spite of the thing he wanted to ask. There was something irresistible about the mood in the room, something that was lifting him, carrying him along like a tide. 'Whatever you're cooking up and whenever you want to eat it is fine by me. It's your show.'

Her cheeks filled with a smile. 'Okay.' She turned back to the chef. 'We'll go with twenty minutes.'

Kristopher nodded and then he was turning, disappearing through the door.

'Now, drinks.' Maddie was launching herself at the bar again. 'I'm having a G & T.'

'I'll have the same.' Not his usual drink, but suddenly appealing after the all the dust and grit of the day.

He watched her pouring and mixing, the nimble movements of her smooth, toned arms. She was graceful, effortlessly elegant in her understated outfit. Beautiful. And also suddenly, somehow, right in front of him.

'Here.' She put a clinking glass into his hand, then lifted her own. 'Cheers.'

'Cheers.' He touched his glass to hers. 'First legal gin and tonic—'

'Or...' Her eyes lit. 'We could toast the elephant?'

He felt his lips twitching. 'I think the poor elephant has had a tough enough day already.'

She chuckled. 'You're on form tonight.' She took a sip, then set her glass down, stepping back a little. 'So, tell me all about it.'

'*All* about it?' He felt a smile rising inside. 'Are you sure?'

Her chin lifted. 'Absolutely.'

'All right.' He sipped, taking the moment to enjoy the anticipation in her eyes. 'So, when I got there, the bull was clearly agitated but I couldn't see any obvious injury, so I darted him, and then I found the problem.

'Which was?'

'An abscess on the underside of his dominant tusk. Fortunately, it wasn't huge, but it was dripping pus and—'

'Eugh!'

Right on cue! No one grimaced quite like Maddie. It was why it was so much fun to tease her. He pushed down the smile that was jumping like a flame inside and shrugged a fake apology. 'Sorry! I'll spare you the gory details.' He lifted his glass to his lips, not drinking. 'You don't want to hear about the lancing...and the draining...and the irrigating...' Her head was tilting, her eyes beaming out a warning. He felt his smile breaking free. 'And you especially don't want to hear the details of how we medicate...' She was coming towards him now, narrowing her eyes into his, a smile curving at the corners of her mouth. He felt a gleeful spark exploding inside. 'How we have to clear out the rectum so we can shove a handful of antibiotic paste inside.'

She stopped in her tracks. 'You've had your hand up an elephant's bottom?'

'Not only my hand.' He couldn't hold in his laughter, couldn't resist miming the action. 'It's more of a whole arm action, to get the antibiotic right up there.'

'All that way?' She recoiled ever so slightly. 'Sheesh! You had a glove on, right?'

'It's more like a wader for the arm.'

Her eyes darted to his shirtsleeve. 'Very noble.'

She was cracking him up. 'Maddie, this is a different shirt, and yes, I have showered.'

She flicked him a mischievous smile. 'That's a relief!' And then her expression softened. 'Seriously though, I think you *are* noble. I'm so impressed with what you're achieving here. You're doing what you always wanted to do, helping animals, working in conservation. It must feel so good.'

The naked admiration in her eyes was touching. He felt its warmth reaching inside, filling him up. 'It does, but then writing an award-winning travel blog must feel pretty good too.'

Her eyes flickered, registering the compliment. 'It has its moments, although nothing that comes close to, you know...' She grimaced, mimicking him with the antibiotic, and then she shrugged a little. 'Compared to yours my life is rather trivial.'

He felt a pang in his chest. Is that what she really thought? He searched her gaze, trying to see behind it, but she broke free suddenly, folding her arms.

'Anyway, what's the prognosis, doctor?'

She was moving him along, but he couldn't stop his

wheels spinning. How could she think her life was trivial? He didn't understand everything, but the fact was she'd had her life ripped away and she'd built another, one that by any standards was a success, in spite of her father and in spite of her fears and her panic attacks. She was stronger than she knew. More determined, more wonderful—

'Kaden.' Her voice broke in. 'Will the elephant be all right?'

He collected himself. 'It should be. We'll keep an eye on him.' He took a sip from his glass and set it down. 'I'll probably have to knock him out again in a week or so to give him a check-up, but he certainly seemed much calmer when we left, and calm is good.' He felt a cold weight shifting. 'Calm doesn't upset travel writers.'

'Oh, my God!' She was blinking. 'Can you believe that I of all people had forgotten about the journalists? Are they okay?'

He swallowed hard, trying to ignore the queasiness that was making a home in his stomach. 'One of them was fine. She has experience of game drives. She said she knows this kind of thing can happen.' His stomach roiled. 'The other one was a little less stoic.'

'Meaning?'

Concern in her eyes, tinged with faint alarm. His stomach clenched. Why had he even mentioned it? Because he was quietly freaking out, because he'd wanted to tell someone who got him, someone who knew that the last thing he'd ever do was play fast and loose with the safety of his guests. But it was a bad move. Selfish. He couldn't finish, couldn't tell her about the reception he'd got from Gerhardus Du Plessis. It would only feed her phobias, and besides, he was probably reading too much into it. Of course Du Plessis had been shaken. Of course he'd needed to vent, and who better to vent at than the actual owner of the game reserve? In the heat of the moment that was what people did. God, it was not as if he was a stranger to a spot of venting himself. And Du Plessis was bound to have calmed down by now because that's also what people did. Hell, through the haze of a champagne glow, he might even be finding some perspective, coming to view the whole incident as a bit of an adventure, something to dine out on.

He inhaled carefully. It was all going to be fine. Not worth worrying himself about, and definitely not worth worrying Maddie about, not when she was looking at him like this, her fingers busy again with that damn pendant. He was going to have to bat away fast, make light of it, for her sake.

He arched his eyebrows in the way that had always used to make her smile. '*Meaning* that I'm down one magnum of Dom Pérignon.'

'Ahh!' Her lips pressed together. 'Do you think it'll work?'

He felt a dull ache starting at the base of his skull. Right now, he didn't care if the sweetener worked or not and he definitely didn't want to devote another second to thinking about it or talking about it because it was killing the buzz. He wanted to see Maddie happy and smiling again, not taking on his woes. She obviously had some sort of surprise planned and *that* was the important thing, the only thing that mattered. How was he going to get them back into that happy zone? And then he knew.

He pressed his lips together. 'Who knows if it'll work?' He made a show of walking towards the door.

'I'm way more interested to know what's going on in the kitchen.'

Quick as a flash, she blocked him, her eyes glinting. 'Oh, no, you don't!'

He felt laughter percolating. Way to restore the buzz.

He arched his eyebrows. 'Oh, yes, I do.' He faked left, went right, but instantly her hands were around his arm, holding him back.

'I *said*, no, you don't.' She was giving him a laser stare, tightening her grip.

He stilled, staring back, feeling his breaths coming short and quick. In a few moments the light in her eyes would change. Trust would filter in and then—

'I'm not letting you go.' Her gaze was gleeful, unswerving. 'I see you, Kaden Barr. I know what you're up to. But I'm older now.' One eyebrow slid up. 'Wiser.'

The pressure of her fingers increased and suddenly the lightning bolts were back, taking off, crackling through his veins, sending heat pulsing into his groin. *Oh, no.* He was getting hard, very obviously hard. But he couldn't make himself move. It was too tantalising, being tethered to this moment, feeling time stretching, everything slowing down, funnelling into this space, this aching, blissful space. Was she feeling it too, the lightning, the pulsing, the wanting? Yes. Oh, yes. He could see it starting, just like old times, that haziness coming into her eyes, the small silent movements of her mouth, her lips parting—

'Ms James.'

The two words hung in the air, dangling on and on, and then somehow—*somehow*—Maddie was moving, gliding effortlessly over to where Kristopher was standing, her voice a warm bright ring. 'Are we good?'

'One minute to go.' Kris's eyes flicked to his, then fixed on Maddie again. 'Are you still eating outside?'

'Yes.' She turned, trapping him in a mischievous gaze. 'You okay with that?'

He nodded, willing his blood to pump in reverse, willing Kristopher's gaze not to drift any lower than his face. 'Of course.'

'Good.' She came towards him, skirt swirling, then breezed on past. 'Come on, then, let's go sit.'

She was killing him.

He followed her outside. No dining table. No chairs. Just the hurricane lamps throwing their warm glow over the decking and the L-shaped rattan sofa unit with its low square table on which there were two napkins, two glasses and a bottle of red, uncorked.

Not what he'd been expecting. He met her eye. 'What is this?'

'Informal dining.' She twinkled a smile, then picked up the wine bottle and put it into his hands. 'I thought it'd be just the thing after a long day spent doing unmentionable things to an elephant. Will you pour?'

He felt a slow spreading warmth, a smile unwinding inside. So nice being with her. So easy, so familiar. But also, confusing as hell. And there wasn't even space right now to sort out his thoughts because she was looking at him, expecting him to do something useful with the wine.

'Sure.' He glanced at the bottle. 'Are you okay with this?'

'Absolutely.' She was settling herself onto a sofa, drawing her legs up. 'I have a wider range these days, but in any case, this is about you and what you like.' Her voice dipped low, softening. 'I know you chose the Sauvignon Blanc for me the other night.'

His heart pulsed. What to say? He had. She knew it. So many things they knew about each other and so many they didn't. Like why she hadn't come back. But letting that thought coil tight was going to spoil things. She was making an effort here, for him. He needed to pin himself to the present and enjoy it.

He poured and set the bottle down. 'You're right, I did choose it for you—'

And then a flash of white caught the edge of his vision. He turned, and suddenly all the tightness inside was loosening. Was this real? Was Kristopher actually coming out with an enormous, sizzling pizza?

He felt his belly starting to vibrate, a chuckle filling his throat. Had Maddie asked his Michelin-starred chef to make pizza? Only she could have done that. Only her. He looked over. She was giggling, her eyes dancing, full of irresistible light.

'What are you thinking, Kade? Good idea or epic fail?'

Maddie! Too funny. Too perfect.

He felt a fresh smile bursting onto his cheeks. 'Good idea. Definitely!'

'Well, that properly hit the spot.' Kaden was topping up their glasses, still smiling like a kid at Christmas.

'I thought it might...' His chef, his ingredients, but still organising it had felt good, had felt like she was giving him something back for all his kindness, for the way he was protecting her from the other journalists even though he didn't think they were a threat, for the way he'd held her when she'd been upset, both times. But it wasn't only to thank him for all the things he was doing for her. It was also for that stricken look he'd had on his face when Jerry had radioed in the news. In that moment she'd felt the weight of the responsibility he was carrying, the immensity of Masoka and everything that went with it. As soon as she'd got back, doing something nice for him was all she'd been able to think about, to bolster him, to show him that she was in his camp. And if it hadn't been for the journalist who apparently wasn't being stoic, then maybe it would have been working too. As it was, she could see a journalist-shaped shadow hovering at his back, and she wasn't convinced that the champagne he'd sent was going to chase it away. Or maybe that was just her. Maybe other travel writers did accept 'gifts,' in which case, maybe everything would be all right.

'Why?' He was lifting up her glass, holding it out. 'Have I been walking around with pizza-hungry eyes?'

She felt the brief scorch of his fingertips as she took it. 'Not exactly, but you always used to crave pizza after rugby, and it struck me that wrestling an elephant was likely to be a bit of a scrum, so, you know, it figured.'

'Intuitive!' He put his glass to his lips, smiling. 'Funnily enough, I can't remember the last time I had pizza.'

'Me neither.' She smiled to mask a little sinking feeling. 'Most of the time it's fine dining.'

His eyebrows flashed. 'Knives and forks.'

'Yes, lovely food but…' She didn't want to dampen the mood but there was something about sitting here with him in the mellow glow of the lamps that was making her want to talk, and maybe he wasn't interested, maybe that's why he'd hardly asked her anything about herself, but right now she didn't care. She wanted to talk to him like she'd used to, letting her cracks show, because he was safety, the one she'd always been able to talk to. She put her glass down. 'But I miss this, you know. Lounging in comfy clothes, eating pizza…' She felt her ribs tightening. Did she dare to push the thought over the line, say it out loud? His eyes were narrowing into hers, interested, gently prompting. She took a breath. 'I miss having someone to eat pizza with.'

'Someone?' For a long moment his eyes held her and then slowly his face stiffened. 'What on earth am I supposed to do with that?'

Her heart stumbled. Pain in his eyes, *finally*, bright, and obvious. Is this what she wanted, is this what she was about, goading him, prodding the sore spot to see how deep it went? She felt a filtering darkness, something stirring. Yes. *Yes!* Having a showdown hadn't been part of the plan but somehow half a bottle of Pinot Noir had brought her here and there was no going back now. She didn't want to. She wanted to face this, had to know. She had to measure what she'd done to him because otherwise how could she ever make amends, put them back together again? She swallowed hard. Because that's what she was thinking about, wasn't it? Fixing them. Subconsciously, it's why she'd put on her flirty jumpsuit that first night, why she'd provoked him into tickling her when they'd been watching the dogs. Everything she'd done was about getting behind his gaze to see what the chances were of putting things right.

She ran her eyes over his face. But that thought had only suggested itself because of what he was projecting. It wasn't just her. He was driving things too, responding to her cues. That game of tag he'd started before dinner, heat in his eyes, that loaded moment. God knows, if he'd been cool and distant from the outset, if he hadn't pulled her into his arms in that lovely warm way at the airstrip, she'd have been sitting in her Lina James box right now instead of sitting with him here under a star-lit sky. So it wasn't all her. He was here. She was here. And maybe right now he was angry but that was okay. He had the right to be.

'I mean, seriously...' His tongue travelled across his lower lip. 'What do you want me to say?' He lifted his chin, mouth twisting. 'Am I supposed to feel sorry for you?'

Her heart clenched. His eyes were wet at the edges. *Her fault.* She'd caused him this pain, and she was going to take it all, everything he needed to lay at her door. She'd see him through to the other side because on the other side there was love. She could feel it and that's the only thing that mattered.

She took a breath, tightening her gaze on his. 'No—'

'Because I was there for you, Mads, always. I *was* your someone, but you...' He was shaking his head now, twisting his glass back and forth. 'You didn't come back. You didn't give me a chance.' His eyes emptied. 'Why? Why didn't you come back? All those plans we made...' His voice was cracking, tearing her heart out. 'Uni... Edinburgh...not to mention the small matter of for ever. Remember that?' His gaze sharpened. 'Remember?'

Hiding under forbidden daytime covers, that so soft light and the warm smell of his skin, their bodies mingling, tangling, the taste of his mouth, seeing nothing beyond the glow in his eyes, words rising, floating free in whispers.

'This is for ever, Kade, you and me. For ever...'

Suddenly his glass was clattering down, and he was getting up, his voice mounting. 'I would have walked through fire and back for you, do you know that? Do you?' He was grinding out words, leaving her no space to interject. 'Wasn't it clear enough? Didn't I say it often enough? I mean, *how* couldn't you have known?' His eyes were loud, practically pulsing into hers, and then suddenly they were filling again. 'You didn't have to be alone. You could have had me...' And then his gaze was retreating, his voice shading back to bitterness. 'But I guess I wasn't enough...'

She felt a black hole opening up inside, her organs disappearing into it. How could he think that?

Because you let him.

'Let's just get it over with, shall we.' He moved to the veranda rail, wanting to distance himself no doubt. 'You found someone else in Paris, didn't you?' His hands flapped. 'And you figured that, what?' Bruised eyes blazed into hers. 'Kaden's a clever guy. He'll work it out for himself eventually?'

'No!' Her heart cracked. 'I didn't... I never...'

Breathe! You are here, you are alive, you are going to fix this.

She got up and went to stand in front of him, loading her gaze with everything, loading her voice. 'You're so wrong.' His eyebrows flickered faintly. 'I can see why you think it but you're wrong. There was no one in Paris.' She could feel her sinuses growing hot. 'There's never been anyone.'

'Never?' His throat was working. 'No one?'

'No.'

'I don't understand.' His fingers went to his eyebrow. 'So if there wasn't...then why? Why the hell...' He seemed to run out of words. The rest was in his eyes, shock, confusion, incredulity and…a flicker of something that looked like warmth coming back.

She felt that warmth turning her inside out. Why indeed? Because looking at him now, all the reasons she'd clung to so tightly didn't make sense. But then maybe making sense didn't matter any more. What was important was talking. Explaining.

She took a breath. 'Believe me, ever since I got here, I've been asking myself the same question.' His lips parted slightly, and she felt a tug, a stab of desperate longing. 'I see you now, the same as you always were, but… I got it into my head that you wouldn't want…'

'What…?' Suddenly his hands were on her shoulders, warm and gentle, his eyes reaching in. 'What wouldn't I have wanted?'

She felt a burn starting. 'I thought you wouldn't want to have anything to do with me, because of Dad, because of your family being so upright.' He was frowning, shaking his head, but she had to finish. 'I was so ashamed, Kade. I still am. Overnight Dad was a stranger—a criminal—and Mum was telling me not to trust anyone, not to contact anyone. All of a sudden, I was in Paris living with a woman I'd only ever met twice before, and I couldn't talk to you…' The burn was scalding her eyes now, prickling. 'I couldn't see you. My heart was breaking, and I couldn't *do* anything, *change* anything. And then, after Dad was sent down, I don't know, everything felt so hard, the thought of slotting back in. I wanted to see you, but I just couldn't face you, in case you'd changed, in case you didn't want me.'

'No, Maddie, no.' His voice was cracking. 'How could you have ever thought—'

'I was so knocked back, that's how! I couldn't see any

good in the world. Just getting out of bed in the morning was an effort. I wasn't sleeping. I still don't. It would have killed me if you'd given me the cold shoulder, Kade. It seemed easier to go forward, to become a different person, than to go back—' his eyes were swimming, making hers swim too, making a sob swell in her throat '—but I never stopped loving you, you've got to believe me, so don't ever think that, okay, just don't!'

'Oh, God, Madeleine, Maddie…' He was looking at her as if he couldn't take enough of her in and then suddenly his hands were cupping her face and he was lowering his mouth to hers.

She felt her breath stopping and then her heart. Same tingle, same warm perfect lips, same clean skin smell, but there was that soft rub of stubble now, that extra height, that irresistible manliness. Her heart struck up again. Was this happening too fast? Should she be resisting? Maybe, but she couldn't think of a reason to, not while his lips were moving over hers, teasing hers apart, making heat rise and liquid pool. She didn't want to resist. What she wanted was exactly this—him—right here, right now, with every fibre of her being.

She caught his face, kissing him back, parting her lips for his tongue, feeling its wet heat working its magic with every firm stroke, bringing her core to tingling life, her nipples, her skin, the roots of her hair. She could feel her body trembling, her pulse rushing, then slowing, then pulsing thick and hot. He smelt so good, felt so good. She couldn't get enough. She slid her hands down his neck, over his shoulders, felt him responding, pulling her closer, pressing himself hard against her so she could feel every hot throbbing inch of him.

'I. Have. Missed. You. With. All. Of. My. Heart.'

He was filling her mouth with the words as his hands roamed, caressing her breasts, circling her nipples, then sliding down, one hand under her buttocks, the other between her legs.

She went for her waistband, but his hands were already there, tugging it down. The linen whispered against her legs as it fell, and then his hand was back, his palm hot, moving slowly. She closed her eyes, clinging to his shoulders as he slid his hand inside her G-string, whimpering as his fingers began to move. He groaned a low groan, stubble grazing her ear. 'You feel so sweet.' His fingers zoned in, lingering, circling. 'So incredibly wet.' She felt her pulse spike, an explosion of heat in her veins. Teasing fingers. Well-timed words. He was killing her softly. Like he always did. She could feel her control going, her senses skewing. It was too sweet. Too bitter. Bittersweet. But somehow words were forming, coming out.

'Don't stop, Kade, please don't stop…'

But he was doing what he always used to do, delivering just enough to keep her hanging on a pulse beat, dangling, and then he released her, finally, and she was tipping over the edge, seeing stars, shaking around his fingers, trembling, then falling back, coming down.

'Oh, God, Maddie.' He was kissing her again, softly now, deeply, making her head spin all over again.

'Kaden…' She put her hands to his face, wanting to say something, but somehow words weren't enough.

His lips came to hers again. 'It's okay, I know.' And then he was leaning away, hazy-eyed, smiling. 'Let's take this inside.'

CHAPTER EIGHT

KADEN BLINKED AWAKE. Sharp fingers of sunlight were poking through the shutters, prodding at the walls. So different to the pale glow of dawn. He turned his head, felt warmth blooming in his chest. Maddie was asleep, hair mussed, a slight flush in her cheeks. No wonder. They'd seen in daybreak with a last, slow assault on each other's bodies before finally curling up, exhausted.

He shifted onto his side so he could look at her. Sweet lips, that feathery sweep of her lashes. Seeing her like this, lost to the world, her expression peaceful, it was hard to believe she was an insomniac. His belly pulsed. Peter Saint James had a lot to answer for, the treasury man with the opposite of the Midas touch, laying waste to hearts, minds, lives. Maddie had been so full of light and life, and now... He slid his hand across the pillow touching her hair with one finger. She was still full of light and life, but she was also damaged. Wary, fearful, so knocked back that she'd thought he wouldn't want to see her, that he'd have turned his face away if she'd re-appeared. Wrong, as far as he was concerned, but still, there was some truth in what she'd said, wasn't there? He only had to think of his own father and that miserable Eurostar journey back to London...

'Look, son. I know you think you're in love, but you mustn't look for her—do you hear me? You mustn't. We need to keep away from that family. There's a lot at stake. God, Kaden, we've had Peter and Natalie over for dinner because of you kids, but now they want to question me too. "Routine," they're calling it. They're going to be asking me if Peter ever alluded to any of his property dealings, if he ever mentioned any names...'

Which, thank goodness, he hadn't, but Dad's face had been grey all the same, and he hadn't deserved to be burdened like that, not when he and Mum had only been trying to be friendly with Maddie's parents because of *him*, because Maddie was his girlfriend and had been for two years by that time.

But if his own father, a good man—decent—had been telling him to forsake Maddie, then there'd have been others, withdrawing, making polite excuses. Facing that, enduring that, after everything she'd already been through, when her anxiety levels were ramped so high that she was having panic attacks, must have felt impossible for her. He got it. At least, in his head he did.

He rolled over, staring up into the white gauze of the mosquito nets. Last night he hadn't been thinking. Emotion had swept in and taken him over. There she'd been, crying, telling him that she'd never stopped loving him, that there'd never been anyone else, and he'd cracked like a shell, lapped it all up. It had been impossible not to kiss her, impossible not to want to love her. And it had felt so right. All night long it had felt right between them. No holding back, bodies and words flowing. *I love you. I love you*, they'd said to each other over and over. His heart twisted. But she'd said it before, hadn't she, then stayed away, and even though he understood her reasons all the way to his bones, one hundred percent, there was a small voice in his head whispering that if she'd loved him enough she'd have come back to him, whatever it took, that just because she was saying it now didn't mean she wouldn't leave him again.

Cruel voice.

He couldn't listen. Didn't want to.

He eased himself out of the bed, pulled on his jeans and slipped through the doors onto the veranda.

The sun was well up. Warm. Tempered by a faint breeze. He glanced at his bare wrist. His watch was inside somewhere, along with his shirt, and his shoes, and his heart. *Oh, God!* What to think? How to feel? Last night had been sublime, feeling her again, so close, her fingers trailing, the sweet taste of her mouth. When he'd been walking here yesterday, he'd never imagined that he'd still be here this morning, never in a million years have imagined that he and Maddie would spend the night making love, feeling so present, so alive, crying out with it, not caring, because they'd always been vocal, always let it all out. But now what?

He went to the rail, lifting his gaze to the treetops. What did he want? In spite of his doubts, in spite of everything, did he still want her? His heart stopped, then started again. Yes, with every beat of his heart, but there was so much to consider. In many ways they were the same as they'd always been, but they were both different too. Twelve years older, twelve years different. She had her Lina James life, lonely perhaps, but still it was the life she'd made. She had a diary full of commitments and obligations. And he was here in the back of beyond building the dream he'd invented to replace her, but this dream was his life now, and not just his. He had his staff's lives to think about too, obligations of his own, projects on the go. Every cent was invested, every ounce of his energy.

Would Maddie ever want this? Would Masoka suit her, the wildlife, the insects? Would this life appeal to the girl who'd stumbled backwards because of a tadpole? And if it wasn't the place for her, could he see himself giving it all up for her? An ache bounced between his temples. So many questions. How could he even begin to answer them when the world was skewed on its axis, when his heart and his mind and his body were reeling?

'Hello, you.' The warm shock of her arms going round him gave way to a different kind of heat as her breasts melted against his back. He felt the soft press of her lips on his shoulder blade. 'You left me.'

He swivelled to face her, feeling his breath catch. Still mussed, still naked, even more beautiful than he remembered. He pulled her in. 'I left you to sleep.'

'I was sleeping, wasn't I?' She smiled up at him. 'I can't remember the last time I slept till after ten.'

Not his usual thing either but since Maddie had arrived, nothing had felt remotely usual. He kissed her nose. 'Not wanting to rain on your parade or anything, but we didn't go to sleep until six. We've had four and half hours, tops!'

She tossed her head coquettishly as if she still had her Tresses mane. 'And yet I feel so good.' Mischief darted through her gaze. 'There's clearly some strange alchemy at work.'

Love in her eyes. Unmistakable. Real.

He felt his heart lifting, a smile breaking loose. 'You can call it that if you like.'

'By any other name, huh?' Her eyebrows flickered, and then she was sliding her hands up and around his neck. 'So anyway, what does a girl have to do around here to get some breakfast?'

Those eyes. Those lips.

'Well…' He bent his head, tasting her mouth for a long, tingling moment. 'The dining room is closed now so a girl would have to order room service—'

Except that would mean Precious delivering a tray along with more of those deep knowing looks, the ones she'd been giving him ever since he'd asked her to deliver Maddie's note. And then, of course, Kristopher would be the one preparing the breakfast, Kristopher who'd seemed to be smiling in stereo last night. And what about Chanda? And Jerry? They'd hear about it, not that it would be breaking news because they both knew that he never took anyone on a one-to-one game drive.

Basically, his whole staff must know by now that there was something special about Lina James. They'd pop if they knew the truth, but he couldn't tell them anything yet because nothing was resolved. It's not as if he and Maddie had spent the night talking. He held in a sigh. But they needed to, needed to talk, and to listen to each other. It seemed heavy in a way, getting into all that after just one night, but then they *were* heavy, weren't they, heavy with history, and for him, there was that tiny speck of insecurity that he'd like not to be feeling. Talking was the answer, but maybe not here, under the watch of kind but curious eyes. Somewhere else. Somewhere where it would be just the two of them with a skeleton staff who were used to keeping themselves invisible. He felt a smile coming. Lucky for him he had such a place.

He kissed her again.

'—or we could go out for breakfast.'

'Out?' Her eyebrows flickered. 'Out where?'

He felt his lips twitching. 'Somewhere.'

'Intriguing.' She was scrunching her face at him, miming inscrutable. 'And what should I wear for this somewhere breakfast?'

He couldn't hold in a chuckle. 'More than you're wearing at the moment would be fine, at least for the journey.'

She was laughing now, eyes sparkling. 'I don't know what you're planning but I'm getting a good feeling.'

Good feelings. Warm feelings. They were the feelings he was getting too, the feelings he wanted to run with, to believe in, but talking was the only way he was going to get there, and they needed to be at Tlou for that. The sooner the better.

'Hold on to that thought.' He freed himself from her arms, backstepping towards the doors. He'd call ahead, ask the staff to prepare fruit salad and pancakes. She'd always loved pancakes, with maple syrup, and a drizzle of cream. And he'd ask them to find a jug too, a nice big one!

Her lips quirked. 'You're looking mighty pleased with yourself all of a sudden.'

He grinned. 'It's probably got something to do with the view…'

'Oh…' She pivoted a little, arching her back, eyeing him over her shoulder. 'You mean this view?'

Long legs. Smooth, shapely buttocks. He felt heat stirring in his groin, a powerful urge to sweep her up and take her back to bed. But going back to bed wouldn't get them to Tlou, would it? And that's where they needed be. At Tlou, there'd be plenty of time for everything, loving, talking. God, after all these years it felt like a dream come true, the prospect of being alone with her, just the two of them.

He forced his eyes upwards to meet her teasing gaze. 'Exactly that view, as well you know.' She was going to be so thrilled with Tlou, the whole *Out of Africa* thing, but he wasn't going to tell. Keeping her dangling was so much more fun. 'You get ready. I'll see you out front in twenty.' He stepped back, faking an afterthought. 'Oh, and you'll need an overnight bag.'

She looked over, felt her heart skipping for the hundredth time. Kaden was perfection. Thick copper hair blowing back from his forehead, shades perched on that fine straight nose, lips just the right amount of full, lips that had always fitted to hers so perfectly. What was he up to? Did she even care? She felt a sudden luxurious warmth unfurling inside. No, because whatever he was planning was making him smile and his smile was more than enough. Contagious. She could feel it aching in her own cheeks. Her body was aching too, in the sweetest way, because of him. She bit down on her lip, feeling a bubble of happiness fizzing through her veins. Had she really just spent an entire night making love with this gorgeous man, this man who also happened to be the love of her life? Yes, with bells on! Those tanned hands, loose on the wheel; maybe they did venture into some unsavoury places, but it's the last thing she'd been thinking about last night when they'd been moving over her body, lingering, caressing. Those hands. Those fingers. They still seemed to know everything about her, how to bring her to the brink, how to tip her over the edge. Muscle memory.

She felt a quiver low down in her belly and looked away, stretching her gaze to the *veld*. Thinking about clever hands was only stirring her up, and getting herself all stirred up while they were bouncing along to Kaden's mysterious breakfast venue was pointless. Better to be concentrating on the waving yellow grass, and the scrub, and the wildlife, all things she needed to write about in her blog piece, which was still there to do, even though things had taken a turn.

She lifted her eyes to the sky. So wide. So blue. Had it looked quite this wide, quite this blue, before? Had the herd of giraffe she'd seen from Jerry's Land Cruiser looked quite as graceful as the animals that were busy lolloping through the acacia beside them? No, and no, and no. Today everything was looking better, sounding better, feeling better, because of Kaden. *Oh, God!* How could she focus on the landscape when there was this feeling inside? Love, topped up so it was brimming, spilling out. Impossible to hide, impossible to hold in. Last night, she'd laid it all out so he would know that she loved him, had never stopped loving him. And all through the night she'd told him over and over again. And he'd said it back, eyes blazing with it. *'I love you, Maddie.'*

She looked over again, feeling warmth surging. Were they really falling back into place? It's what it felt like, but there was still so much to say and to work through. Saying *I love you* to Kaden was easy because it was true, but it didn't mean that everything else would be easy. Where did they go from here? This place was his life, his passion. Asking him to share it with her, asking him to let her in on the strength of one blissful night, felt audacious, even if it's what she wanted. Yes, he seemed to have understood why she'd let him go, but the hurt he'd poured out to her last night had deep roots. It had been there in his eyes, and there'd still be fragments left, words jumbling in a corner in his mind saying that in spite of

everything she *should* have contacted him, that her love
for him should have trumped everything. Nothing she
hadn't thought herself, tortured herself with, over the
years. But thinking about it now was too hard. Hard
thoughts were nothing next to the allure of just diving
in and drowning, splashing around in all the love, and
the joy, and the happiness, feeling the bright zing of it,
zinging the bright feel of it. No sleepwalking here, not a
chance! She felt a smile rising inside. Probably not much
sleep ahead either but what did sleep matter when her
senses were trilling.

*You are here. You are alive. You are safe. You're in
love.*

'You okay?' His eyes caught hers over the top of his
shades.

She felt a tingle prickling to life, travelling up her
spine. Something in his gaze was conjuring a memory...
those limousines...those long rides home...the game
they'd used to play... Her pulse skipped. Did she dare?
She felt her pulse skipping again, then drumming, beating fast. It's not as if there was anyone to see them, and
maybe he wouldn't bite anyway. Her belly clenched. But
if he did...if he did, then it was no less than she deserved.
She was twelve hungry years behind the curve. That was
a lot of catching up.

She pressed her lips together, holding in a smile. 'I
think so.'

A familiar light ignited behind his gaze. 'You *think*
so?' His hand fell from the wheel, landing on her thigh.
'What does that mean?'

She felt her insides vibrating and tightening at the
same time. Laughter wanting to come and something

else too. She pushed up her sunglasses, fastening her eyes on his. 'It means I'm not sure...'

His chin dipped. 'Could I do something to help?' His hand slid upwards, exerting a tantalising pressure. 'I mean, you're a cherished Masoka guest. I want you to be one hundred percent okay and to be absolutely sure about it.'

She bit her lips together hard. She could feel her body responding to his words, to his touch. She shifted a little, detecting wetness between her legs. 'What do you suggest?'

His eyebrows flickered and then suddenly the vehicle was slewing to a stop, bowling dust into the air. He removed his sunglasses, setting them on the dash carefully, and then he sat back, gesturing to his lap. 'I suggest you come to sit here.' His eyes darkened a little. 'Just slide on over.'

She felt a giggle coming. How could she ever have imagined that he wouldn't bite when he always had? She shot a glance at the handbrake. 'It's going to be more of clamber.'

'Here, let me...' In one swift movement strong hands were reaching under her, scooping her up, and before she could blink, she was sitting astride him, feeling the intimate warmth of his thighs beating through the fabric of her skirt. His eyes lit with a smile. 'Hello there.' And then his hands were moving, travelling up her arms to the straps of her vest. He hooked his fingers in, eyes dancing. 'Do we like these?' She felt her breath hitching low down in her throat, and in the far distance, a smile tingling. *Game on!* She shook her head, holding his gaze. His eyes flashed. 'Didn't think so.' He lifted the straps off her shoulders, pulling the garment down, freeing her arms one by one, until she was naked to the waist. She felt her mouth drying, her pulse thundering. 'Comfy?' His gaze was playful, darkening, and then his hands connected with her breasts, his thumbs tracking a slow route over her nipples, once, twice, three times. She felt her breath catching, her back arching involuntarily, white-hot darts arrowing into her core. *Clever thumbs.* She wanted to stay, clinging to the moment, losing herself in it, but that's not how it worked. It was her turn now, to tease him back.

With difficulty she blinked him into focus and locked on, catching her lower lip between her teeth. 'Actually, no…' She moved, keeping the movement small, watching its effect on his face. 'I'm not quite comfy yet…' His lips parted in a low gasp. She shifted again, moving her hips, closing in by degrees until she could feel his full hard length right up against her. 'Oh, dear…' She rocked against him, feeling her pulse responding, thickening, seeing his focus hazing. She exhaled against his forehead, holding in a smile. 'There seems to be something in the way.' She pushed against him again, eliciting a low groan of pleasure that made her insides clench.

'Really…?' His voice sounded tight.

'Yes.' She brushed her lips over his, going for his button, undoing it. 'It might need some further investigation.' She sucked his lower lip into her mouth, feeling him opening, surrendering, feeling her limbs turning to liquid. 'Just this now…' She toyed with the tag of his zip, waiting for a beat before giving it a tug, because rushing had never been part of the game. He let out a heavy sigh as she freed him, a sigh that yanked tight a string of nerves in her core. She stroked him, feeling her focus narrowing. Hot, rigid, silky. He felt so good. She wanted to take him into her mouth, but the steering wheel was behind, trapping her. That left her hands, her fingertips, a little imagination. She stroked the pad of her finger across the liquid tip of him, felt her pulse spiking as an animal noise erupted from his throat. She swallowed hard, doing it again, and again, tormenting him, tormenting herself, until suddenly she couldn't stand it. 'Kade—'

'I hear you.' He started pushing at her skirt, trying to hold it away. 'Can you manage?'

She went for her underwear, felt her knee shearing off the seat. 'I can't…'

'Hang on.' His arm was going round her, holding firm. 'Right, lean.'

She leaned, letting his strength take her, feeling laughter suddenly vibrating through him, which set her off laughing too. He was tugging at her G-string, wrangling it down between fits and bursts, until finally, it twanged over her foot. He gasped against her. 'God, this was so much simpler in the limo.'

She felt another giggle shaking loose. 'You're not quitting, are you?'

'After all this effort?' He was levering her upright again. 'No way! I offered you one hundred percent satisfaction, and I'm going to deliver it.' And then his face fell. Suddenly he was blinking, looking confounded. 'Damn it, Mads, I'm sorry, but I didn't exactly come prepared for extra vehicular activity.'

A good name for their old game.

She twisted, reaching into the footwell for her bag, feeling a little glow of satisfaction. 'Well, lucky for us, I'm a regular Girl Scout. I grabbed some goodies out of the bathroom at the lodge, just in case.'

His face was incredulous. 'In case we got jiggy in the car?'

'Not specifically, but—' she felt a giggle shaking free as she tore the foil and eased the condom over him '—it's been known is all I'm saying.'

His gaze heated, then softened. 'Certainly has. For the record, you're a genius.' And then his mouth was on hers, warm and urgent. 'Time to finish what we started.' She could feel his hands going underneath her, lifting her, steadying her, and then it was easing herself down, feeling her short breaths running out, her awareness narrowing to the deep, delicious connection, the sensation of being two in one. She closed her eyes. Moving could wait. This deep feeling was too heavenly, too warm, too perfectly intimate, to break.

'Look at me, Maddie.' His voice was low, compelling. She opened her eyes into his, felt her breath catching on his molten copper gaze. His thumbs moved over her cheekbones. 'I love you.' And then he was pulling her in, taking her lips, teasing with his tongue, reigniting the flames until she couldn't not move, couldn't not rock. And it was too divine, this slow moving, this pulsing of skin, and heart, this building ache, beating onwards like a drum. And then he was moving too, with her, meeting her, making the ache inside ache more. And his kiss was deepening, his tongue scorching hers, stroking hers to the rhythm of their bodies. She felt a cry filling her lungs from the inside, his body driving into hers, deeper and deeper, pushing her higher and higher onto a sublime wave that wouldn't stop rising. 'C'mon, baby, come on.'

Her breath stopped, her senses spiralling upwards again. His voice always did that, pushing her higher, but it was too much, this hanging, trembling on the edge.

She needed it to stop, needed release. 'Please, Kaden, please...'

His mouth softened against hers momentarily. 'I love you, Maddie.' And then he was pushing, and she could feel herself going, tipping over the edge, everything tingling and clenching, and she could feel him releasing too, his body pulsing into hers, both of them gasping, trembling, holding on tight, shimmering back down to earth. For a long moment there was stillness and closeness and the warmth of his cheek against hers, and then sounds were filtering in, and smells. Dust, sweet grass.

'Wow.' His cheek twitched against her suddenly. 'I was not expecting this.'

She nuzzled in, feeling a smile coming. 'In spite of strong evidence to the contrary, neither was I—'

'I don't mean that.' He produced a low chuckle. 'I mean the audience.'

What?

She yanked up her vest and twisted round, heart going, and then she felt her insides buckling, laughter bubbling. Beyond the hood, a herd of impala was standing, their eyes locked on, ears twitching. She bit down hard on her lips. 'Do you think they saw?'

'Yep.' Kaden was shaking with laughter now, tears running down his face. 'Some of them have got actual popcorn.'

CHAPTER NINE

'I CAN'T BELIEVE that Tlou didn't even cross my mind, not even when you said to bring an overnight bag.' Maddie was trailing her fingers over his chest, tracing little circles. She lifted her head, kissing him softly. 'You've clearly addled my brain.'

He felt a smile unwinding. 'More than your brain, I hope.'

'Oh, yes.' It was a heavily laden, yes, accompanied by a deep, mischievous look. 'Believe me, you've left no stone unturned.' Her lips grazed his again, setting off a jumping jack in his veins. 'I'm addled from head to toe.' She nuzzled her face into his neck. 'You're very good at addling, always were.'

'Right back at you.' Which was why they hadn't set foot out of the tent since breakfast, why the super-king-size with the canopy drawn around—*'more romantic,'* according to Maddie—had been their sole domain for the past four hours.

He ran his fingers along her arm, felt her snuggling in. The problem was that making love with Maddie was the only thing he wanted to do. She made him feel alive, present, not neutral, like Fran. He drew an uncomfortable breath. Poor Fran. What they'd had was nothing to this and he should have known, should never have let it continue. And Fran should have known too. Or maybe Maddie was right. Maybe Fran hadn't noticed because her heart had never properly been his either. Perhaps her heart had always belonged to the dream of Africa. It's what they'd started with after all, what they'd always had in common. Maybe, at least partly, that's where her tears had come from that day. Not crying for him so much as for everything that went with him, the work they were doing together, the passion they shared for the *bushveld* life.

He held in a sigh. Crossed wires, tangled emotions. Too late now to be pondering all that. Now Maddie was back and, no question, his heart was all the way in. He was beyond addled. God, she'd even had him in the Land Cruiser with the impala watching!

He closed his eyes. Limos. Land Cruisers. Whatever. When it came to Maddie, he was a lost cause. Every time she touched him with that look in her eyes, he could feel the tunnel opening up, sucking him in all over again. Maybe this was the phase they had to go through to get to the next one, the one that involved talking and planning a new for ever. It's what he wanted: a new for ever with her, and he wanted to tell her, read her reaction, hear her say it back. It's what he'd brought her here to do, what he'd imagined them doing alongside the loving, but bringing it up was hard. It felt like a too-high step.

He felt a band tightening around his chest. But it did, still, need to be resolved because way off in the distance, several times removed, he could feel his nerves chiming, a cold fear rinsing through his heart. Old hurt breeding new insecurity. How deep was her love? How true? Deep and true enough to see them through this time? That's what he really wanted to ask her, but how could he? It would only put his doubt on show, make her think that he didn't believe the reasons she'd given him for staying away. Good reasons. He could see it. She'd been so young, so uprooted, and the world was cruel. It all made sense, and yet that insecure speck inside kept jumping up, trying to bite him.

Ridiculous though, surely, because there was no reason on earth for her to vanish again. She knew now that he didn't care about Peter's mistakes or about his release from prison or about his shameless cash-in-on-a-scandal book. He'd told her straight that none of it reflected on her. She just had to believe it—believe him—shake off the shame she'd taken onto her own shoulders. She had to believe that she wasn't tainted, wasn't worth less, because of her father.

His heart contracted. She wasn't worth less, but she *was* damaged, fragile in places. It's why he needed to pick a careful path through his doubts, why he needed to find the right way into the *What do we do now?* conversation. He could help her, show her that she was better than her father. He could give her a home, show her the meaning of love and loyalty. All she had to do was let him, but to get to that place, they needed to be digging into the scary stuff, communicating beyond the curtained boundaries of the super-king-size.

He turned to look at her, felt his heart filling. She was sleeping, and…she was here for three more days. Three. More. Days. That was plenty of time. The right moment for talking was bound to arise. He just needed faith, needed to slow himself right down and enjoy the ride, speaking of which—he squinted at his watch—they'd need to be on their way in less than an hour.

He felt a tingle, then a smile was coming. Another surprise, hopefully on point. He couldn't wait to see her face.

Was this actually happening? She felt a smile breaking free, a tingling thrill of happiness. Was she really rising into the air in a basket beneath a towering balloon, a balloon that Kaden was piloting? The burner above her head was roaring, throwing down warmth, and the guys standing by the truck below were laughing and waving, laughing at her openly, because she'd been as excited as a kid from the moment Kaden had pulled up at the launch site. The basket had been on its side at that point, the balloon half filled, the burner going full tilt. Now they were upright and rising fast. The truck and the laughing faces were getting farther away, and the view was expanding. Trees, scrub, red earth, yellow grass and, in the distance, the sun, glowing orange, low in the sky. Heartbreakingly beautiful. And Kaden had planned it, kept it a secret, even kept it secret that he was the pilot—him. It had only clicked after they'd clambered into the basket and the other three guys had stayed where they were. That's when the penny had dropped, along with her jaw.

She turned to look at him. Mischief glinting in his eyes, his smile still twitching with his magnificent surprise. 'Am I forgiven now?'

She felt a tug of guilt. She hadn't exactly jumped for joy when he'd pulled her out of bed. For once she'd been hard asleep, reluctant to move, well, frankly, a bit moany, but he'd paid no attention. He'd plied her with strong coffee and a bag of freshly made *koeksisters* and bundled her into the Land Cruiser, telling her it would be worth it.

She wound her arms around him. 'You're forgiven to the max. The real question is, am I? I was a proper grump.'

He laughed roundly. 'You were, but I was prepared for some hefty grumbling. It's not like we've had a lot of sleep and you never did like being woken up…' One eyebrow ticked up. 'Remember that time after the Kingston Ball…?'

'Oh, God.' She let go of him as the memory surfaced, taking shape. 'When we fell asleep in the pavilion—'

'Starkers under a picnic blanket because we'd been having a little fun.'

She felt a smile coming. 'I remember.' They hadn't bargained on falling asleep afterwards, hadn't bargained on that sudden rattling at the door.

He was shaking his head, chuckling. 'You wouldn't move. You kept telling me to let you sleep and I was panicking big-time, trying to get you to get dressed, thinking it was old man Kingston about to walk in on us.'

Moonlight spilling through tall windows, Kaden's warm limbs suddenly untangling from hers, his low, urgent whispers tickling the edge of her consciousness. *Maddie! Wake up, Maddie!*

'I was tired. I'd had that early shoot, remember, and the punch was aptly named. Knocked me right out.'

'You never could take much alcohol…' A warm, indulgent look came into his eyes. 'Anyway, I managed to get you moving, *eventually.*'

'All for nothing too, if I remember rightly, because by the time we crept out, whoever it was had gone, so we could have stayed put.'

'But not this time.' He reached up, adjusting one of the burner levers. 'I'm guessing you wouldn't have wanted to miss this…'

'Definitely not.' She looked past his eyes and into vast innards of the balloon. Just nylon and hot air holding them aloft, but she felt safe. Always safe with him. She met his gaze again. 'I wouldn't have missed this for the world. It's incredible.'

A smile spread over his face and then his attention shifted. 'Check out the zebras.'

She followed his gaze and felt her breath catch. The animals were galloping, a herd of thirty or so, sleek-flanked, graceful, powdering the dust as they went. 'Are they running away from us, from the balloon, I mean?' Orange and white, with the black Masoka logo blazoned across. From a zebra's point of view probably alarming.

'I don't know, maybe. I can't see any sign of a predator.' He blasted more heat into the balloon and then his eyes came to hers. 'But then zebra spook quite easily, like horses, so it could be anything. Maybe they're just enjoying a canter.'

He looked so confident, so in control.

She turned back to the view. He'd achieved so much in twelve years, becoming a vet, then coming here, taking on this vast wild kingdom, launching what was clearly going to be a profitable business so he could stretch himself further, fund other, worthy endeavours. He'd spared no expense at Masoka, renovating the lodge to the highest degree, building luxury accommodations, and, as for the bush camp... Canvas, yes, but that's where the similarity to camping ended. The bed was vast, made up with impeccable linens, and the outdoor shower was a work of art with its polished copper fittings and a drench head the size of a dinner plate. Meals were freshly prepared and served by a contingent of staff who remained invisible at all other times. There had to be at least three of them, probably eight at the bigger bush camp, and maybe thirty more at the lodge. Guides, chefs, bar staff, housekeepers, managers, cleaners, pool people, spa therapists and beauticians. Kaden was employing a lot of people, and then there were contractors too, the builders who were building the schools and medical centres he was putting into the local communities.

And with all those plates spinning, he'd still, somehow, learned to pilot a hot-air balloon. He was a force of nature, always had been. Full of ideas, full of energy and passion. He'd filled these past twelve years to the brim and there was bound to be more, because Kaden had always been a 'more' kind of guy.

She bit her lips. There was so much to discover in him, so much she wanted to know, but it was going to take time and time wasn't her friend. She was supposed to be leaving in three days. Her stomach clenched. She didn't want to go, but how to say it, how to steer the conversation that way? And even if she managed it, asking to stay felt like a demand she didn't exactly have the right to make, not after having stayed away like she had, causing him all that pain. Not her fault, plenty of reasons, but facts were facts. She *had* hurt him, and now they were in the throes of whatever this was, talking about love, acting like lovers, but the thought of putting a seal on it, even though it's what she wanted, was churning her up inside. What if things went wrong? What if she hurt him all over again?

She felt her heart contracting. She loved him so much. He didn't deserve to be hurt again, and it wouldn't be her intention, ever, but she wasn't the person she'd been. Yes, Kaden was safety. With him she could feel Madeleine Saint James coming back to life, shining bright, but she could also feel the snipped wires and jagged pieces inside, latent panic leaping like a flame. Who was Kaden in love with? The girl she'd been, or the woman she was now? Any conversation about the future had to take account of the woman she was now, but how to do that when she didn't know herself who that woman was. It was all too hard to think about. If only she could stay in this moment, suspended in the dream she'd been living ever since he'd kissed her last night. If this moment could last for ever, then everything would be perfect.

'Mads…' His voice broke into her thoughts. 'What are you thinking?'

Her chest went tight. If only she dared to tell him her actual thoughts, get it over with, but she couldn't. Not yet.

She took a breath and turned to look at him. Eyes full of the sunset, full of warmth. It was a bolstering kind of warmth. She felt the tightness loosening a little, something steadying inside. 'I was just thinking that I still can't get over you with this balloon. I mean, there's got to be a story that goes with it, and then I was thinking that there must be so many stories…' She felt a burn starting behind her lids. 'Things I don't know, all the things I've missed.'

'Hey.' His hand closed over her shoulder. 'It's the same for me, with you.'

The tightness inside flexed, shrinking around a germ of bitterness. 'You haven't missed much where I'm concerned.' A life spent hiding—running—not connecting with anyone or anything. She swallowed hard. 'I'm a cul-de-sac.'

A frown flashed through his eyes. 'No, you're not! You're the strongest person I know. You took a devastating situation and you built back. You turned things around, carved out a career that loads of people would give their eyeteeth for. Queen of the elite travel scene is no small achievement.'

She felt something give. They were the things she told herself all the time to shore herself up but hearing them from Kaden's lips made them seem more real somehow, true even.

His gaze was softening with a smile. 'You're a powerful woman, Maddie. Think about it. You could make or break Masoka with a single well-aimed sentence!'

'I'm not going to break Masoka.'

'Pleased to hear it.' He squeezed her shoulder gently and then his hand went back to the lever above his head. 'Anyway, going for the silver lining, at least we've got plenty to talk about. We should embrace it, get digging and delving.'

Finding silver linings. That was Kaden. Force of nature!

'You're right.' She felt a lightening inside, her smile returning. 'So, honestly, I have to know, why ballooning, because in the whole time I knew you, ballooning never even broke the surface.'

'That's because it was never underneath. It was a total whim.' He blasted the burner briefly. 'When I was at Kruger there were some guys running an operation there. I used to go along sometimes to help them set up because it was something different. They took me up a few times and I loved it, so I found out about piloting, did the training and got myself a licence.'

'Just like that?'

'Yep.' He grinned. 'Then, when I took over here, it seemed like a no-brainer to put ballooning on the menu, not that I pilot the excursions. The guys who brought it out for us run the show on a day-to-day basis, but with a bigger basket. I just fly for fun in this little picnic basket.'

'I love your picnic basket. It's cosy.' And then suddenly she couldn't not slide her arms around him, couldn't not let her admiration flow free. 'You're quite something, Kaden Barr. Proud father to wild dog pups, intrepid vet, pilot of the skies and—' she couldn't resist '—red hot in the sack, as well as in at least two different types of vehicles.'

He laughed. 'What can I say?'

A spark of mischief flared. 'Have you ever—'

'No!' Instantly his hands were on her arms, putting her away from him. 'Don't even think about it. The balloon pilot's handbook is very clear about what is and isn't allowed in flight.'

'Okay.' She smothered a giggle and turned. 'I suppose I'll just have to content myself with this astonishing view.'

'Perfect! Hold that thought.'

She ran her eyes over the landscape. What a thought to hold, drifting through the sky with Kaden, birds gliding below, impala scattering with white tails flashing and, beyond, a small group of giraffes flowing sedately through a loose stand of thorn trees. She felt her heart swelling, a sigh escaping. 'It's just like *Out of Africa*. I can almost hear the score playing...'

And what else...? What else was playing inside her head? What was she seeing in the distance? A future, for them, here? A future with him?

Stop!

This was crazy. He needed to put a lid on his insecurity right now and focus on the moment. They were having a good time. She was thrilled with the balloon ad-

venture, thrilled with the views, and she'd just been prop-
ositioning him. That was a thought worth holding on to.

He checked the burners, then went to stand behind her,
wrapping his arms around her shoulders. And this was
another thought to hold on to. Maddie melting against
him all warm, safe in his arms, right where he wanted
her to be.

She twisted, looking up. 'Is this allowed?'

'Yes.' He kissed her, keeping it brief just in case the
tunnel sucked him in again. 'The grouchy pilot says it's
fine since we're nicely on target for the landing site.'

She smiled, then turned back to the view. 'But I don't
want it to end.'

Neither did he, not while the sun was sliding towards
the horizon like this, not while she was here with him—
impossibly—drifting over his adopted home. A pang
caught him in the chest. Where was home for her? He
didn't even know. So many things they didn't know about
each other.

He buried his lips into her hair. 'Where do you live
when you're not travelling?'

'Mum's place near Marseilles. She bought it after Dad
was sentenced. It's got a little apartment on the top floor
that I use as a bolthole.'

At least she had a base, and Natalie. He hugged her
tighter. 'How is your mum?'

'Okay. Well, dismayed about Dad's book, not that
she's said anything.' She wriggled, swivelling round to
face him. 'We don't talk about him.' Her eyes clouded.
'He's a taboo subject.'

On whose insistence? He felt a frown coming.
Sounded like Natalie was calling the shots and Maddie
was, what, falling in, going along with it? Figured. Just

yesterday she'd said that thing about how everything had been a million times worse for Natalie than for her. Had that mindfulness kept her from pushing her mum to talk about things? If so, it meant that Maddie had never got to talk about things either. No wonder she still had all that hurt, and hate, stuck inside.

'The book thing is so hard, not knowing what's in it…' She was chewing the edge of her lip which was the nervous thing she did when she wasn't twisting her pendant about. 'I mean, I really don't want to look at it in case there's personal stuff in there, but at the same time, if he's written about me and Mum, then there's a part of me that does want to know.'

Fear in her eyes, that scrawl of pain.

His heart seized. Why the hell couldn't Peter Saint James just disappear? Why couldn't he be the one hiding his face for shame? Didn't he care about Maddie, about the hurt he was causing? Didn't he have a scrap of imagination, a shred of decency inside? Unbelievable! He exhaled, pushing it down. Anger wasn't going help Maddie, wasn't going to take away her pain. Pain had to be managed, like with the elephant. Lance the abscess, drain the poison, then disinfect. Shift the dynamic towards healing. Maybe that was the answer, right there.

'Mads, I can't believe I'm saying this but maybe you should check it out. At least you'll know what you're dealing with.'

'Would you look?' Her gaze was wide, trusting. 'If it was your father, your father's book?'

'I think I'd have to, yes.' He felt his stomach tightening suddenly, his pulse gathering. Could this be the moment he'd been waiting for, the moment to talk about the future? It felt like it, felt like an opportunity. He took a gentle hold of her shoulders. 'You know, you don't have to be alone with this. We could order the book online, check it out together over a bottle of wine...' A light was coming on behind her gaze. Love. Gratitude. He licked his lips. Final push. 'The only thing is, there's no same-day delivery service out here so it would mean waiting.'

She blinked. 'Waiting...?'

'Yes, for a bit.' His mouth was drying. 'Or longer. It would be fine by me, if you wanted to wait...stay, I mean, for longer...for as long as...then I could be with you for the book and for—' He felt tightness cramping in his chest, panic rising. Why wasn't she saying anything? Did he need to be more emphatic? Maybe he just needed to be plain.

He licked the dryness off his lips. 'What I'm trying to say—ineptly—is that I don't want you to go, Mads, not when we've only just found each other again.' He put a hand to her face. 'I love you.'

For a moment she was still, and then her eyes were filling, tears sliding out. 'I don't want to go either, but the thing is, what's coming into my head right now is that I'm scared, scared of wrecking things, scared of hurting you again.' Her face was crumpling, tearing his heart out. 'I don't want to hurt you, not again.'

'Oh, Maddie.' He felt tenderness rushing in. 'You didn't hurt me on purpose.' And she hadn't stayed away because she didn't love him either. He could see it now, shimmering through her eyes, quivering on her lips. She was trapped inside her own fear and shame. If only Natalie had helped her more, let her talk, let her release it all, then maybe things would have been different and she'd have found a way back to him, but it was too late to worry about that now. The past was written. It was the future that mattered. He smoothed her tears away with his thumbs. 'We were dealt a bad hand, that's all, but we've got another chance.'

'We have, but I'm a mess, Kade. I know it.' She lifted his hands away from her face, and then her eyes were on his, shadows moving through. 'Parts of me are the same, but the sameness doesn't reach all the way in. There's all this other stuff going on inside, fear that feels like it's closing in, and I can't stop it, can't stop feeling it. I love you, Kade, I really do, and I want to think about what happens next, but there's a bigger part of me that wants to stay right here, *literally* in this moment, in this basket, drifting along, just the two of us. I don't think I can process more than this—'

'Which is why we need to take the pressure off.' He took hold of her hands. 'We need to give ourselves time to just be, time to fill in the blanks, find new feet and maybe to grow back.' Her gaze was filling again, softening, lifting his spirits, making his pulse fly. 'I'm talking about trying, that's all. No pressure. No promises. Just more time.' He felt a smile coming. 'More wild dog pups, more ballooning. You up for that?'

She was looking at him as if she couldn't fit enough of him in, and then she was smiling all the way to her eyes. 'What do you think?'

CHAPTER TEN

'WHAT ARE WE going to tell Chanda?'

'Nothing she hasn't already worked out for herself, I imagine.' Kaden's eyes came to hers, smiling eyes. 'I think we can assume that the whole staff is up to speed by now. Taking you to Tlou was a bit of a giveaway.'

And moving from her guest lodge into his rooms when they got back—in T minus ten minutes—was going to clinch it. But it wasn't quite what she'd meant. She stretched a hand to the back of his neck, playing with his hair, feeling a knot tightening inside. 'What I mean is, should we tell everyone my real name or what?'

'We'll tell them whatever you want, whatever you're comfortable with.'

The knot pulled tighter. Why hadn't she thought about this before, the actual practicalities of staying? Up there in the balloon, Kaden had made it all sound so easy, talking about adding time to take the pressure off. No promises. No expectations. Just her, staying for longer, so they could keep catching up, keep filling in their blanks, so they could keep on loving each other. Trying to build back. At Tlou, believing in that dream, living it, had been easy too. Dining under the stars by the fire with a hundred lamps glowing, then bed...which hadn't involved a lot of sleeping but at least when sleep had come it had been deep and blissful. And then this morning, she'd opened her eyes to the hazy whiteness of mosquito nets and him, sitting there smiling down at her, a jug in his hands...

'Your hair needs a wash...'

'Ah! That explains the jug.'

'Of course! Someone told me two days ago that if she was staying at the honeymoon bush camp, then she'd want to replicate the famous hair-washing scene from Out of Africa, *so here I am, jug and soap at the ready. I also have a poem...'*

'A poem?'

'If it's good enough for Robert Redford...'

She felt a smile curving on her lips. He'd led her outside, parked her on a warm boulder, leaning her back to wet her hair.

'I say poem, but it's more of a limerick, really...short and sweet, like your hair.'

'A limerick?'

'I wrote it myself, but don't worry, you're not going to be out a job any time soon.'

'So let's hear it...'

'Okay. There was a young lady called Maddie, who was prone to throwing a paddy, if she was woken up quickly, 'cos it made her quite sickly, or if not sickly, then at least pretty crabby.'

She smiled again, sliding her eyes over his face, feeling the love swelling inside, flowing out. He was everything, the only one she'd ever wanted, the only one who mattered, so why were the jitters coming back, why was she suddenly feeling the weight of her father and everything that went with him—betrayal, shame, fear—pressing down on her, crushing the joy inside? She bit her lips together. Maybe staying was the problem. It wasn't that she didn't want to stay because she did, with all her heart, but staying in one place for more than a few days at a time was counterintuitive. She was a rolling stone, had become one because constant motion was safety. Changing places. Changing faces. It was a decade-old habit, one she was about to break, so maybe that's all it was, nerves chiming because she was about to step out of her comfort zone, but also into one, because that's what Kaden was, what he always had been, her comfort, her joy. *Gah!* She was a bundle of contradictions. No wonder her nerve ends were fraying. If they could just resolve the niggling problem of her name, then maybe it would help.

She took a breath, swallowing hard. 'The thing is, Kade, if we tell them that I'm Maddie Saint James and that we go back a long way, then, given what we've been doing, that's going to make more sense to them than if I'm Lina, who from their point of view has just arrived and within minutes seems to have snagged the boss. If I stay here as Lina, there's a good chance they'll be thinking to themselves that I'm a bit fast and loose, and I'm going to see that in their eyes the whole time and I couldn't bear it because I'm the total opposite, as you well know, but then telling them my real name could be a risk. I'm not saying they'd do it and I feel awful for even thinking it, but as I said before I'm messed up—and this is messed-up me talking—but if they know who I really am, then maybe they might be tempted to contact the press, sell me out for money—'

'Stop!' In one swift movement Kaden had pulled over and switched off the engine. His hand went up, removing hers from the back of his neck. 'Are you listening yourself?' His eyes were bruised, incredulous. 'My staff would never do that. They're like family, a family I pay extremely well for their discretion, and loyalty. I've built Masoka as an exclusive, private venue...' He was shaking his head, his eyes narrowing. 'You know that! We've had travel writers here this week, but my target market is the VIP market—celebrities, politicians—the kind of people who require absolute, one hundred percent discretion. My staff know it, and respect it, so please, don't denigrate them, Maddie. I'm one hundred percent sure of them.'

Even as his words were settling, she could feel words of her own rising from some place deep inside, springing out of her mouth before she could stop them. 'And yet in front of them, right from the first day, you called me *Ms James*, not Maddie, or Ms Saint James, so you can't be *that* sure of them!'

His face stiffened. 'It was *you* I wasn't sure of! That first day I was simply respecting the name you were using. It would have been rather presumptuous of me to start bandying your real name around before we'd even talked about it, don't you think!'

Her heart clenched, then her stomach. He was right. About everything. And she was... She squeezed her eyes shut, sealing in the tears that were suddenly scalding her lids. She was snipped wires. Jagged pieces. She was being unfair, ridiculous. Paranoid.

'I'm sorry.' She bit her lips hard and braved his gaze. Cool. Bruised. She felt her heart buckling, her tears sliding out. 'I'm so sorry... I don't even know where that came from...'

'I do.' His eyes held her for a long second, and then his expression softened. 'You're safe here, Mads. How many more times must I say it?' And then he was moving in, pulling her against him, stroking her hair. 'You need to find some faith.'

She closed her eyes, melting in, feeling the tension inside loosening. So easy having faith when his arms were around her.

His fingers moved to the back of her neck, stroking. 'Anyway, maybe I have a solution for the name thing.'

'What? Calling me crazy?'

He chuckled. 'You are, but no. I'm thinking that if it's going to make you feel better, for now we could go with Lina, and say that it's Lina and I who go back a long way. That way, no one is going to think you're some shady lady. Does that work?'

It was the perfect solution; one she might have thought of herself if she hadn't been so busy spiralling out of control. She felt more tears sliding out, a sudden overwhelming gratitude swelling in her chest. 'It does.' She swallowed hard. 'It's perfect. Unlike me. I'm a mess.'

'You're just scared.' His arms wound around her tighter. 'You've been scared for a long time, but we're going to fix that.' She felt his lips moving in her hair, her heart melting as he whispered, 'I promise.'

'Welcome back, Mr Barr.' Chanda's smile wasn't quite as effusive as usual. *Strange.* Her eyes flicked to Maddie. 'And Ms James… How did you enjoy Tlou?'

'It was wonderful, thank you.' Maddie's eyes came to his briefly. 'I loved every second.' Her cheeks were flushing a little. 'It's quite something being out there, under canvas.'

'It certainly is.' Chanda folded her hands on the reception desk, then folded them again the other way. 'I'm glad you enjoyed it.'

He felt unease stirring. Bad enough Maddie having a little outburst in the car, but at least he got the roots of it, understood where it came from. This low-key, grave-eyed version of Chanda was something else altogether.

'So, Mr Barr...' Chanda's eyes came to his. 'I was wondering if I could have a word.'

'Of course.' The sooner the better. There was something wrong and he needed to know what it was. 'Shall we go into my office?'

'Yes.' She was already moving. 'That would be best.'

'What about me?' The flush in Maddie's cheeks was gone. Now she looked pale. Face. Lips. He felt tension seizing his shoulders. She was clearly thinking that Chanda wanted to talk about *her*. Unlikely, but if he didn't invite her into the conversation, what kind of message was that going to send to her about faith and trust? And what kind of message would it send to Chanda about the relationship between him and Maddie if he didn't ask Maddie to join them? It would create the exact impression that Maddie wanted to avoid, that she'd tempted the boss to a little holiday fling. At least he could nip that one right in the bud.

He held out his arm to her, loading his smile with as much reassurance as he could muster. 'You, too.'

Chanda stalled, her eyes widening. 'Mr Barr?'

'It's fine, Chanda. Lina's a very old friend. Whatever you want to talk to me about, you can say it in front of her.'

Chanda inhaled and then she smiled. 'Of course.'

Moments later, he was closing his office door behind the three of them, feeling the quick hard beats of his pulse bouncing between his temples.

He looked at Chanda. 'So, what is it?'

Her face dropped like a stone. 'It's this...' She went

to his desk and picked up a newspaper that hadn't been there when he left, a broadsheet that she battled with for a moment before handing it over, opened out. Her lips pursed. 'It's the *Johannesburg Gazette.*'

He looked, felt his lungs collapsing.

Danger Top of the Menu at Masoka Game Reserve!

He read on, blood roaring, until the words blurred, shifting, and floating on the page. He blinked, forcing himself to read the name of the journalist, even though he already knew: Gerhardus Du Plessis.

'Kaden?' Maddie's anxious voice filtered in, jerking him back. 'What is it?'

He lowered the paper so she could see.

'Oh, my God.' Her eyes flew wide. 'Is that the journalist you sent the champagne to?'

His heart clenched, then his jaw. 'Yes.' He felt an edge drying sharp at the back of his throat. 'And guess what? He even thought to mention it.' He pushed the paper at her and went to the window, staring out blindly.

He hadn't truly got it before, the way his dad had been after the Saint James scandal broke, all those callous-sounding words about forgetting Maddie, about staying away from her and her family for the sake of the business. He hadn't got it then because he'd been seventeen, because he'd been too busy dying inside, but he got it now. His dad would have been thinking of Barr's business reputation and market position, but he must also have been thinking about the staff, their livelihoods, the livelihoods of their suppliers, all the cogs in the Barr's machine, because that's what he was thinking about right now. His staff and their livelihoods, all of which depended on

Masoka ranking high, pulling in the right clients, making money. One freak incident, one wretched article! He felt his gut twisting. After all his hard work, Fran's hard work, everyone's. Renovating the place to the highest standard, building the lodges, hiring the best chefs, the best guides, the best of every damn thing. The best, most reliable vehicles, the *safest* vehicles, which was why Du Plessis was still alive, but he hadn't written that, had he? No. He'd simply dragged Masoka through the dirt and sunk in the boot by mentioning the champagne.

He dragged his hands down his face. He should never have resorted to Dom Pérignon. What had he been thinking? Or maybe that was the problem, he hadn't been thinking. He'd lost his cool, felt panicked, worried for Jerry and the two journalists, worried for the elephant too. He'd been a fizzing ball of overreaction instead of the calm businessman he should have been. Never again.

Next time he'd explain that there was always a degree of danger attached to going out on a game drive, a small risk of injury that was clearly outlined in the terms and conditions. He'd politely and kindly draw their attention to the clause about guests agreeing to participate in game drives at their own risk. And then he'd point out all the different ways that those risks were minimised, via highly competent trackers and guides, via the constant two-way radio communication between the vehicles so that animal movements could be advised, and warnings delivered. And he'd emphasise the quality of the vehicles themselves, their stability, and rugged strength. There were cheaper safari vehicles available, but he'd bought the best, not skimping, not compromising, because he was his father's son, only interested in delivering quality and satisfaction. And then maybe, once he'd explained all that, he'd offer to add a complimentary extra night to the affronted guest's stay, using the time to build back the goodwill.

He sighed. All very well having good ideas now, but for there to be a next time there needed to be a business. He bit his lips together. He couldn't let this throw him. He couldn't let Du Plessis tilt him off his axis, not now he'd come this far, not when he had staff to think about, plans in motion. Being calm about it, getting things into perspective, what was the readership of the *Johannesburg Gazette* anyway, and the travel section at that? Was the article likely to be syndicated? Maddie would know. Travel was her business after all.

He turned. She was still reading the paper. Did she look paler than before or was it just the light bouncing off the page that was making it seem that way? He looked at Chanda. Her face was serious, her lips still pursed. He felt a germ of a smile starting, warmth flooding in. Chanda was clearly taking the Du Plessis piece personally. The whole staff would be because as per his earlier conversation with Maddie, they were loyal, invested. They were family. And he wasn't going to let them down by falling apart over this. He was better than that.

He raked a hand through his hair. 'Okay, so maybe it's not the write-up I was hoping for, but we've got eleven more coming right? Have we had any feedback from the journalist who was with Du Plessis?'

'Birgitte Sommer?' Chanda was shaking her head. 'Not yet, but she's still here. She's leaving tomorrow.'

'Right. Well, hopefully she'll be kinder. When I went to see her, she seemed okay about what happened. Ma—' He bit down on his tongue. Had Chanda noticed his slip? He couldn't bring himself to look. 'Lina?'

'Yes.' Maddie lifted her gaze from the paper, blinking. 'What?'

She looked distracted, stricken around the edges. He felt a knot yanking tight in his belly. If he'd known what Chanda was going to show them, he'd never have included Maddie in the conversation. It was obviously churning her up, feeding her anxiety about journalists. He should let her go, give her an excuse to leave so she wasn't having to hold it together in front of Chanda, but first he needed her opinion.

He went to stand in front of her. 'What do you think the chances are of the article being picked up?'

She shrugged a little. 'He makes some general points about safety in game parks, but there's not enough meat in the article itself to give it real legs.' Her eyes clouded. 'Your biggest problem is the headline. It's hooky so it's going to attract some attention.'

Not what he wanted to hear but at least she was telling him straight. He liked that. What he didn't like were the shadows moving behind her eyes. She was taking this all too hard. Harder than he was. He held in a sigh. The sooner she was all moved in with him the better. Once she was under his wing, he was going take care of her, dedicate himself twenty-four-seven to chasing those shadows away. He was going to bring back the Maddie Saint James sparkle.

'Do you want to go?' He leaned towards her, lowering his voice. 'Pack your stuff.'

If she went to pack now while he was catching up on other business with Chanda—filling Chanda in about him and Maddie—then Tumo would be able to bring up her things.

She nodded. 'Yeah.' Her lips pressed together. 'I'm so sorry about the article.'

'Hey.' He gave her arm a squeeze. 'Don't stress. Really. It'll all be fine.'

She handed him the paper, blinking. 'I hope so.'

She hurried through Reception, head down, heart pounding fit to explode. Why the hell had that damn Du Plessis article gone over the page? If it hadn't, she'd never have seen the other article.

She crashed through the doors and stopped, waiting for the knife to stop twisting. How careful she'd been this week, coming here in the first place, binning the paper that had been left for her every day without even glancing at it, avoiding news sites and social media, and then suddenly, without warning, there it had been right under her nose, a huge smiling picture of her father, a still from some stupid talk show, and that headline: *Where Are You, Madeleine?* What was that even about?

She felt a sob expanding in her chest. As if he was interested! As if he even cared! She squeezed her eyes shut, sucking in a deep breath, forcing her feet to move. But worst of all, *worst of all*, was that picture of herself—inset—a still from the Tresses advert, the one where she'd started off with her hair up in a ponytail, then tugged out the clip so that her hair had tumbled down. Of all the pictures to use, the one with her hair off her face, so that the whole picture was just her face, like a Wanted poster. The only difference between then and now was her hair colour. Anyone at all who saw that picture and who'd seen her without her shades on would join the dots, know for sure that she was Madeleine Saint James. She felt tears burning behind her lids. Nice one, Dad, pulling her back into the spotlight just to blow her cover, exposing her, destroying her all over again. The sob inside struggled upwards, filling her throat. All that hard work, all that steeling herself, pushing through the pain and the panic to create a version of herself, a wary version admittedly, but still a version of herself that was free, able to move through the world on her own terms. And now…

Now Chanda knew, and probably the whole staff too. She'd felt Chanda's eyes on her when she'd turned that page, seen the flicker of acknowledgement there when she'd dared to glance up, and she hadn't been able to say a thing to Kaden, hadn't even been able to signal to him, because he'd been staring through the window, rubbing his head, caught up in his own crisis, thanks to Du Plessis.

She swallowed hard. Poor Kaden. He didn't need all this grief, or the grief she'd given him earlier, implying that his staff might sell her out. Hurt in his eyes. Annoyance. No wonder. Everything he'd said was true. His staff were loyal. She'd seen it for herself, Chanda's obvious chagrin over the article, her demeanour towards Kaden: protective, verging on the maternal. Maybe that's why he'd seemed to rally so quickly, because he knew he had the support of a good team. Maybe that's why, when he'd touched her arm, he'd seemed so grounded. *'Don't you stress. Really. It'll all be fine.'*

She slowed down, lifting her gaze, letting it drift through the tree canopy. Would everything be fine? She breathed in, filling her lungs. The sun was still shining, wasn't it? The sky was still blue. Maybe the Du Plessis article would prove to be a hiccup, nothing more. Maybe the eleven articles to come would knock Du Plessis's piece out of the field. And of course, her piece would count for a lot because her posts always got a lot of traction. So maybe Kaden's faith was well-placed. Which just left her own faith, her own crisis…

She walked on, tuning in to the trilling of the cicadas. The cicadas didn't care if she was Lina or Maddie, they'd keep on trilling anyway. And Chanda, and Precious and Tumo and Jerry, didn't care who she was. They cared about Kaden, and about Masoka, same as her. She touched her pendant, noticing its smoothness. Maybe it didn't matter if her Lina James cover was blown because she was staying here, wasn't she, where it was safe, where she was going to be surrounded by kind, loyal staff. She felt a little lightening sensation around her heart. And now, going for the silver lining, now at least she'd be able to stay as herself, being herself, not worrying about what was going on in London, what her father was saying about his South African co-conspirators. Whistleblowing. Masoka was private, exclusive, respectful. Here, she could be Maddie. Here she could be free.

She felt a sudden springiness in her feet, a smile coming. She *was* free. Free to be with Kaden, free to love him, free to be his support, his port in a storm. Right here, twenty-four seven. She'd help him see off Du Plessis. Maybe she could help him on the website side of things too, writing regular Masoka newsletters, facilitating engagement, building client loyalty. All things she could do in her sleep. Kaden was right. God, he was so right. Everything was going to be fine, was going to be better than—

'Madeleine?'

She froze. Birgitte Sommer. Somehow. There. Phone in hand. Aimed.

'You *are* Madeleine Saint James, aren't you?'

Move! Why weren't her feet moving?

'I'm sorry. You're in shock.' Birgitte's mouth twitched into a tight smile. 'I shouldn't have sprung myself on you like this, but I'm leaving tomorrow, and I'd really like to talk to you. Are you going back to your lodge just now?' Birgitte's eyebrows arched. 'We could walk and talk.'

Walk and talk?

'No!' The word exploded from her mouth, and then suddenly, miraculously, she could feel her limbs again, her feet, feel her blood pumping, strength flowing. She dragged in a breath. 'How dare you. I'm not walking and talking to you, or anyone.' She could hear the hysterical edge on her voice, feel the pain and anger rising, boiling over. 'Just leave me the hell alone. Leave me be.' She aimed a strike at Birgitte's phone, sending it flying, and then she sprinted, running to her lodge, heart pounding and twisting, not looking back.

At the door, she fumbled with the key card, stumbling inside, then fell back, heart pulsing in her throat. How could she have ever thought she'd be free? Safe? She wasn't safe, and she was never going to be free. There was always going to be a Birgitte stepping out in front of her, after a scoop, a headline. She felt her sinuses tingling, tears burning, sliding down her cheeks. And because there was always going to be someone after her, she was never going to find peace, never going to get better. Kaden thought he could fix her, but he couldn't because this was the reality. *Her* reality. Her father had publicly hitched her to his abominable wagon, and it was going to keep rolling and rolling and rolling. She felt her legs giving out, a shudder racking its way through her. He didn't love her enough to be a good man for her, but he wasn't letting her go. She was like Marley, and he was the chain. She was going to be dragging him around for ever, and if she were to stay, then Kaden was going to be encumbered too, and she wasn't having it. Wasn't. He deserved better. He deserved happiness and success, every good thing in the world. He didn't deserve to be lumbered with a liability such as her.

CHAPTER ELEVEN

'I THINK IT's wonderful news about you and Ms James.' Chanda's eyes were glowing, full of warmth. 'It doesn't do anyone any good being alone, especially a young man such as yourself.'

At least Maddie wouldn't have to worry any more about anyone thinking she was some kind of predator. As he'd suspected, going off to Tlou had sparked some furious speculation, but he'd given Chanda the bare bones, that they'd been an item in the past, so that was settled.

He smiled. 'Thanks, although frankly I'm not feeling particularly young right now. I messed up with Mr Du Plessis and I seem to be reaping the whirlwind.'

'It'll work out.' Chanda smiled and then suddenly her smile was fading. 'Mr Barr, I want to say something but I'm not quite sure how to say it.'

His heart clenched. Not more difficult news. He drew in a breath, digging out a smile. 'I always find that straight up is best.'

'Okay, well...' She pursed her lips. 'The thing is, I know—we *all* know—about Ms James, that her name is really Madeleine Saint James.'

He felt the muscles in his face stiffening. 'How?'

Chanda picked up the paper again, thumbing through, and then she turned it round, putting it into his hands.

His heart clenched for a second time, taking his stomach with it.

Peter Saint James was smiling out at him from the page, still handsome in spite of his twelve years inside, and—*Oh, God, no!*—Maddie too, smiling out of a smaller picture, an old Tresses shot, cropped tight. Aside from the dark sideswept fringe, she looked the same. Exactly the same. His slid his eyes up to the headline: *Where Are You, Madeleine?*

His throat went tight. How could Peter have put that in the press, and the photo? He swallowed hard, trying to make his voice work. 'Chanda, did she see this?'

Chanda blinked. 'I think she did, yes.'

No wonder Maddie had looked bleached, stricken. And yet she hadn't said a thing. She'd calmly answered his question about the article, hiding whatever was going on inside, a swan gliding over a mirror lake, but underneath... She'd have been melting down, falling apart, and she'd been doing it alone instead of pouring it all out to him.

He threw the paper down, pulse banging, and looked at his watch. Nearly a whole hour with Chanda, going over everything, and all that time, Maddie had been alone, stewing.

An hour...

His heart seized. It shouldn't have taken her more than an hour to pack and get back here. And she wasn't here, was she?

Oh, God!

'Chanda, can you call Tumo, please, right now? Find out if he's gone to get her bags.'

'Of course.' She bustled out.

He pulled out his phone, swiping and stabbing at the screen, putting it to his ear. Maybe he was panicking for nothing. Maybe she'd seen the picture and was cool. No. On no planet whatsoever was Maddie going to be cool with this. He paced, holding his breath to the ring-ring, churning to the endless on-and-on, caving to the click.

Voicemail.

'Mr Barr—' Chanda was back, eyes wide. 'Tumo did go for her bags, but he put them in Clive's Jeep. She's gone to the airstrip.'

'No…' His heart was collapsing. This couldn't be happening. *Couldn't!* Not a second time. He wasn't going to let it happen. He wasn't seventeen any more. She belonged with him. They belonged together. Whatever she was thinking, whatever she thought she was running from, he was going to fight for her, show her that he was there for her whatever it took.

He ducked past Chanda, sprinting through the building, through the doors, running hard until the door of the Land Cruiser was in front of him. He yanked it open, started the engine and stamped on the accelerator, tearing out of the compound, not even braking for Richard's bridge.

She pressed her back into the wall of the little terminal building, clamping her arms to contain the shuddering that wouldn't seem to stop. There were two planes on the apron, two pilots pottering, exchanging the odd word.

She pulled her arms in tighter to quell another shiver. They didn't know she was here. They wouldn't have heard the Jeep because she'd asked Clive to drop her at the back of the building, and not to rev the engine on

his way out. And she'd asked him not to tell anyone—
Kaden—that he'd brought her here until he got back.
She'd figured she'd be long gone by then, but for some
reason she was still here, glued to the wall, unable to
make her feet take those last steps.

She closed her eyes, feeling the burn. Eyes. Throat.
Heart. Why was she stalling? She must get onto one of
those planes for Kaden's sake. Staying was only going to
taint him by association, bring more Birgittes to Masoka,
sniffing around, hunting, and she didn't even understand
why, because she was nothing, had nothing to say. She
wasn't remotely interesting or important, but they'd keep
on coming, keep on tripping her up, making her hateful
and angry, and she couldn't inflict that on Kaden as well
as everything else, have him suffering her moods and
all her paranoia, not after he'd worked so hard to bring
Masoka to life. He deserved only the best, because he
was best person she knew, the kindest, dearest, most
beautiful soul, a beautiful soul who loved her.

She felt her heart buckling, twisting like wreckage.
And that was the problem. Now she was here, just metres away from the planes, the thought of leaving him, of
actually going through with it, was unbearable. He had
so much love inside, so much faith, and she loved him,
with every screwed-up fibre of her being.

He'd be there now, wouldn't he, with Chanda, one eye
on the door expecting her to walk back in with Tumo and
her bags. That's what he was expecting; meanwhile, she
was here, stuck and trembling. *Oh, God!* She felt more
tears seeping out, winding down her cheeks. What was
she supposed to do? If she got on the plane, she'd be hurting him, and if she went back, she'd be hurting him. It

wasn't a choice at all, but she *had* to make a move, push the button, choose the blue or the red—

'Maddie...'

She screwed her eyes tighter, biting her lips. *Maddie, Maddie, Maddie!* That was what he'd be calling out now, going through the guest lounge, feeling worried, maybe striding along the path to her lodge.

'Maddie.' Warm hands gripped her shoulders. 'Maddie. What are you doing?'

She blinked. *Kaden!* Her heart leapt. It was him, really him, right here. His dear face, his beautiful soul, but he shouldn't be here, or—*no*—it was her who shouldn't be here. She should be on the plane. Why hadn't she got on the plane, why couldn't she move, decide, feel anything except this pulsing joy?

'I saw the paper, Mads, your dad, your picture...' He was rubbing her arms gently. 'You should have said something. Why didn't you say something?'

Pain in his eyes. *Her* fault. All her fault.

'I couldn't...' Her voice felt thick in her mouth, smeary. She swallowed hard. 'You were upset about Du Plessis. You had enough of your own stuff to think about and—' she felt her stomach hardening, darkness closing in '—and I'm sick of everything always being about me and my problems, my stupid dad—'

'But they're not just your problems.' His face was tender. 'They're mine too, because everything that upsets you upsets me, so when something like this happens, I want to know, so we can work through it.' His gaze tightened on hers. 'You don't have to hold it all inside. Maybe your mum never wanted to talk about your dad, but I want you to talk to me. I want to hear it all.' And then he was shaking his head, all the hurt inside showing, the confusion. 'Just taking off like that, without a word, why would you do that to me?' Tears were welling at the edges of his eyes. 'I don't understand. I thought you loved me. I thought we'd agreed—'

She put her hands to his face. 'I do love you, so much.' She bit her lips together hard. 'But then, Birgitte…'

On the path. Tight smile. Phone primed.

'Birgitte what?' His gaze was sharpening, hardening. 'What happened?'

She let her hands fall. 'She accosted me on the way back to the lodge. She was filming me…said she wanted to talk. "Walk and talk," she said, as if we were friends, and I—' she felt a sob rising, filling her throat '—I was so angry, because of Dad, putting my picture in the paper like that, inviting all this in again, so I let her have it. I smashed her phone and ran, and then I realised that it's never going to stop, whatever we think, whatever we want, and I was thinking about you and Du Plessis and all the work you've put in here, and about how if I stay, then I'm just going to be liability, a hairshirt, always prickling, irritating, and I don't want that for you. You deserve better.'

'Oh, Maddie.' He looked away for a beat and then his eyes fastened on hers. 'Do you know what I did when your mum told me you'd gone to Paris?' He ploughed a hand through his hair. 'I followed. I went after you.'

'What?' Her heart pulsed. 'I don't understand… I mean, you didn't even know where I was staying, so why?'

'Why?' His eyes were blazing suddenly, full of passion. 'Because I knew you needed me, and I wanted to be there for you. It's as simple as that. You're right, I didn't know where you were staying, but I wanted my love to do some work, understand? Some actual work. And walking the streets looking for you was better than just sitting on my hands.'

She felt her heart turning over, hurting. Even though he hadn't known where she was, even though it had been a fruitless mission, he'd gone after her, doing the work.

'And it's what I want to do now, more than ever.' He was shaking his head, his gaze softening. 'I don't care what comes. I don't care about your dad, or about the papers, or about Birgitte. I love you, Madeleine Saint James, and my love is strong enough to do the work, to do whatever it takes, because otherwise what does it mean? It's just words.'

Like her dad. Words in the paper, showmanship. Nothing behind it. Nothing real. Nothing there of any worth at all. But Kaden was worth something. He was everything. Maybe it was time to make her love do some work too. Believing in him was a start. Believing in them. She felt warmth filtering in, a fresh warmth that felt hopeful and pure.

He was taking her face in his hands, wiping her tears with gentle thumbs, and then suddenly he was smiling. 'For the record, if you're a hairshirt, then I can't wait to slip you on, but we'll have to go back to my place for that.' His lips came to hers for a long moment, warm and firm, drawing a tingle through her veins. 'What do you say?'

His place. His home. Hers now too. No more doubts. No more running.

She felt tears budding and spilling and then a smile arriving. 'I'm saying, yes. I'm saying, sorry. I'm saying, Kaden Barr, I love you with all my heart. And I'm saying, please, take me home.'

EPILOGUE

Six months later...

'WHAT HAVE YOU got so far?' Birgitte was looking at her with that funny little tight-lipped smile of hers, a smile that was apt to widen and brighten in a heartbeat, or equally, to draw tight, depending on the circumstances.

She toyed with the notebook in her lap. 'Not much, but I have been rather busy...'

'Excuses, excuses...' Birgitte picked up her glass, chuckling. 'Anyone would think you'd been organising a wedding...'

She felt a smile coming. *Birgitte!* Who'd ever have thought that they'd become firm friends? Letters of apology simultaneously crossing via the reception desk, hers apologising for smashing Birgitte's phone; Birgitte's apologising for the way she'd approached her on the path. From there, somehow, things had progressed. A few weeks and scores of emails later, Birgitte had finally persuaded her that writing her own story would be good for her, cathartic. And Kaden had agreed. But then he'd proposed, which had taken her eye off the ball just a little bit.

She felt a lump thickening in her throat. Tomorrow, she

was marrying the love of her life on the veranda where they'd had that first dinner all those months ago. Just a small wedding, which, in truth, hadn't taken that much organising. Mum was here, and Renée, and Kaden's parents and his sister and her boyfriend. Grandma Barr too. They were all outside on the front veranda with Kaden, drinking sundowners. She could picture his face, his eyes full of delight, his ready smile, pride in it. Masoka was doing so well. The Du Plessis blip, which is what they called it now, had been short-lived. The other reviews, and her own, had brought those first bookings in, and the now the ball was not so much rolling as careening full speed ahead. Nothing less that he deserved.

Kaden. Her rock, her shelter, her safety. Her one and only love. For ever. He'd probably be looking about him now, wondering where she was. Would he be feeling a twitch of anxiety in some corner of his beautiful soul? It hurt that he might be, but if he was, then it was all down to her. She was better than she had been, better by a mile, but it was still there inside from time to time, that jumping anxiety, and Kaden knew. Because he *knew* her, all her snipped wires and jagged pieces, and he loved her all the same.

'So are you going to read it out or what…?' Birgitte's eyebrows were at maximum elevation.

She looked down at the notebook. She didn't need to open it to know what it held.

My father's name is Peter Christian Saint James. I grew up thinking he was a good man, a kind and honest man. In truth, I idolised him as if he were, indeed, a saint. The hardest lesson of my life was learning that he was the opposite. This is my story…

She swallowed hard, meeting Birgitte's curious gaze. 'No, it can wait…' She put the notebook aside and got to her feet. 'But Kaden can't. He'll be wondering where I am, and I can't have that, not on the night before our wedding…'

Birgitte set down her glass and then she was looking up, her eyes full of warmth and shine. 'You really do love him, don't you?'

She felt her heart filling, exploding softly. 'Oh, Birgitte, you have no idea.'

* * * * *

COMING SOON!

We really hope you enjoyed reading this book. If you're looking for more romance, be sure to head to the shops when new books are available on

Thursday 1st September

To see which titles are coming soon, please visit

millsandboon.co.uk/nextmonth

MILLS & BOON®

Coming next month

CAPTURING THE CEO'S GUARDED HEART
Rebecca Winters

The Eiffel Tower stood 1063 feet tall on the Champ de Mars, not that far from the jewellery store. Anelise noticed the seven-thirty traffic moving toward it had grown heavier, but she couldn't take her eyes off the engagement ring and bracelet.

"It's hard to believe that some people can actually buy the kind of jewels I'm wearing. Tonight, a man put sparkling jewels on my finger, wrist and ears. I know I only get to wear them for a little while, but I've been granted an old wish. When you conceived the plan to expose the culprit, I never dreamed I'd have the time of my life doing it with you."

Nic had to stop for a light and looked at her. "If you want to know the truth, I've never had more fun and I find it astonishing that there's a woman alive this easy to work with, let alone please."

His words found their way inside her until they reached the parking area outside the famous monument. "It's a good thing I've already ordered dinner. From the look of the crowd gathering, we'll be lucky to make it before closing time."

"Except they wouldn't close knowing you're coming," she quipped. Together they made their way through people taking pictures and entered the exclusive elevator taking them directly to the restaurant. His strong arms went around her as they ascended, making her feel safe and cherished. *Remember this isn't real, Anelise. Don't get carried away.*

The maître d'hotel met them the second they stepped inside. He fell all over Nic after greeting him.

"Marcel? May I introduce my beautiful fiancée, Anelise Lavigny."

"It's my great pleasure to meet you, Mademoiselle Lavigny," the older man said with a twinkle in his eyes. He showed them to a table with lighted candles, centred at the window overlooking Paris. The other tables had been placed further away to give them privacy.

Nic reached for her left hand and massaged her palm. "So far we've aroused the insatiable curiosity of everyone in this room including undercover journalists. By the time we finish dinner and leave, it's possible the person responsible for bringing us together will be among the diners."

"Let's hope so."

The sommelier poured the vintage wine Nic had ordered. He raised his glass and clinked the one she was holding. "To the most successful adventure of our lives."

Anelise couldn't help but smile.

Continue reading
CAPTURING THE CEO'S GUARDED HEART
Rebecca Winters

Available next month
www.millsandboon.co.uk

MILLS & BOON

THE HEART OF ROMANCE

A ROMANCE FOR EVERY READER

MODERN

Prepare to be swept off your feet by sophisticated, sexy and seductive heroes, in some of the world's most glamourous and romantic locations, where power and passion collide.

HISTORICAL

Escape with historical heroes from time gone by. Whether your passion is for wicked Regency Rakes, muscled Vikings or rugged Highlanders, awaken the romance of the past.

MEDICAL

Set your pulse racing with dedicated, delectable doctors in the high-pressure world of medicine, where emotions run high and passion, comfort and love are the best medicine.

True Love

Celebrate true love with tender stories of heartfelt romance, from the rush of falling in love to the joy a new baby can bring, and a focus on the emotional heart of a relationship.

Desire

Indulge in secrets and scandal, intense drama and plenty of sizzling hot action with powerful and passionate heroes who have it all: wealth, status, good looks…everything but the right woman.

HEROES

Experience all the excitement of a gripping thriller, with an intense romance at its heart. Resourceful, true-to-life women and strong, fearless men face danger and desire - a killer combination!

To see which titles are coming soon, please visit

millsandboon.co.uk/nextmonth